EIGHTY DAYS OF SUNLIGHT

EIGHTY DAYS OF SUNLIGHT

A Novel

ROBERT YUNE

Thought Catalog Books /
Prospecta Press
Brooklyn, NY

Published by Thought Catalog Books, a division of The Thought &
Expression Co., Williamsburg, Brooklyn

in association with Prospecta Press, an imprint of Easton Studio Press,
LLC, P.O. Box 3131, Westport, CT 06880
www.prospectapress.com

For general information address hello@thoughtcatalog.com; for
submissions to Thought Catalog Books
manuscripts@thoughtcatalog.com

Founded in 2010, Thought Catalog is a website and imprint dedicated
to your ideas and stories. We publish fiction and non-fiction from
emerging and established writers across all genres. Learn more at
www.thoughtcatalog.com/about

ISBN 978-1-63226-044-4

Printed in the United States of America
First Printing: June 2015

10 9 8 7 6 5 4 3 2 1

Cover design by Nick Kinling

DEDICATION

For my parents, Kathy and Douglas Stevens; along with my grandparents, Robert and Lois Baum, Mary-Louise Engebretson, Joan Stevens, and Douglas Stevens Sr.

CONTENTS

Part I. THE BINDERY

Part II. IN A CATHEDRAL CITY

Part III. MOONLIGHT MILE

PART I

THE BINDERY

1

IF I HAD A HAMMER

Every year, the Boy Scouts of America throw a delightful weeklong festival called Jamboree. Scouts from all over the nation gather and attend workshop stations to earn merit badges. The camp I attended was not Jamboree but rather New Jersey's equivalent. Instead of camping next to scouts from Hawaii and New Mexico, we got boys from Camden and Paterson. I was not looking forward to it. I hated being a Boy Scout. Also, there would be other Asians there, possibly other Korean-Americans. My father, brother, and I were from an all-white town and I enjoyed the small thrill of being exotic.

Our father stressed acting white. Had we settled elsewhere, this could have worked out beautifully: I picture us sitting in wicker lawn chairs, sipping umbrella drinks as our friends cheer Secretariat to victory. But we'd immigrated to a small town near Trenton and our father took a job in a cannery. There, being white meant country music and sports. For my brother Tommy, aged fourteen at the time, this meant football. This was fine with him because it combined his two favorite things: hitting people and being rewarded. I was eleven. I joined the Boy Scouts because I enjoyed being away from my brother.

And my father. His coworkers nicknamed him "Overtime" and mostly he just sat and stared at the television. *When* he was home. Late at night, he flickered in the dull glow of infomercials—that's my only real memory of him from the time. After reading *Animal Farm* in school, I started calling him "Boxer," after the industrious horse. Tommy and I called him that until we graduated from high school. He died a few months later and then it wasn't funny anymore.

Boy Scout camp. My underwear and T-shirts were neatly folded in my pack; as we ate breakfast and waited for our father to finish packing the van, my brother sat at the table pretending to read the newspaper and probably said something like, "Have fun at Girl Scout camp." I probably called him a bastard and he probably attacked me. He played football and I was fat: If you're male and have a brother, you know what this means. At that age, he liked to throw me to the ground, take off one of his socks and wrap it around my head, trying to tie it in a knot. This may have happened that morning.

"Boy, Boxer's *shuuure* gonna miss you, Gayson. Your asthma and your bedwetting."

I told him it was *Jason*, as he well knew, and added, "I'll see you in hell, Tommy." I said this a lot when I was eleven.

———

It was a three-hour drive to the camp. My friends Mike and Clay were in the back of my father's van with me. There was another kid with us, Jonathan. He was new, so of course we only talked to him when the Scoutmaster made us. I remember he played a video game. This was before cartridges and 3-D; back then, a video game consisted of a plastic case, a motor, and a scrolling plastic sheet. It made an annoying whir like a camera rewinding, but the van mostly drowned it out. I was too cool to acknowledge my dad, too cool to think of anything else once Clay told me about the Rifle Shooting merit badge. This was the one merit badge station anyone cared about. Of course, we had to go to the Rabbit Raising and Leatherwork stations, but none of them compared. "Twenty two calibers," Clay said. *Bolt action, motherfuckers.*

For those who have never fired a gun, I'm not sure I can explain the attraction. It's not a rush of power, it doesn't make you feel like a god. It's not about violence or power, it's about the light smell of oil when you work the bolt to chamber a round. The profound engineering of death nudging you in the shoulder after each shot, a crisp report of cause and effect. It's strangely addicting, firing a gun. One almost reaches Zen after a few hundred rounds. The world contracts to just you, the target, and perfection. Breathe in, and pull the trigger as you breathe out.

They taught us gun safety, of course—I think that was actually the point of the merit badge. And of course it was supervised, on a gun range far away from camp. But we eventually got to shoot. A .22 round could fit inside most pen caps, but they were rockets to us. Bolt-action rifles, as I said, American made, and if I remember correctly, you loaded seven rounds in a clip, pulled the bolt, and fired downrange at a paper target. We were like little soldiers with our beige uniforms and rifles. When we shot, we leaned behind a sort of wooden shelf at the shooting range and beside us were small dividers which held a coffee can full of ammo. Coffee cans—I'll never forget the heft of a tin can brimming with death.

The sixth and final day of camp, there was water in the tents from an overnight rain and our packs were mildewing. The novelty had worn off especially for the city kids, but we were all tired of eating hot dogs and campfire eggs off tinfoil. We were all picturing our homes that day.

Jonathan, the little fucker playing video games on the drive to camp, was, of course, in my troop and he was also in my noon Rifle Shooting merit badge class. On the last day of camp, he stole a handful of bullets from the shooting range. Little .22 shells, I bet they rattled pleasantly in his beige shorts pockets. No one knows why he did that and no one knows why later that night he walked up to our campfire and tossed them in. If there's ever a campfire with young boys around it, someone's always throwing something to the flames. Nobody noticed the bullets. At first.

Here, I have to pause to explain, in general terms, how a bullet works. After the trigger is pulled, a striking pin hits the flat bottom, or rim, of the cartridge, setting off a small primer cap. This ignites the main charge of gunpowder; the explosion propels the lead slug down the barrel. But when you throw a bullet in a fire, it settles, sits calmly, and explodes. The heat warps the lead, which breaks into fragments and becomes shrapnel when the primer and powder simultaneously ignite.

So there I was, sitting by the campfire, sipping orange astronaut Tang from an aluminum canteen and singing "If I Had a Hammer." Popcorn! I looked up from my little spiral-bound songbook to be greeted by molten shards of lead. The world shut off like an old TV and then I was in the hospital. "They look like teeth," my father said, looking up at the glowing X-ray of my skull. Little canines—doctors are still afraid to remove them.

I don't know what happened to Jonathan, whether charges were filed or anything. Occasionally, I consider looking it up, but nothing comes of it. I suppose it's because I know the answers I want can't be found in newspapers. Sometimes, when I'm fighting though another weeklong migraine or waiting in some therapist's office, I wonder why Jonathan did it. *What did he want?* As if any motive could be distilled to a single sentence. Maybe it was like a science experiment, an attempt to bypass that clumsy delivery system of wood and metal, get right to the result. I imagine him digging his fingers into the can, feeling all that ribbed lead. All the possibilities, different paths they could take. Most of the time I can forgive him.

I liked the hospital. It was near Princeton and my room had a gorgeous view of trees, a concrete walkway, a perfectly rectangular, well-kept lawn. I had my own room and cable TV. Tommy had to be civil to me when there were people around, and there were always people around. My father often brought me meals and even though the food couldn't have tasted very good, I thought for some reason that he cooked every meal. I actually pictured him wearing a chef's hat, whittling down an infinite pile of carrots just for me. And it made me feel a little better. I wasn't physically ill—I just had headaches where every thought felt like an echo, headaches where my eyes throbbed and ached. "Maybe they'll explode," Tommy said helpfully after the doctor handed me some pills and left. They told me there wasn't much they could do, just treat the symptoms.

During those weeks, legal documents, release forms, and insurance paperwork circulated through my room like sterile air, neutral and powerless. In the real world, two important things happened: My father lost his job and made a friend. I don't remember it well, but my father probably decided he didn't want to shorthand his production line any longer and quit. At any rate, he spent a lot of his time in the hospital's chapel. I've never been there, but I picture it having giant angelic stained-glass windows, a balding sad-eyed nondenominational preacher, and plenty of literature about coping, grieving, coming to terms. It was in this environment that my father met "the doctor," as if he were the only one on the planet. Eventually, to our father, he was the only one who mattered. Near the end of my second week in the hospital, our father introduced him as "the doctor" to us, so we called him that. We were scared of him. Our father wasn't in the business of explaining things, so for years we weren't sure how they'd met or what they'd talked about. The doctor was once chief of surgery at the hospital, but he'd recently retired. They'd both lost jobs—maybe that was enough of a bond for them. Years later, I asked Tommy about it.

"Dad just said, 'We prayed together,' as if that explained everything. He was best friends with you if you prayed with him. I guess that was the secret," Tommy said. Of course, neither Tommy nor I had ever prayed with him. We were too young, too savage for him to consider us fellow Christians. He probably could have found a support group in Trenton, but there weren't many fathers in Princeton whose sons had bullets in their heads. He must have felt very alone, and there must have been something solid, immovable in the doctor—his white beard, his bushy eyebrows, his intense blue-eyed stare—that immediately earned our father's trust.

At any rate, I was released from the hospital after nearly twenty days. I'd actually felt okay after the first week, but I'd faked my headaches to stay longer. We were all sad to leave the hospital's soft white comfort, the clean antiseptic smell, the chaos banished to emergency wards and morgues. But now, my father was jobless and we'd probably have to move. It must have been hard for him, his pride, but my father asked the doctor to watch us while he searched for a new job. And the doctor accepted.

2

THE SPIRIT BOWL

I didn't know about resonant frequencies, how the right vibrating pitch can shake buildings apart. But I could feel something shifting around me—perhaps those lead shards in my brain, perhaps my brother's anger at leaving our old house. All I knew was that our father was surrendering us. There was a sense of being carried to the end of the world, to this new forested edge of New Jersey, but mostly there was just the hum of tires on the highway. My brother and I were too young. People tried to shield us from our capitalized disasters: Dad's Job Search, Moving. We wanted to believe them, so we folded our panic deep into our suitcases.

A dirt road jarred us from our stupor. We sat up and bounced as our father gripped the steering wheel in surprise. He stared at the directions on the passenger seat. None of us expected dirt roads in America—not in the early 90s, the height of history and progress. Then, as if to chide us, a mansion appeared like we'd seen on television, white and colonial with a phalanx of trees on either side. The front door opened and the doctor walked down the driveway to meet us. He and my father hugged and watched with vague disapproval as my brother Tommy and I dragged our luggage up the long driveway. A few minutes later, the doctor's wife came out to help us.

"Think of this as a vacation," our father said to us in Korean, by way of farewell. "Behave or I'll kill you." Us, standing in the driveway. The black heel of his shoe, tension in his shoulders as he shifted into reverse, turned his head, and backed down the driveway. The doctor's wife smiled at us as if to say *Everything's fine*, but we knew better. Our father wasn't going far to search for a new job, but there was something ominous about his departure, as if everyone sensed his journey didn't guarantee success.

———

The doctor and his wife were generous, kind people. We were not, fourteen-year-old Tommy and I. I'd spent the first few days like a magpie stealing for a nest while our hosts were busy preparing meals and scrubbing our muddy footprints from the carpet. Our first Saturday night in the mansion, I emptied my pockets onto my bed sheet. I'd collected a #1 Ticonderoga pencil, some photographs and heart-shaped paperclips, a black marble. The exploring and theft were thrilling enough, but as I looked over the items, a different feeling settled in my young brain. The photographs weren't merely trinkets—their combination of paper, gloss, and image offered the closest I'd come to honest answers. What happened if my father didn't find a job? My work with the photographs felt more like divination, calling forth meaning from the pictures. It felt like detective work: research, interrogation, report filing. It would be a long night. My brother was reading, sitting Indian-style and looking at the nude tribeswomen in one of the doctor's *National Geographic* magazines. He had a bowl of popcorn which he lifted to his mouth like a horse eating oats from a bucket. His focus on these two tasks meant peace, at least for a while.

The first photograph I'd stolen from the doctor's office, frame and all, was of the doctor and my father, taken sometime when I was in the hospital. They're at a restaurant, the kind where a plastic swordfish hangs on the wall behind their table. This was so strange for me—back then, it was hard for me to picture them anywhere else but the hospital.

The doctor is wearing his usual suit, except with a lemon-yellow tie, and in the picture has just tossed something in the air. It's blurred by motion, but it looks like something made of paper. Next to him, my father's about to laugh, clapping his hands. There's a high contrast: my father, a proud anvil of a chest with broad shoulders, a shock of thick black hair. The doctor was white, pale compared to my father, with white hair, even back then. I couldn't get over the look on the doctor's face. He was laughing, which must have sounded hearty and generous. I stared at the two smiling patriarchs, so stern and unknowable in real life. This photograph felt more forbidden than pornography, and even more precious.

A few pictures popped out when I slid open the frame, stuck to the back of the first. They were mostly old people I didn't know, but one was a Polaroid, some distant relative of the doctor's, I supposed. The face was contorted and marred by fingerprints now permanently burned into the paper. It was an elderly white man with fierce bushy eyebrows. His open mouth was the only source of emotion, bellowing at the height of some kind of electric madness.

I leaned it against the lamp on my nightstand and watched him scream out the open window. There were feathery insect sounds and peeper frogs, a desperate struggle for survival in the matte black outside.

Our alarm clock was a non-digital relic that read 10:50 PM. "Hey fatty." My brother had silently moved to stand next to my bed. "Where did you get those from?" he said, moving backwards to stand on his own bed, the whole time staring into my eyes. He was about a foot taller but slim, like a stretched out, uglier version of me. We were dressed nicely enough in denim shorts and pastel polo shirts, but we both had the same unfortunate haircuts, newly crafted for our vacation by our father with a barber's kit he'd bought at a garage sale. They were frustratingly close to the popular crew-cut-plus-rat-tail, but they more closely resembled flat tops, gelled with a flammable waxy substance. Tommy discovered the flammability our first night: I awoke to see a glowing orange disk float under my bed and then hit the wall. There was still a black spot we couldn't clean—we knew they'd find it someday.

I swept the trinkets over the photographs and pushed the pile behind me. "The doctor's wife gave them to me," I said.

"You're a freaking liar," he said, shining a flashlight in my eyes. I squinted, wanting only to sleep. The flashlight clicked off and he vanished, replaced by a reddish afterimage and a stabbing pain behind my eyes. "The doctor's gonna find out," he said, his voice ominous in the dark room.

"You're gonna tell?"

"Doctor's gonna find out about you."

"Gonna tattle?"

"You're done for," he kept saying.

"Tattle tale tit..."

"Shut up now. I'm going to bed," he said.

"Went and had a fit—" A bowl of popcorn flew like artillery and landed all over my bedspread, the kernels intermixing with my precious artifacts, which I'd just hidden under my bed. "Damn it," I said, hopping to the floor.

"Serves you right, thief." He pulled the covers over his face.

I removed the popcorn and rearranged the pile alphabetically. I had to rely on the moonlight, which required me to stay in front of my window, locked open to let the late summer breeze in. I worked quickly, leaning away from the window, a thin screen the only protection from many-legged bitey things. There was a shrieking noise and wind chimes—Tommy said no, he couldn't hear anything. "And shut up, too." While I was re-sorting the photographs in chronological order, a crashing sound and what might have been a human voice screaming sent me to bed, the thin bed sheet tight over my face. I could barely breathe and stayed this way for a long time, muttering curses. After a lull in the evil noise outside, I shed the covers, stood, and slipped the open-mouthed Polaroid under my brother's pillow.

———

It was around 9 AM when the curtains opened with the snap of sparrow wings and the room exploded with light. "The doctor wants you up," the doctor's wife said. They were our parents until our father returned, that was the rule. It was easier to follow their directions: Don't swear, wear shirts to the dinner table (and the rest of the time), blah blah, so we did most of the time.

I stomped down the wooden stairs and slumped over the table. I sat in the chair next to the telephone and ate my cereal slowly until the doctor walked in. He was in his sixties, with worn lines in his face and a permanent frown. He had the look of a man who went long stretches without eating. He wasn't skeletal, but he had deep eye sockets and the first pair of blue eyes I'd ever seen in person. Icy. He looked like an explorer, someone whose closet held leather suitcases, khakis, collared expedition shirts. Even now, when I picture him, he's traveling through the wilds of Alaska on a dogsled or screaming orders through a hurricane to the crew of a doomed sailboat. But he was, as I'd mentioned, a retired chief of surgery. Doctors watched people die and conjured babies from blood and screams. There was something awe-inspiring about this. But someone who trained groups of doctors? Even adults—the mailman, supermarket cashiers—seemed intimidated by him. To Tommy and me, he seemed like one of the pre-Christian gods, inexplicable and terrifying. He was hard of hearing and since we were raised never to raise our voices to adults, he would glare and move closer as we spoke. We would back away, which confused and annoyed him.

Shortly after we arrived, he retreated to his study and my brother and I avoided him, trying to shove each other into the pond in the backyard and going on drives with his wife. We thought about them I suppose the way millionaires think about their butlers. On rare occasions when we had to address them, we called "the doctor" exactly that, as our father did. It never felt right to call the doctor's wife Mrs. Cedric, the same way one might feel calling the First Lady Mrs. ____. So, "the doctor's wife" it was. Years later, I would learn that calling a surgeon a doctor was like calling a human being a primate. But he allowed it out of friendship with my father, who, despite his fluency, was not a native speaker and may have had trouble pronouncing the title. Asian languages have a complicated relationship with the letter "r": *doctull* sounded better than *suell-a-jin*.

That particular morning, though, the doctor's wife must have insisted on some meaningful interaction between the men in the house. The doctor's wife was hosting her annual summer party that week, so our job was to pull weeds in the tomato garden. The garden was surrounded by a chain-link fence to keep out deer, and there was a path in the middle made of rotting boards. The doctor seemed strangely underdressed in cargo shorts and a white tank top. It was already unbearably hot, the insects trying to escape the humidity by flying into our hair, our sleeves and ears. I wiped the sweat from my forehead and pulled at a dandelion, but the root broke off and remained in the ground. Shrugging, I threw it in the bucket. The doctor picked through the plants, putting the good tomatoes in a plastic Cool Whip container. The rest he mashed into the dirt with his foot.

"There's a beast in here," Tommy said, holding up a small brown frog. He bounced it a few times in his hand.

With some effort, the doctor stood up and walked over. "That's a toad. *Bufo americanus*, that's the scientific name. A native of the New World and of course plentiful here in Princeton." At times like these, he spoke louder and gestured as if he were addressing a note-taking class of lesser surgeons. "There has been talk of changing the nomenclature." He laughed to himself. "And perhaps they will. Simpler language for a simpler era."

"We need a hero to slay this beast," Tommy said. He turned it over and stabbed at it with his finger.

"The only beast to be slain here is indolence," declared the doctor.

"Hey Jason, you want to take a picture?"

"I do not," I said, glaring at my brother.

"Jason's a photographer. A idealogerrr. He takes pictures," Tommy said in a singsong voice, emphasizing *takes*. Very clever. He pretended to throw the toad at me and I flinched. I gave him a look that said, *You got me, OK, now stop.* The doctor kneeled and frowned at a tomato plant as he fussed with the leaves.

A dirt clod hit Tommy square in the chest and exploded. Some of the dirt went into his nose and eyes. He shook his shirt and snorted, then stepped toward me. "You piece-a—"

"Knock it off," the doctor warned.

"Did Jason tell you about his collection?" Tommy said, brushing off his shirt.

"What did you say?" the doctor said.

"Tell the doctor what you've been doing with his magazines," I screamed, pointing at Tommy. "And why you stole those photographs and hid them under my bed," I shouted, my eleven-year-old mind flushed with my own brilliance. Tommy's face reddened as he stood up. He threw his bucket across the garden and opened his mouth to scream but stopped. Later, we found out he'd had a panic attack and fainted. But at that moment, it was terrifying the way he simply collapsed—dropped straight to the ground. The toad hopped from his hand. After a few seconds, it became clear this was all not a joke.

"Oh my God," the doctor said. I ran into the house without a word, my mind swimming. He must have thought I was going to call his wife or the hospital. But really, I was running upstairs to our bedroom to hide the evidence, that black-magic photograph under Tommy's pillow which had, for all I knew, just killed my brother.

Tommy survived his brush with the dark arts. If voodoo actually worked and had I arranged my curses just right, perhaps he would have turned into a toad. Or we could have switched places: He would become a fat kleptomaniac and I would become good at making farting noises with my hands. I don't remember much about his return from the hospital, but I do remember talking to my father. There was a lot of noise in the background, wherever he was. I pictured a diner, bells, and clattering plates. A newspaper in front of him, opportunity after opportunity circled and crossed out. "All is well—that's what everyone says. Tell the truth about your brother," he said.

"All *is* well," I said, quickly handing the phone back to Tommy.

After he hung up, my brother sat smirking at me, kicking his legs in the tall chair. He was sitting behind an enormous wooden bowl of cherry tomatoes, making a whistling noise as he tossed one in the air and caught it in his mouth. Anxiety, the doctors at the hospital had said—he should rest for the next few days. He smiled and said he'd sure miss working in the garden.

Even though the doctor wanted me to continue weeding, his wife intervened and said we brothers should spend some time alone. So we sat facing each other at the thick oak table in the kitchen. Tommy picked up the magnifying glass the doctor used to read the newspaper and looked through it at me. "Dad just said he's only taking me back. Only room for one," he said, blinking his massive bloodshot eye.

"Liar." To Tommy's credit, he never verbally blamed me for making us move from Trenton. He knew it would have resulted in what we called "the smackaround." Our father felt bad about what happened at the camp—he'd supported my Boy Scout career, after all. But I'm not sure Tommy at that age really linked me to what was happening. To him—to both of us, actually—life just kind of happened around us. The only constant was that we were free to attack each other when no one was looking.

"And he's gonna get me a freaking wheelchair 'cause of all my anxieties. And then I'm gonna run your fat ass over with it."

"Hardly," I said, looking down at my belly. He made some more fat jokes.

"Shut up." I flipped through *The New York Times* on the table, searching for the funny pages.

"You're gonna live in the forest and eat toads. *Buffoonus Americanos*. But someday, a toad will eat *you*."

"Shut up...hospital boy," I said. It was a mean thing to say, but I didn't back down.

"Dad said he's coming back for me next week. Maybe no one's coming for you," he said, standing to examine a wooden elephant displayed on the bookshelf behind us. He walked out of the room, leaving me to ponder the very real possibility that even the doctor and his wife would vanish and the fruit in the bowls on the table would rot and I would sit and wait forever.

The next week, Tommy took revenge. After all, he'd been made to pass out, to look weak in front of the doctor. Someone had to pay. Still feeling a little guilty about calling him hospital boy, I picked out the rocks he snuck into my food and didn't tell anyone when I woke to find him putting my hand in a bowl of warm pond water. I think it was water, anyway. But as the week went on, my patience and sympathy ran out. I began plotting.

It happened when we were in the doctor's study, playing a new game he'd invented: Whoever could go the longest without speaking would receive a coveted flashlight, a little metal penlight that resembled a light saber. After a period of silent taunting, we decided to ignore each other. Tommy stood on a chair, trying to reach the anatomy books at the top of the bookshelves. I stared out the window at the forest outside, reviewing my plan. The doctor was somewhere upstairs, listening.

After mulling over my brother's transgressions, I put my plan into action. I really didn't have anything to lose. There were two doors to the study and since the doctor was upstairs, he'd have to come through the one closer to us, which was currently closed. It was perfect. I walked over to the desk and opened the cigar box partially hidden by a stack of magazines. Now I had Tommy's attention. I pulled out a cigar and with some effort bit off the tip like I'd seen in a cartoon. I spit the tobacco into the wastebasket, wiped my mouth, and stood listening for a few moments. I found a Zippo in a desk drawer and flicked it open. *What the frig are you doing?* Tommy mouthed. A few moments later, I heard the doctor creaking down the stairs slowly because of his bad knees. But Tommy didn't seem to notice. He kept waving his hands, as if to say, *What the frig?* I held a finger to my lips and he sat down, mesmerized. Usually, he was the first to act. *No way. You wouldn't frigging even*, he was thinking. I ran the cigar under my nose, relishing the freshness of the experience, the texture and the exotic scent, so different from the taste. I flicked the lighter, waving the cigar over the flame. Tommy sat down, a look of awe on his face. *Holy crap*, he mouthed. He waved his hands and sort of bounced. *My insane little brother—*I sincerely hope there was some pride in his gyrations, even if it was only one of several emotions he was trying so poorly to contain. I closed my eyes and put the cigar in my mouth.

"What's going on in there?" came the doctor's voice. He must have smelled it and was now really hoofing it down the stairs. I raised my eyebrows and took another puff. My brother looked at the door, then at me. I still hadn't put the cigar down. *Holy crap!* Then, just as the door handle turned, I tossed the burning cigar in my brother's lap and bolted through the open door.

The doctor's wife drove a purple car. Even though it was streamlined and sporty-looking, I usually would have been embarrassed to ride in such a girly colored vehicle, but I didn't mind that day. I slumped in the back seat, staring out the window. The seat in front hid most of the doctor except a bit of white hair that rose above the headrest like a cloud. I had my new flashlight but couldn't see the beam in the sunlight, so I pressed my forehead to the cool window and watched the scenery.

She drove through a grid of mansions and thick trees. "There's Einstein's house," she said, slowing as we passed a little white house with a big porch. It was too small and plain, I decided, looking around for the real house, which I imagined as a solid-gold mansion shaped like a mushroom cloud. We turned the corner and I couldn't see the block anymore. The doctor pointed to a baseball field. He started to say something but caught himself.

"You don't play baseball, do you?" he asked me. I said no, that was my brother. I could barely walk up a flight of steps without passing out. Tommy was rotting at home doing some kind of punishment for smoking a cigar—I couldn't wait to tell him about this drive. It smelled like freshly mowed grass outside and someone was burning a woodpile somewhere. The doctor closed his eyes again. I rolled down the window and stuck my hand out to catch the wind.

It was around noon and the sun would have been a problem anywhere else. But this was Princeton, where everything was old. The town absorbed rather than reflected, and there was a certain softness to the old mansions, like stones along a river or the worn pages of a book. It would have hurt my eyes to stare at the glossy fences and mailboxes back in our first American house in Trenton.

Scattered houses gave way to green fields, streaks of yellow wheat at the borders. She drove a few miles on a bumpy dirt road. "We used to buy all our veggies here when I was a girl," she said as the road got dustier. She had short hair, almost like a man's, and was wearing a pink summer dress with white flowers on it. At the farm, the doctor gave me money and let me pay for the vegetables—the responsibility was part of my reward, he said.

We took a different route home. I was tired, but the scenery was enough for me to forget about my father's job search, about what would happen when he returned. Out the window were things I'd only seen on TV, the opposite of Trenton's concrete and razor fence. It occurred to me that without even trying, I had found what my father was ultimately searching for: paradise and harmony.

After taking the corn, squash, and other veggies to the kitchen, I checked on Tommy, who glared up, then turned over his essay on integrity and honesty. He took out a pencil and wrote *I'm going to frigging kill you You turkey turd burger.* I probably did something obnoxious like click my flashlight on to shine it on the page. *Your frigging DED man,* Tommy wrote. Then he erased it and went back to work.

The same day, the doctor's wife was unpacking boxes in the attic, which was basically an entire floor above the bedrooms. Hoping to find more trinkets, I volunteered to help. We worked by the windows at the far end of the attic where there was nothing but a wide expanse of worn wooden floor. There was a haze in the sunlight and dust—late in the day when I was tired, it seemed as if all the boxes had simply evaporated.

She wore a purple bandana with a floral print on it. From

pictures I'd seen, she didn't look much older than she had on her wedding day. Except she had really long hair then, down to her waist. And it was darker, still blonde but not almost white. She was a small woman. I could see it especially in her wrists and hands as she lifted some wine glasses to the light. They had a date etched in them, but before I could make them out, she wrapped them in brown paper and placed them in a small box. Watching her repeat this process with various items, I forgot about my father for a while. But he surfaced again as we taped up the box and together slid it across the room. "What happens when my father comes back?" I asked, meaning, *What happens if he can't find a job or can only afford to take one of us with him?*

"Well," she answered carefully, "I suppose you'll keep living with your father. When he finds a job." This prospect did not excite me, but I'd been living with him my entire life. Somehow, I thought I could stay in Princeton forever. Because I was special, because I was wounded, because I was so different than my father and brother. At the time, it seemed like such a small, pathetic hope—a sort of droopy thing I'd finally exposed. As we packed boxes in that attic, it seemed like opportunities were being strangled and cut off, new blank spots on a map. It didn't occur directly to me because I never considered what a job was and how the accident had affected my father. But it was beginning to dawn on me that I was somehow the cause of the current panic. The doctor's wife was standing over me. Deep in thought, I was about to sit down on the box when she grabbed my hands. Without thinking, I held on and let her pull me back up. "We're having a party tomorrow," she said. "Let's forget about that for now, shall we?"

Tommy and I spent the rest of the afternoon shucking corn for the party. After we finished, I retreated to the living room to sit in my favorite chair. It faced a brass bowl that held a bundle of dusty firewood. The house didn't have a TV, so the bowl took its place. When a car passed in front of the windows, the bowl's seams and dents shifted with the light. I watched, idly wondering about all the millionaires driving past. The drapes were porous and the world outside looked blissful.

Inside, there wasn't much to look at. On the wall above my chair was a red-and-white rug depicting rows of alien-looking stick figures holding hands. The carpet was light brown. There were magazines on the coffee table, but they were big words, tiny print, and even the pictures were boring. The only other thing in the room was the flea trap, which had a little bulb above a tray of amber sticky paper. Sometimes I'd watch and commiserate with the bugs stuck on their backs, legs waving in the air.

Tommy walked in and sat down. He was planning something stupid and mean—I recognized that bored, predatory look in his eyes. He looked at the flea trap, then at me. I left quickly.

In the living room, I could pretend to read magazines, but I knew it would only be a matter of time before the doctor spotted me wandering around the house and assigned a chore. I considered my options and walked right into his study.

"Bored?" the doctor said. I shook my head. He laughed. "Of course not." I stared at the hole someone had burned in the carpet with a cigar.

"Tommy wanted to know if there were any chores he could do," I said.

"Tommy said that, did he? What a thoughtful brother you are," said the doctor, laughing. I backed away slowly, figuring he wouldn't notice. I planned to exit the room in this fashion. "Work is...important for a man," he said finally. "It's a shame I don't have any for you."

My eyes fixed on a blue-and-white striped bowl at the top of a display cabinet. There were more colorful bowls in the cabinet, but they didn't hold my attention. "You like pottery?" the doctor said, as if he were about to give me something. I nodded, responding more to his tone. "You have good taste," he said, walking over. He lifted the bowl from its stand and shook a dead spider from it. "This might very well be the capstone of my collection. Anasazi." He raised his voice a little. "The Anasazi were American Indians who lived in the Mesa Verde, near New Mexico. Leslie," he said, gesturing to his wife, "attended college in New Mexico. The best archeological minds are still trying to figure out how these people lived, considering the lack of food in the area. No one knows where they buried their dead. They found small burial sites but not enough for such a large settlement. They did migrate to the Mesa Verde, upon which they built cliff dwellings—have they taught you any of this yet?" I shook my head. "The Anasazi are also problematic because one day they simply..." He held his hand out in a fist, tightened and opened it, shaking particles of nothing onto the carpet.

"Disappeared?" I said.

"About the same time this bowl was made, actually. Eleven hundred AD."

I sat down in the chair opposite the desk. "And they just left this behind?" I said, eyeing the bowl.

"Among other artifacts."

"Why did they disappear?"

"Ah. Another mystery. Some scholars believe there was a drought. Or disease. Some...explorer recently found evidence of cannibalism among the tribe. This...claim could always be some fiction, something to scare up some fame and grant money."

"Cannibals." This wasn't history. It couldn't be. My brain turned this Anasazi puzzle over and over. In the lingo of the era, it was a paradigm shift. I'd just learned that entire civilizations could impossibly exist and then vanish. The ground under my feet was not as solid as I'd believed.

"They left carvings, but no one has been able to decipher them. I've come to believe this bowl came from a dubious source," he said, holding it so I could see the full pattern inside. Four blue, pencil-thin stripes curved toward a vanishing point in the center. The bowl was about the size of a salad dish. It certainly didn't look more than eight hundred years old. But even now, my memory flashes to that pattern, perfect—as if machined—against the cream-white interior. I wanted to hold it, impatient to trace my fingers along its pale slopes.

"A spirit bowl. It may be the only such surviving. Usually when the bowl's craftsman died, his kinsmen smashed the bowl to set the spirit free. Dubious, as I said, that this one is still intact. The man I bought it from has since gone the way of the Anasazi, so to speak." He laughed.

"Can I hold it?" I said.

With some effort, he put the bowl back on its stand in the cabinet. "Did you say something?" he said.

Tommy walked into the room. "What's shakin'?" he said. I wasn't about to surrender this new secret.

"Come help me set the table," the doctor's wife called from down the hall. She entered the room to lead him out.

That evening, I stole a bottle of port during the party. I had first admired the bottle itself, made of cut crystal. But I really began to covet it when the doctor noticed my interest and moved it to the top of the liquor cabinet. But he forgot to lock it and there were so many chairs in the basement that obtaining the bottle wasn't a problem. I would drink some, it would taste like liquid Skittles, and I'd fill the difference with water. Since the doctor didn't drink anymore, no one would notice. I was proud of this plan.

I sat at the desk the doctor used to tie flies, which was stacked high with clear plastic craft boxes. I flicked on the fluorescent magnifying light and swiveled it to survey the feathery objects and wicked-looking silver tools arranged on the desk. If my father didn't return, I could help the doctor. He could say, "Tweezer-thingy" and I would hand it to him. I took a sip of the port and tried to keep a straight face. My mouth burned as I swallowed, my throat convulsing against the liquid. *This stuff's gone bad*, I thought. But I'd committed to the plan. I took a less enthusiastic sip, listening to the party above. I could make out the light classical music playing through the old stereo speakers. I loosened my tie and stretched my legs, pressing my back against the chair. Tommy would be too busy trying to charm people to notice my absence. But the doctor wouldn't. I walked up the stairs, feeling queasy. I figured it would pass.

There were some new paintings in the living room. There was a seaside European town (lots of blue and yellow lights) and a purple seascape in the kitchen. I stared at them for a few moments and moved on. Color swirled around me, most of it late-summer pastels in the women's dresses.

My wandering took me to the doctor's study, to the bowl inside, but the door was locked. I put my ear to the door and heard a faint humming, as if people on the other side were having a hushed argument. A passing party guest gave me a disapproving look and I moved on.

There were enough people that no one really noticed me. Some waved or tried to engage me in conversation, but I just nodded and moved on like I was looking for something. I drifted among the crowd, completely at the mercy of gravity and my own tired legs. Tommy was holding a snifter of sparkling grape juice, talking to some older men. "Here's my little brother," he said, grabbing me by the shoulders. But I shook free with porcine grace and fled the room. My head felt like it weighed a million pounds. It was getting harder for my neck to hold it up. *I'm not gonna freak out*, I mentally repeated to myself.

Before Princeton, there were times I'd grab the wrong cup at breakfast and gasp for breath after taking a sip. I remember how our father's coffee burned our eyes—Tommy and I had contests to see who could stare into the acid steam mug the longest. This party was supposed to be my first step into the adult world that ran on burning liquids and sat glassy-eyed for days on end. But I'd effed it up and suddenly had the feeling that this misstep would lead to a long, unpleasant stumbling.

I found myself on the back porch, sitting at a picnic table. The cool breeze woke me up a little. Through the screen door, I watched the doctor inside. People waved and shook his hand, but he never really stopped to talk. He was smiling, or at least doing his best. He slid open the screen door and sat down across from me without saying a word. He started to say something, then caught himself. Looking back, I think he was about to ask whether I was having fun, but the answer must have been clear. There were a couple of people outside smoking, but they didn't see him. The breeze already a distant memory, I felt the humidity creep beneath my shirt, around my neck. I loosened my tie again and took a deep breath. I sat on my hands, feeling them press against the wicker seat. The doctor sighed and stood up slowly, trying to hide the pain in his knees. As he passed, he put his hand on my shoulder as if to say, *I know exactly how you feel*, then returned to the crowd.

My brother was too busy entertaining party guests to notice

that everyone else at the party was white. I felt naked when I suddenly realized this, strangely exposed. But Tommy didn't see that we were guests, that we didn't belong and now wouldn't stay much longer. Somewhere in the wilds of New Jersey, our father's search was drawing to a close. After he found his job, we would be whisked from this moneyed purgatory forever. The weight of that finality was as overwhelming as the humidity outside. One giant opportunity lost.

Maybe I'd been on the ground for hours when someone lifted and carried me. I tried to open my eyes, but all I could see were the beige carpeted stairs.

"Are you a cannibal?" I asked. The man shifted me in his arms and I heard the doctor's voice.

"Truly your father's son. I hope you remember this," he said.

I said something like, "Please don't kill me," and may have offered up my brother as an alternative. But beyond this easy and automatic betrayal, meaning detached itself from words. The hallway wasn't long, so the trip to my room must have been just a few minutes.

"Damn, you're heavy," I remember him saying. His knees popped as he set me down on the bed. The chilling insect noises entered through the window. The doctor put his hand on my forehead. It was huge and cold and after a few seconds everything went quiet. Everything flowed away from me—only calm and sleep remained.

"Good night," I managed to say, out of habit. He laughed quietly and left, turning out the light behind him.

I had a strange headache the next morning, as if I were viewing everything from behind a wavy glass. Sounds were more distant, as if underwater. But I was able to get dressed and walk downstairs with little difficulty. The clock on the microwave said 6:04 AM. I poured myself some cereal. It was nice eating alone, I decided. I could sit and think all I wanted without anyone interrupting. As the sun came up, I worked a little in the garden. I knew I was in a lot of trouble but somehow wasn't worried. I'd survived the party and that was enough. No one mentioned anything at lunch and I considered the possibility that no one had noticed my drunkenness at the party. When dinner came and went and I went upstairs to bed without incident, I considered myself safe—a miracle.

But that day, I watched everyone closely as I anticipated my punishment. I watched the doctor's wife sort through what seemed like centuries of memories in the attic. She was throwing away so much. The doctor spent the afternoon in the garden, holding up tomatoes and lecturing to some invisible class. Tommy threw rocks at ducks in the pond. Events like these were commonplace that summer, but somehow I was beginning to see their actual shape, everyone trapped in their own sad little worlds. Of course, I hadn't jumped in front of the bullet, hadn't invited the accident. But it felt like the bullet's path had somehow been preordained just for me. It was as if I'd been cursed, and my family would forever suffer because of me. And, of course, I couldn't have articulated this feeling when I was eleven. But it was there.

The headache became a sort of dull static in my mind. I still heard the noises at night, but now there were new ones, a new buzz on the telephone line when I spoke to my father. There was a hysteria beneath his calm voice only I could hear, certain words that shook when he said them. In the gray diners of New Jersey, he sat next to a stack of want ads as tall as he was, a red-eyed scarecrow of doubt and failure. I knew my father would burst into tears if I said the wrong thing. I couldn't sleep. This new humming was shaking me apart and only I seemed to feel it. Sick and sleepless, I became lost among the signs and wonders, the late summer delirium thickening my blood.

The night before my father arrived, everyone pretended to be happy. He would arrive in time for dinner and would share the news then. Everything would work out. I heard this phrase a lot back then, but there was a desperate hollowness behind the words. There was something behind the fear that bred and multiplied. Where *would* we go from here? I had that feeling again: Here is the yawning edge of the ocean and I'm leaning over too far, dizzy.

Realizing it might be my last chance, I touched the spirit bowl that night and instantly regretted it. The blue lines, slightly indented, were exactly as far apart as my fingers—I remember that very clearly. The bowl felt strangely damp, fevered. I spent the rest of the night upstairs in bed, curled up and wondering what it all meant. I knew how records worked—what awful song had those blue grooves worked into me? I laid awake and waited for my father to arrive.

3

A BOY NAMED SOO

My father arrived just before dinner and said he had an announcement. At the dinner table, I sat across from him, my fat hands gripping the table. Something had been welling in my chest for the past week. "Everything will work out" was a lie pulled taut over the big mystery and didn't change the fact that my father had returned with bad posture and a sad smile. My chest tightened and I could hardly breathe. Everyone at the table wanted desperately to run away as my father cleared his throat and stood. It was unbearable, yet we all stayed. I took a few breaths, drawing nothing. Like an asthmatic looking for an inhaler, I ran from the room. It felt good to run, let my legs carry me away. I was in the doctor's study when I stopped to catch my breath, the blue-and-white bowl above me. People were coming, but I didn't care. I stood on the bottom shelf and grabbed it. The heat and glory of it, back in my hands.

"What do you have, Jason?" my father said. Apparently he didn't know anything about pottery, either. Maybe he thought I was hungry and getting cereal. He forced a smile. He patted my head as I passed him and followed me out of the room. "Where you going, tiger?" he said. *Tie-guh.*

"Oh my God," the doctor said. "Jason—"

I ran through the kitchen, past all of them. They reached out to grab me but I kept running, pushing someone's hand off me. Tommy—here he was grabbing my shirt, but I got away. Now came the real yelling and commotion. "He's lost it. Call a SWAT team," Tommy yelled. Because Princeton had lots of those.

Upstairs, our bedroom. I scrambled out the open window onto the gable and stood with one leg balanced on either side. It was starting to get dark out—the grass below was blue. The stars emerged in new constellations. I held the bowl in my hands and looked around, amazed at the sudden change of pace. I greedily sucked in the night air.

"He's in here," the doctor's wife said. She took a step into my room. "What are you doing with that, darling?" My father started to crawl through the window.

"Snipers," Tommy suggested helpfully.

There I am—that's me on the roof. Eleven years old and I've climbed the summit of Mount Princeton. At that moment, I know exactly what I'm doing. With all this tension, the bowl has to break. I press it between my sweating hands—it's charging somehow, I can feel the current shaking my heart until all I hear is the rush of my blood. I can see my family through the window, advancing. I back to the edge and everyone stops. Everything stops except the ringing in my ears. And when the world—lines and grids of light, the outline of the United States—when every ear in the universe has leaned toward this one rooftop in Princeton, I hurl down the bowl and watch it shatter, the pieces sliding down the roof. They fall glittering to the lawn below and I feel the universe exhale. And then my foot slips on a crumbling shingle, and I'm falling.

All I remember was my body just beginning to twist as I hit the ground. And I was back in the hospital. My father and brother moved without me to a small town in Pennsylvania, where he'd found a factory job. He couldn't lose another job because of me, and the doctor agreed to take care of me until I was better. My father saved a lot of money on food alone, and that must have pleased him. There was a vague agreement that he would eventually return to claim me. Maybe there was a handshake involved or a signing of papers: I picture a mahogany desk and a pen on a metal stand, but the whole thing was probably an informal affair. *Sure, we'll watch him for a bit, monitor his symptoms. Until he gets better.* But I made sure not to get better. I exaggerated my headaches, came up with strange new symptoms. After living in a Princeton mansion, there was something shabby and sad about my father's thick work pants, his rough hands. I hated him for that, for how much he embarrassed me. And if I didn't hate my brother, it was nice to use the bathroom without worrying whether he was going to burst in and throw something at me. It was nice having my own bedroom.

And even if they didn't say it, the doctor and his wife were happy to have me. Maybe they liked having someone youthful around. Maybe the doctor's wife knew I would occupy her husband's time, give him purpose in his restless, unhappy retirement. My father and brother occasionally visited and called. I never asked to return and I suppose my father let me stay in Princeton because he wanted the best for me. Maybe even then, he understood that I viewed him and Tommy as painfully cheap and shabby: T-shirts in church, ice in the wine. But there was a distance between us even when we all lived in the same house. I simply didn't like either of them. We never bridged the distance and, looking back, it's almost shameful how quickly we grew comfortable with the widening gulf between us.

Eight years passed uneventfully. I enjoyed brief celebrity as a miracle child, a beneficiary of medical science but mostly fortune. I used the story on prospective friends in high school and later on dates. "Really? You drank ten beers at the Alpha Sigma Pi party you snuck into last night? *I have a fucking bullet lodged in my brain.* I'm in a medical journal. Two, actually. Yes, ma'am, I'm fine, although I used to black out when I was younger. How did it happen? Well, let me tell you..." It was a good story, and I was quietly accepted into this different family, this different community. There was school and so many activities. Although it would be nice to imagine a growing nostalgia for Tommy or my father, the truth is that I rarely thought about them, if at all. This was my new life, and we'd all moved on. No sense getting sentimental about it. I was happy, and I supposed they were happy.

I even got a new name, sort of. "Soo Kyo," my parents named me when I was born. It means "remarkable establishment," especially appropriate in my new home. When I started school in Princeton, my teacher looked at the roster. "Sue," she said, shaking her head. "That won't work." I told her people usually called me Jason. (Only my father used my Korean name, and only when we were alone in the house.) My old name vanished, only to emerge for correction at the beginning of each new grade.

I tried for months to get the doctor and his wife to legally change my name. I'm not sure why it was so important to me back then. I didn't like being called "Sue" the first week of every new grade, even by the other Asian kids, who had secret names like Ryu or Lee, that rare name which passed as normal in either world. I wanted to make my new life official somehow, to use the immovability of law to wall myself from that old ghost family in Pennsylvania. The doctor and his wife refused. I think it was the permanence—they were afraid to claim me, afraid of changing something fundamental that remained inaccessible to them. There was a mysterious depth behind Han Soo Kyo, those three syllables, property of a nation an ocean away. The doctor and his wife weren't imperialists, just temporary caretakers. To Jason the great faker who'd prolonged a sick leave in paradise for eight whole years. Jason the heir to everything Princeton offered.

Like my old name, these issues rarely came up and were easily dismissed. I would like to make it clear that my childhood was not spent in existential torment over cultural identity or familial obligations. I considered my family low-class and cheap; I didn't consider Korea at all. When I looked in the mirror, I was checking my sideburns or, later, for acne. I spent my youthful time and energy on school and friends, sunlight and grass. We explored the neighborhoods and later the mysterious, impenetrable world of girls. There were books, homework, procrastination, cars. Obsession with music (Guns N' Roses, The Stones, Led Zeppelin). Like most boys, there was a summer where I was obsessed with knives. Those eight years passed uneventfully in the way I suppose most childhoods do.

It wasn't until after high school, after I graduated from my prep school, that I was forced to consider what I'd so readily surrendered. My father was dead. He had committed suicide in his small faux wood-paneled living room after working a double shift in a factory. I drove to Pennsylvania to attend his funeral, figuring it was the least I could do.

4

DARKNESS ON THE EDGE OF TOWN

The doctor and his wife accompanied me. Leslie, I call her Leslie now. After living with them for a few years, she insisted on it. The doctor remained as intimidating as ever as I grew up in his house, and I could never bring myself to call him anything but.

They didn't say much and it was a long drive from Princeton to Pennsylvania. In the long silences, I thought about my other family, how our mutual absence must have affected each other. How often did my father think of me? I hoped it was more than three or four times a year. How strange to think that for almost half of my life, we had just been a quiet emptiness in each other's lives. There was little doubt in my mind that to my father I was a clever little weasel who traded his family for a better one and didn't look back. Who knew I could so quickly learn to tie flies, my little fingers effortlessly looping and flourishing? On weekend trips with the doctor, those flies arced brilliantly as New England sunlight flashed off the calm ripples. And all the while, my other family lived a world away, down in a shabby little factory town.

The funeral had the usual rituals, unremarkable except for the fact that the preacher spared the few in attendance the clichés that my father had moved on to a better place, *et cetera*. It had been a suicide; there was no mention of heaven.

Tommy walked in just as the preacher started to speak and even though he saw the doctor, Leslie, and me, he sat on the other side of the aisle. He was wearing khakis and a faded long-sleeve T-shirt. I supposed it was his only black shirt, but it seemed a bit informal. On the other side of the aisle were three or four people, dressed appropriately in collared shirts and ties. I'd never seen them before and assumed they were coworkers at the factory my father had worked at. In total, there were about ten people in attendance.

As soon as the preacher stopped talking and the benediction started, Tommy stood and walked quickly out of the church. I followed him, trying to think of something comforting to say.

"Where are you going?" I said, catching up with him in the parking lot. He stood in front of his car, as if he couldn't wait to leave.

"Nice of you to show up," he said, ignoring my question. *At least I was on time,* I wanted to say, but didn't. His face showed more anger than grief. It was a little hot out, being June, and sweat beaded on his forehead. I looked down, trying to think of something to say, something that didn't sound like it came from a Hallmark card. It looked like he'd recently drawn on the toes of his shoes with a black marker to cover up the scuffs.

The doctor and his wife walked up behind me. I turned and looked at them—the doctor was dressed in a black suit I'd never seen before. It wasn't new, but the threads near the lapels sort of glimmered in the sun. His beard was perfectly trimmed and his shoes were made of soft leather. Leslie wore a simple black dress, a modest diamond pendant hanging from a fine gold chain around her neck. My black shirt and slacks were new—Leslie had bought them for me the day before. I suddenly became aware that I smelled like new clothes, a chemical smell, like an upscale department store.

Tommy wore an almost-scowl as he appraised us, the same look native Brooklynites give to European tourists. "He would've been glad you came, the three of you," he said as he dug in his pocket.

"I'm sorry for your loss," Leslie said quietly.

Tommy took out a bundle of keys and leaned against the side of his car. I thought he was about to get in and dramatically drive off, so I backed away a few feet. The doctor and Leslie followed my lead.

"Here," Tommy said, tossing the keys at me. They fell through my hands and landed in a dull metal heap on the asphalt. I stared at them, confused. "You know, you became his favorite after you left. I never understood it," he said with a smile that almost looked genuine. "*My milac-uh boy, bullet in the head. He lives in Pince-ton now,*" leaning back a little and opening up his throat, sounding eerily like our late father. "Miracle boy. He'd tell people all about you. And there I was. I'd just stand there. I guess he thought you were the future," he said.

"That's not true," I said. But really, I had no clue what our father had thought or said. I wasn't there.

"Those are the keys to the house, which our father left to you. I'll drop off the paperwork later." I picked up the keys and held them out, as if offering them to my brother. Tommy explained that he'd inherited the urn, the ashes. According to the lawyer, he was in charge of "disposal." "You forgot your own father and that's what I got." He looked right at the doctor with an expression that said, *If he forgot his own father, what chance do you have?*

I turned to the doctor, who was looking at me the same way someone does when they're trying to determine the species of a particularly messy roadkill. It wasn't horror, necessarily—it was as if he didn't recognize me. It was like he saw me as a lump of smiling flesh pulled over something otherworldly and cold, tentacled. I felt my face flush hot and red as, a second later, he composed himself and both he and his wife started to say I was actually a very dutiful son.

Tommy cut them off by opening his car door. He weakly slapped the steering wheel and then turned back to me, leaning back on the door. "I'm going to investigate dad's death. I want to know why, and I swear I'm gonna set it right." *And I don't expect anything from you,* he didn't say. He drove off. I picked up the keys to my new house.

After I dropped the doctor and Leslie off at the airport, I called the colleges at which I'd been accepted and deferred my admission. College could wait—for now, I needed to find out why my father had killed himself and, if possible, set things right. My father couldn't grant me forgiveness. But Tommy could forgive me for leaving, I thought. If I found the right answers.

My new house was a small, one-story prefab with white vinyl siding. The blistered white paint fell off the side of the doorframe as I fumbled with the ring of keys. The deadbolt popped and I stepped through the door into the empty house. I'd only visited a couple times and none of it seemed familiar. None of the keys would open the bedroom doors, so I spent the night on the couch trying to ignore the knocking pipes, the sighs of the boards as they expanded in the early summer heat.

Wilkes-Barre, Pennsylvania, is one of the only hyphenated cities in the U.S. There are two pronunciations: Wilks-*Bar* or Wilks-*Bury*, and residents have been arguing over the correct one ever since the city was founded. (There's a third pronunciation, Wilks-bear-*ugh*, but it's only used by the most dull and ignorant of city residents.) During a stand-up gig there, Jerry Seinfeld remarked, "What does it say about a city when the people who live there don't know how to pronounce its name?" It is not named after John Wilkes Booth, as my brother once bragged to me when he was in middle school. Rather, it is named after Mssrs. John Wilkes and Isaac Barré, colonialist sympathizers in Parliament.

Wilkes-Barre is situated in a quiet valley, sitting atop what was one of the largest coal fields in the nation. Huge sections of the city, fast food chains and strip malls, are built on slag piles, broad plains of spent anthracite. Occasionally an old mine shaft will collapse and swallow an entire house or business. They call it mine subsidence and sell insurance for it. More slag piles sprawl outside the city and burn. On clear days, when the underground fires are hot enough, you can see the black smoke diffusing into the horizon.

My father's neighborhood is fairly rural, populated with descendants of Polish coal miners moving outward to escape the noise and crime. And isolated, long stretches of road with nothing but forest to one side. On the other, there's an ancient rock wall guarding empty tan fields. In the spirit of such a neighborhood, everyone was suspicious of new faces, even though I wore khaki shorts and polo shirts.

A few days after I moved in, a spotted black dog wandered into my front yard still trailing a leash. I picked it up to lead him to his rightful owner. I passed a few people before finding the right one, and they all demanded in their own way that I explain my presence. *Oh my Gawd, another one of them. Asian invasion.* Could it be me joyriding down the street, gleefully smashing their mailboxes? Mailbox hockey, it's called, and did I know it was a felony to damage or otherwise molest a mailbox? At the time, people were setting fires to barns all over the state. Blame it on pre-millennium tension or Satanism or someone looking for a cheap thrill. To quell their fears, I introduced myself and asked about my father. I hoped someone might have answers. I didn't know what I was looking for exactly: a cryptic phrase he might have uttered that day, some warning signs that went ignored. I went door-to-door down the street, but no one had talked to him that day. In fact, most of his neighbors didn't know about his death until I told them.

Where my father lived, the coal smoke is almost invisible. There are a couple grocery stores close to the house, a Burger King, and two churches. It's the kind of calm prosperity he must have found comforting. He had, I think, a manageable sort of American dream which was more concept than ambition: a feeling of almost-home, of vaguely static space.

After a few days, I ran out of neighbors to interview and started cleaning. I didn't throw anything away at first, figuring Tommy and I would go through everything when he showed up to drop off the deed and other paperwork. The house was crammed with books, which made sense because my father worked in a book factory and must have been allowed to take damaged copies home. Someone else cleaning the place would have been surprised to see twelve copies of *Patriot Games* replacing a missing leg on the kitchen table or, upon opening a kitchen cupboard, having five or six little orange copies of *Travels with Charley* fall to his feet. Then there was a little wall of books at the foot of my father's bed. Most of them were Harlequin Romance novels, chosen (I hope) for their uniform size and thickness. Above the three feet of romance, there were five or six books standing up, the back covers facing him. Maybe he liked the pictures: Danielle Steel is certainly one of the more photogenic and attractive authors out there. Others...I think he liked the praise, something about the language of the blurbs, the energetic little bursts of praise: "Haunting and lyrical." "Drop what you're doing and READ THIS BOOK." "Important. Vital." The first day I moved in, I put them all in boxes and moved his monument to the basement. "A tour de force."

Tommy's room was locked. He relished the symbolism, I imagine. It probably took him days to set it up: I am Tommy, an enigma wrapped in a mystery locked behind a padlock sealed with wire and a dollar store lock. Hear me roar. Inside, he'd vented his frustration over not inheriting the house. I was prepared for the mess but not the smell. He'd destroyed everything he couldn't take, splintered chairs and smashed windows. There were a few books inside: *The Aenid*, Roget's Thesaurus, but they'd been torn and stained. Ever the paragon of maturity, he'd taken all the food out of the refrigerator (I'd wondered why it was empty) and spread it around his room. A gallon of milk soaked into the mattress, flies buzzing. There were piles of blackening food all over. The smell was indescribable; it seeped into everything like an infection. It took weeks to erase it.

There was no way to know now, of course, how my father felt about me. His presence was in every room and there was a sense of the unresolved as I cleared out the house. I packed endless small dishes and bowls and the traditional brass *bulgoki* cookware into boxes, slid them down the too-narrow hallways. There were things I didn't understand and didn't know how to dispose of: a jar of battery acid, a box of shotgun shells (he'd gotten rid of his guns after my accident), a shopping bag full of cell phone charms. Even halfway through, it became obvious that I'd never be able to erase his presence. Maybe that's why I inherited the house—a quiet pleading in the stillness of everything, the books and piles of junk meant to say *remember me*.

But it was obvious that I'd lost him long before he died. His death was only a marker letting me know when I was to start missing him. I couldn't speak Korean, so I couldn't call our relatives overseas. I could have found a translator, but I didn't want to explain why I'd abandoned the language. I didn't want to remind the family of how my father had died. Tommy had kept the language; he would have to lead that part of the investigation.

Besides books, our father had few material possessions, none of them particularly revelatory. I couldn't read the Korean papers, so I carefully stored them in manila envelopes. I looked for our father in the house's one or two photo albums. I looked for him as I finished bottles of liquor he'd hidden throughout the house.

I was talking to Leslie on the phone when I realized that I had other responsibilities. "You've taken care of the bills, right?" she said. I pictured the lights turning off the moment she said it, the opposite of the epiphanic lightbulb appearing over my head.

"Of course," I said calmly, looking at the unread piles of mail on the kitchen table. I'd been so busy sorting, mired in the almost-grief following loss. I was eighteen, a child of privilege who vaguely understood bills and commerce. "Everything's totally under control," I told her.

My friends back in Princeton had already started summer college courses and the house I'd inherited felt uncomfortably large. I needed money, but I also needed answers. The house's size amplified everything, my confusion echoing off those faux-wood-paneled walls. I'd given up packing by this point and had piled the rest of my father's belongings in a small mountain in his room. Probably some of Tommy's stuff, too, which was strewn around the house. I would deal with it later.

I put in an application to the old factory, the one my father had worked in. Someone there knew what had happened. After all, he'd taken an entire bottle of pain pills right after finishing his shift. This didn't seem like a coincidence. I thought it was a brilliant plan, sort of like going deep undercover. Once I gained the trust of my father's blue-collar coworkers, they would tell me everything. My father would come alive once again in funny stories and anecdotes. The factory doctor, the one who had prescribed those deadly white pills, would explain the suicide in a way that made perfect sense. Afterwards, I would leave and continue my life.

I got into my car and drove my father's daily commute into Wilkes-Barre, speeding toward steaming piles of black rock, past thin forests and junkyards stacked high with cars, rushing headlong to my father's fate, telling myself that this would not take long. It was July and the year was still young.

Tower Manufacturers Incorporated is located in a huge manufacturing complex on the other side of Wilkes-Barre. It's still there: You can go there late at night and throw rocks at the warehouse windows like the local kids. But inside those long, unpainted concrete walls, they still recycle paper and keep records in restructured mine tunnels. They print posters and vinyl banners. But mostly, they manufacture books. Paperbacks of all kinds, over a million a day.

The HR rep was a red-faced man with a brown mustache. I didn't recognize him from the funeral, but I found myself wishing he'd attended. There was something comforting about his solid working-class face that reminded me of hot dog-eating contests, conservative values, #24 on the back of the family vehicle. The plaque on his desk said Paul Gricyznski. "Call me Mister G.," he said as I shook his hand. The air conditioner was on full blast and the office was freezing. Mr. G. informed me that I would be working as a press text assistant. "Don't worry about training, they'll do that when you get there." He handed me some papers which I signed without reading. Since I was new, I'd be working midnight shift, 11:30 PM to 7:30 AM. My father's shift. I shrugged and said I was a night person anyway. "Great," he said. "The shift starts on Sunday at 11:30 PM and ends on Thursday at 7:30 AM. So you get Friday and Saturday off." I said that was great. "Just go through those double doors marked BINDERY," he said. "See you Sunday."

And that was it. I didn't mention my father—the interview was so short I didn't have time. (Had he noticed the resemblance, the same last name, and given me the job quickly out of pity? Did my presence make him uncomfortable?) I thought about asking something simple on the way out but didn't. Even then, I knew enough not to be direct. From my AP Psych courses, I knew the situation was delicate. Perhaps his coworkers blamed themselves, perhaps there were things they wouldn't eagerly share with a dead man's son. I feared a direct approach would scatter any answers into a deeper, perhaps unreachable silence. Following the new employee checklist Mr. G. gave me, I bought a pair of steel-toed boots and thought I was prepared for my first day of work.

5

TOWER

The coal mines were empty long before my father and Tommy arrived in Wilkes-Barre. The rest of the area's industry had deserted the country after NAFTA. This left Tower Manufacturing the region's largest employer by default. Just about every family in the towns outside the city had a relative who worked "down at Tower," often shortened to "down Tower" so it sounded almost like "downtown." It wasn't uncommon to find two or three generations of a family spread out on the factory floor. In fact, Tower was almost an institution: We had a union, a bowling league, employee picnics and Family Day, discount bus trips to Atlantic City. Couples met there, romance flourishing in the heat like orchids in the tropics. People died there.

Push through the thick double doors and you enter the bindery. The smell is the first thing that hits you. It's hard to describe, industrial glue. It's nothing like the dead horse smell of Elmer's or the dangerous tang of model glue. It's a heavy, acrid smell with a chemical aftertaste. It never quite washes out of your hair or clothes. You get used to it, although some people get headaches. You get used to that, too, I suppose. I've had headaches ever since that bullet kissed my brain, so it was hard to tell where they came from.

Directly in front of the doors is "the smoke shack," a small concrete room fronted by long rectangular windows like an aquarium. Inside, people sat on benches, as if on display. They angrily blew long streams of smoke toward the fluorescent lights. The foreman met me in front of them and proceeded to give me a tour of the factory. He didn't look at the smokers as we walked past. "I see you in there, I'll yank you out," he said. "Kid like you's got no reason." I said nothing. I recognized him from my father's funeral and there was a flash of recognition as he saw me. But he didn't say anything, perhaps out of respect for my privacy. Or perhaps he felt it was part of his job to attend his workers' funerals.

We continued our tour of the bindery. Walkways marked by double yellow lines formed a maze that faded in the distance. The foreman listed various production lines as we walked. "There's Line 5," he'd say. "Line 8. 7's over there." He waved to the workers. They waved back.

Walkways snaked around blind corners and ended abruptly. Even if they'd given me a map, I still would have had trouble finding my way around. The machines formed walls in this maze and were generally squarish with scarred metal casings, chest-high and ranging from six to twelve feet long, hinged by conveyor belts into curving production lines. Most were painted gray or olive green.

In the time I spent at Tower, I didn't learn much about the foreman. He was missing the pinky on each hand. What else...he wore jeans even on the hottest days. Thick brown hair, slicked back by some magic antique oil. He had a worn face with a well-trimmed beard and looked like someone who once bowled a perfect game. I never found out what really happened to his hands. I got a lot of stories, most of them bullshit. Some said he'd lost them in a hideous industrial accident here at Tower, others said it was a story to scare new employees. At any rate, the union folks knew. I've always suspected they simply refused to tell me—me, a smartass kid unworthy of knowing such a detail about such a man. (Here, *man* is used as the ultimate compliment.)

There was enough room between the yellow lines so we could walk side by side. He leaned down and yelled directions and names as he pointed at things. Everyone had to yell to be heard over the machines. The noise, that's the second thing to hit you. The whole place was a riot of unsettling sounds. I wouldn't learn the names until later, but I learned to sort them out. The blade assemblies beat steadily like war drums. The gatherers made pneumatic pocks and sighs. The forklifts whirred, their drivers cursing at pedestrians, and the binders made a rushing noise, the swell of the industrial symphony. Once you put in your earplugs (the foreman gave me a look that said *you idiot* and handed me a pair), everything sounded like the ocean with a seashell to your ear. I could still make out the sounds, though. Occasionally a strangled voice would yell cryptically over the intercom or a strange rattle would start in the machines, like the one you try to ignore in your car, turning up the radio to drown it out.

"Line 14. Here we go," the foreman said, stopping. I suddenly wished I'd paid attention during the walk there. No way could I find my way back. We stood next to an orange oval-shaped machine as long as a boxcar. Sitting in the center was a large metal vat with a few aluminum pipes that rose upwards and ran the length of the ceiling. There were more machines, but before I got a good look, the foreman whistled and a man leaned around from behind a machine. He was fat with a shiny bald head.

"Here's your new belt man," the foreman said, gesturing to me. The fat man glanced at me and nodded.

"Well, good luck," the foreman said. "Your journeyman here'll help you out. You need anything, just give me a call. They'll show you how to work the intercom." I said okay, thanks. He started to walk away. "Oh, and keep your hands out of the machines," he said, waving a truncated farewell.

"Well, get over there," the fat man said, pointing to an area where the conveyor belt connected to one end of the oblong orange machine. There was a gray-bearded man there. Behind him were three refrigerator-sized metal bins. I ducked under the conveyor belt and stood next to him. I was now a belt man, whatever that meant. The conveyor belt was supported by a green metal frame. The belt itself was a darker green with the texture like old rubber. The man beside me looked as if he hadn't slept in a very long time, which made him appear older than he was—probably only in his mid-thirties. His arms were long and sinewy.

"You the new belt man?" he said.

"I think so," I said. Between the noise and the earplugs, every word was suspect. But it was quieter next to the conveyor belt, where we were insulated from the noise by the bins. There was a new whirring noise and a group of rectangles appeared in the orange oval-shaped machine.

"That's the binder," the grizzled man said. Something inside the binder spun like a carousel and a series of booklike objects flew out, stacked one atop another, and came down the conveyor belt toward us. He pulled one off the belt. "This is a *double*," he said, handing me the long booklike object.

"Makes sense," I said. It was two of the same books attached end-to-end in a long rectangle with two covers. He turned it over and two Dean Koontzes looked at us, like contact prints from a mall photo booth. The cover of the book hung about an eighth of an inch over the edges of the pages like a taco shell. The edges of the pages were rough. I handed it back and he tossed the double into a large blue dumpster on the other side of the belt.

We stood there for a long time. There was a clock, but when it felt like I'd been there for hours and saw that only fifteen minutes had passed, I forced myself not to look. It took a few hours, but I learned the grizzled man's name: Ted. Ted wasn't much of a talker. His exhaustion seemed a lot like a drunken stupor. I doubted he'd remember me the next day, so I figured I had little to lose. Hoping for some easy information, I asked if he knew my father. He didn't say anything for a long time and then pointed at the fat man the foreman had introduced as a journeyman. "That's Dale. He's in charge of the line. And yeah, he does look like a prick."

Eventually, I gave up talking and decided to focus on the job. Ted's job, apparently, was to watch the conveyor belt. On the conveyor belt, thousands of Dean Koontzes stared up at us, smiling benevolently. The books fell stacked from the orange machine: They sort of resembled dominoes after they've fallen, or stairs. A giant staircase in motion passed us, made of Dean Koontz.

Every few minutes, Ted would grab a double off the conveyor. Sometimes he'd quickly put it back, but occasionally he'd make a disgusted face and throw it into the large blue dumpster. I weathered the boredom until lunch, which came at 3:30 AM. I went to the cafeteria and bought a sandwich from a vending machine. Afterwards, someone in the union was kind enough to walk me back to Line 14. Ted came by and picked up his coat and cooler. He gave me some advice, most of which was lost among the roar of the machinery. Before he waved goodbye, he leaned in and pointed to a metal shelf welded to the oblong machine. "Don't sit on that 'cause it hurts your balls."

And he was right. I'd almost fallen asleep sitting on that metal shelf when the entire binder jerked and shook. After making sure no one had seen me fall to the ground clutching myself, I resolved to be a better worker. I moved back in front of the belt, where I could see the whole production line with all its workers and machines. I could also see the factory's rear wall, made of large tan bricks. Sometimes, janitors in tan jumpsuits would pass by and appear to wink out and vanish, at least in my blurry 4 AM mind. A man with an eye patch walked over and stared at me. He had thinning, rat-colored hair that almost reached his shoulders. As he trained his one unblinking red eye on me, I knew instantly that he'd murdered at least one person. He was looking for an excuse to make it two, it seemed. I was thankful the belt separated us, although it probably wouldn't stop him for long. As politely as I could, I yelled "Yes?" but he didn't respond. I figured it was best to ignore him and tried harder to look busy.

Bored, I decided to pull a double off the belt every seven minutes and forty seconds. Sometimes I'd put it back and sometimes I'd throw it in the dumpster. I'd even perfected Ted's disgusted scowl. For a long time, it seemed like nothing was going to happen. A little after 5 AM, the one-eyed man left. Around 6:30 AM, a startling noise erupted from the machines at the opposite end of the conveyor belt. I'd later learn this was called a "death rattle." An entire section of the belt stopped and the doubles started to pile up and fall. I watched in horror as twenty, fifty Dean Koontz heads nosedived to the dirty concrete floor.

"What are you doing?" said a man in a blue jumpsuit. He was pale (everyone on midnight shift was) with white hair and a sparse beard. He leaned down to grab a handful of the doubles (I'm going to call them "books" from now on) and arranged them in a stack along his forearm. In one swift movement, he placed all of them into the metal bin behind me. Then he reached over to the conveyor belt and pulled an even longer stack of books off. "I've been doing this since before you were born. How sad is that?" he said. "Princeton Academy Track, huh?" nodding toward my shirt as he put another armful of books into the bin. "You *could* help me out, track star." I copied his sort of scooping motion, took a short stack of books off the belt and placed them in the bin. "Now you got it," he said, pulling off a stack four times longer. "You just graduate?"

"Yeah." The rattling noise stopped and the conveyor belt started moving again.

"I'm Cal," the man said, shaking my hand and gesturing to a name patch on his blue jumpsuit. (Some of the union workers wore jumpsuits for some reason.) He had a broad face and watery blue eyes. He was friendly (unlike the other albino types literature had warned me about), and it showed in his face. Months later, he told me he'd worked for the census. People were always inviting him into their houses—that kind of face. He said he'd started out as a belt man and was now a trimmer operator. I told him that despite my extensive training, I had many questions about my job. He laughed. "Basically, your job is overflow management. When the books pile up in front of

47

you, put them in the bins. When there aren't any books on the conveyor belt, empty the bin on it. Keep the product moving." He told me not to worry about the machinery. "Looks cool, though, doesn't it?" It did. The blade assembly that cut the doubles into two separate books was a junction containing four hydraulic arms: Two pumped down and two pushed up, creating a shaky kind of rhythm. There were smaller arms that rocked and pumped and the whole machine had a neat industrial look to it, all couplings and pneumatic tubes, asymmetrical and slightly angled away from us in line with the conveyor belt. Further downstream on the production line, six workers packed the books in boxes, which someone else stacked onto wooden palettes. Occasionally, a forklift carried them away.

I felt better about the job now that I had some understanding of it. Cal had a sharp voice: not mean or harsh, but it was a clearer pitch than the foreman and Ted's gruff rasp. He didn't mumble or grunt like some workers. He told me about his kids and how he coached middle school girls' basketball, had a daughter that age. A coach's voice, yelling from the sidelines—that's a better description of how he sounded. We talked about some other stuff. I remember he told me not to wear Princeton-branded athletic gear to a rural factory in Pennsylvania. "Even if it is a book factory." He might have saved my life with that advice. He didn't know much about my father, even though they worked on the same shift, in the same area, for decades. He seemed friendly—and besides, he'd helped me out, so I didn't press him. He watched the conveyor belt spin for a few minutes and didn't say anything.

"What do they do?" I asked, pointing to the three men sitting behind desks.

"They're trimmer operators. Dale, that (fat bald) slob over yonder, is the journeyman. The boss of this line. But the trimmer operators run and maintain the blade assembly."

"Specialists," I said, trying to sound smart as I stood there in my Princeton Track T-shirt and pre-stressed jeans.

"They're special all right." Cal repeated that he himself was a trimmer operator on a neighboring production line. He pointed to his machine, a giant two-story behemoth. He looked up to see the man in the eye patch, who had silently returned. Eye patch man walked over and stood by fat, bald man. They were about ten yards away. Together, they stared at us.

"You know who I am, right?" I said. Even though Cal hadn't been at my father's funeral, I could tell they'd known each other. Pity shaded the way he looked at me, even though he tried to disguise it. It was the same look the foreman gave me: *I'm sorry you're the son of a suicide victim. Pretty selfish thing your father did.* The silence became awkward and I blurted out, "Can you tell me where my father worked?" I looked over at the two staring men, but there was no way they could have heard me. Cal glanced over his shoulder at his two-story machine. I couldn't see the expression on his face.

"I gotta run," he said, jogging toward it. And maybe there really was something wrong with it, because as soon as he reached it, he pulled off a metal panel and started fiddling with the wires.

I woke up the next afternoon with a sore back. Although I hadn't done much, I'd strained muscles I didn't know I had. I considered staying home, but at 11 that night, I had energy and nothing to do. The highway, the hallway, the bindery, punch in at the time card reader. Pushing through the double doors, I exaggerated a limp and held my back, hoping the foreman would assign me to a new area. Maybe I'd get an easy job like packing books into boxes. That way, I'd have five people to talk to. But I wasn't surprised when the foreman sent me back to the Line 14 belt. I went without complaint. It was just a summer job, after all.

Factory work teaches respect for infinity. You watch time liquefy. It freezes and flows, the whole eight hours evaporating at an uneven pace. The blade assembly might go an hour without breaking, or it might break every five minutes. Pick more books off the floor. Repeat. Sometimes workers from various lines would tamper with the clocks, slowly inching them forward—a minute one day, thirty seconds another—so they could leave for lunch earlier. Of course, nobody messed with the time card machine and the foreman would occasionally reset everything, but I found that if I walked a certain path, I could lose or gain a few minutes, as if moving through uncharted time zones. Before I knew it, I'd already lost a week.

Occasionally during my time down at Tower, I'd make the joke that I needed that job like a hole in my head. The joke never got the laughter it deserved, although I never really put it in context for anyone. I didn't tell my famous Boy Scout camp story anymore. Too many details to get lost in the noise. But the job gave me a lot of time to think about the metal shards in my brain, how the vibration and noise might be moving them toward virgin regions of my cortex. And then there was the conveyor belt assembly, which had several yellow and black warning illustrations of stick men losing fingers. It was a time for growing ulcers, new pills and less sleep. You could hear it everywhere if you listened: The hole in the ozone layer would bring cataclysmic flooding. The Y2K glitch would turn the nation into a Mad Max-style wasteland. The publishing industry was fucked. Tower, the last factory standing, was about to close. It became its own kind of white noise, an electricity in the air fueled by the idea that everything in the world had gone horribly wrong. Somehow, everyone's history had accumulated and accelerated to messily crash into everyone else's. And somewhere in the noise was a signal waiting for me like a star's final pulse: my father's voice with a message just for me.

But despite the era's bottled hysteria, we still punched in and did our jobs. Although he couldn't always be there to help, the foreman looked out for me. Perhaps my father had told him about me, about my frail health. Perhaps he spoke with pride about how I was being educated at Princeton, how I was the one member of the family who was definitely going to make it. At any rate, help arrived my second week. As if he were already impatient with the progress of my investigation, Tommy got a job down at Tower.

6

THE MSV

I hadn't gotten used to sleeping during the day. During the summer, the factory produces its maximum of about a million books a day. Line 14 made maybe 50,000 a shift and most of them were falling on the floor. I was ready to quit.

A few minutes before lunchtime, I heard the foreman's voice repeating the same speech he'd given my first day. "Keep inside the yellow lines. A number of years back a kid on midnights got hit by a fork truck." The union called forklifts *fork trucks* for some reason. "Wasn't paying attention. He hit her in reverse, ran her clear over. Crushed the pelvis and all the ribs on the one side. Don't worry, she's okay now but I'm guessing you don't want to spend your summer in the ICU. So. Keep inside the yellow lines and check before every corner." A dozen teenagers gathered across the belt from me. They were college students, hired to help during the busy summer months. They stared at me, wide-eyed. One of the college kids stuck out because he was Asian in this predominantly white factory. I gave him my best *fuck you* smile—it was Tommy. He turned away and circled behind the group.

"Jason here's a college student, too...how's it going?" the foreman said.

"Could be worse," I said.

"You're damn right," he said. Although the union labeled me a "college kid," I still didn't have definite college plans. I'd had so many opportunities growing up: I had a solid GPA and a diploma from a prestigious private school in Princeton. I could wait a year or two to enter college. But if I went without finding out what happened to my father—it would have felt wrong. The mystery would have haunted me. At any rate, I couldn't explain this to my coworkers. It was easier for my investigation if I just blended in.

As I walked to the cafeteria during breaktime, the college kids moved on with their orientation. Most of the girls had tans, souvenirs of booze-soaked vacations in Ocean City, Senior Week T-shirts with signatures markered on the back. Seashell necklaces and tie dye. As they moved down the aisles, the union workers turned to stare. Bright colors! Firm teenage breasts!

Tommy sort of broke off from his group. He walked toward me, and I could tell he was composing his thoughts, trying to figure out what to say. Suddenly, a forklift carrying a huge stack of paper swerved at him, missing him by a few feet. It sped off, a few sheets of paper flying in its wake. Tommy stood there, breathing heavy and looking around, the panic slowly waning. Our eyes met, but there was nothing I could do. He looked over his shoulder and jogged to catch up with the orientation group. It would be easy to compare the college kids to a school of exotic fish, peeking and nervously darting across the walkways. At any rate, they were soft and blurry and in no way prepared for the factory's crushing monotony. I took comfort and a strange kind of pride knowing Tommy wouldn't last a week.

Coming back from lunch, I saw the foreman and my brother standing in front of my bins. "Tommy here's gonna be your helper," the foreman said. This made sense. I don't mean to imply the foreman thought, *Hey, let's put our two Orientals together.* If I were dishonest or lazy, it would be easy to paint my fellow workers as semi-literate, unwashed hillbillies who emerged from the border towns to (ironically) churn out lit-a-chure. But that wasn't the case. There were swastikas carved in some of the bins and someone graffitied *Jim E-- sucks nigger cocks* in a bathroom stall, but there was stuff like that at my preparatory school. Some of the union guys (Dale and Eye Patch, for example) didn't like us, but race probably had nothing to do with it. Everyone there hated us college kids—some of the white kids got treated worse. The foreman put us together because he noticed our last names and put two and two together. Maybe our father had shown him pictures of us as kids; maybe this is how the foreman had watched us grow up. At the very least, he probably assumed we were used to working together, helping each other.

"Nice to meet you," Tommy said, offering his hand. I didn't want to disappoint the foreman, so I shook it. He gripped my hand much harder than he had to. After surveying the area with disgust, Tommy tried to appeal to the foreman, who had already left. Tommy and I hadn't spoken since the funeral, and it pleased me that he was so surprised to see me. And unhappy, because I'd taken the initiative, beaten him to this part of the investigation.

I should point out that I wasn't fat anymore. A steady teenage diet of self-denial, track, and diets had taken care of that. Although it would have been great if Tommy was now the fat one, he wasn't. While I'd grown tall and thin—willowy, I admit—he'd inherited our father's stockiness, a grappler's body type. His face was broad and he'd grown his hair out long, almost shoulder length. He was wearing a dress shirt and tie and looked much different than he had at the funeral. "You look ridiculous," I said.

"So what do we do here?" he asked me. He gave me a look that said, *What did* you *do to get stuck here? And why am I here with you?* I explained my undercover mission as well as my job as a belt man.

For maybe the first time in his life, he actually listened, nodding his head as I pointed out various machines on the line. He was taller than me, maybe about six foot, but he was already pale, more given to sweating than I'd remembered. The blade assembly shut down and we started throwing books in the bin. He was out of breath after five minutes.

———

"Bottle rocket. That's how Jimmy lost his eye," Cal said. He'd appeared suddenly, startling us. Every few days, he would appear out of nowhere and just start talking, sometimes continuing a conversation we'd started a week before. He motioned to the tattooed eye patch man, who was now sitting at a desk, reading a newspaper.

"See, (your journeyman) Dale and Jimmy"—he nodded with his chin toward one-eye—"were good friends way back. I guess this would have been about ten years ago. Fourth of July. And one night, well they get to drinking and decide it would be smart to shoot bottle rockets at each other. They still make bottle rockets, right? Okay, well Jimmy took one in the eye. I'd imagine that was pretty painful," he said, shaking his head. "And then it exploded." The three of us looked up in awe at the man in the eye patch, trying to imagine that kind of blinding—literally—pain. What was the last thing he saw with that eye? I imagined a brilliant flash, like a red sun winking out. I remembered that I had a bullet in my head. For a second, I felt a deep compassion. I wanted to tell Jimmy that it was okay, that I understood. Then, I got over it and wanted to shoot a bottle rocket in Jimmy's other eye because he was a creepy leering motherfucker and we all wanted it to stop.

"Rock and roll," Tommy said, smacking his palm on the conveyor belt.

"There's a lesson for you boys. Think about it," Cal said.

"Don't mess with fireworks," Tommy said. He kicked the back of a bin and a cloud of dust rose from the top.

"God," I said.

"Take a look at them fans," Cal said. Everything in the factory was coated with thick gray dust. "Paper dust from the trimmers mixes with the oil and engine exhaust, sticks to everything." He pointed to my coffee mug, which was covered by a copy of *Where the Red Fern Grows*. To Tommy, he said, "See, he's got the right idea. If you don't cover your coffee, it turns to Jell-O."

"That's fucking gross," Tommy said.

"You ever blow your nose after a shift?" I said. Cal nodded and shrugged. Your snot looks like tar. Cal smacked the leg of the belt assembly with a book and tossed it into the blue recycling bin. "Cake. You know how that French queen said, 'Let them eat cake?' Well, back then, cake was the crud that built up on the bottoms of the peasants' pots and pans." I offered Tommy some paper cake but he declined. "Let them eat cake. No wonder they decapitated her royal highness."

"*Calvin Jones to the MSV. Jones to the MSV,*" called the intercom.

"Gotta run," Cal said.

Talking was the only thing that made the job bearable. Technically, we didn't "say" anything to each other. Even though it was a little quieter on 14, we still had to yell, drill the words into each other. "I think Cal knows something about our father's death. What do you think?" I said to Tommy.

"Which reminds me. I have the paperwork for the house in my car. I'll bring it in after lunch. Store it in a safe place." He quickly changed the subject and told me about his college life in Pittsburgh. Tommy was an art major (art!) at Carnegie Mellon University in Pittsburgh. I told him a little about my graduation, about what I hoped to learn about our father's suicide. I confessed that I really didn't like the factory and had been considering Leslie's offer to return "home," as she put it. But.

"You got a new home here," Tommy said.

"About that. If you want, you can stay with me. Save on rent money, *et cetera*."

"I'm staying with friends. The house is yours now," he said. "I'm not going back."

"What about your stuff?" I said. In addition to the garbage in his room, he'd left several boxes of stuff in the basement: an electric guitar, a really heavy amp and speaker thing, a few boxes of VHS tapes, and awful-smelling football pads.

He shook his head.

"I really don't understand why I got the house, anyway," I said, by way of apology.

"You got it because he didn't want me to have it," Tommy said, raising his voice over a new banging noise coming from the machine.

Even though his refusal to set foot in the house felt petty, I let it go. There were things I didn't know and I began to understand how he felt about not looking back, especially as I thought about how I'd feel after leaving this summer job.

One day in early June, Tommy asked me, "Dad. Where did he work here?" I was embarrassed that I'd been working there over a month and still didn't know. When I asked the union members about my father, they would say something vaguely positive and change the subject. And in the past sleep-deprived month, I'd put aside my detective hat and retreated into survival mode, leaning hard on the daily routine. I'd gone to Tower with something in my heart that I kept quiet, even to myself. Back then, to name this desire would have destroyed it, made it wither like burning plastic. I wanted my brother's forgiveness. I thought that if I found the reason behind our father's death, I could tell Tommy. With this one act, I could erase the hatred and jealousy that had built up while I'd been absent. When Cal stopped by, I took a risk. Even though he'd run away the first time I'd asked, I asked him where exactly our father had worked.

"The MSV assembly," he said, pointing to his own two-story machine. Apparently, he trusted me now.

"He worked on the same machine as you?" I asked.

"Yeah. I got transferred there after..." There was an uncomfortable pause as he thought of a nice way to say "your father killed himself," and I broke it by asking if my father had worked with the other two guys on the MSV. Maybe they could tell me about him.

"No, by himself."

"Seriously?" said Tommy.

"Yeah. The Japanese bought that heap back when we still published magazines. Then the Germans retrofitted it to make smaller books, like kid's books. But it ran like crap. I guess 'cause he was Japanese he knew about the setup and the parts, maybe."

"He was Korean," I said.

"Yeah. Well anyway, management finally let him make some changes and it runs a heck of a lot better now. Course, it takes forever to set up but then it just runs its cycle and finishes."

"Cool." We watched the MSV for a while and I pictured all the tiny parts inside, all the precision gears and hydraulic joints, crude circuitry, coiled pneumatic guts. I spent a lot of that summer staring at that huge bleached two-story machine, wondering how a single man could command such a behemoth.

And on long days, when the damn clock wouldn't move or when we'd arrive and someone had peed in the corner of a bin or when we were literally knee-deep in thin slippery books and another union worker/comedian walked by to yell, *"Boy won't this job make you study harder in school?"* and laugh, I'd think about my father's old machine. I'd take a deep breath, close my eyes for a second and the world would dip into beautiful silence just long enough for me to finish the shift, to push through the double doors, punch my time card, and stumble into the morning sun.

At this point, thick dust had grown on my detective hat. It felt good to shake it off, watch a cloud form in the air as I put it back on.

7

SMOOTH OPERATORS

From my previous description, you might think there were only four of us on the line: my brother, myself, fatty, and eye patch. But there were the specialists. Since they never introduced themselves, we gave them nicknames: Dale was hairless and fat with a sort of baby face, so he became "Baby"; the staring eye patch man was "Cyclops."

There were three machine operators. They dressed in factory couture—instead of jumpsuits, they wore shorts and wife beaters (tight-fitting tank tops often modeled by domestic violence suspects on *COPS*). "Fang" had prominent yellowed canines, "Hunter" wore a mesh camouflage hat with his hunting and fishing license clipped to the top, and "Zombie" had eye bags and a jaundiced waxy face. It looked like they'd dug him up, chanted a spell, and drew a path from the graveyard to the factory in salt and runes.

Fang started eating around midnight. When he was done with his candy bar or potato chips, he'd crumple up the wrapper and throw it in our general direction. When we were busy, it would hit us. Otherwise, we were careful not to give him the satisfaction. Sometimes he'd throw it at Hunter and the two would wrestle. And even though we prayed they would crash into the machines to be horribly mangled, it never happened.

For most of the shift, Baby and Cyclops sat at their work desks and read newspapers, hiding them when the foreman came around. Reading was forbidden in the book factory.

Our workspace was a yawning vacuum. There would be a pleasant, druggy sort of haze over everything and then the blade assembly would bite down with a kick that you'd feel in the hollow of your chest. Confetti-sized scraps of paper would fly from the blades and the night would get longer.

Zombie's job was to sharpen the blade assembly's knives, which were bigger than a riding mower's blades and must have been heavy given the way he carried them. He was okay, probably the operator we hated the least. Sometimes, when the other operators went on smoke breaks, he would pick up the garbage his coworkers threw at us. Sometimes he'd talk to Cal when he stopped by.

Cal. They made a movie a few years ago set in a distant future. Because the dumbest people reproduce in the largest numbers, the people of this future have lower and lower IQs. When a regular guy gets transported to that future, everyone thinks he's a genius. Their savior. That movie barely counts as fiction in my opinion, and they must have based that regular guy on Cal. Witness his daily routine: He arrives on time to his shift and spends the first hour or so doing actual maintenance work, climbing up and down ladders with Spray Nine and rags. When he has downtime, he actually cleans his area so the intakes didn't clog with paper dust. When his machine breaks down, he shuts it off, brings his toolbox to the machine, and *fixes it.* Gasps of amazement. Give this man a winged trophy and our finest virgins soaked in olive oil or whatever. This man Cal doesn't simply kick the machine and glare at it with furious indignation when that doesn't work. He's usually finished by 1 AM, everything running smoothly. For the next hour, he re-sweeps the area with a push broom and reorganizes his toolbox. Then he sits and stares at his machine for a while and checks the books for defects. Sometimes he talks to the other two operators on his line or eats an apple. Around 2 AM, he utilizes his leisure time to visit Line 14.

I couldn't ask about my father directly, but I hoped the right questions might lead to an accidental revelation. So I asked Cal about the foreman, how he lost his fingers. "He used to be a journeyman. That's how it works...you start out as a box stacker or belt man and after a few years you become a machine operator."

"So all those guys used to be belt men?" Tommy asked.

"Yeah," Cal said, looking toward the pot-bellied men sitting at the long desk. "Back then, things were a lot nastier. Their machine operators weren't as nice." He gave a bitter almost-laugh. "This was before the machines had auto-shutoffs, back before we got the ISO certification we're so proud of. Anyway, you see those clamps on the binder? They pick up the cover and pages and hold them together while the glue's applied..."

"And the foreman got his hand caught in a clamp," Tommy said.

"Yeah. Machine bit him, which is why you're supposed to shut the machine off before fixing them." He shook his head and pointed to the binder. "See how that carousel machine spins around? Well, it grabbed and dragged him. Back then, they didn't have pneumatic shutoffs, so they had to take the machine apart around him. So he was just hanging there. He eventually passed out. The good news is they were able to save most of his hands." We shuddered, flexing our fingers.

"God," I said.

"Keep your hands out of the machines," Cal said. Like I said, the man's a genius.

We ate our lunches outside. I found an old stairwell that led to the factory's roof. I've never been one for heights, especially after a childhood incident involving a bowl and a roof, but we were far from the edge and I forced myself not to look down. We ate next to the air conditioning vents above the offices, where we'd stretch out near the Freon ducts and let the chilled air evaporate our sweat, the heat and tension in our bodies rising toward the cold black sky.

"I've been thinking about hiring a realtor," I said one night in late June. At the time, home prices were rising. I figured if I sold the house before I was done working at Tower, I could just rent an apartment. And even if I still didn't know why my father had committed suicide, I could at least live comfortably while I tried to figure it out.

Tommy's hair had grown a little past his shoulders. He sighed and ran his fingers through it, Kato Kaelin-style.

"But you're going to need to move your stuff out of the basement. Plus, there's a lot of your father's—our father's stuff. That we need to go through."

"I don't want you selling the house," he said.

"You're going to have to sort through the stuff eventually," I said. I made up my mind to be firm with him. I'd done some research: There was roughly $90,000 on the line. That's how much the house across the street had sold for.

"I want to scatter dad's ashes during *Chuseok*. It's like the Korean Thanksgiving, but with more ancestor worship. Families gather—"

"I know what *Chuseok* is. The autumn harvest festival. I didn't forget everything, you know." Tommy didn't say anything. I figured I could put off selling the house until after autumn. But I hadn't expected him to show interest in Korean culture, much less honor our father in a traditional fashion. I supposed our father would have liked it, the two of us getting together in an ancient ritual. Still, it was surprising, given that Tommy still refused to set foot inside my house. He was full of surprises.

Speaking of surprises, there was one in Tommy's workday. Sometimes when he walked through the factory, on his way to the cafeteria or bathroom, a passing forklift would swerve at him, veering away at the last second. An exhausted Tommy would leap out of the way just in time to see it vanish around a corner. This didn't happen every day, but the minute Tommy let down his guard, half a ton of steel and diesel came flying at him. This happened as we walked back from lunch that day. I explained the situation to Cal when he stopped by 14. This was called "buzzing," he told us. A hazing practice that had mostly died out after too many people died. "Someone's got it out for you," he said.

"Why me? I don't get it," Tommy said.

"Don't bother trying to figure this place out. You'll go crazy," Cal said. "It's probably boredom, nothing personal. It's not right, but it happens. If you manage to see his face, you let me know." By 4 AM, the caffeine pills and coffee scraped at our thinning guts. My vague pulsing headaches became sharper, more defined, but I didn't tell anyone about them.

Aside from the paycheck, the best part of the job was the pride. We were midnight shift and we were the best, even though we had to spend the first hour fixing what afternoon shift did to our machines. We made more books than day shift, even though they had the most experienced workers. We made more books despite the exhaustion and overloads of coffee, caffeine pills, energy drinks, amphetamines, and God knows what else.

Of course, accidents and injuries were off the charts, but fuck it, those came with the job. Scar on your leg from the time a cheap wooden palette fell apart, shearing away a ribbon of skin? Scrapes on your forehead from the time you collapsed from heatstroke? Make sure that smiling company VP sees it when he visits the factory in his dress shirt and Looney Tunes tie. When he asks you for the fifth time what college you attend, feel his soft hand against yours and ask yourself how long this man would survive on the belt. As you go home, you see on the company bulletin board that *midnight shift, motherfucker!* is once again #1 in production. It wasn't much, but wealth, safety, and healthcare were off the table, so we clawed for that #1 like drowning men.

Accidents and injuries started my father on his tragic path—there was no doubt in my mind that he'd injured himself on the job. Many of the union men wore back braces, and Cal said that my father's injury was most likely to the lower back or hand. But Cal had an easy job most of the time, ever since my father had fixed the machine. The pain pills my father had taken were a fairly low dose and he hadn't refilled the prescription, so it wasn't that the pain was unbearable. He was on the best shift.

Late in June, we arrived and the air lines were clogged. They

62

couldn't run the pneumatic gatherers, so we couldn't make books. After sweeping the floor for the fifth time, we wished the machines would start up, give us something to do. Staying awake was a constant issue during midnight shifts. I was going to omit Tommy's drug use, but I think his nasal fixation started from a desperate attempt to remain conscious at work. Little known fact: A contact lens case makes a perfect container for cocaine. I'd catch him emerging from a Freon pipe alley on the roof, wide-eyed and rubbing his nose. I pretended not to understand why he would sometimes swing from obnoxiously talkative to a scary, sort of seething quiet. When he was talkative, he was actually interesting. Eight hours a shift, 37.5 hours a week—this gave us a lot of time to catch up. He'd tell me about his classes at Carnegie Mellon University, where Andy Warhol had once attended before dropping out. Then he'd use big words while he talked about his singular artistic vision.

"*Art major*," Cal said, raising his white eyebrows in amazement. I wasn't the only one surprised by this. By this point, Tommy had been wearing the same dirty T-shirt for the past three days and his jeans were stained with machine oil and grease. Tommy looked like he should be playing a murder victim on *Law & Order,* certainly not discussing things like "plasticity" and "issues inherent to the medium."

"Art major," Tommy confirmed.

"Just like Hitler," I said. Cal snorted and started munching on a hot dog he'd brought from the cafeteria.

"That's funny," Tommy said, not bothering to look over at me. He took out a marker, found a non-dented length of the bin, and sketched spiky-haired Calvin pissing on the Tower logo.

"What's your planned major again?"

"Communications," I said.

"Just like that janitor over there," he said.

"Ha. Aha, ha," I said. "If this art thing doesn't work out, there's always com—"

"How are those hot dogs, anyway?"

"Delicious. 'Round here we call them tube steaks," Cal said.

When the mechanics arrived to fix the air lines, Baby and Cyclops stood at opposite ends of the binder, both looking very pissed. Factory work is a numbers game and their numbers were way down—we might not be listed as the #1 shift on the board tomorrow. The head mechanic said something to Baby, then walked over to repeat it to Cyclops.

"Must be awkward for both of them, working together," I said.

"Yeah," Cal said. "Been like that since it happened. Haven't said a word to each other. He'll never admit it, but Dale's still beating himself up about it."

"Why doesn't the foreman assign those two to different areas?" Tommy asked.

Cal laughed. "Maybe he went to high school with them. Maybe he doesn't care much for either of them guys." He scratched his neck. "Or maybe if the foreman separated all the feuds here, we'd need a much bigger factory."

Lunch came and went—still no air. Not all the college kids left after the first week. The union guys were real nice to some of them. Normally, we were almost too tired to pay attention to the college girls but one of the cutest ones, a short redhead, was bending over to stack boxes. She swept her area, then bent over to gather up the paper scraps. We watched her for hours. She had short hair, a Manhattan pixie sort of look, ending just below her ears. Her hair (just a little too red to be natural) was nicely layered: I pictured her spending 9-10:45 PM styling it, teasing all the old union cocks as she flitted by, twitching her ass and innocently arching her back as she walked. It must have taken practice to get right. *Can you touch your elbows behind your back?* was an old high school trick, but some of the college girls were trying their little hearts out. She made it look effortless, just like that hair. I pictured her red hair bouncing in layers as I rammed her from behind. I already knew how her voice quivered just before rising to a shout. Cal pretended not to be interested. He was married. Married men didn't think about stuff like that, he said, walking back to the MSV. I wrote my flame-crotched beauty a missive. It read:

Is this a library? 'Cause I am *checkin'* you out. Meet me by the men's room, 10 mins.
—Secret Admirer

"I don't know," Tommy said.

"Too direct? Come on, with all these books around..." I said, laughing.

"Let's find out," he said, walking toward the redhead.

"Don't you fucking dare," I said, chasing after him. I tried to grab it out of his hand. He shouted to Strawberry Shortcake, who looked over just as I tackled him. Trying to push me off, he crumpled the note into a ball and threw it toward her. The foreman must have heard because he ran over. As we explained we weren't fighting, he spied the note on the floor.

"Knock it off," he said, picking it up and walking away.

"Don't worry, he'll throw it out," Tommy said as the foreman opened the note and read it. He turned back and gave us a strange look.

"I didn't write it!" I yelled.

"Yes he did! Ten minutes, he'll be there!" he shouted.

"Get back to fuckin work!" Baby screamed.

"Great work, communications major," Tommy said. After they still couldn't get the air working after lunch, we got sent home early, right before the caffeine kicked in. While we walked through the parking lot, we tried to wake ourselves up for the drive home. Standing outside his car, we made up variations of Tower Manufacturing Inc.'s initials. Tedious, Monotonous, and Incompetent. Toothless Morons Inbreeding. Too Many Idiots. Thoughtless Maniacs...

"Incompetent?" Tommy said.

"We already used that," I said, resting my hand on top of the open driver's side door. "Speaking of incompetent."

"It's five in the morning. Cut me some slack." He sat down behind the wheel and started to close the door, but I didn't move my hand. I asked him if he thought our father had a feud with someone.

"Because do you think it's possible someone killed him and made it look like—"

"Stop," Tommy said. "It wasn't murder. It was *this place*." He pulled hard on the door and I barely got my hand free before it slammed shut.

On days like that one when I couldn't sleep at home, sometimes I'd grab a book. My father had several books by one author, a woman I'd actually met when I was younger—a prominent woman of letters named Ms. ——. Why he kept her books I'll never know. Every other book you could buy in a grocery store, but not these. I like to think it's because she listed Princeton as her home on the biography on the back cover. I like to picture him reading it. No holographic covers or letters from the author on the back—just solidly crafted stories, daring escapes, and sad desperation in the sun-bleached suburbs. I spent hours reading Ms. ——.

After I put my book down in my huge room in my huge house, I looked around and felt the cavernous spaces around me growing. In Princeton, right after I'd fallen off the roof, I remember lying on the ground and staring at the doctor's mansion. The world was sideways and I was cold and alone, my worst fear made real. A second later, as if in answer, there was a wooden slap of the door and my brother and father were running to me. I had a responsibility to my family still. I couldn't escape to the fictional suburbs forever.

But what was I supposed to do? Tommy seemed to connect our father's suicide to the factory, but I wasn't so sure. Our father had Cal's job, and he really didn't seem stressed. I thought about the Harlequin novels in his room. Were they a clue? Could our father have been involved in a disastrous romance? Maybe he was diagnosed with a painful incurable cancer. If answers were outside of Tower, they would be hard to find, especially for someone who slept during the day.

My headaches increased, probably due to the stress. A doctor came to the factory every week as part of some health insurance plan. I learned that he'd worked at the factory for the past two years. I made an appointment.

8

THE SNAPPING TURTLE

"Tell me a story," I said to Cal. It was around 3 AM and Line 14 was running smoothly. I was bored and Tommy was several feet away, sweeping the floor, which we were supposed to do during downtime. A clean workplace is a safe workplace.

"Well, you know about foreman, right? Every summer, you college kids want to know how he lost his fingers." He was holding a broom and turned it over and scratched a little oval in the ground with the end of the handle. "He lives out in the sticks and there's a little pond on his property. And, uh...well, one day he decided to get rid of the snapping turtle living there. Well, lo and behold—"

"Wait, you told me he'd lost them in a binder!" I shouted. Tommy looked over, but he was too far away to hear us.

Cal laughed. "He did. One day he brought that snapper to work—"

"My God, you've been lying to me all along," I said.

"My stars and garters." Cal smacked part of the belt assembly with his palm. It stopped immediately and I started filling the bin. "Can you believe that?" he hollered to Baby and anyone else in range. "I help this kid, I run over here with my bad knees to help him—I bring him coffee." He stared at me with mock incredulousness. "I brought you coffee," he said, leaning back

67

and staring at me as if I was a Mormon trying to push my way into his house. I smacked at the belt but nothing happened. I filled the bin and started on the second one. I didn't mind. "I work my arthritic wrists to the bone picking books off the floor, and what does he do? Call me a liar?" I had filled almost half the second bin when Cal smacked the same spot that had stopped the belt. Nothing. "Crap," he said. He helped me for a few minutes and then the intercom called him back to his own line. "Sorry," he said. Tommy put down the broom and helped me fill the bin.

"That's not funny. Wait," I said. I knew he felt bad, but I also heard faint cackling as he jogged away.

"Tell me the truth," I said to him the next day. I'd arrived early and waited by Tower's front entrance. I followed him to the MSV, where the face on the covers was that of my father's favorite novelist. Even though she wrote a book every other year and we published all of them, I took it as a sign. Ms. ——. She had a delicate face with shiny black hair in the glossy photo on the back cover. I wondered what she was doing at that moment. The weather in Princeton would be humid, the landscaping crews working fast to prepare the university's campus. Did my father think about Princeton when he saw her? Did he think about me?

"Oh come on," he said, leaning over the channel where the books flew by. He reached in and grabbed a book, frowning as he leafed through the pages. "Does it really matter?" The book's cover flapped as it flew toward the dumpster.

"Hey, be careful with these. Seriously, where did he really work?" I said. Cal looked around, sighed and pointed to the Line 14 belt, where Tommy had just arrived. He noticed us and waved.

"Ah," I said, nodding toward my brother. "The whole time my father worked here, he..."

"It's not like it was when I started here. We have a bigger union now, longer lines to manage. Fewer openings. I'm sorry," he said quietly, making a helpless gesture with his hands. "I just..."

"No, it's all right," I said to nobody in particular. I said I had better get to work.

"Are you sure you're okay?" Cal said. I nodded. I was fine, I really was. He stared at me for a few seconds, then turned and walked to his workbench.

The oil and grit in the air stuck to the back of my neck and itched. Anger seldom moves in a straight line. It would be so much easier if it shot like a bottle rocket—forward trajectory and then a crisp report, the mathematical beauty of cause and effect. But in my experience, cause and effect never quite line up. Most angers tend to hover like humidity teeming with gnats. Without an outlet, it builds inside until one tiny thing at the wrong time sparks an epic freakout.

Although they never quite went away, my headaches were manageable in high school. A few hours into the shift, I went to my appointment with the factory's doctor. I figured I'd been working at Tower long enough to earn a reputation as a nice person, a hard worker. I hoped the doctor would be comfortable enough around me to tell the truth.

Everyone called him "Dr. Jim." He was in his early thirties. Like many men during that time, he sported a goatee. His office was small and near the foreman's, with a modest wooden desk surrounded by three office chairs. The walls were tan and blank. Dr. Jim placed his hands on both sides of my head and ran his fingertips across my temples. He felt my jaw as I opened and closed my mouth. He said that, unfortunately, there was little he could do but prescribe something to control the symptoms. He started writing a prescription in a small notebook.

"You know who I am, don't you?" I said.

He nodded without looking up. "Your brother came here last week asking about your father. A very angry man." It didn't occur until later to ask whether he meant my father or brother. "This is a prescription for painkillers. There are new medications for migraines, but I'm not sure they'll work for your...condition."

"You know about the bullet?" I asked, surprised.

"Your father talked about you. For what it's worth, I am sorry about what happened. Yes, I wrote out the prescription, but...a lot of workers here have back problems, or broken fingers from the machinery, or cuts."

"Was he in that much pain? I mean, maybe he had something else, like cancer?"

Dr. Jim gave me a tentative, searching look, as if I'd asked a trick question. After a few seconds, he said, "Your father had a disease. As a society, we don't tend to think of it that way, but we should. I don't want to go into details, but his drinking was likely a factor."

"He didn't drink himself to death, though. He took pills. That you gave him."

Dr. Jim looked up at me. He'd been staring at the pad, underlining something. He started to say something and hesitated, rolling his chair backwards a few inches. "You didn't see him near...the end. Factories can be stressful work environments. There's monotony, fatigue, outflow pressures, work-related injuries. It's well-documented. But this is something you should discuss with your brother. You know that alcoholism is genetic. You and your brother both—"

"My father wasn't an alcoholic," I said, louder than I'd intended. I felt my hands shaking. A strange twisting in my stomach. I knew my voice would sound shaky, so I sat for a few seconds staring at the beige carpet. The person who had sat in the chair just before me must have been heavy and restless—there were deep grooves in the carpet fibers, a tight path. For me, an alcoholic was someone who drooled and beat women. My father had raised a son and kept a job. Nothing made sense.

"This is something you should talk to your brother about," Dr. Jim repeated. He placed the prescription slip on the desk across from me. I picked it up.

"You don't know what you're talking about," I said. I left, not bothering to turn and see his reaction.

To be fair, he didn't understand my investigation, which had suddenly concluded. I wasn't sure I would last the summer—I couldn't imagine working for eight years as a belt man. Sometimes it took a few beers or shots of vodka for me to fall asleep, but I could imagine drinking more heavily, especially if I looked around at the gray, dusty factory and realized that my entire future was contained between its brick tan walls.

And Dr. Jim certainly didn't understand my relationship with Tommy, who still thought our father was a successful machine operator. There was a look of pride, some indistinguishable light in his expression when my brother looked at the MSV. I couldn't take that away from him. As I stood next to Tommy at the bin, I realized why Dr. Jim had looked at me so wearily. Tommy had grown up with our father, of course. He knew about the alcoholism and after he'd started work at Tower, he'd quickly figured out that the factory was to blame for the suicide. And it was, in a way. My investigation was over, but I couldn't quit yet.

I gave up on trying to earn Tommy's forgiveness and started watching him carefully. Occasionally, when he looked at Baby or the other machine operators, I'd see a strange expression on his face—not rage, but the same blank expression of a jackal surveying his prey. There was something eerie and inhuman about it. I remembered what he'd said after the funeral: "I'm gonna find out why and *set it straight*."

I could have quit the job and gone to college, but I wasn't going to abandon my brother. I knew he was planning something, taking a road that would end in prison or worse. My only option, I decided, was to keep working, to somehow hold on long enough to defuse his bloodlust. And the summer wasn't even halfway over.

9

THE CAULDRON

I've exaggerated my headaches for pity, as an excuse not to do things, and once upon a time to prolong my stay in Princeton. But too often, I don't have to pretend. Some headaches deserve names, as they give great storms—the worst is when my head feels jack-o'-lantern hollow, the pulsing gray mass scraped out and piled on a newspaper on someone's kitchen table. Still, somewhere in the void, there's a dull ache. Or maybe it's the opposite: My head is full but the ache is a tiny emptiness. A hole through which sense and reason vanish, the crumbling cork a lone splinter of lead.

Heat causes this particular type of headache, or so the doctors think. Which is strange, because the last one happened late at night, when it felt like the world's only source of heat was coming from the lamp on my desk. But maybe the damp heat of the past is enough to cause halos and blindness when seen clearly.

In late July, a heat wave swept up from the south and coiled around us for the rest of the summer. This was normal and compounded the summer rush the union always dreaded. But a new work order complicated things. Tower's VP signed a contract promising 38 million books by the end of the month, the deal consummated during a golf tournament, or so the rumor went. The numbers were a fact, though, an ultimatum on the bulletin board. Unfortunately, factory work is a numbers game and we could only bind a million books on a perfect day. July has 31 days.

Weekends became mandatory and the union received memos warning that "Due to Tower's contractual obligations," shifts could be stretched from 8 to 12 hours. "THANK YOU FOR YOUR UNDERSTANDING." The machine operators were angry because the heat bent tiny coils and pins in their machines, keeping the overweight, sweating men chained to the diesel-powered machines. The heat rising off them warped everything. I was still reeling from my visit to Dr. Jim, my discovery there. Tommy continued to endure the job with a grim determination.

Especially angry over the new scheduling were the forklift drivers, who received a memo informing them their shifts were now 10 hours long and since there were so few of them, calling off meant instant termination. As the summer wore on, they grew more and more upset that they had to sit in an upholstered seat drenched with 10 hours worth of the last driver's swamp-ass and crotch sweat. Lysol and towels only do so much, one of the female drivers told me, explaining why she'd bolted a small puke bucket to the frame.

Imagine this: You're barely twenty years old, more or less a native of the area. You're trying to raise money for the $400 your books and brushes will cost next semester. After eight hours, you only have the time card reader on your mind. You can feel it grip the stock paper of your time card, the whine of the ribbon as the dot matrix printer records your shift, spits it back up to you, and with it springs your freedom for the next sixteen hours. Almost there—you're between the yellow lines, safe, and maybe you're starting to get a hard-on as you picture that sexy gray machine on the wall. A blur of hard rubber spinning on concrete, a forklift comes from behind, swerves toward you. Part of the frame clips your ear as it passes. *That's even closer than last time*, you think, almost detached. Wait, what the fuck just happened? Anger takes energy and you don't have any.

You move forward, hoping it doesn't happen again and march toward the machine, reaching forward in anticipation.

The few remaining summer workers were profoundly disillusioned with our jobs, with being at the mercy of people at whom we'd snicker if we passed them on the street. To add insult to injury, the union started using the free/damaged books bin (frequented most by college students) as a spittoon.

The few college girls, well I told you about them. If Halloween gives girls predisposed to sluttery the excuse to dress as sluttily as possible, every day down at Tower was Halloween. The factory was a place of no consequence, a twilight world where they could practice flirting, hone their skills before the meat grinder of dorm life and Greek mixers. The union ladies didn't much like it when girls half their age catwalked through the bindery every summer, taking the easiest jobs and snatching all their blue-collar Romeos. But the college girls were tired and tired of being leered at, tired of the whispering and graffiti. And the heat—the fucking heat. So many people passed out or called off that the bindery couldn't run at full capacity. Management was all clipboards and frowns. Like I said, it's a numbers game and triple-digit heat in a concrete rectangle just doesn't add right.

Eleven thirty: a cloud of the last shift's body odor. Smeared blood on the corners and more dents in the bins. Arguments increased, my brother and I bumping into each other as we filled up one, two, two-and-a-half bins. *What happens if we fill all three?* Tommy kept asking.

Termination if you hit someone, period, kept everyone in line. Occasionally we'd see a shoving match broken up before the foreman came. You could feel hate move through the factory, work its way beneath your fingernails. It worked its way as a sort of itch into my blood and a few shifts went by where I didn't think about my father at all. Darker things filled our hours now. Tommy and I kept quiet and did our jobs. I didn't talk to him about our father because it seemed to upset him. There was a flush of almost-shame in his face, and he would just stand and stare off into space. The main thing we talked about were our fantasies, which no longer included teenage girls. Our coworkers' behavior and the heat mutated them into imaginary murder sprees. We'd kill Zombie first. "I'd shoot him in the knee," I said. "After he falls on his face, I'd roll him over and shoot off his fingers, give him lobster hands. Then the stomach, then take out his other knee and just as he started to curse God, like *really* curse, I'd shoot him in the face, send his fat ass straight to hell."

"Nice," Tommy said.

"See, Hamlet knew the deal. Who says literature's useless?"

Tommy took out his knife and sharpened it on the metal edge of the conveyor belt. "Cyclops, I'd stab him until he was just a big red hole."

"I'd just shoot him in the eye. It'd be quicker, stop that goddamn staring."

"I prefer a knife," Tommy said. "But whatever it takes to get the job done."

We'd kill everyone quickly enough except for Baby, who we'd shoot in the crotch. What would that look like? I saw some guy's testes explode in a motocross event on live TV. *Oh, the humanity!* This would be a slow-motion sort of thing, his balls exploding into strings of pearly liquid, dripping through his fingers as he clutched his red, white, and blue jeans. Tommy's forklift driver—well, we'd run him over with his own machine, put a wheel right next to his face and stomp the accelerator, watch his terrified expression peel right off.

I was looking forward to leaving Tower for many reasons, but mostly I looked forward to having my humanity back, a mantle I could put on when the school year started. If someone died violently on TV, I wanted to feel sad or shocked or whatever the TV wanted me to feel. Back then, I pictured the dying as various coworkers, and that kind of sunny Technicolor sharpens teeth into fangs. When we were too exhausted with our pretend-bloodlust, my brother and I fumed in silence until 7:30, when we'd walk into the sunlight, too itchy and worked up to sleep.

Quiet fuming aside, you'd think Tower would have liked how my brother showed up for work on time, didn't complain or mouth off to the shift coordinator. He worked smart and stacked carefully—most belt men slam and jam when the machines are in overdrive. But Tommy got frustrated when he couldn't do his job right. Despite the drugs (and he wasn't the only user in that plant), he put forth a genuine effort. He didn't stare off into space or daydream. There was a chiding energy to it, something even that forklift driver must have felt, anger swelling until he absolutely had to buzz him. For those who'd given up a long time ago, those who'd grown bitter from the heat, the monotony, there must have been something about his spirit that ate at them.

"You're killing yourself to save the stereotype," I said one day to the model minority beside me. This was a typical spectacle in July: machines shaking to death and we couldn't fill the bins fast enough. But the hotter they ran the machines, the faster that tall Oriental worked. Unlike the other one, the one who seemed satisfied at just knowing why his father killed himself, who just shrugged, slopped the books, and waited out the summer. I always suspected they ran the machines faster as a "fuck you" to Tommy and I didn't appreciate being along for the ride. A few minutes passed and he turned to me.

"You ever notice that the foreman doesn't check to make sure we're here on 14 every morning? He doesn't check the stacking in our bins. He's hardly ever over here," he said.

"He doesn't do that with Cal, either," I said. We were back to race again, although I suppose I brought it up. Actually, Tommy brought it up with his step-and-fetch-it routine. He might as well have walked in wearing a graphing calculator stuck inside a pocket protector and started measuring our daily output.

"Cal's been here for decades. The foreman doesn't babysit us because other people worked hard and proved themselves. We've climbed here because we're standing on his back," he said, nodding to the MSV. He didn't have to, but he said it anyway, "The foreman sees dad in us."

As far as I was concerned, my undercover investigation was over. My father was dead, and he wasn't coming back. And here I still was, babysitting my brother to make sure he didn't murder someone. It would have been the perfect time to tell him the truth, let him know just how far our father had made it with his hard work, but I let it go. If he wanted to continue our father's imaginary legacy, so be it. "I don't give a fuck how he sees me. That's his problem," I said, the blood rushing to my face. My life was complicated enough. I didn't care what anyone thought, how anyone looked at me. All I cared about was finishing my shift and eventually finishing the summer. I figured Tommy would calm down by then and just go back to college, to his bullshit art degree. In the meantime, if the foreman wanted to hang baggage on me, fine. But that didn't mean I had to carry it. "It's just not fair."

"You think anything about this place is fair?" he said with a bitter laugh. "Do what you want to do," he said, making it clear that in its own way, his Herculean effort was for my benefit. As part of a summer tradition, our trimmer operators were placing bets as to which of us would pass out first. And even though I'd carried him most of the summer, I started hiding Tommy's water bottle, stayed a few minutes extra in the bathroom when I knew he was up to his waist in books. I didn't appreciate his tone, and there was something about his little speech that pissed me off, the insinuation of betrayal. No way was I gonna drop first.

10

FAMOUS DATES IN AMERICAN INDUSTRY

The factory pulled the trigger on a Monday in early August. Looking back, there were signs: a scythe moon close to midnight, the air thick with insect sounds as we moved through the parking lot. Moonlight gleamed off someone's thermos, bloodshot eyes lit green in the sodium vapor lights. The parking lot was always full of menace, a maze of cars and slow traffic cut off from company eyes. Every parking lot is scary if it's full and poorly lit, but this one was at the center of all the feuds and hungers. Who knows what tensions were released on that hard blacktop? I knew to keep my eyes forward, my head down.

The factory pulled the trigger on a Monday in early August. Looking back, there were signs: a scythe moon close to midnight, the air thick with insect sounds as we moved through the parking lot. Moonlight gleamed off someone's thermos, bloodshot eyes lit green in the sodium vapor lights. The parking lot was always full of menace, a maze of cars and slow traffic cut off from company eyes. Every parking lot is scary if it's full and poorly lit, but this one was at the center of all the feuds and hungers. Who knows what tensions were released on that hard blacktop? I knew to keep my eyes forward, my head down.

By 11:45 that night, my brother still hadn't shown up. It was strange but I figured he had a good reason. Perhaps carrying the mantle of racial expectations had finally crushed him. Working alone was fine because the machines were running at a reasonable pace. The shift started with a food fight between Fang and Hunter and then some horseplay. But Fang tripped and fell into a circuit box, which knocked out the power to our entire line. I calmly waited in the dark and talked to Cal. By midnight, Tommy still hadn't showed up. I figured he'd called off sick.

The electricians fixed the circuit and the lights came on, thousands of fresh volts surging through those fluorescent tubes. The flash triggered a wicked headache, but that was the least of my problems. Although we had light, the intake and ceiling fans weren't working. I guess I'd taken them for granted because now the air was thick and oppressive, as if the heat and dust crowded out the oxygen. The electricians were nowhere to be seen and I knew Baby wouldn't call them back. There was a fan mounted on a plastic stand by the other line. It was turned off and a group of ladies who worked the automation machines were a good twenty yards away, sitting and talking. I dragged it over and tipped it so it at least moved the air. A few minutes later, one of the older ladies dragged the fan back to their line and shut it off.

"That's *our* fan. Shoo," she said when I walked over. I said, *Look,* my hatred building, and then I heard the foreman.

"Jason, where's your brother?" he asked.

"Didn't he call off?"

The foreman looked at his clipboard. "Here's the call-off list. Not on here."

Shit. "Uh, yeah. I mean, of course he didn't call off. I thought you were talking about my buddy Cal, who *did* call off."

He gave me a strange look. "Cal's right over there. And he hasn't called off in twenty years."

"Exactly. That's why I was so confused." I wiped the sweat from my forehead and almost patted the foreman on the arm as I thought up an excuse. "Yeah, Tommy, he's in the bathroom," was all I could think of. I felt sick from the heat, but this obvious lie made it worse.

"Well I need to talk to both of you, so don't go anywhere when he comes back."

"Okay, but he might be in there a while. He's uh, having problems. Shitting. But I'll tell him," I said.

"You do that," the foreman said.

The foreman returned a little after 2 AM and I lied again, saying Tommy'd run off to the bathroom a few minutes ago.

"Is he okay?" he asked, tapping his clipboard on his leg.

"He's fine. Probably something he ate."

"Well you give me a holler when he comes back." Holler. How I miss that word. Around 2:30, the foreman appeared again and I wondered what could be so important.

"Still in the...yeah," I told him, shaking my head.

"That's funny because I just checked the men's room," he said. *Fuck.* "And nobody else has seen him all day. Funny how he punched in right after I talked to you."

"Well, he's forgotten to punch in before. It's possible he's in the medic's office. I've been thinking about going there myself for this headache," I said, which was true.

"I hope you're not fucking with me."

"Um, it's possible he might have gone home," I said.

"Well if he did, you tell him don't bother showing up tomorrow."

"Now that I think of it, I think he went to a different bathroom this time. Like somewhere else. 'Cause the last one was, uh, making him sick...er. You know how they never clean those things."

The foreman took off his glasses and cleaned them on his shirt. He took a deep breath and his eyes widened a little. "You tell him I'll be mighty pissed if both of you aren't in my office by four."

"Will do," I said.

During lunch, I ran to the parking lot, hopped in my car, and sped to my house. I didn't own a cell phone (few people did—this was the late nineties, after all) and had reluctantly used the pay phone at work. I remembered the numbers of a couple of his friends and left a string of messages, but I had no clue when he'd receive them. I was headed back to the house to look for more phone numbers in his old room. Nearly blind from that headache with my empty stomach writhing, I was running out of steam when I spotted him. The job had taken its toll, I saw as I pulled in my driveway. Tommy's car was parked there at an angle and he was passed out in the driver's seat. His car's engine was still running. Whether he'd gone there out of habit or he'd gotten my messages, I'd never know. His face was zombie-like and slick with sweat, pressed into the steering wheel. I turned off the ignition, pushing his face off the wheel to wake him. I could almost see the vapors of cheap vodka rising from his pores, condensing like cold air as he breathed. He groaned some curses.

"That's my boy," I said. "Come on, Tower needs you. See that light in the sky? It's like the bat-signal. *Thomas Han to Line 14. Thomas to 14.* Now stand up."

"That's the moon." He was now on top of the girl in the passenger seat who couldn't have been older than sixteen. She was one of those confused Hot Topic girls you see in the food court of any mall, putting on her black lipstick as she glares at the yuppie sheeple exiting the Cinnabon. She wore black fishnets and her black hair had recently been dyed and sloppily cut (perhaps that night) into something resembling a pageboy. As I checked for a pulse, I noticed a spider web tattoo on her neck, right below the ear.

"Jesus, Tommy," I said. I shook her a few times but she didn't wake up. Maybe she was dead. I checked my watch and dragged Tommy inside my car. "Sorry," I yelled to the girl as I backed down the driveway onto the street and stomped on the accelerator.

"Received a complaint about you boys," the foreman said to us, sorting through an unstable mountain of clipboards on his desk. The walls of his office were painted a dull yellow, made of the same huge bricks as the factory's outer walls. He looked over at Tommy, who was leaning forward in his chair. His shirt and hair were wet, his pants flecked with vomit. He ran his fingers through his hair and a few droplets of water flew onto the foreman's desk. A damp smell of alcohol filled the room. "You all right, son?"

"Not your son," Tommy mumbled.

Either the foreman didn't hear him or pretended not to. He pulled out an orange slip of paper. "It says here you two been harassing a fork truck driver." Tommy's head jerked up, his eyes focusing on the paper. "Says you've been throwing books at him, calling him names."

"Oh my fucking God," Tommy said. He wasn't very articulate, so I explained the situation. Tommy made an angry helpless gesture with his hands, then fell silent.

"Well that very well might be true," the foreman said, "but I gotta deal with these people year-round and you kids are only here for three months. Anyways, this"—he held up the orange slip—"might very well be bullshit, but I still have to give you a warning. I'll keep an eye out, but I got a factory to run and I can't be everywhere at once."

"He's been harassing *me*. Ask anyone," Tommy said.

"I have, but he's got witnesses who swear they...if you'd said something first—"

"Whatever," Tommy said, getting up to leave.

"So what's going to happen with the complaint?" I said.

"It'll stay on file, which for you guys means nothing. I'll mark down I gave you a warning and we discussed things. All right?"

"Can we file a complaint? Like a counter-complaint?" I said.

"Sorry, you have to be in the union," the foreman said. Tommy staggered back to 14, but I stayed and filled out another application. I told the foreman I'd been planning to work there full-time anyway. This was a lie, of course. But college had faded to a dim hope and I didn't have anything else going on. I had failed—in the chaos of working the midnight shift, I still hadn't realized why my father had killed himself. I didn't have any friends and I never really hung out with Tommy outside of work. By this point in the summer, I was sleeping during the day and into the evening. Tower was slowly becoming the only thing I knew.

"You sure about this?" the foreman said.

"I am," I said with a nod that emphasized the finality of my decision. "My father," I said quietly, unsure of how to finish the sentence. *My father would have been proud of me?* No, that wasn't it at all. But I couldn't back out now. Everyone else at the factory had been evasive about my father, as evasive as they were about the foreman's missing fingers. I wanted one thing—a story, something that would bring him to life, just once. And then, I suppose, I would want something to explain how he felt about me as I grew up hundreds of miles away.

"Your father was a good man, I think, but he had a temper. He would have handled this differently. I'm proud of you."

"How would he have handled it?"

"Hey, don't tell anyone you're trying to get in the union, all right? Because then, they'll really mess with you." The blood was pounding in my ears as I waited for my revelation, so maybe he didn't hear me—maybe I'd spoken too quietly, afraid to shout over the factory noise like I usually did. Or maybe he didn't want to step into my family business. I never really gave up trying to learn more about what I'd lost. Maybe when I was in the union, things would change. "And close the door on your way out," he said.

Baby was pissed because of the power outage, so he ran his machines at a breakneck speed after lunch. Even though he wasn't in the best of moods, Tommy did his best to keep up. He looked confused, as if he wasn't sure where he was. Even though I told him to go rest somewhere, he insisted on helping. The fans never got fixed and every few minutes we'd get dizzy and have to stop, have to ignore Baby's yelling and the Cyclops eye of judgment. We were so drained there wasn't any anger left in us, just a strange instinct to do our jobs, finish the goddamn shift. I wiped the sweat off my forehead with my already-wet shirt and took a deep breath.

Why didn't I quit? I didn't think about it at the time. I suppose I kept working there because if my father could work there for eight years, I wanted to honor that. Tommy and I didn't talk much about our father—when we did, there was a cold look in my brother's eyes. Well before the suicide, I suspected there were domestic problems, anger issues. It must have been horrible to have lived in that house. But Tommy at least respected what he saw as our father's legacy at Tower. He saw his own work as a way to keep the family name and reputation alive. And if he wasn't going to quit, neither was I.

We were binding *Moby-Dick* (one of my favorite books, of course) for the coming school year. It was a large run, in the millions. Sixteen old-growth trees make a ton of newspaper and there were seven thousand tons of paper for this job. Tommy's worst fear came true when we filled the third bin. It was an incomprehensible moment as we stood in front of an immovable wall. We yelled for the journeyman but no one came. And then came the death rattle, of course. The blades stopped and books fell on the floor. We were up to our waists by the time Baby walked over, an *Oh my God* look on his face. It was a monumental occasion, filling all three bins. Baby gave a speech (spittle flying, furious pointing that must have strained his whole arm). "Famous dates in American industry: January 13, 1951. Mr. John Peabody discovers that if he plays dumb for long enough, other people will do his job for him. He gets moved to an easier job, where he plays dumb and gets an even easier job. How about that? *How the fuck about that?*" If I had a gun, I would have shot him. Even now, I can imagine the recoil, that jumping pain in the wrist. One full magazine until just clicks, *nothing to see here* and I'd calmly wait for the red and blue lights. But. We just stared as he continued his speech, the fat on his double chin and beneath his arms jiggling with indignant fury. He shut off the binder. More wild gesturing as he turned up the green conveyor belt and started throwing books on it. "Get to work, twinkletoes!" he screamed at me.

"If you want quality, stop rushing the machines," Tommy yelled. We'd had just about enough.

"Shut the fuck up and Do. Your. Job," Baby said. We fucking college kids thought we knew everything. Baby grabbed a handful of books and without looking threw them in the garbage. Look how many books we were wasting. More spittle and yelling.

Tommy slipped and the stack fell over. Things went so bad that Baby, now hoarse, actually waded in to help us, shoving us out of the way. The area thickened with sweat, alcohol, glue, and we were all soaked. The oil in the air clung to us, blackening our necks with that familiar itch. The human mind and body can only take so much. As Baby's wet, hairy forearm brushed my mouth as he pushed me into a full bin, I bounced to the ground and vomited. I remember this very clearly—my face was only a few feet from the floor. I'd eaten watermelon that day and my puke was a weird pink color, almost like Kool-Aid. The consistency of snot, probably, it splashed all over the concrete floor. And then, as the smell rose, my mind shut down. I don't know if it was the heat, the headache, or the smell, but I suddenly couldn't see a thing. More sickness erupted and I couldn't breathe. It felt like my organs were rushing out of my nose and mouth. I grabbed at a bin and held onto the handle for my life. When my vision returned, nothing had changed. I could see Tommy and Baby's boots as they continued to unload the third bin at the far end. Maybe they hadn't noticed. I grabbed a book and sopped up what I could, spreading the smell. Everything muted in that nightmarish fog as we struggled to keep the line moving, hold together Melville's innards. Tommy saw me and waded over to help. *No, we're not shutting down the goddamn line*, someone said. Fang, jovial after a half-hour cigarette break, returned and playfully winged a book at Tommy as he was helping me up. It clipped him, the cover scratching him near the eye as it helicoptered past.

Tommy's knife came out in dream time. I had a vague sense of what was about to happen, so I grabbed at my brother's shirt. It ripped and he catapulted forward. I watched Fang's boots and ankles as he turned to run. I slumped on my back and lifted my head to watch the whole scene play out upside down. Fang picked up the intercom phone and dropped it when he saw there wasn't time. He'd probably never seen a college kid fight back before, much less pick up a knife. He kept backing up. Cyclops crossed his arms and stared.

The foreman came from nowhere, probably drawn to the vacuum of silence around our line. He moved between them and started yelling, his voice rising above everything else. *Thomas. Put the fucking knife down, NOW.* As Tommy went after Fang, someone ran behind him and grabbed his arm, tried to wrestle the knife away. Somehow, I stood and moved into the group, which had quickly turned into a dogpile, all gristle and bone. Someone fell hard on top of me. All I saw were frantic legs and a steel-toed boot coming right at my face. *Who was that meant for?* I thought as the gray world began to spin. A kaleidoscope of scrambling limbs. But my last thought before I passed on the dirty, oil-soaked concrete was *Please don't let me die here.* The parking lot or an ambulance, but please God, not here.

11

SATANISTS

"It wasn't that great of a job anyway," I said to Tommy. It was about 7 AM, both of us sent home early following the unpleasantness which had just ended our shift. During the scuffle, Tommy had injured his hand, which was curled by his side. I was driving him home in his car. He had been terminated and I had to report to the foreman before starting my next shift.

"I'm not done there yet," he said. We drove in silence, the cool morning air rushing in through the windows. I told him that some people do fine down at Tower. Cal, for example, made a good living and didn't seem to mind the hours. But. Tommy thought our father had an easy job at Tower, Cal's job, but he never thought to ask why our father started drinking more, why he killed himself. If he'd pushed those questions like I had, he might have found out the truth and the summer would have ended differently. Tommy was only interested in one question: Who can I hold responsible? And it seemed like the answer was: *everyone at Tower.*

"Dad killed himself right before the summer. He didn't want to face another one. Think about it." I said nothing. It made perfect sense. "Here, go down that dirt road. I want to show you something," he said. After half a mile of brown dust and potholes, there was a red barn, two stories high and as long as a strip mall. To be more specific, it looked more like two barns attached to each other in an *L* shape, the longer section parallel to the road. It was surrounded by weedy patches that poked through the gravel drive, growing thickest under the downspouts. Two windowed gables jutted from the roof and I thought I saw a white shape inside flutter past. The roof was green with moss.

I parked the car and we walked toward it. I was wearing nylon soccer shorts and the tall weeds brushed my legs, leaving behind a buzzing, itchy feeling. The air around us smelled pleasantly of dead grass and dry wood. It was quiet and I took a deep breath, hoping the old Pennsylvania magic would heal our aching backs and arms, the pastoral space an antidote for Tower's claustrophobic horrors. I followed my brother until he stopped in front of a gap between two imposing wooden doors which stood about twenty feet high. He reached in and flicked a light switch inside the doors but nothing turned on. After a few tries without success, he shook his head, turned sideways, and vanished through the opening.

The only light in the room came from a tiny window far above our heads and Tommy cursed as he stumbled through the room. I took small steps as my eyes adjusted, pushing against stringy cobwebs thick with dust. The light gleamed off the metal objects in the room—an old tractor, maybe, scattered machine parts. Somewhere in the room Tommy crashed into something. "Fucking chair," he said, knocking it over. There came a fluttering sound, wings beating above us in the darkness. I covered my head with my hands, waiting for something to swoop at my face.

"What was that?" I said as something brushed my leg.

"Birds," Tommy said, his voice distant. "You'll see."

"No, it was something else. Shh." There was a faint rustling behind us as something began to stir. I felt the eyes of a vast, wild public—rats and the compound eyes of spiders.

"That's enough." Tommy was just a few feet ahead of me and we felt our way through the room, the silence interrupted by metallic scraping as we kicked wrenches and screwdrivers.

We passed a tractor and shuffled further into the darkness. My heartbeat grew louder, the blood thick in my ears. "Here," he said. A door opened and light streamed through the dust we'd kicked up. I quickly jogged through, slamming the door hard. Tommy looked back at me. "What?" he said.

"Nothing," I said, trying to catch my breath and hoping there was another exit somewhere.

We walked through a long concrete hallway lit by several lightbulbs running the length of the ceiling. Beneath us the ground was patterned green with mildew, which serpentined up the crumbling white walls. The echoing sounds of wingbeats grew louder.

"Pigeons," Tommy said, kicking a hollow bird carcass as he walked. It skidded and hopped across the dirty floor. A faint aroma of death rose and mixed with the hallway's earthy smell. So much for the bucolic scenery. In just a few minutes, we'd gone from *Charlotte's Web* to *Deliverance*. The other bird corpses we passed were just a red splotches and scattered rings of feathers.

"What happened here?" I said. Rounding a corner, we entered a room as tall as the barn itself and a good third of its length. The morning light entered in through a row of tall windows, falling in even bars across the room. The floor and walls were thick wooden planks and the high wooden rafters arching above us gave the room a vaguely cathedral-like feel. The room's size dwarfed the red pickup truck parked in the center. Tommy walked toward it.

"I used to work here. Mowed those thirty acres out front. See all this bird shit?" He pointed to the floor, speckled white and inches thick in places. He waved around to the rafters, where there were several sloppy-looking nests. "Well, it became a real problem. Built up so bad the sediment and smell would destroy the barn. So after work, we mixed whiskey with birdseed and set it out. After the birds got drunk, we grabbed the shotguns and cleaned house."

"I didn't know you could get birds drunk," I said.

"You missed out. I bet in high school you didn't even get the first day of hunting season off." I shook my head and said I wasn't even sure when that was. He looked at me with infinite pity. "Your bourgeoisie education..."

"Your hillbilly education. I'm surprised you even know the word," I said, cutting myself off as I heard myself say it. I would have been snotty anywhere but felt especially wrong to say it in this bucolic temple. And I mean it—bird shit aside, the scale of this place alone lent it majesty. Not to mention the dull red paint, Americana bursting from every handmade joint in the thick square rafters. The crushed silver and red Budweiser cans in the corner, the 12 gauge in the truck's gun rack. Tommy didn't say anything. A pigeon cooed, the sound echoing softly off the walls. Aren't pigeons related to doves? I pictured them fluttering and diving through the barn, careening into walls before exploding in a hail of buckshot, raining down as red mist and feathers.

"Well I've learned something today. I remember Dad always saying you should learn something new each day."

"That's good advice," Tommy said.

"Did *you* learn anything today, Tommy?" He slid open two thick wooden doors. The sound of the wind and insects returned along with those light, summer smells thick with pollen.

"A lot, actually," he said as a sparrow flew in through the doors. He reached under the pickup's seat and grabbed a revolver. Holding the gun in his good hand, Tommy cocked his head and followed the bird's flight.

We took a break around noon, having chased three or four birds through the barn, running down stairs, across lofts, up ladders as he searched for the perfect shot. As we returned to the pickup truck, he fired off his last six shots at a pigeon ahead of us. Plumes of dust erupted from the pocked ceiling, trailing away as wood chips fell on us. "It's a good thing we're trying to save the barn," I said as he opened the driver's door to the truck and sat down. I walked around and got in. He tossed the gun between us and stared straight ahead at the barn's thick wall.

"God damn it," he said, looking at his hand, which he rested on the steering wheel. His knuckles were purple and scraped, some of his fingers swollen from the recoil. He tried not to appear concerned, trying on an "isn't this cool" expression.

"Here," I said. There was an old white tank top in the pickup. I ripped it into strips and wound it around his hand, which was surprisingly warm. His palm was rough, the joints of his fingers deep red with paper cuts. I tucked the loose end beneath the wrapping.

"You're going to a doctor about that, right?" I said. He made a noncommittal noise and sat staring at the bandage for a while, as if surprised by my gesture.

The silence was too long. "If you were a horse," I said, motioning to the gun. "You know, I could take care of you."

"Ha," he said. He closed his eyes and leaned back on the headrest. "Right." What Tommy didn't know was that, despite my aversion to firearms, I'd gotten over my fear of them after several pheasant hunting trips with the doctor.

"Here." He reached under the seat and handed me a plastic bottle of cheap whiskey. What other treasures did the truck hold? I took a pull, trying not to cough. My eyes watered.

"Too strong?" He took a swig, then another, and took a deep breath. "Nothing."

"Fuck you," I said, glancing at the label. "I put this on my pancakes."

He put a joint in his mouth, lit it, and took a deep breath. "Here. To a day of firsts," he said, his voice strained as he tried not to exhale. I took it.

He looked around the room, through the open doors for a while. "God," he said, taking another deep drag. We sat in silence, passing the bottle back and forth.

A pigeon flew into the barn. Startled, Tommy grabbed the revolver and shot through my open window, the revolver an inch from my nose. I made a conscious effort not to flinch. A cloud of gunpowder stung my eyes, stuck to my nose hairs. "Shit," he said as the bird spun in midair, hit a wall, and fell to the ground in a heap. He grabbed the truck's roof with his good hand, pulled himself out the window, and walked over.

The bird's wing was torn almost completely off and blood pooled around its body as it flapped the other, trying to fly away from us. It looked right at us, pleading an aria as it shook its head. Tommy was out of ammo, so he picked up the shotgun and fired a round, the plastic shell ejecting and bouncing on the concrete. A cloud of dust drifted up.

"Christ," I said, looking out the barn's windows, expecting the farm's owner to appear. "Can we go now?" Tommy seemed upset at the first bird he'd actually hit that day. It wasn't that he felt guilty, really. I think he felt the same as I did, that it felt unsporting, the birds confused and trapped in this large wooden enclosure. Plus, if we were interested in shooting anything, it wasn't birds.

"You going to work tonight?" Tommy asked me.

"Sure, why wouldn't I?" He didn't respond, keeping his eyes on the fire. He'd reassured me that we had permission to hang out here, so we drove back to Tower and retrieved my car. After that, we built a roaring fire with fallen branches and gasoline. Even though we hadn't talked much, it was nice spending time with him. Even more pleasant because we were free from the tyranny of the clock, the machine operators. Darkness was just beginning to fall and obscure the barn, which we could barely see from the field. It had rained a little, so I was sitting on a blanket while Tommy had perched on the hood of his car.

To our right there was a long mound on which grew a row of apple trees. In the middle were two stone cisterns left over from when the farm housed cattle. "Why do you ask?" I said, but he had passed out, or at least pretended to. The fire was smoldering and my head pounded. I was exhausted. The only things keeping me conscious were adrenaline and caffeine, and I could feel them evaporating from my bloodstream. On an impulse, I walked back to the barn and found my way to the red pickup. I felt around for the revolver but it wasn't there and neither was the shotgun. Even as I walked to the barn, I knew I wouldn't find them in that pickup. They were in Tommy's car. We'd had some target practice earlier today and now he was planning to sweep through the factory like the angel of death. Tragic Massacre Imminent.

He never locked his car and I found both guns hidden in the

back under a blanket. I grabbed them along with a coffee can full of ammo. Part of me wanted it to happen, to see Fang and Baby ripped to pieces by a hail of righteous lead. But eleven-year-old me walked by my side, a fresh stream of blood pouring from his forehead, a reminder of unexpected consequences, of innocent bystanders. I quietly circumvented the dim glow of the fire.

Breathing deep as I tried to balance it all (the can held well over a hundred rattling .38 rounds, a few shotgun shells), I walked up to cisterns and put the guns on the circular stone wall of the tallest one, about three feet above the ground. I looked down, pausing to admire the moon's reflection off the still, black water, the smoothness of the stone walls. Weighing the consequences of inaction, I took a deep breath and pushed the guns into the cistern. A few seconds later, I heard a splash. I dumped out the coffee can, watching the shiny brass shells rain toward oblivion.

I turned around in a panic when I heard Tommy approach and he was right in my face. Something sobered him up fast.

"Tommy, how are you?" I said, forcing a smile.

"Where are they, Jason?" His voice had a vicious undertone to it, mostly denial, but also an edge of panic.

"I'm, uh, glad you asked. 'Cause I was just cleaning them when this badger thing jumped out of the bushes. We should go—"

"Jason, where are the guns? The ones that aren't yours?" I backed away from the cistern and he followed me.

"They may have fallen into the cistern," I said finally, getting ready to run. He tackled me around the waist and we fell together down a hill. Before I could stand, he started choking me. I coughed and pushed at him, desperately grabbing his arms. I remember they were thick and veiny. In comparison, my hands must have felt sadly feeble to him. He cursed and let go. I fell back, coughing, the cold wet grass the only thing I could see or smell.

He ran toward his car, got in, and threw it in reverse. He'd parked it behind the barn in what looked like a solid patch of earth. But his car, that old Dodge Dart had settled in, tons of Detroit steel sunk deep into what was now mud. It made a hideous noise, the tires spinning mud into the air. "Fuck!"

"Wait. Just wait," I kept repeating through the fog of a new headache. I pounded on his window and told him to stop. He got out, doubled over with exertion. He walked to the hood of his car and started pushing.

"We're fucked," he kept saying. "And yes, this is all your fault."

"Can't we just go?" I said. My car wasn't stuck. Because I hadn't parked in the mud. He continued to spin the wheels while I pushed on the hood. Over the roar of the engine and spinning tires, it almost sounded like we were back at work. I made several helpful suggestions.

"I'm sure as fuck not coming back for mine after this," he said. "Not after they find their guns missing. No, I can't just buy more guns. Seriously, with what—and my boss will want to know what happened to the old ones. No, stop. Stop. No, I can't afford to lose my fucking car, either. (Not all of us have wealthy benefactors.) Push harder. Dickhead."

My shoulders couldn't take any more, so I came up with a plan. "Satanists," I said, holding up my hands. The car shot backwards a foot and then sunk even deeper.

Tommy got out and looked. "You threw the guns in the fucking cistern," he said as if he'd just realized what had happened.

"Yeah, but I have a solution. Follow me," I said. We went into the barn and found some spray paint. I drew some sloppy pentagrams and Tommy broke some windows. "Yes, I'm positive this is our only hope," I said. I sprayed a crude cat skull on the wall. I told him that he needed to think like a Satanist.

Since he was still processing his outrage over the guns, it was easy to persuade him. He squatted and defecated a few feet in front of the red pickup. "This is kind of brilliant," he said, the novelty blunting his shock and anger at the guns falling into the well. I cut my hand and smeared some blood on the handle of the passenger side door of Tommy's stuck car. I found a marker and wrote, "We are not Satanists. We tried to help," on the windshield and we left in my car. Two crises averted. When we came back at night a week later, Tommy's car was still in one piece. Someone had pulled it free of the mud. It looked like they'd washed it, too.

12

WAR AND PEACE

The foreman gave me a broom and demoted me to janitor for the week. Ostensibly, it was punishment, but I knew he was giving me some time away from Baby and the rest of Line 14.

"Watch out for fork trucks," he said. It was late August and the summer hires could feel the end. I knew fall would set us all free. The college kids would head off to their campuses and I would...well, I didn't really know. But it was a pleasant sense of release. Tommy was somewhere orbiting the factory and I was fairly sure I'd averted his murder rampage. There was no one to supervise me, so I wandered, stopping to chat with Cal. I knew enough not to celebrate when I saw Baby and Fang doing my job on the belt. Cyclops was gleefully running the binder in overdrive, looking very satisfied as the machines broke down and books piled up. It should have felt good, but even then, I knew those two would spend the rest of their lives feuding in the dirt and heat. Every summer, kids would arrive, young men just like them in another life, one they could still remember, before these sullen, know-it-all kids they'd have to train this summer, and a new group the next. Maybe that was the part my father hated most, even more than the heat and exhaustion. It would have felt unsporting to gloat—any victory was fleeting in that place.

I decided to check out the press, Tower's print division. I'd imagined it would be the complete opposite of the bindery. Spotless with sleek, modern machinery. "And everybody's real nice," I said to Cal.

"Especially the midget."

"What?"

"Yeah. I don't know exactly where he works in the press, though," Cal said.

"Get out." Occasionally, Cal's stories checked out. I had time to verify this one for myself.

"Maybe he makes those little books. Like the ones you see near the counter at bookstores," I said.

"Short stories. That's for you to find out," Cal said. I told him I'd send a postcard.

I found strange things that week. I quickly walked through aisles of trenchlike blade-sharpening machines, hard metal gnashing beneath black water. When I asked about the midget, someone pointed to the baler room, located in a sublevel beneath the factory.

Romeo the Trash-rat didn't know anything about a midget worker, but he did give me a tour of his little domain. Romeo was in charge of all the baler room workers, affectionately referred to as "Trash-rats" by everyone else. He didn't know where Tommy's Asian friends were, only that they'd quit a few weeks ago. I didn't really follow up—I only asked out of bored curiosity. Romeo was a thin white guy with a scraggly mustache and at 19 was not much older than me. He wasn't particularly handsome but he did have three children, hence the nickname. He was chatty—most people down at Tower were. Helps pass the time. Anyway, the baler room was where the factory recycled. "All the leftovers and excess paper in those blue dumpsters gets sent right here," he said, handing me a dust mask, "then it gets baled up by these machines, hay during harvest."

The area was about the size of a high school gym. Two conveyor belts in the center fed loose paper into long machines that looked like airport baggage scanners. Four-foot cubes of shredded paper came out the other side, where masked workers stacked them. The ceiling was forty feet high, a platform with flights of stairs to reach it. A mass of metal pipes ran the ceiling above, large enough for a man to crawl through. In places, the pipes looked tangled and formless like a den of snakes but were difficult to see because thick paper dust swirled around us. A solitary worker shoveled up paper flakes that accumulated in little drifts on the floor.

"What do you do with all this paper dust?" I asked, watching the man with the shovel.

Romeo said, "Well, some of it we recycle as packing material. But we dump a lot. You know that crick that runs next to the factory?" I nodded. "Some days it doesn't run too fast."

I returned to the press. It had a similar layout as the bindery, except with wider corridors and taller machines, each at least three stories high. They resembled the platforms you see on industrial cranes, a windowed, fluorescent-lit control room at the top. I climbed the tallest machine, stopping at the second story. A six-foot-tall roll of paper hung suspended by hooks attached to a rod and unwound through slots and rollers throughout. A single, continuous sheet of paper unspooled around and over me, making a strange whispering which occasionally changed pitch. The energy it gave off felt electric, the tiny hairs on my forearms sticking up.

Aside from the occasional forklift, the only noise was the crisp sound of paper unrolling. When I stood long enough without moving, I almost heard a human voice in the rush, a ghost in the analog process. I climbed to the overhanging control room, the outer wall one long window of pale green glass overlooking the press. There were panels of gauges and colored lights along with a gearbox with several levers. At the desk in front of me, there was a little orange plastic chair placed atop a wooden crate. Also, a tiny denim jacket hanging on a hook to the rear of the office. *Holy shit!*—I had officially entered midget territory.

I thought about everything he must have gone through to make it up there, all the obstacles he had to overcome as he slowly and literally climbed the factory itself. He'd finally made it and this room, shielded from paper dust and noise, was lasting proof that his hard work had paid off. Every day, he sat in his little chair and overlooked the factory like a little foreman, his head high as he captained this t-rex of a machine. High above the tension, I sat in that little chair and looked out at the factory's other half, a feeling of suspension and weightlessness as I rose with him. It felt like anything was possible.

The next week, it was back to the mental midgets at Line 14. I returned to my job behind the belt without fuss. Baby had saved up his venom during the week, but I worked through it without complaint. Cal walked over. "Welcome back," he said, sipping his coffee. The binder stopped, so I got a break.

"How was your week?" I asked him. His daughter's basketball team had won a championship game and he'd started another job during the day, driving a delivery truck. He said school was coming and clothes are expensive. "By the way, did we ever make that summer production goal?" I said.

"Yes, no thanks to you. Next month, they want us to make fifty million books."

"Ha. I'm so ready for that," I said. The binder started back up and then sputtered to a halt.

"So are the machines, it looks." I swept the area, then curled up in a bin to finish an entire Ms. — — novel. It was the pattern of the words, the rhythm of the sentences. They lulled me into a rare calmness and I almost forgot in that seven and a half hours that my father was dead, that my brother had tried to murder several coworkers, that college was far away. The story itself kept my mind active, the neurons firing in perfect synchronicity without delay—it was reassuring and somewhat remarkable, given the paths they had to travel around those lead shards. The shifts passed uneventfully, the hours covering the unpredictable spasms. A week later, Tommy returned.

Tower always came through when I needed help. First, they sent my estranged, drugged-out brother who pissed off the machine operators and almost went on a killing spree. Now that I was alone, the foreman assigned a woman named Gertie to help me out. She was an elderly woman, probably in her mid-seventies. I'd seen her in the press delivering little samples of paper to the machine operators. "What's your name?" she'd ask me. "What do you do?" Then she'd ask a series of pointless follow-up questions, nod, and wander away. Half an hour later, she'd appear and ask my name again. I had gotten used to working by myself and felt relieved that she didn't offer to help.

The third hour in, I didn't wait for her to ask the usual questions. "My name is Jason Han," I told her. "H-A-N. Yes, there used to be two of us here. I'm going to college soon. No, I don't know where yet." She looked at me wide-eyed. Maybe I could read her mind. Maybe I was a traveler from a distant future. The possibilities were endless. After lunch, she walked over carrying her cooler, a Harlequin Romance novel balanced on the top.

"If you want, I can tell you exactly how that ends," I said.

"Have you read it?"

"He has," Cal said.

"No. Don't even have to."

"Are you a writer?" she asked. I shook my head. A loud rattle, and I stacked some books in the bin.

"Don't listen to him," Cal said. "He's a writer if there ever...ask him about the love letter he's writing you." As we finished filling the bin, she looked at me as if I were an angel just starting to glow.

"Oh my," she said.

"Isn't it funny. Working here and I've never met a writer." She rubbed her head. "Do you write mysteries?" she asked.

"Everything," I said, patting her on the shoulder, "is a mystery." Especially how this factory was still operating.

We had some down time and then *The Art of War* came down the belt. "Is this you?" she said, tapping the brushstroke portrait of Sun Tzu on the back cover.

"God damn it," I said. Eight hours of this with no end in sight. It felt like a joke about someone's personal hell. "Imagine Sun Tzu—ageless Sun Tzu—working undercover here at Tower. Must be making sure these idiots don't screw his book up." I waved to Baby. She stared at the book's cover.

"Isn't that something," she said.

"Write this down: *Wait long by the river and the bodies of your enemies will float by.* No seriously, write that down. Right there. They'll know what it means." It wasn't a Sun Tzu proverb, not even close. I'd seen it on a poster at a record store, but it sounded ominous enough to express how I felt at the moment.

"That wasn't nice," Cal said. "Gertie used to work here, but they forced her to retire. Now she comes anyway." This I simply couldn't believe.

"It happens a lot to people who have been here forever," he said. He couldn't explain it. "Seriously, you can see her sitting in the parking lot half an hour before the shift starts. Nobody has the heart to remind her. Maybe she doesn't have anyone outside the factory to talk to." She died a few months later and no one seemed to notice.

Tommy might have learned a little about art in college, but he was still my brother. I picture him playing football, using those quick instincts to grab an impossible pass and shake off defenders. But even before that, he was someone who acted quickly, all synaptic flashes and muscle spasms. As for myself, I'd developed a tendency to assess and observe, break out the T-square and graphing calculator while the world spun around without me. When we met at the bar later that night, he spotted the copy of *The Art of War* in my car and spirited it away to his house. He must have studied it, too—and by studied, I mean "looked at the cover for a while and became enraged by the industrial glue smell that had seeped into the pages." After hours of study, he came up with a Plan, capital P.

I'd taken to spending my lunch hour exploring the factory. The landscape fascinated me. There were the mysteriously named departments: Five-Color, Security Impound, Fork Truck Hub, Mine Storage I and III. And then I saw Tommy walk out of the Receiving Department carrying a claw hammer. I stopped in my tracks, feeling as if someone had physically slapped me. We eyed each other and he walked over and told me it wasn't what I thought. The receiving department was far away from the bindery and insulated by boxes, so we could speak quietly. My voice started to shake before I even got the first word out, so I just stared at him. I shook my head and gave him a look that said, *Not here, not now.*

"I'm just here to do this one thing." All that week, Tommy had snuck in and stalked his nemesis the forklift driver. We walked together for a while, me keeping an eye on him. I didn't quite believe him and suspected he had a cache of rifles and bombs somewhere. "Shh," he said. Tommy pointed to someone in the shipping department. He was asleep in his forklift, nearly hidden by a maze of boxes ten to thirty feet high.

"No," I said.

"Stay here," Tommy whispered, nodding toward him.

"No," I said louder. It sounded like someone else's voice coming from me.

Tommy paused and tightened his grip on the hammer, then loosened it. In the summertime, workers often prop open doors to let the cool air in—he walked from the room and must have left through one of these, presumably the same way he'd entered the factory. Once my heartbeat quieted to the point where I could hear myself think, I decided I'd call him after work and we'd talk it out.

But I never got the chance. Later that day, someone entered the factory and found that forklift driver, who was a thin man with long brown hair and a scraggly mustache. He must have been sleeping, leaning forward to rest his head on the forklift's padded roll bar. That day, he was wearing black denim cutoffs and, for some reason, a short-sleeve dress shirt and tie. There was a steaming plastic 16-oz. coffee mug in the forklift's cupholder and whoever attacked him first threw it in his face. After that rude awakening, his attacker threw him to the ground and beat him viciously enough to make a caveman sick. The police later determined only steel-toed boots could have caused that much damage: five broken ribs, one of which was driven into a lung, a shattered spleen which had to be removed, both collarbones broken. The sheer force of the kicks to the ribs damaged the forklift driver's *spine*. All ten fingers were broken—a pinky and thumb had to be amputated. But most of the damage was to the skull: His brain was so damaged that by the time his assailant was through, he barely had IQ enough to make bubbles in the blood gushing out his nose. The last time I checked, he was still in a coma.

The police questioned everyone, but nobody knew anything. I guess it would have been different had the forklift driver been murdered. Management seemed more concerned about a lawsuit, which never happened. The police investigation stalled. This was an internal matter, and our laws—the laws of pent-up anger and vengeance, the laws of cause and effect—outdated polite society's. On a management level, all doors were required to remain closed during all operating hours (a rule everyone ignored) and security cameras were installed above the main entrance.

They never caught the attacker. No one said anything to me, although I'm sure a couple people thought I was responsible. I didn't mind people thinking twice before they spoke to me. I'd like to say that I felt sorry for the forklift driver and that the attack's sheer viciousness was unwarranted or disproportionate. But I wasn't sorry. For me, the forklift driver became a sort of sacrificial lamb. The factory had taken our family's patriarch, and actions have consequences.

I did have a sense—it felt almost peaceful or comforting, I'm ashamed to say—that the universe had righted itself by redirecting the violence in that factory toward someone more deserving. It was something I had little control over, and I was glad that people were now leaving me alone. I was relieved I didn't have to look over my shoulder when I walked to or from my line. The forklift drivers steered clear of the college kids. In fact, everyone backed off the college kids, even if only for their few final weeks. It didn't bother me at all that the forklift driver's three children (Aurora, 19 months, Joshua, 4, and Kacee, 9) were left without a parent and became wards of the state. Tommy snuck out of town shortly after the attack and went back to his college in Pittsburgh. I went back to Line 14.

13

AN OPEN GATE

I got my union card in September. By then I'd forgotten why I'd even applied (to file an official complaint about that forklift driver). But there it was: my union card, sitting in my new mailbox. It had my photograph on it along with a magnetic stripe and a hologram of the water tower that once stood in the middle of the complex.

The foreman shook my hand again when I walked in, showed me my new locker. They never hired a replacement for Tommy, so every day I'd walk in early to see two tough-guy afternoon shift men walk out. At 7:30, two big, bad day shift motherfuckers would walk in and stare at me, wondering how this tiny Asian dude outpaced them day after day. By being super-competent, that's how. Don't forget to check the board, bitches: We started and finished half a million Tom Clancy books. You know, the thick-ass ones with so much glue that it burns the hair off your forearms? They're 500-plus pages, a width that fucks up the machines. But you wouldn't know that. Have fun with Nora Roberts, jerks.

Days and nights ran together. Since the week starts Sunday night and ends Friday morning, you're never sure which day is which. Past midnight on Monday is technically Tuesday. And it really didn't matter because the world around you stops and only Tower continues. There's only the job—the belt and three bins, hustling. After a while I found a rhythm and timed my movements. It was repetitive, sure, but it was a good beat, one I could move to. My coworkers on 14 treated me with a grudging respect now that I wasn't a summer worker. No one threw garbage at me. When I got bored or restless, I thought about Cal, or the midget. If they'd made it, so could I. I wasn't my father, but I wanted people to remember and associate my family with me. And my success, which would come soon. I'd abandoned my father once, but now I could stay and tend to his legacy. People stopped asking when I was leaving for college.

Cal eventually forgave me. The first month or so he refused to even acknowledge my presence. "Another lifer. What a waste," he said when I proudly showed him my card. "Hey, take a look around," he said, pulling me by my arm so hard it felt like my shoulder had separated. He walked me through the bindery, past men in back braces, knee braces, stained shirts, old Gertie's ghost shuffling around. My father's ghost. "Twenty years. Fifteen years. Thirty years. Hey Williams, did you plan this as a career?" *Hell no. Get the fuck out. Isn't he in college?* We passed a gauntlet of exhausted, worn-down men staring at their machines. "Look at them smiling faces," Cal said. "The foreman assigned Gertie to you to show you your future." He threw up his hands and walked away.

But he got over it. We hung out at Tower picnics and family day. At work, there were long stretches of comedy and standing around, lazy conversations with my new friends. Most of the union workers were nothing like the grotesque caricatures on 14, I learned. I was paying the bills, I was young and fast and on the best shift. The foreman and Baby relied on me, which was something I'd never felt before. People outside the factory were scared of me, gray-faced and walking through the supermarket at 7:45 AM. I'd carved out a place for myself, became an insider in this hostile environment. As much as I loved the doctor and

Leslie, Princeton was a reward I hadn't earned. They have bar-restaurants all over where middle-management types go to feel blue collar. I belonged to a working class world and I swear to God, I miss it still.

Even Cyclops warmed to me. During the course of the year, he got a large tattoo on his left arm. It appeared piece by piece, spreading like a weird skin disease. I'd stare at it whenever he walked past, trying to figure out what it was. Even when it looked complete in November, I still wasn't sure. Water tower? Bulldog, perhaps? But he must have noticed me staring because one day when I was coming back from break, he walked over and showed me.

It was a smiling, naked pixie holding a flaming demon skull in both hands. The skull had a long, thick tongue that wrapped around the woman's waist and disappeared up between her legs. It was very detailed, of course—one of the most tasteless things my eighteen-year-old eyes had ever seen. Of course I couldn't look away. Cyclops turned his wrist and flexed the muscles in his arm a certain way, making it look like the tongue was pumping in and out of her. Then he nodded at me and walked away.

It was a momentous year outside, the whole world trembling as the millennium rolled toward us. All over, people were building cinderblock bunkers and buying guns. And fucking, too, checking off every possible sin before the wrath of Armageddon. There was a charge to the air and everything swirled. It felt like we, bloated with sin and history, had been pushed to the edge, our momentum about to carry us over and into the abyss.

I'd been working at Tower for eighteen months when a phone call woke me up. It was Thanksgiving. I answered it and the voice on the line said, "Wow" and hung up. Half an hour later, Tommy showed up outside my house, banging on the door.

"Do you know what time it is?" I said as I stumbled through the kitchen to open the door. The clock on the stove said 5 PM. I had work in six and a half hours.

"Christ, you look terrible. And take a shower," he said, leaning back. Half-awake, I invited him in. He shook his head. His car, that old Dart, looked like he'd crashed it a few times, but he still looked the same. I took a shower and went back to the door, my hair dripping and steam rising from my skin.

"Shouldn't you be in college?" I asked him.

"Ha," he said. It was unseasonably warm out that evening and he was wearing a red tank top and a pair of brown corduroys. "Where did you get that?" he said, looking at the glass in my hand. It was a clear blue tumbler filled with wine.

"Found it in the bathroom," I said.

"Pour me a drink," he said, standing outside the screen door. He looked at the empty kitchen behind me. I'd put most of the house's contents in storage. "I've been seriously thinking about putting the house on the market," I told him, hoping he might stop being dramatic and sit down at the kitchen table so we could talk like normal people. It had been well over a year since our father's funeral.

He drank a sip and tossed the thick remnants into the flower bed. "This is only good for a few days after you uncork it. Even then, you have to refrigerate it."

"What?"

"You know that, right?"

"Yes," I lied. This explained why I'd been getting sick lately.

"Don't put the house on the market yet," he said, leaning his forehead against the screen, pushing it in a little. "I still have dad's ashes. I want to honor him during *Chuseok*," he said. Which required both of us to build a shrine inside the house my brother refused to set foot in.

"*Chuseok* was last month," I said. I'd circled it on the calendar. The house next door had recently sold for $135,000. The owners moved to Florida and their daughter went to college.

"We'll celebrate next year. Together. As a family. I just need a little time." I nodded. I was stunned a little by how the word *family* struck me. I hadn't thought about it for so long and now it felt strange, something caught in the passage between my lungs and mouth.

"Come on, let's go for a drive," my brother said, jerking his head toward his car.

He insisted on taking an unopened bottle of wine, so I brought it to his car along with my dinner in a cereal bowl. "It's rice, butter, and barbeque sauce," I said, looking with disgust at the look of disgust he was giving my supper. "Where are we going, anyway?"

"You'll see," he said, lighting a cigarette as he barreled onto the highway. He was driving toward Tower, which made me nervous. We hadn't talked since he left Tower for Pittsburgh and we never discussed what happened to the forklift driver. What had been broken was broken. There was nothing else to say. I felt slightly less nervous after he pulled onto the dirt road leading to the old farm. He parked the car in the gravel, got out, and walked to the red pickup in the barn. He found the key under the floor mat and managed to start it, the dead bugs on the dashboard sliding toward us, dust rising from the hood.

It was a surprisingly smooth drive down the dirt road adjacent to the farm. He drove past an orchard and stopped beside a metal fence. We got out of the truck and followed a dirt path uphill. It was still warm out, winter impossibly far away. It started to get dark and the only sign of late November was a slight sting in the air when you breathed in too deeply.

"Almost there," Tommy said, panting. We reached the crest of the hill and he walked to the center, cocking his head as he looked down at the scene below. He nodded in approval. "Here," he said, motioning to the area with a sweep of his arm, as if unveiling a prize. Along a lonely stretch of road, there was the skeleton of a barn, bleached and leaning perilously over the rest of the yard, an old school bus abandoned in the half-acre of weeds and debris, and a couple junked cars. The bus was scarred by .22 plinkers, the windows smashed. Nothing out of the ordinary for the area. Near the barn, there were piles of old farm tools rusting together. To the right was a horse. It was dark brown and sleeping, its head almost touching the ground.

Aside from an involuntary flicking of the tail, it didn't move. I surveyed the wreckage and shrugged.

"Wow," he said, looking at my pale arm in the dying light. He held his up next to mine.

"Midnights. Soon I'll just vanish."

He sat down and pulled out a little Ziploc bag. "How is work, anyway?" he asked, licking the paper.

"You know."

"Still on 14?"

"Yeah, but I have more responsibilities," I lied. "And they're training me to be a trimmer operator."

"Whoa-ho. You'll get fat again," he said, rolling the joint and licking it again. He waved it under the lighter to dry it.

"It's fate, really."

"Getting fat? Hand me that," he said, gesturing to my food. "Look, it's like soup. The butter alone—"

"You know what I'm talking about." Did I have to say it? "Our father. Sometimes you see three or four generations in the bindery. Oedipus fought his fate and that just made it worse. Me, I'm just not the tragic hero type."

"Just tragic," he said.

"Thanks."

"Hope things work out better for you. I'd hate to see you in the city blind and wandering," he said.

A few minutes of silence. He slid the cellophane off his cigarette pack, dumped the remaining buds in the plastic pouch, and sealed the top with his lighter. "Is that what you're learning as an art major?" I said.

He lit the joint and puffed furiously. "How's the W-B? Heard the streetlights in Market Square are rusting and falling over."

"Just one or two. How's Pittsburgh? Heard the steel industry closed down." I took another drag, my head already feeling lighter. I exhaled slowly, feeling the aching muscles in my back unwind. Neither of us spoke for a while.

Finally, I said, "God, is there any water here?" to break the silence, tonguing the roof of my mouth. He brought out the wine. It was dark enough that I couldn't read the label. He drove the pickup truck up the hill and parked it backwards so we could sit in the bed to enjoy the scenery. I could feel the cold metal through my jeans as we sat and even though there was a blanket in the truck, neither of us bothered with it. It was a pleasant cold, the temperature just low enough to make you sit up and pay attention to everything, a cut-glass clarity that occasionally glared into the marijuana haze. We passed the bottle back and forth and watched the headlights of cars as they passed through the skeleton of the barn.

"How long you in for?" I said, wondering how long our conversation had lapsed into silence. The words came slowly, falling out of my mouth.

"Just today. I'm delivering a message."

"Like Grandmaster Flash." No response. "You drove from Pittsburgh. Ever heard of a phone? Or mail? Carrier pigeon—"

"Stop. Seriously. You're going to feel idiotic for saying that."

"This wine isn't bad," I said.

"If you want me to forgive you, fine. I don't care that you left. You escaped a horrific living situation, and you get to remember dad as a nice person. And you got the house. But you're just wasting your time punishing yourself. And if you think you're gonna do better down at Tower, you're just embarrassing yourself. Because you're not better. That's the message." He took a drink from the bottle.

I didn't say anything, and Tommy continued talking after pausing for two or three seconds. But if I'd said anything during those few seconds, it would have been "I don't need your forgiveness." But I did. Tower was a penance for abandoning my family. If I hadn't faked headaches in the hospital, my family would have stayed in New Jersey. My father might have become a foreman in the cannery. If I had grown up in the same house, maybe I could have saved him, convinced him to get help. A lot of things might have been different had I stayed. But now his former workplace had become everything to me: a penance, a paycheck, a hope for a better future, a place to see friends, somewhere to belong. But I could feel the cold immovable thickness of the wine bottle and knew how the story would end. It became clear as the light glinting off the dark curved glass:

Tommy's message was the same thing my father would have said. I knew I had to leave.

"Eventually he's going to die there," Tommy said, jerking his head toward the horse. "And then they'll throw him on a conveyor belt, make glue out of him." He stood up and walked toward the barn. There was the sound of an engine starting and then he was gone. It took me a few seconds to realize what had happened. I sat for a while, waiting for him to return. Finally, I realized he wasn't and that he'd taken the keys from the pickup. I grabbed the blanket. The cold settled on my skin as I stared at the scene below. The night air sobered me, the breeze lapping away my buzz. I remember staring late into the night at the gate he'd left open, at the horse that would never pass through.

The shift I worked after that long walk was one of the worst. It's amazing what people can get used to. I could suddenly feel my cells and organs dying as the seconds ticked away. It wasn't really a decision for this to be my final shift down at Tower—I absolutely couldn't stay any longer. But I would finish out the goddamned shift. I thought about my father, working beside me like a ghost. I wondered when he realized that this is all there was for him. I wondered when he'd given up. It struck me that I hadn't thought about him for so long. Force of habit, I guess. But I could feel it like an ache in my forearms and spine: the exhaustion that comes with factory work, the eternal insomnia that accompanies the midnight shift. I wouldn't want the last thing I breathed to be of oil-soaked paper dust, industrial glue, potato chips, and farts. In the end, it must have seemed to my father that the only control he had was to choose his method and time of death. At 7:30 AM, I swept the area clean. I had to leave, but I forced myself to stay for one last ritual.

I walked down the staircase to the baler room. I guess they don't run it every day, or maybe my last shift was Friday with no weekend overtime. At any rate, the room was empty and eerily silent, a thin sheet of paper dust on everything. As the dust I'd kicked up settled, I sat Indian-style in that slaughterhouse of literature and wrote a letter:

Father,

The animals circle in the forests surrounding us, drawn to the heat and lights but never illuminated. I've swept the line clean and they've got tons of old-growth forest spun through the press, awaiting our hungry blades. The machines ache and sigh as I write this, unable to bear the stillness. Everything and nothing has changed in your absence: There's a rival plant opening in Buffalo and we've lost contracts with some major publishers. Somewhere, they're inventing an electronic book to replace us. Another industry unsettles—the sugar-glazed electronic beast stalks our paper world.

From every possible angle, our enterprise here is in peril. How appropriate that now, at the end of a savage millennium, my little paper world should collapse. I won't mourn it too much—I've fed on ashes and dust for too long, I think.

I'm leaving following a record shift (how little those numbers mean now that I'm a retired union man). And I trained a replacement, the proper thing to do. He's a recent parolee and will last two weeks, I predict. But Wilkes-Barre feeds off the interstate, and there will always be someone to take his place.

Myself, I'm a college kid again, heading off to Pittsburgh, where I should have been all along. One day you wake up and everything's wrong—I've come to understand what this does to a man. Fitzgerald once said there are no second acts in American life, but I'm still heading west. This factory was a detour and there isn't much to support this beyond hope, but if you catch it early enough, when there's still time to fight the current, maybe there's such a thing as a clean break. Tomorrow, I head down the interstate. It will be exhilarating, I think, after all the stillness here.

I know this place is not my birthright.

They say old Steel City's reached its peak, but I'm going to see for myself.

And then I signed my name.

Call it a vision, call it a daydream, call it something I saw because I had to, but as I stood in the baler room, I saw my father sitting in his living room, sitting in his chair. He's pouring the pills in his mouth, surprised and annoyed at how much liquid it takes to wash the whole bottle down. As he starts shaking and his heart gives out, he's trying to say something. Even as his bowels give out and he slumps forward on his chair, a coffee mug full of vodka falling to the ground. He's trying to say something in another language, something deep and round.

Korean. His head is rolling, arching his back, trying to see blue sky in the narrowing horizon, something to remind him of the blue-green *Dong Hae*, the East Sea he never forgot, rows of earthen pots drying in the sun—anything but concrete, ash, unbreakable metal. I can't understand the words, but I know what he means. Never again the piercing stink of New Jersey canneries, never again the queasy industrial glue.

I tucked the letter into the waiting heap and left footprints in the dust behind me. At Tower, I'd tried on my father's life, the one he never wanted me to have. The exhaustion and sadness now had a logic, the long hours and sacrifice now made sense. And when he saw the chance to send me to a better life, it wasn't done with a capricious shrug. I now had to bear the weight of that sacrifice and hope. I left the room. The time card reader spat my hours back at me, and I tucked them carefully in the holder on the wall.

Cal surprised me on the way out. He was waiting next to the front entrance, staring at my car. We were alone in the parking lot. "You okay?" he said. I nodded. "You didn't seem in the mood to talk today."

"I don't know," I said. I wasn't good at goodbyes, I suppose. The truth is, I was in a hurry to leave—anything keeping me there was dangerous. Because the factory offered the comfort of friends and a steady paycheck.

"Well all right," he said. "See you tomorrow." I nodded and we walked to our cars in silence. Later, I told myself he must have understood. There must have been times he'd thought of leaving, pointing his car in one direction and speeding off, feeling the wind peel his old life away.

14

ARRIVAL SURVIVAL

Tommy lived in Oakland, one of Pittsburgh's largest neighborhoods. You turn onto the exit just as the city's skyscrapers appear ghostly on the horizon. Beyond are the rivers. During the drive, I pictured my disintegrated letter floating through Tower's crick, making a journey parallel to mine. Up the long hill of Bates Street, the thin, hairy trees lining Route 376 merge with civilization and you see the forest encroaching one or two barely standing brick houses painted aqua green. You wonder who would live in that hinterland before you pass under hulking iron bridges to come out the other side into civilization proper, with its mini marts and scattered billboards and squat brick row houses.

Pittsburgh. Steel City. Iron City (beer). Distance from Morgantown, West Virginia: 78 miles. Pittsburgh, the "Paris of the Appalachians." Distance from Paris, France: 3,987 miles.

True story: A man walked into a bar wearing a yellow stocking cap pulled over a baseball cap. His glasses fogged up. "Damn, it's cold out there," he said. His stocking cap read "Big 7 Ben." He pulled it off. Underneath, his black baseball cap read "Ben at Work."

Ingredients in a Roethlis Burger ($7), invented at Peppi's on

the North Side and widely imitated by any number of city restaurants:
  half a pound of ground beef
  two Italian sausage links
  three eggs, scrambled
  grilled onions
  American cheese
  three tomato slices
  Kaiser roll, toasted
  half a pound of mayonnaise

True story: She grabbed her bottom lip and pulled it to the side, exposing her pink gums. "Heah," she said, pointing. She had the Steelers logo tattooed on her gums. She let go, rubbing her face. "Just wanted to be true to my roots." The Steelers don't have cheerleaders—what's the point?

Pittsburgh: eighty days of sunlight a year. Andy Warhol had to flee to sunny New York. The Warhol Museum downtown has a fully stocked bar—it's the first thing you see when you walk through the door. Their happy hour sucks.

Primanti's restaurant. "Almost famous." Almost not a stupid motto. Fries on your sandwich, between the bread, above the coleslaw and meat. At first, out of convenience for truckers. Now, because—who cares?

Working steel mills in Pittsburgh: The imposing Edgar Thomson plant in Braddock, the Irvin Works plant in Dravosburg, the Clairton coke plant, the U.S. Steel plant in the Mon Valley. How many does your city have?

"Seriously," Tommy says. "And by the way, how many Super Bowl rings does Wilkes-Barre have?" This is the Pittsburgh Tommy knows and loves. And defends to the death when I bring up the gay quarterback, who wasn't even—and besides, he's gone now so would I please stop bringing up that unpleasant piece of history? Pittsburgh has four Super Bowl rings, one for each finger and now we need one for the thumb. He tells me I need to think more positive.

"What about Princeton?" he asks. We had Einstein, I tell him.

He's worth at least two Super Bowl rings, I think. "Two at the most."

He is quick to point out that Pittsburgh's fractured geographically, neighborhoods connected only by its bridges. Tommy's city includes the whole region, the scattered neighborhoods and towns outside the city, authentic Yinzer enclaves. They sound intimidating: McKee's Rocks. Freedom. Braddock. Blawnox. Carrick. Some of them have charming names, he tells me: Moon, Cranberry, Butler. Muse. "Butler's where they have those roadside blanket stands. You know, the ones with horses and wolves on them." I tell him that sounds real nice.

Oakland is a busy neighborhood in east Pittsburgh, a "cultural district" that contains a business district, three universities, several residential neighborhoods, and several hospitals, all crammed into half a square mile. Hospitals. There are five thousand, seven hundred and fifty-nine hospitals in the United States and most of them are in Oakland, situated amidst a maze of one-way streets and conveniently located atop one of the steepest hills in the nation—Pitt students call it "Cardiac Hill" as they pant their way to Trees Hall. Let's pour out some liquor for the old stadium before we roll downhill. The new stadium—sorry, "events center"—looks like an Austrian Museum of Banking (this is not a compliment). Plus, it's named in honor of some Important Rich Dude—a harbinger of things to come, I fear.

Downhill to the Cathedral of Learning (hurry, before it they rename it the *Capital One Cathedral of Learning*). In the 1920s, Chancellor Bowman commissioned the structure, prompting workers and students to call it "Bowman's erection." No one knows why it was built: I like to picture Chancellor Bowman enjoying the panoramic view of Oakland from his castle-like mansion overlooking the city. *You know what this area needs?* he says to no one in particular. *A thirty-six-floor Gothic skyscraper.* He throws his snifter of brandy on his lead crystal window, watches a tall amber stain run drip onto Forbes Avenue, the new axis upon which Oakland would turn. He turns and pulls his robe tight around his chest. *We'll begin tomorrow.*

And so they built the Cathedral of Learning, the second tallest free-standing university building in the world, and certainly the most phallic. "If you get lost at night in Oakland," sorority sisters tell each other, "just follow the huge glowing penis." The huge glowing penis will safely lead you home—this is just the beginning of a liberal arts education.

There are more unicorns in Pittsburgh than taxis, so let's start this tour on a bus. "Spare some change? Spare some change?" Shake your head and the beggar, a skinny black man in a dirty blue bomber jacket, will move on. A few feet and you can't even hear him. Amidst the sound of the bus' massive diesel engine, there are blaring horns muted through the windows. It's a hot day in late August and your seat smells like old Pepsi and new urine. The bus seats are 80s relics, fuzzy and brightly colored with red squiggles and electric blue triangles. The colors somehow make the smell worse. The bus moves a couple feet forward and stops. "Aw hell no," the man sitting next to you whines into his cell phone. "Goddamn Pitt students." Indeed. It's Arrival Survival week, meaning a swarm of bright-eyed Pitt freshmen are descending upon Oakland. They push their belongings in Pitt-issued housing carts, bright yellow and the size of the clothes carts at laundromats. Look down and you can see inside. One student has his filled entirely with ramen noodles. And then there's the usual: computers, clothes, vacuum cleaners, fans, mini refrigerators. As the bus inches by, you spot a freshman girl pushing a cart filled to the top with stuffed animals.

"Got any change, change?" Meet Sombrero Man, one of Oakland's many panhandlers. His broad, dirty face is shaded by an authentic-looking straw sombrero. Occasionally, freshmen steal his hat and hang it like a trophy outside their dorm windows. He always gets a new one, though. No one knows from where.

Sombrero Man's on the move, and so are we. It's a dense

neighborhood—this entire tour only covers about four blocks. Now we're passing another Oakland landmark: *Diplodocus carnegii*, the huge bronze dinosaur outside the Carnegie Museum of Art. It's tall and as long as a school bus, its thin neck stretching to overlook Forbes Avenue. A sign below reads *Please do not climb on the dinosaur*. Although it seems impossible, I know it is actually possible to climb up the dinosaur's stocky legs and onto its back. It is a difficult task, however, even with Thunderbird and Wild Turkey wings lifting you up.

On with the tour. We're sitting on the stone wall outside Pitt's Law School. This is one of the things I liked to do instead of going to class. You can see everything from this wall. Since the streets are so crowded, you can't ride a bike on them. Instead, people ride their bikes down Forbes, weaving through four lanes of traffic. They fly, too, sometimes faster than the cars. A burst of horns and shouting interrupts me and we looked to see a car heading down Forbes the wrong way.

Oh yeah. This happens a lot during Arrival Survival—and here, you thought it was just a clever rhyme. There's a poorly marked intersection where Forbes Avenue changes from being a two-way street and abruptly becomes a one-way. If you don't turn down a side street, you face the very real prospect of a head-on collision with four lanes of oncoming traffic. Next to this intersection is the Carnegie Museum of Natural History. It's a huge stone building adorned with statues: bronze Copernicus and Shakespeare guard the entrance. From the roof, statues of great pioneers and architects gaze down pitilessly at the scene below. A minivan stops in the middle of this trap/intersection. Horns blare. As it attempts a K-turn, a few cars speed around it.

Oh, and check this out: A Pitt student stands up from the stone wall and looks up and down Forbes. There are cars coming, but he's late for class. There's a crosswalk about a block away, but whatever. This is a shortcut. Will he take it? Without hesitation, he puts his head down like a bull and charges across the street, his overstuffed purple backpack bouncing. He makes it! This is an everyday occurrence: Just about every hour from 9

AM-3 PM you can watch waves of Pitt students playing real-life Frogger. Good thing the hospitals are so close.

Down Forbes, you can see the scaffolding tunnel. They've been working on that building for the three years I've been here. It will be Sennott Square, home of Pitt's new business school. Parts of the façade are made of hard plastic meant to resemble marble. There's going to be a little strip mall on the bottom floor and probably a Starbucks or two, academia sitting comfy atop commerce. It is rumored there's going to be a Vespa dealership on the ground level. Vespas in sunny Pittsburgh! They'd be better off selling canoes.

Speaking of transportation, there's one last thing I'd like to show you—one final stop on this tour. "Excuse me, excuse me," a young man in a red shirt says, interrupting me. He runs ahead of us, facing us and walking backwards. "Please, my man," he says to me. He's in his early twenties, about my age (21), white, with a scraggly mustache and a neon-green baseball hat. We stop. I exhale in disgust. "My car broke down on the Boulevard of the Allies yesterday."

"Sorry," I say.

"It's out of the shop, I mean they're done with it on the shop—you know the Exxon down there—and anyways I need it to get to work." I tell him I don't have any money. "Come on," he says, looking at you, pleading. He says there's four grand worth of tools in the back. He can repay you. His inflection is so perfect, his eyes pleading. He could be faking, or is that genuine sorrow behind the "I'm ashamed I have to ask" tone? That look in his eyes...one can't fake that, right?

Enough. I say something rude to him and walk away. You look back at the man—maybe you're even wondering if you have any ones or fives. He's good. And maybe he's telling the truth. Either way, that's the third time his car has broken down this week.

My first day in Pittsburgh. My brother took me to The Original Hot Dog Shop, a small restaurant in Oakland. The menus above the kitchen area were charming 70s reds and oranges, carefully hand-painted. The colors and fonts reminded me of the boardwalk stands in Ocean City. The whole place had a strange odor, like stale cigarettes and cheap beer. After placing our order, we walked past a corner where a couple body-bag-sized potato sacks sat as if on display and sat down at a table. The adjacent wall was thick with high school graffiti. Someone with a very sharp knife had carved "Megalize Larijuana" next to my chair. Returning to the counter to pick up my order, I watched the cook lift the basket out of the fryer and put a small paper tray (the kind you get burgers on at a carnival) on top of it. Then she flipped the entire thing over, overflowing the tray with freedom fries. *Yes, I'm sure I got your order right.* "Small" *means* "ridiculously gigantic" *here. Deal with it,* the look on her face said. A little stunned, I walked back to my seat.

As we picked at our fries, I told him I'd applied to some colleges in Pittsburgh and hoped to hear from them soon. "So what's new back home?" he asked. I told him about Tower's newest lawsuits.

"Ha. From crippled workers?"

"No. Line 16 was making porno books..."

"Those *Blue Moon* ones?"

"Erotic fiction. Yeah. And Line 21 was making Bibles, right?" Tommy laughed. He understood. This sort of thing probably happened every summer. Before the books were bound, someone took a few pages from the porno books and put them in the Bibles. And vice versa.

"Rock and Roll," he said, clapping his hands. "Imagine their faces. Brilliant." He promised to take me on a tour that day. "What about the foundation? It's the site of Carnegie's old house, down by the Waterfront. The house isn't there anymore. I don't know if they moved it or what, but the stone foundation is still there...raised a good twenty feet off the ground, like a platform. Sometimes people hang out there. Mostly scumbags." I told him maybe later.

"When you said you were taking me to the Dirty O, I thought it was a strip club. Or, like, Hooters, except the waitresses talk dirty to you."

"No, it's 'cause of the weird layer of grease on everything." Behind us, a MoCap Boxing arcade game started its cycle:

cheering, a mumbled announcer's voice, and then some flashing lights. After three or four cycles, my head started to hurt.

"That's not yours," the man behind the counter said. He was one of the cooks, a tall black man whose twin brother worked the pizza counter. This would prove to be a complete mindfuck in subsequent visits when I was profoundly intoxicated and the red and orange flashing neon was brilliant and fascinating. But at that moment, he narrowed his eyes at the would-be thief, a grimy-looking white man already wearing a thick down winter jacket. The thief continued lifting the beige peacoat from the back of a chair and turned to leave, coat still in hand.

"Mother*fucker*," the man behind the counter said. He *jumped over the counter* and tackled the man, getting in a couple shots to his face before wrestling the coat away. The homeless man fled, slipping on the greasy floor until he grabbed the door handle and burst out onto the sidewalk. The cook stopped at the door, yelling profanities. He picked up the coat, brushed it off, and carefully set it back on the chair before returning to his place behind the counter. The whole time, Tommy kept eating.

"You should have splurged and gotten cheese," he said.

"It was like five dollars," I said, still processing what had just happened. A businessman walked up the stairs from the bathroom, picked up his peacoat and left, completely unaware of the previous drama. I took a sip of my drink, noting how unfazed Tommy had remained through the incident. No one else seemed surprised. "My kind of city," I said.

"I said you'd like it here. What took you so long?"

PART II

IN A CATHEDRAL CITY

15

AN EXORCISM

The garbage truck rolled down Atwood Street for the sixth time. It was midnight and although most students were indoors, the weight of their lifestyle squeezed the garbage onto the street. The day before classes started, it was waist-high—furniture left behind by hastily exiting graduates and shiny appliance boxes from new student tenants. This was the Oakland neighborhood in Pittsburgh, my senior year in college.

The truck stopped and two garbage men stepped over bloated bags of rotting food and flung the lighter bags into the truck. In about a month only the heaviest refuse would remain: air conditioners, refrigerators, cracked tables, and abandoned couches. Eventually, even these would vanish, spirited away by desperate students and thrifty landlords. Earlier that day, I found a perfectly good vacuum cleaner and a microwave that still had the plastic sheet over the clock, thrown out because it wouldn't fit in someone's car.

After decades of complaints from townies, the University of Pittsburgh finally rented contractor-sized dumpsters and stationed them on every street of the student ghetto—Atwood, Meyran, Bates, and Semple. They'd filled long before Arrival Survival and people continued to pile garbage around them, making them impossible to tow away. That was how it was in

Oakland: We didn't own the neighborhoods, they had always been there, and we didn't think about them much. And so we treated the place like a rental car, eager to test its boundaries with impunity. The way drivers gleefully drop neutral bombs and smoke the tires, we packed our rooms with wires and electronics to the point they bulged and snaked out the windows. We threw bottles off rooftops just to watch the impact's glitter, we let garbage bags sail like tumbleweeds. Occasionally, we'd see the indigenous inhabitants—old Italians, mostly—cleaning the cigarette butts of their front lawns or community clean-up rallies. And on those days, we felt bad. But mostly, the neighborhood did not belong to us, never had, and we were amused with our squalor. A microcosm for the nation, perhaps, but I really hadn't seen much of it by this point. I waded through the junk around the Bates Street dumpster and pulled myself onto the rim and crouched there, searching for anything worth taking.

"Shouldn't you be studying?" someone said. I lost my balance, stepping forward into the tangled mess of furniture at the surface. I looked up. Tommy leaned out the window, face lighting in a flash from his Zippo.

"Did you piss on this?" I called up. He did, I bet, right out his window. He took a drag, the floating orange dot glowing brighter.

"What are you doing down there, anyway? Dumpster diving? I expect that from a Point Park student, but *you*? What would your chancellor think?" I ignored him, wiping my sleeve across my nose.

"Well, it wasn't just you, from the smell of it," I mused. I pictured waves of nimble young men scaling the surrounding trash wall, wading to the center of this massive blue dumpster just for the privilege of peeing on it. I found a small card table and slid it down the side of the container.

"God, do you really need that? Look, I'll buy you a table." I didn't respond as I looked at the treasure around me through the angular shadows cast by the streetlight. Finally, I walked to the middle of the dumpster.

When in Rome. I unzipped my jeans and watched my arc of

piss shine in the streetlight. As I climbed down, a police car slowly drove by.

"*You,*" a loud, amplified voice called. A spotlight in my eyes stopped me in my tracks. The cruiser's windows were black and I couldn't see inside. I grabbed the card table and held it in front of me like a shield. "*I repeat, what are you doing?*" The car door swung open.

"There's a body in there," I yelled, panicking. I waved and pointed wildly. "God help us all!"

"*What?*" the voice boomed. An obese police officer struggled out of the car. Dragging the table, I ran around the corner to Tommy's house and pounded on the door. Eventually it opened. In my excitement, I slammed it shut and winced. After checking the peephole for a few minutes, I saw no one had followed me.

"Happy birthday," I said, setting the table down in the bare living room. I didn't know how old he was, but at least I remembered the date.

"Thanks," Tommy said.

"I'll wash it off later."

"I'll hold my breath." Now that I think about it, he was about 23. It seemed like yesterday I was walking through the double doors down at Tower. That whole year felt like a bad dream, our father's house now a million miles away.

"We should celebrate, old man," I said. I found some Banker's Club gin in his fridge and we finished it as we watched the scene unfold just below his window. More police cars arrived and five or six cops surrounded the dumpster, waving flashlights and gesturing. One cop managed to pull himself up onto the lip and almost slipped a few times as he picked through the rubble, hurling cabinets and chairs to the sidewalk. "God, look at them. They live for this. You just hit the big time, fellas. No more telling kids to turn down that gosh darn music."

"Maybe they'll actually find a body in there," Tommy said. A spotlight jerked toward our window. We snuck down the fire escape and headed to the bar.

We stayed until last call. After that, we looked for a party. It was the usual hunt—neither of us knew where it was or if any of the usual houses would admit us. But by 3 AM, we'd grown restless and I could see in Tommy's eyes that he was seeing the night's promise fading, thinking it might save us a lot of walking if we just went home. But there could always be a party just over the next hill. Tommy decided to head to the Hill District, the actual ghetto just outside Oakland. I tried to reason with him even as we moved further uphill, up the weird brick-paved streets where sneakers hung from power lines like drying meat. Someone once told me that hanging shoes meant a drug dealer lived in the house below. If that was true, there was a dealer in almost every house. "You know that people inside those houses are aiming Glocks and nines at us, right?" I said. If that wasn't the case, I knew they were watching—the curtain pulled aside and not looking away when I spotted them. We were literally at one of the city's edges and could actually see the forest that separated the city from the wilderness beyond. "You know, Tommy, there are horror movies that start like this."

"When Oakland was in its prime, all the rich people lived here, above all the smoke and dust. But the steel industry left..." We passed more weedy front yards and crooked, slanting houses. Small groups of black people on porches watched us pass and the night got colder. Somehow, the history lesson wasn't reassuring.

The last neighborhood stretched up on a slight curved incline. Beyond was a dense wall of forest. With a row of pointy little houses on each side, the street resembled the bottom half of a huge snout, the moonlight shining off the worn brick road like a long dry tongue. Even though I just wanted to collapse in my bed at this point, I hoped there was something in this neighborhood—if not, Tommy might head into the woods. But there was a blue light in front of a house near the end of the street. It reminded Tommy of Kmart and he reasoned, in his 3 AM logic, that the light meant discount liquor and weed. I told him it probably meant they'd shot out the red lights on a police cruiser, but he walked toward it just the same.

That blue light was gone when we showed up but sure enough, there was still a party there. The stairs leading up to the porch were lined with brown-skinned people. A couple were bald and I distinctly remember how the streetlight reflected off the scars on their heads. Tommy called out something in Spanish and a squat Mexican-looking kid ran up the stairs and brought a skinny dreadlocked white dude to talk to us.

"Either of you speak German?" he said. We looked at each other. He repeated his request, his glassy eyes constantly refocusing. Tommy said he was born in Hamburg and could speak several dialects, no hint of an accent. I claimed the same and our gatekeeper nodded, clapping his hands and yelling to the people inside, "Check it out. I found them," he said. He put a cold hand on the back of my neck and guided me through the house and down some stairs.

The damp basement was lit by black lights that made the white stripes on Tommy's shirt glow like ribs. Glowing graffiti and tags floated around us and there were twenty or so college-age drunks nervously gathered.

"Maybe they want us to fight to the death," Tommy said.

"God, I hope so. Remember, this was your idea. I fight dirty, too." I said, looking at the anxious crowd. In my three years of college, it had occurred to me in a couple dim, morning-after flickers that crashing parties late at night probably wasn't the safest endeavor. But we'd stayed in Oakland. The two of us fed off the strange fellowship that came with being college students. In the early morning hours everyone became more generous as we forgot each other's majors and finally stopped asking. And if someone had weed, they'd be happy to share as we huddled in some back bedroom. But the people around us weren't mostly rich white kids from the Philly suburbs. They probably weren't attending any kind of college—they were an entirely different nocturnal crowd, and they'd blocked the stairs, the only exit I could see. Had they done that on purpose?

A shaggy-haired white kid walked down the steps. It was his party, I think, as much as anyone can own such a thing. Everyone parted to let him through. Leading us to a dark corner, he reached down to a strange lumpy shape and pulled away a blanket, revealing a sleeping police dog. It was a large German Shepherd still wearing the orange K-9 vest. Someone was vomiting upstairs—I think she was vomiting, anyways. Otherwise, it was quiet.

"Fuck," I said quietly. I hadn't expected this at all. My stomach churned beer and cheese fries with all its might and I swallowed hard to keep it all down.

"Well, get to it," the shaggy-haired kid said.

"What?" Tommy said, looking down at the sleeping animal.

"We need to get rid of it," shaggy hair said.

"Like an abortion," someone in the crowd said.

"How did you get it?" I said, looking for another exit.

"That's not important. We need it to leave and that's where you come in. They train these things in German and you're both German." Like I said, not college students.

"Is it really a police dog?" I said, stepping closer to examine the sleeping animal. Shaggy hair clapped his hands and the dog stood up, sniffing the air. It had a black muzzle with cinder-gray markings on its chest and back. It looked royal, dignified, and I said maybe we shouldn't disturb it.

"Jason speaks better German than me," Tommy said, pushing me toward it.

Someone in the crowd must have noticed we were Korean. He reminded me, "Remember, talk to it. Don't eat it."

"Do it, Jason," shaggy hair said, his eyes wide with anticipation. "Make it leave. Exorcise the beast." As the crowd yelled encouragement like "Do it motherfucker!" I shouted every German word and number I knew, making martial hand gestures to punctuate my commands. I remember looking at Tommy and thinking *happy freaking birthday* as I stood in the center of this delinquent but not yet murderous crowd. I looked up at the still-blocked stairs, hoping I'd have enough energy to make a quick break when the SWAT team kicked in the front door, cracking skulls as they tore across the house in search of their canine partner. My hands started shaking. After the dog failed to respond to "Ich bin ein Berliner!" the crowd began muttering. Someone upstairs played a catchy rap song on the stereo and they began to disperse, moving toward the beats. I slipped into the crowd, deciding I'd repay Tommy for volunteering me either by stealing something valuable from him or punching him in the kidneys hard when he wasn't expecting it. I suddenly felt a little better.

"We're gonna die in this house," I told him as he walked over.

"Don't worry. I'll get it to leave and we'll be heroes. You'll see," Tommy said, squeezing my shoulder. The shaggy-haired kid nodded. I followed the crowd upstairs. There are literally a million dialects of German, I told them. It's possible the dog was trained in another one. Maybe the dog was deaf. It made perfect sense. What they needed was sign language and I didn't know canine sign language. People mostly agreed, saying things like "good effort, bro," and someone handed me a coffee mug full of beer.

After a few drinks with the crowd upstairs, my hands stopped shaking. I was at home amongst the drunks. Sure, it was a slightly different crowd—people were either high-school age and trying to look older or in their thirties and trying desperately to look younger. There were a few black people at the party, but most of them left in a big group half an hour after we arrived. Most of the rest were white kids in baggy jeans and puffy jackets. Still, most people had already gone home, and this was my favorite time, the post-celebration haze. There was a mutual respect in the air for everyone's party stamina.

And I guess I'd been talking about my legendary ability to consume alcohol, because at some point in the night, a kid with a beard dared me to drink something called "Rocket Fuel." Rocket Fuel is the name of an actual mixed drink (consisting of 151, Grey Goose, and blue Curaçao), but his version consisted of maybe several shots of grain alcohol, a few shots of 151, and half a can of National Bohemian, all mixed together in a plastic Big Gulp 7-Eleven cup and set aflame. Watching the top of the cup melt, I made a toast to the room, to the Hill District and the 1974 Pittsburgh Pirates before throwing it down. Shortly afterward, I collapsed on the couch.

Another weird thing about those twilight hours is that you become invisible even as people introduce you, passing around your name and studying your face. Even as you become ubiquitous, you're still part of something blurry and fast-moving, almost impossible to track as it winds through its phases. Or more like moods, the party a generous, capricious multicelled organism. Everyone's blissfully anonymous, liberated. Instant friends (just add alcohol and stir gently) slowly turned back into strangers as the sun rose. Though I might spend hours in a conversation that ends in mutual hugs (or more), the next day I could pass the same girl and all the love and awkwardness would have already faded to something faint—a blush, a wink from across the room, heat after a campfire.

The next morning I woke up around noon with a girl standing over me. Watching me. She didn't say a word. The sunlight was blinding and I really didn't get a good look at her face. But I was relieved to see I was in my house—or rather, Tommy's house, where I'd recently moved to save money. I was on the couch where I usually slept. I didn't remember walking home. It felt as if my world had been turned upside down and shaken several times during the night. Everything just felt a little off. It was a familiar feeling. I coughed and went back to sleep. This young woman business was too much to deal with at the time.

An hour later, she was still there. She'd closed the curtains—filtered through them, the noonday sun was blue and little dust particles floated like embers. She had short brown hair, this girl, and she was going through my stuff. Her back was to me, and she was bending over as she grabbed a T-shirt and moved a pair of boxer shorts with her foot next to another clothes pile. I tried not to stare at her ass, even though it was right there. I wasn't sure who she was, if she was dangerous at all, and leering at her seemed unwise given my tenuous grasp of the situation. Maybe she was a cop. I leaned my head against the rough canvas back of the couch and tried to remember. I had a headache, but her face seemed a little familiar. There were poker chips and cards on the table, but everything had been neatly organized, so there was no way of telling. She must have heard me moving around.

"I thought you people were supposed to be clean," she said playfully.

"Just the Japanese. The rest of us are complete slobs," I said.

"Quite the scavenger," she said, looking up at the wall above my bed. I rolled over and looked up at the orange reflective Boulevard of the Allies street sign, the tacked pictures and postcards and concert posters.

"Postmodernist." I sat up and rubbed my temples. I thought about introducing myself but figured we'd probably met earlier that night. From my location I could see a bunch of blankets thrown on the kitchen floor. I wondered if the two of us had done anything on those blankets.

She was pretty, sure, better looking than most of the girls I found wandering around my apartment on Sunday mornings. Her light brown hair was parted slightly to the side and there was something about the way that blue light struck it, the way her hair curled around her ear and reached down to her neck in almost ragged strands that looked strangely elegant and made me think of tall thin grass and seashells, a fleeting childhood memory. She was wearing a denim skirt and a green and white Le Tigre track shirt with a flip collar, the outfit topped off with a pair of striped knee socks and black boots. The light flashed off a red glass bead bracelet on her wrist. She had an almost sleepy look as she leafed through my mail. Maybe we were married now. This must be what waking up at noon in Vegas feels like.

She picked up an envelope stamped "URGENT—PAST DUE" in huge red letters and held it up. "Watch this," she said. After finding a permanent marker, she wrote "DECEASED AND IF YOU DONT MIND WE'VE HAD ENOUGH SORROW" on the envelope in large block letters. She held it up again, as if toasting me, and tossed it back on the coffee table.

"Does that really work?" I said. She nodded and grabbed another envelope. I stood up, grabbed the phone, and walked to the bathroom. *I'm probably still legally drunk*, I thought to myself. I sat on the toilet and called Tommy's cell phone. "There's a chick in the house," I told him.

"Kate," Tommy said. He waited.

"Well, Kate's *cleaning* the house."

"I'm in the kitchen," he said and hung up. I opened the door. Tommy stood up and waded through a sea of blankets. Kate had completely thrown back the curtains and opened the windows and, blinking, we strained to see her again in the suddenly brilliant living room.

Using sworn statements from all parties involved and utilizing the power of my own imagination to fill the gaps, I have reconstructed the following events of the night we met Kate. Here's Tommy in that ghetto basement. After a blitzkrieg of German words, words he thought were German, and words that sounded German, Tommy sat on the basement steps and stared at *das hund*. This hairy dilemma, this four-legged question mark. Faint laughter and music drifted down to him as he stalked through the basement, turning over the problem in his head. He caught sight of a large, white brick wall and an abandoned box of art supplies on a table. The police dog sat unmoving, its eyes following him as he moved a beer-pong table away from the wall and with his foot pushed some stray beer cans aside. After rummaging through the box, he pulled out a permanent marker and began to sketch the dog on the white basement wall, drawing its large brown eyes first. He'd finished the outline and was grinding out the dog's markings with the Sharpie's nearly dry tip when a young brunette walked down the steps.

"Nice," she said as she passed the Turner and Hooch show. She picked up a shoebox.

"Uh, do you live here?" he said.

"Used to. Just getting some of my things." She took a closer look at him. He was tall, much taller than she was, but thin. Wiry arms. Still, he had an attractive face and a strong jaw. Not cute, she decided, too serious-looking to be cute, but definitely handsome. He had the bed-head haircut of the sensitive artiste, meticulously groomed to look as if he'd just rolled out of bed. She wondered how long it took him to style it.

"Oh," he said, not knowing what to do.

"Your brother is throwing up," she added.

Tommy shrugged. "Wait, how do you know he's my brother?" he said.

"Ha," she said. Carrying a box to the steps, she paused to look at his drawing, studying the thin strokes he had made with the marker. The portrait of the sitting animal had depth and a surprising amount of detail but still lacked something.

"I'm coming back," she said. She hesitated, but returned with a plastic cup filled with acrylic paint tubes. "I don't like this brand. You can have the rest." She spoke quietly with the slightest hint of a backwoods accent, unconsciously drawing out certain words. "Couldn't find any brushes," she added. Tommy grabbed a piece of cardboard and began mixing the paints. She plugged in a lamp and noticed his watery eyes, glazed from the alcohol, but focused with a newfound resolve on the impromptu basement portrait.

Holding his makeshift palette, he paced and added color with his hand, feathery shapes and odd swirls at places. With the black paint, he added lines with his fingers and made more cryptic shapes, occasionally looking at the real dog as if seeking approval. She watched him for a few minutes and then moved closer. "Go ahead," he said. "There's no orange, so I'm not drawing the vest." He offered her the palette and she began to smudge brown paint on the wall with her palm. Tommy stole a glance at her pale arm, slender and pale as she traced her fingers down the wall, an almost feline gesture, he thought. A thin double-stranded glass-bead bracelet jumped on her wrist, crossing and uncrossing as she streaked paint over the rough wall. She stepped back as she moved to a new section, her gray eyes lighting as she imagined the finished project. Tommy thought about painting a picture of her slender hand, adding soft light to reflect off the fine white hairs on her arm, to sparkle off the bracelet's helix. This was, sadly, a time when bell-bottoms had made a comeback and influenced the denim fashion world. She wasn't wearing bell-bottoms, but her jeans flared out a little at the base. Above it, she wore a hemp belt and a blue and white tie-dyed shirt. Tommy remembers her being barefoot, but that doesn't make any sense, not in that beer-soaked basement. She wasn't quite a hippie chick, not with their unshaven legs and vegan politics. But she took a page from their fashion playbook and made it cute.

"How did we ever get away from this? The brushes...you can't feel it like this," she said. When they were finished with the browns and blacks, Tommy took a tube of gold paint and began to draw a circle behind the sitting, painted dog's head, a sort of Byzantine halo. "Archetypes. The beast in the jungle," he said and she nodded, wondering what he meant. She caught the Sinclair Lewis reference, wondering if he meant it. After drawing the outline, he handed her the palette. She finished the painting using broad strokes with both hands.

"Well there it is," Tommy said as they stood back to admire the iconic portrait, a mass of brown fur and muscles staring back serenely from a dirty white background.

"Should we sign it?" she said.

"Let's not."

"Romantic," the young woman said, instantly regretting it. She flipped her hair a certain way in the hope he would think her last statement ironic. She walked over to the dog, looped her finger in its collar, and said something quietly. The dog shook itself and stood up. She led it up the steps.

"They train them in Dutch now," she said as he followed her. "I bet you tried German."

"Yeah," Tommy said, surprised. His father once said to learn something new each day. "Is that how you got it?"

"I had nothing to do with it." And although we crossed paths with that dog again, I never found out how it got in that basement.

While they were finger-painting, I was barricading myself in the bathroom to a soundtrack of cuss words. Someone lit a piece of paper on fire and pushed it beneath the door and I stomped it out. It was bad weed or some rude comment, but the shaggy-haired fellow and a friend accused me of being a "narc," among other things. After chasing me to the bathroom, they held their siege for what seemed like hours. "Open up, narc," one yelled, beating on the door. Making sure the lock held, I peed in their shampoo, carefully re-screwing on the caps. Opening the cabinet beneath the sink, I stuffed all their toilet paper and paper towels under my shirt, using my belt to secure the bulky package. I stood up on the toilet, crossed myself for some reason, and pulled myself through the window. I dropped to an alley below, sitting on the cold ground and trying to catch my breath.

Silent except for the clicking of his nails on the concrete, the German Shepherd ran past me, bounding into the night. Tommy appeared, a pretty brown-haired girl by his side. They walked up to me—she was trying hard not to laugh. "This is Kate," Tommy said, motioning to the girl. I looked down at my shirt and sighed. "Kate, meet my brother. He has a bullet in his head," he said, as if that explained everything.

"Nice to meet you," I mumbled. I offered my hand and she shook it with a surprisingly strong grip, leaving behind streaks of gold paint.

16

THE PROGRAM FOR THIS EVENING...

We waited outside Club Laga, a local concert venue located above a record store and the dirtiest Chinese restaurant in Oakland. There were a few local urchins sitting outside, all denim, hair dye, and attitude. Kate arrived and we went upstairs. I remember two or three staircases littered with flyers, posters, and a graffiti wall apparently reserved for middle schoolers. Occasionally, there would be someone sitting on a stool talking on a cell phone. It wasn't clear whether they worked there or were simply posing as inept ticket-stampers.

The concert was Kate's idea. She'd taken some promo photographs of the band and had free tickets but didn't want to go by herself, so she'd called Tommy a couple days after the party. Club Laga's main stage room was the size of a high school gym, except it had balconies covered with chain-link cages. A middle-aged man intercepted us on the way in. He wore thick emo glasses, a pleather vest over a white dress shirt and skinny clip-on tie. A plastic badge on his vest said "EVENT STAFF."

"Whassup, folks," he said, looking at our outfits. Tommy and I were wearing jeans and sneakers, but he had on a CLEAR LIGHT T-shirt because we were there for a Doors cover band and this T-shirt was some kind of inside reference.

I was sporting my favorite hooded sweatshirt from my days

at Tower. It was frayed around the hood's edge and had some holes in the sleeves. Kate's hair was in a sort of 60s housewife style, curled up at the edges with sweeping bangs. Horn-rimmed glasses and a floral shirt with a flip collar. The whole ensemble was topped off by a long black skirt and a pair of Converse All-Stars. Skinny tie nodded in approval. He flashed Tommy and me a look that said, *Hope her fashion sense rubs off on you fellas.* "It's a big night for the Nü Doors. A huge opportunity. So here are the rules." He looked down at a little index card. "You *absolutely* need to smile," he said, making upwards motions with his index fingers to the corners of his mouth. "Okay? Okay, number two. Sing along, even if you don't know the lyrics."

"What?" Kate said.

"And three, just pretend the cameras aren't there," he said as he wrapped fluorescent pink bracelets around our wrists. "Big night, big night, yo!" he said. "Howdy," he said, looking past us to inspect the next group who arrived. I stood in line to buy drinks. When I came back, the band was tuning up. Tommy and Kate were standing real close to each other. She leaned in with her mouth close to his ear, which wasn't necessary since it hadn't gotten loud yet.

"Hey," I said, handing them their drinks. I was about to say something witty when a voice came on the sound system.

"Ladies and gentlemen. Here is your band, The NÜ DOORS!" The man onstage started clapping and whooping and the crowd followed his lead, even though none of us had any idea who the Nü Doors were. A camera crew took up position on the edges of the stage, lenses pointed at us.

"They weren't called that before," Kate said, squinting at the band tuning up onstage.

The announcer on the stage went on, declaring them, "The BIGGEST thing to come out of the 'BURGH since CHRISTINA AGUILERA!" Less applause this time around. The band took the stage shortly afterwards. The lead singer apparently couldn't commit to shaving the sides of his head, so he sported a fauxhawk, his hair gathered up like a paintbrush and gelled. He kind of looked like a troll doll. The fact that his hair was dyed neon green didn't help. He was wearing a T-shirt advertising his own band, acid-washed jeans held up by a leather belt with squarish spikes on it, and finally Doc Martens which for some reason had red laces.

"Sup sup y'all," he said into the screeching mic. "We got some nü shirts and gear, so make sure to check out the merch table." Just like Morrison at Nü Haven. I liked him. Seriously, there was something amusing about this hapless corporate shill, his faux nostalgia and the ironic way their bass player (!) and drummer wore matching 80s-font MTV T-shirts. But it was the weekend and even if we couldn't have a genuinely good time, at least we could pretend. The three of us would have happily watched them try, clapped and cheered heartily. But then they started playing. At the time, it was popular to sing in the style of Ruff McGruff, which would have made them sound like Creed or Nickelback covering The Doors. But their image consultant must have been an *American Idol* fan, so they mixed in some blue-eyed soul. By the time he reached the chorus and stretched the word "fire" to twelve syllables, the three of us were anxiously picking at our wristbands. We looked at each other.

Kate held Tommy's hand, looked into his eyes, and made a dramatic (but probably heartfelt) look of apology. They nodded at me and I led the way to the exit. Which was guarded by skinny tie man. To the sound of "Come on baby, light my fie-*yuuuuuur*-ur" repeating in the background, Kate and Tommy made a plan and Kate walked over to distract tie man, who was standing in the middle of the doorframe, his hands propped tight against the sides like a toddler fence. With the cameras rolling, he wasn't going to let us ruin the shot. I looked up at the balconies, which were covered with a chain-link fence that ran from the floor to the ceiling. They were meant to separate the under-18 from the over-21 crowd, but they really looked like cages. And through these cages, the kids were glaring down at us. At first, I figured it was because we could drink, but that wasn't it. No way were those kids going to pay $4 for a Yuengling. I looked around, suddenly self-conscious. All the kids in the crowd were wearing jeans and T-shirts, basically the same cut and generally the same brand. Even Tommy's shirt blended in with all of the other novelty T-shirts. There was something suffocating in this realization, that we had all donned the same labels, eaten the same manufactured food in our microwaves, and come down here for the same prepackaged concert experience which would be resold over any number of airwaves. From a distance, it looked like we were all trying to be the guys onstage. "Try to set the night on fieueueueueeeur." I looked at the crowd, who would yell and dance and point when the cameras walked by, then kind of settle and dance, happily playing the role of a rock audience. Occasionally, someone crowd-surfed. When we looked back, skinny tie and Kate were gone. Tommy turned the handle and pushed at the door. It was locked.

"Are you fucking serious?" I said. He threw his shoulder at the door, but it wouldn't budge. "Is there another exit?" They were now playing the opening notes to "Hello, I Love Yü," which was a bad Kinks rip-off even in the 60s. Tommy heard it too and backed up a few steps to get a running step before kicking the door. It opened a few inches, the striker plate stubbornly holding the door closed.

"Where's Kate?" he yelled to me. I looked around but couldn't see her.

"This one's for my homies. And all the fine ladies, the *hawt hawt* females," the lead singer called out. "Are yooooou ready?"

"I don't know. Kick it again," I yelled. Kate was partly responsible for this abomination, anyway. Tommy hesitated but there she was, running toward us. Skinny tie was behind her, carefully carrying a $20 rum and coke until he spotted us and quickened his pace, the drinks spilling as he chased her. Tommy gave her a kind of salute, backed up for one final kick. Sweat and heartbeats and ringing in the ears, the three of us broke on through and ran as fast as we could down those crack-house steps, the momentum carrying us onto the solidity of asphalt and sidewalks, floating neon and night air.

But college isn't about parties, police dogs, or tribute bands. Occasionally, academics rears its ugly head. A condensed history of my college career: Here I am in my first semester, shiny new books stacked on my desk, eagerly leaning forward as the professor writes her name on the board. My grades arrive and Leslie's so moved that she calls me crying. The doctor congratulates me by saying, "It's about damn time," but I can hear the pride in his voice. "Well done," he says by way of farewell. Click.

The next semester, there's some stubble on my chin and my eyelids are drooping a little. I have last semester's academic success to repeat. Also, there's a constant choice: Do I call that girl back, maybe go out tonight, or do I honor my father's sacrifice at Tower by studying? It's an easy decision but a constant drain. I spend a lot of nights making ramen noodles in a coffeemaker, sitting alone at Tommy's kitchen table under a pale fluorescent light. I sharpen my pencil and open a textbook. The headaches return.

When I was hiking with the Boy Scouts, they said an item carried by hand, outside your pack, feels like it weighs five times as much. Although it wasn't physical, carrying the expectations of the living and the dead began to weigh on me. Suddenly, I was struggling to catch up. The doctors said the migraines were caused by stress. The pain wasn't the issue, but focusing through it felt like I was looking at everything through a downpour, the sounds of the world muted through the rush. During this blurry period, I'd look around the auditorium-sized classroom to see 300 students blankly staring toward the professor. It felt like a boring movie I wanted to walk out of. High school all over again. After the lecture came the rote call-and-response. It felt like everyone was playing their part: student, teacher, brilliant antagonist, vacant-eyed burnout arriving fifteen minutes late. By the last year of college—by the time we met Kate—I stopped attending class on a regular basis and everyone seemed happy to continue their roles without me.

I spent much of my new spare time at the protests. I can track my entire college career though them. Apparently I wasn't the only student not interested in class. After 9/11, the students busy with anti-racial-profiling demonstrations threw their energy into protesting the upcoming Iraq War. "Get the U.S. out of Iraq," their picket signs said, even though we weren't in Iraq yet. There were the anti-gay demonstrations ("Adam and Eve, not Adam and Steve") from religious fringe groups, the same groups who printed poster-sized photographs of aborted fetuses and posted them on the side of U-Haul trucks that slowly circled the campus. These were followed by fervent anti-anti-gay or anti-anti-abortion protests, often on the same day. Commuters in the already-congested neighborhoods grew angrier, sometimes weaving through streams of protestors, who jumped out of the way screaming in indignation.

We'd survived terrors imagined and real from Y2K to 9/11 and now, as we entered our new millennium, we'd developed a fervent passion not to repeat the mistakes of our parents. Bloodthirstiness, racism, greed—it had to go. And the best way to rid ourselves of these evils, we decided, was to wave signs and yell slogans more or less in unison.

Or maybe there's a simpler explanation that had little to do with that particular time period. Students nurtured by the myths of the melting pot, immigrant rags-to-riches, the benevolence of papa government, *et cetera*, were now faced with internment camps and Selma, colonialism and Third World debt, Uncle Sam the crack dealer, bombs over Baghdad (the song and the actual event). There was the energy of a youthful army gathering, a group whose only model was what they knew of the sixties (sit-ins, dreadlocks, Day-Glo body paint and wild dancing), a group starved for attention who moved as a giant headless mob fueled by throbbing left-wing/right-wing outrage machines. Free Tibet was so last season. Did you know there were people dying by the millions in Sudan Liberia Somalia East Timor? Get the U.S. out of Iraq! *How dare you when those soldiers give you the freedom to* I'm an American! If you don't like it, go back to _____ and take a bath while yer at it. The IMFG8WTO are controlling the world, don't you see? They must be stopped by God hates fags. God hates bring them home NOW! *Pitt contracts to companies who contribute to the growing military industrial prison complex.* For God so loved the world that he instructed me to print a pamphlet and hand it to you food not bombs love not war, because the richest countries are using debts incurred during colonialism to ensure that brown-skinned people are starving and subservient Socialism NOW, because that's the only way to get healthcare because GOD HATES FAGS, pay university workers a living wage and bring them home now.

Everyone was screaming at each other. On the radio, news and talk shows, the streets. Even beyond the performative aspect, it seemed like there was a perfunctory aspect, a sort of ritual. The "(God and Country) freedom" crowd was compelled to make a statement, to which the "(civil) liberties" crowd was forced to respond. It wasn't fascinating like a train wreck. It was more like watching a huge multilegged bug flail around with its legs in the air, making a horrible noise as it writhed in circles. And don't get me wrong—all the noise could have added up to something, except for the location. Most of the University of Pittsburgh's newer campus buildings were built in the 1960s, in an era where students regularly sat-in and shut down campuses for weeks at a time. With this in mind, architects designed buildings to be riot-proof.

The university was well-equipped to ignore protests, just or not. But the campus itself encouraged fragmentation and scattering in a place—above all others—whose goal was the gathering of knowledge, the assembly of peoples and cultures. And don't get me wrong; I certainly didn't want Berkeley to be recreated by those naïve poseurs. I didn't know how to solve the problem and so I dispersed myself. I didn't realize at the time how draining the whole atmosphere was because I had so much energy back then, liberated as I was from academics. But it seemed like any contentious conversation back then became a sort of grinder into which all issues went in and came out a blank exhaustion, a vague expanding headache. Some days, I did my best to leave that irresolvable storm behind me.

It took effort—everyone in Oakland had their hand out. The Nü Doors wanted my money, love, and worship. The university wanted my money and attendance. The protests wanted my attention, they desperately wanted me to wake up, get educated, and join a revolution. There were panhandlers and students who desperately wanted to be crowned homecoming queen, exhausted fraternity underlings harassing me to pledge. The university—all symbolic with its trio of vented beehive-looking tower dorms—vibrated with all this energy. All that spare time. All those souls to save. All those unguarded youth. I remember feeling—it wasn't even a fetus of a thought at the time, just a sort of swirling almost-consciousness—that the world was slowly pulling me apart. I could feel it in my aching neck and knees, the heaviness in my shoulders. Soon, there would be nothing else to drop out of.

October in Pittsburgh is cold but beautiful, the maple leaves outside the university shedding their majesty onto the worn stone walkways. At our house on Bates Street, it was warm and beautiful, the beaded curtains ringing with their own music, the steel-era mirror above the mantle twinning the LP sleeves, woven Chianti bottles turned into candleholders, sketches by Tommy and Kate. This is the three of us late at night on weekdays. The couch on our porch is nicer than the couch inside, but it was too heavy to bring in. We're inside tonight, sitting on a pink floral couch from the 1920s. There is a lime-green carpet beneath us that has been at the house since the 1970s, and parts of the house look like a garage sale is trying to break out. That whole year, the three of us sometimes spent entire weeks together. We read books and passed them around—I turned Kate on to Ms. ——, the only author whose books rested on the shelf above my head, a little piece of Princeton in the Steel City. We loved her so much that Kate enlarged the photo from the back of her book and put it on the refrigerator, her wise staring eyes gazing down in pity as she staggered in for another drink. We listened to old jazz, Miles Davis on repeat.

"Hey, what's the difference between 'red' and 'electric red'"? Tommy said.

"What are you talking about?" He handed me the back of the LP sleeve, the garage-sale vinyl smell wafting through the room. I passed it to some kid named Trapper and he passed it to Kate.

"The same difference between a chair and the electric chair," I said.

"Whoa—ho-ho."

I was the clever one that night as *Aura* spun slowly on the old turntable, and then some Firesign Theatre, and then some real Doors as the sun came up. Some old friends walked unannounced through the unlocked front door. Tommy had a record player—he liked the skips and pops. There was something romantic about the analog process, the glow of light on the wooden speakers, the inconvenience of vinyl. It would probably surprise the previous generation to learn that we'd discovered some of their secrets and pleasures. And certainly, we weren't the only ones in Oakland listening to solid state record players bathed in cigarette smoke and dim red and green lights.

Down in the beautiful squalor, in a house that vaguely resembled the Broadway set of *Cats*, the garbage and overcrowding of college squalor was both hilarious and strangely normal. An hour-long conversation about the film *Showgirls* was normal. It was like a music and book club mixed with a support group where we'd smoke joints and complain about our parents until we forgot we were smoking joints. Even when we weren't high, we listened to each other, eager to follow the trajectory of each other's thoughts, happy to untangle the world's problems. I like to think this was closer to the spirit of the 60s than the poorly choreographed performances parading their way through the city. I don't know what I'd expected from college, but it certainly wasn't the thirteenth grade I'd sporadically attended. And though it wasn't idyllic and we certainly weren't our own little three-person university, it wasn't exactly a drum circle. There was some kind of exchange in those long, vague hours.

But Tommy's house wasn't Shangri-La, and it was only a matter of time before cold reality walked through that unlocked door. The world of commerce and academics was outside sharpening its knives, and no amount of wine or marijuana could hold it back.

17

LIGHT MY FIRE

One day you're moderately rich from your factory job. On the way to your freshman English Comp class, you pass a little vendor stand. It's early morning and the girl behind it is very attractive, Nordic features with wispy blonde hair and an eager innocence like the teenage mall sunglasses vendors. And cold—her nipples poke through the thin cotton T-shirt her breasts are straining mightily against. You stop, sign some forms to get a free backpack. A week later, a credit card arrives in the mail. At the end of the year, you move out of the dorms and realize you can't carry everything. You're drunk and late for a party, so you leave your speakers and mini fridge on the curb. Circle of life, college style. You can buy more later. There is no force more powerful, no energy greater than a teenager with a new credit card. One day, you're poor.

To protest my newfound debt, I got a job as a waiter at a shiny new restaurant downtown. I spent most of the day staring out the windows at the stands that sold beaded purses and incense. At the end of the day, we carried empty plates and clean silverware to the dishwashers. The manager was a cokehead and the owner was also a cokehead. It would have made a good sitcom.

One day in mid-October, my manager called me into his office. He informed me that due to reasons he didn't want to get into, our restaurant did not have any condiments. This was a problem especially for the breakfast crowd. He needed me to go around to various restaurants and "liberate" (his term) ketchup, butter, and jelly packets until we could get back on our feet.

"Shouldn't take more than two or three days," he said. As I was leaving, he told me to wear a tie. Nobody would ask me any questions if I wore a tie.

This was about a month after I met Kate. She was amused by the restaurant's predicament and since she wasn't much for going to class, she put on her nicest dress to accompany me. We hit up all the restaurants downtown, then moved on to the Strip District, a section of Pittsburgh famous for its food: wholesale distributors, restaurant supply stores, markets, and restaurants. In the end, we were taking the little condiment baskets right off the tables. A few days into our liberation campaign, someone followed us out of the restaurant and down the street. We had to walk quickly and act normal, which was difficult, given the situation. My hands started to shake, and the contraband ketchup packets I carried suddenly felt cold and slick.

Luckily for her, Kate was wearing a denim baseball cap that day, which helped obscure her face, but she was also wearing black leggings, which made her somewhat more conspicuous. As we walked into Posvar Hall, she tossed the hat into a trashcan.

"In case they're still following us," she said. I tossed the ketchup packets.

I glanced over my shoulder, but the building was empty except for us. Kate's sandy blonde hair was parted slightly to the side and there was something about the way the light struck it, the way her hair curled around her ears and reached down to her neck in nearly ragged strands that looked strangely elegant and made me think of tall thin grass and seashells, a fleeting childhood memory. She was wearing a new coat, a gray Zooey jacket. "It has a funnel neck, 100% cotton. The label says it's 'vapor gray,'" she said when I asked. She talked for a long time about the coat's accessories and virtues as we walked. It looked comfortable enough to justify most of her description.

It was cold inside the building. Posvar Hall looks like a Neo-Brutalist concrete bunker, designed during the 1960s to be riot-proof. There are no central meeting areas, just hallways. Above one of the largest corridors hangs a metal sculpture made of spikes and triangular metal sails.

"In honor of shrapnel," Kate noted. It didn't look very well secured and I just wanted to get out from under it. Because Posvar Hall was built over Forbes Field, the Pirates' old stadium, it makes sense that the building contains a replica of the old Pirates' home plate. It does not make sense that above the west entrance hangs an antique airplane, about ten feet across with a canvas-colored bi-wing.

"In honor of flight," I should have said. Kate, my brother, and I were graduating soon. None of us planned to stay in Pittsburgh. Somehow, that made her even more attractive. I suppose I associated her with randomness and chance, opportunity. Even if being with her wasn't one of them. The landscape itself echoed my sentiments. Pittsburgh has often seemed to me like a sanctuary, a place for exiles to catch their breath before moving on. After all, few of my professors and even fewer of my classmates were from Pittsburgh. There was also the architecture—the Doric columns and cupolas of Carnegie Mellon University's campus, Pitt's Gothic Cathedral of Learning. Near Bellefield Hall, there is a lone medieval-style stone tower. It isn't attached to the curved concrete-and-glass building next to it, nor are there any signs explaining its existence. It's always felt to me like the buildings themselves were being temporarily stored, to be moved to their respective Gothic or modernist cities someday.

And it felt like Kate wanted everything at once, like she had a metropolitan sensibility bordering on cubism. She wanted to map out the fashion and architecture and culture in pretty layers—and somehow, she was able to synthesize all of it into her speech, into her closet. Kate was not quite my guide, but someone pulling me toward the strange and unexpected. My own unified theory of everything.

"I think we're safe now," she said. She paused in front of the doors. We'd both been thinking the same thing: What if the person following us had circled around and was waiting outside? But of course no one showed up. Kate paused to readjust her boots. We exited Posvar Hall and walked together under the arch of a lemon-yellow sculpture.

At the end of our week as condiment thieves, Kate discovered she'd run out of time for her art projects, all of which were due in a few days. She said it was partly my fault, and of course I agreed. This was the first art class she'd taken since she'd declared art as her major and she regretted she couldn't finish it alone. But I wouldn't be doing much. I would receive credit as part of her creative team. It was academically legal, she insisted.

Once, whilst high on mushrooms, Kate read me the dirty passages from *Lolita*. Humbert Humbert loved his child bride so much that he wanted to pull her open and kiss her internal organs: heart, lungs, spine (Nabokov phrased it better). But if Humbert truly wanted to see inside his love, he should have given her some crayons, sat back, and watched. Kate would have been too old for Humbert, but it was fascinating watching her mind at work, the sketching and calculations.

For the projects, she wrote several pamphlets suggesting that we build concrete trees to replace old-growth forests and arguing that the slaughter of aborigines was okay as long as we preserved their likenesses in wax museums. In addition to the pamphlets (which had several grammatical errors she refused to correct), she drew large cats on orange stock board.

"Panthers," she said. We cut them out and connected pairs of these little orange cats with Scotch tape and twine. Then we walked around Pittsburgh, and it was my job to throw the orange cats in the air so they wrapped around the power lines like pairs of shoes. This was surprisingly difficult and we eventually had to attach rocks as weights. When I was down to the last pair of cats, she bought a bouquet of plastic flowers and laid them down on the street. She took a photograph and we were done.

The second project was slightly more illegal. After we'd

pilfered the day's quota of ketchup packets from Eat'n Park, I drove her back to her apartment to prepare for the last project. I didn't change out of my shirt and tie, my thick black work pants. She changed into a business suit, black stockings, and a pair of boots. On the back of her blazer, she'd draped a blue cardigan-like garment that fell down her back like a cape. She carried several rolled-up posters under her arm and in the other she carried a wooden T-square. I drove and she directed me to a multiplex full of outlet malls and chain restaurants. I parked in a grassy section on the edge of downtown where there was a junction of four billboards facing the freeway. She grabbed her art materials and walked to the billboards, sizing everything up. I picked up her camera and took pictures of her as she looked at the billboard, which she seemed to like. There were thin vines snaking their way up the billboard frames and the entire area smelled of gravel, pee, and sickly yellow weeds.

"Move the car over here," she said. She climbed to the car's roof, grabbed the billboard's hanging ladder, and pulled herself up with an impressive display of strength. My job was to remain on the ground and document the entire thing, so I just kept taking pictures. Kate used the T-square to hold a sticker in place at the top of the billboard and smoothed it out as it unrolled.

The click of the shutter. Grass and gravel. Five more shots from different angles. Kate, determined and staring across at the other billboards. Two of them featured a 50-year old, frizzy-haired realtor. One featured an accident lawyer and the fourth simply declared, "Babies are meant to be breastfed—Ad Council." I took a close-up of Kate using the T-square thing to survey and size up everything. Her signs read, "You don't need" in the same font as the billboard. Just like those "hammertime" stickers you see on stop signs. After she finished, the sign said, "You don't need a dedicated realtor who will work hard for you."

I yelled up that I didn't get it. "Just keep taking pictures," she said. She had to hang from the lip of one billboard to get to the other sections and she moved slowly, hand over hand. At one point she got stuck. I ran to help, but she said, "Goddamnit, keep taking pictures. Even if I die." Eventually, she made it to the other side and managed to pull herself up, chest heaving.

I took her picture as she stood in front of the lawyer billboard with a dejected, confused look on her face. Despite my prompting, she refused to have her picture taken in front of the breastfeeding billboard.

She climbed down, breathing heavy, her hair teased a little from the wind. She lit two cigarettes and passed me one. I stood next to her. She didn't say anything. Maybe she'd had a profound moment up there, risking her life amidst the soaring typography of capitalism to deliver her crypto-Marxist message. Or maybe this was just another day in the life of Kate—stealing ketchup packets and then some daredevil stunts. She brushed a strand of hair out of her face as she exhaled a thick stream of smoke. Camels, those were her favorite brand. She noticed me looking at her and smiled a little, making her hand into a fist and pushing it into me. This gesture meant, *Not bad. We make a pretty decent team, don't we?* But she left her fist on my shoulder for a few more seconds, then leaned into it to push me away. My chest swayed back a little and I instinctively stepped forward. I could feel the blood pounding in my head as I realized this was the first time we'd touched.

There was something in those few seconds where her hand lingered. It felt less like electricity and more like an impression. The fabric of my coat would easily reassume its form, but I knew something had changed. I leaned in toward her because I had to. Her expression didn't change when I turned my head, only inches away. I could feel her breath, quiet and calm, on my face. I could smell her shampoo, the almost-invisible drops of sweat on her neck. She raised her hand to lightly touch her temple, maybe to brush away a stray hair. Sunlight flashed off the glass-bead bracelet on her wrist.

Weeks later, I drove by the billboard. I'd been avoiding that section of town. That year, the Ad Council aggressively ran one ad campaign, and whenever I'd open a magazine to see "BABIES ARE MEANT TO BE BREASTFED," I'd quickly close it, my face hot with shame. Anyone watching me would have thought me a prude. I stopped watching television because the commercials for realtors or accident lawyers reminded me not of Kate, but of that day. I didn't kiss her, of course. I leaned away and the cloth of our jackets touched, our weight leaning into each other before I gracelessly turned and sort of bounced off of her in slow motion. I mumbled something about getting lunch.

As far as I know, Kate never told my brother about that moment and we never talked about it. The space between us was clearly delineated and we could grow comfortable with it, we told ourselves. But as I looked up at the billboard (I had to), I saw that air pockets had formed beneath the words she'd added. They warped her words, themselves a distortion of the billboard's message. It wasn't much, I told myself. It was a near-kiss during a weird art project beside a highway. It wasn't even that awkward when I drove Kate home a few minutes later. But there was something about that day. It wasn't a weight that one carried around like a coat. What was left unsaid was more like a strange buoyancy inside me. I knew I could push my feelings deep, knew they would thrash and quiet. I was old enough to understand that. And I was old enough to know they'd resurface eventually, and I couldn't predict when. "You don't need," the billboards above me said.

18

YOUR CODE IS SUBOPTIMAL

There was a sickness blooming inside me. It started out as a little shard but grew and migrated when I moved to the city. At the time, I thought I'd killed it back at Tower, but we'd moved to an actual city where that shard grew septic and swollen. It happened at my workplace. With all this talk of factories and bad grades, you may have forgotten my ethnicity. Me too, once—hence the sickness.

The restaurant laid off most of the waitstaff in October, but I weaseled my way into the kitchen as a prep cook. Most of the cooks were black and I quickly became aware of how much race mattered amidst the pulpy lumps of tomatoes, walk-in meat freezers, boiling water, and knives. All my life, I'd been taught that racism was an affliction suffered only by whites and my college professors did little to teach me otherwise. But in that kitchen, white people were treated like absolute shit. The other prep cook, George, would fuck up and someone would threaten to "smack the taste out of his mouth." "No pork in that, idiot. What if a *motherfuckin'* Muslim drank that soup?" Someone would mock me for the same error but there weren't any threats. It became apparent that a very old war was continuing in that kitchen between white and not-white, a war where people made small stands and concessions every day. I didn't like it, but after the stress of school and dealing with my brother and trying to contain my feelings for Kate, I was happy that I didn't have to be on the receiving end of a hatred I never understood. But at that time I began to realize that hating and ignoring the endless national obsession over race didn't change a goddamn thing.

———

Any number of things could have triggered it. Pittsburgh doesn't have Asian neighborhoods, which keeps the math-and-gadget crowd on the move. They stay long enough to earn a degree and then take their families and cash elsewhere. But while in Pittsburgh, they move through the city dazed by the byzantine urban planning, the legions of panhandlers, the unreliable public transportation. They gather around Carnegie Mellon University, the city's largest importer of transitory Asians—the five-mile radius around CMU is the best place for lo mein, hands down. They gather in the basement of the Cathedral of Learning, fresh off the private jet and queuing politely in the language labs. They gather in the Hillman Library, which Pitt students call "Chinatown," and the upper campus' cavernous science labs.

Asian people. I wasn't in the library much, but it was inevitable that Tommy and I would pass through large groups of them as they walked to parties at Ginza's Korean Restaurant carrying messenger bags made of gray space-age polymers with bright orange reflective tape, Armani Exchange T-shirts, and shiny black hair. My lord. Even if you saw me following them as I walked to the financial aid office, you'd never assume we were together. Me, I was dressed in a black Pirates sweatshirt with five layers underneath (this is late October in Pittsburgh, after all) and a pair of baggy jeans (loose-fit baggy, not skater or thug baggy—everyone wore their jeans a little looser back then). My Adidas sneakers that kicked down concert doors. My hair was never shiny, no matter how many beers or cigarettes

I consumed. Tommy and I watched them, displayed in the tall windows of the new Asian Fusion Happy Happy Bistro.

If they noticed, they didn't acknowledge us. Observe as they finish their soy-based snacks and sip whole-fruit-based drinks with floating sorghum or bubbles of healthy whatever. That one guy wearing the T-shirt declaring "Your Code is Suboptimal"—he's only half-joking. "Look, one of them just got a call," I said to Tommy. "That phone he's talking into? Your American cell phone would literally disintegrate if you held it next to theirs. Unless, maybe, they're carrying the holographic memory-based models—in which case their phones technically exist in the spirit world of cyberspace, their calls dissolving into zeroes and ones. Maybe you should save yourself time and just throw your plastic-based brick of crap into the jingling cup of the panhandler outside. Or take it to an antique store. These people might not speak fluent English, but they're learning. And they're happy! Look at them. Smiling and joking as they discuss calculating pi or inventing something your brain, atrophied from too much Donald Trump-based reality television, cannot possibly imagine but will include a simplified menu..."

"Well, I'm good," Tommy said. He'd been reading the menu on the window.

"What?" I said. "Did you hear anything I said?"

"I only heard a long whining noise. Eventually, I tuned it out," he said, walking into the restaurant. Even though it would feel awkward to sit next to the group I'd been staring at, I followed him inside. I wanted him to understand what I was going through.

The Happy Happy Bistro was the size of a studio apartment and decorated to look like a third-grade classroom from the year 2030, the ceiling fixtures bright primary colors, paper-thin LED readouts on the walls for menus, brushed aluminum tables.

"I think this place is actually owned by Japanese and stocked with Korean waiters," I said to Tommy. I told him a story about my interactions with a waiter who worked there. "He's that guy over there," I said, pointing to a nondescript short Korean man wearing an apron. "A few weeks ago, he asks me if I'm Korean. So I tell him yes and he nods and walks away."

"So what?" Tommy said, bored.

"Well, I'm here a week later and he asks me again. Except he says, 'You still Korean?' just like that." Tommy laughed and said something about 70s cinema, *Stay strong. Stay black.*

"It might have been a fluency issue," he said.

"So the 'still' part was just—he just threw it in there? Plus, he started saying all this shit in Korean to me. I couldn't understand all of it, so he gives me this look and walks off. The kind of look you're giving me right now."

Tommy took a deep breath. "How am I supposed to look at self-obsessed whining? So now it's race. Anything you can possibly—"

"I never wanted to talk about it. I was here because I like the MSG." Asians, according to Tommy, try to guess each other's ethnicity when they encounter each other. It's like a game, part of an unspoken greeting. He told me this as if I already knew it. Why was this such a big deal? He was sure other minorities did it, too, and probably white people. A tribal thing, dating back to the caveman days.

"So many Asian people," I said. Student organizations, Asian Christian church services, missionaries. I politely avoided them when I could. It wasn't so much ignoring as it was keeping to myself, I explained to Tommy. "I've been to parties without you where there's only one other Asian dude. So what, should I go talk to him just because we have race in common, barely? And seriously, then what?"

Tommy didn't understand why the waiter bothered me. Honestly, it's hard to articulate. From what I learned from my Asian friends in Princeton, they have a term for folks yellow on the outside but white on the inside: *bananas*. It would make a good title for something in a slam poetry contest. It's probably already happened, someone shrieking the metaphoric possibilities: the phallic, fruit, insanity. But that's not me. To me, being a member of a racial group felt too much like being a member of a street gang with its own crude rules and predetermined loyalties and hates. I was happy to remain neutral in that outdated world, to not pay dues to anyone, to drink my beer in peace.

When I was young, I cherished being rare, exotic. Of course, I was neither in Princeton, but I was among the doctor and Leslie's social circle. At gatherings, I always stuck out, bathed in attention. I could fake interest well and this gave hope to people nervous about my generation. People wanted to invest their hope in me, this thin, doe-eyed survivor living among the nation's intellectual and literal wealth. But sometimes it became too much and I just wanted to be left alone. And when she sensed I was uncomfortable, Leslie knew how to change her tone ever so slightly, ask *exactly why* someone thought I was so smart for my age and I'd vanish into the background as a cloud of defense and *I know you didn't mean it like that but some people...* until someone changed the subject and then I disappeared. It was camouflage, my heritage. When I needed to vanish, I could move quietly within the groups of Asian classmates who tolerated my presence because of some unspoken instinct, a begrudging unity that even in their youth they could not deny.

Camouflage—maybe some people can maintain it forever. And maybe I could have, too, had it not been for the fact that I was related to and living with another Asian. I needed space to maintain my equilibrium and the world was eating away the walls I'd built around myself.

Inside the Happy Happy Bistro, my insular little world collapsed. "Here we go," I said to Tommy. But the short little waiter didn't approach us. Instead, he spotted a half-Korean girl at the table next to us. She was sitting next to the kid in the "Your Code is Suboptimal" T-shirt. He looked at her, perhaps noticing her ears weren't pierced, that she wasn't wearing any makeup. Maybe eighteen, honey-brown hair. Her Asianness came through slyly and she was exotic in a vague way, a certain softness. But you could see it in the eyes, the high cheekbones. It seemed like she'd just won an award or something, out with her friends to celebrate. A happy group minding their own business.

The waiter walked over to the group and looked her straight

in the eye. "What are you?" he said. I sat there stunned for a second, feeling so embarrassed for her, and I tried to think of something to say besides "Hey waiter, go fuck yourself."

She didn't look shocked. Even if people never said it, she must have noticed them doing this all her life—trying to figure her out, reduce her to a single term. It's human nature, she keeps telling herself. But here, surrounded by the warmth and comfort of friends, the surprisingly homey feel of the room. To have someone vocalize the demand here. *What are you?* as if trying to determine where to shelve her in a sideshow. *'Cause you're sure as hell not one of us.* And now everyone's staring, especially the two handsome fellows at the table next to you. No one from your group speaks and the silence hangs in the air for a few more agonizing moments. Even if he doesn't know why, the waiter should apologize but doesn't.

"Uh," someone at your table says. A phone could ring or someone could make a joke to break the tension. But it never comes and that fucking waiter just won't back down. To him, the world contains Asian people, who are usually friends or behind the counter. White and black people are customers. Anything else, well—the audacity of something like that to exist in the first place.

"Hey buddy, what are *you*?" the guy at the next table says to the waiter. No, it wasn't me, of course, although for my anger it should have been. I'd been too busy observing this scene and contemplating how it related to my own life. Of course it was Tommy who spoke up, even though he didn't understand what the big deal was. A tiny stand, but one I could have easily made.

"I'm Korean," the man said in Korean, looking him in the eye.

"You're a fucking waiter," Tommy said loudly, giving a little *yeah, fuck you* nod. "Where's our food?" The people from the other table left shortly afterwards, the little brass bells on the doors rang as it closed behind them, the charms on the doorknob shivering.

It was at this point I went through a period of self-questioning, an identity crisis that usually occurs during puberty. I could have backpacked across Europe after high school, but not now. Leslie and the doctor would have funded it, but I wasn't about to call and ask for help. And what kind of answers would I find in Europe, anyway? If everyone was picking sides here in Pittsburgh, I wanted to know where I fit into this war.

As soon as I got home, I made a chart. The question that now occupied my time wasn't how I was going to pass my classes this semester, where I would get the money to buy the next case of beer, etc. The question was the same one the waiter had demanded of the half-Asian girl: Exactly how Asian was I? Because other people really, really cared and would judge me in this game I hadn't realized I was playing. And I was tired of losing. The chart kind of looked like a ladder with "Asian" at one end and "white" at the other. There were demarcations set clearly in between, and I began measuring myself.

19

IF I FORGET YOU, O JERUSALEM

At this point, I was vaguely aware of everything I'd forgotten. I'd forgotten to set my alarm for the midterm on Wednesday, I'd forgotten why I'd gone to college in the first place. I'd forgotten my father's sacrifice, I'd forgotten an entire nation oceans away. What I had not forgotten, even for a second, was a quiet boy named Clay throwing bullets into a fire, a frenzy inside the flames as they exploded, a troop scattering as we tried to get away. Everyone escaped but me and now I was caught in some weird vortex that was ripping away everything I had. Now it was my identity—what was I without it?

Even when I was drunk at parties, I didn't tell my best story. I got tired of people looking for the scars (there's only one, a tiny white spot on my forehead near the hairline). I shrunk when I told it, became the story, and people tired of it. Also, buried in adulthood was the newfound realization of my own mortality, frailty. The bullet in my cerebral cortex was a prophecy of decline and madness, the scar a tiny *memento mori*. I stopped talking about that lead splinter, but how could one not obsess over it?

My father was born in South Korea, a charming nation of engineers stalwartly facing nuclear annihilation. Kim Jong Il, missiles—you know the story. It's something they don't think about until it flares up, one relative told me after my father's wake. It's like loss, an entire nation gone at the end of the war. The North severed at the 38th parallel, the pain returns unexpectedly now and then like a phantom limb. South Korea, *my* South Korea, felt much the same when it returned to me. Between us was a bullet, an ocean, and the mazy passage of time, but sooner or later, everything returns.

———

At his father's funeral, Bruce Lee—*the* Bruce Lee—crawled screaming on his hands and knees. This was the custom: to beg forgiveness, a penance for being absent when his father died. Bruce Lee was twenty-five then. At twenty-two, I'd failed the previous semester and had done my share of screaming and crawling to the point I'd ended up at the Western Psychiatric Institute and Clinic. Kate and Tommy had been dating a few months. It was almost November, the city preparing for another harsh winter. My therapist and I worked on my identity chart and discussed my relationship with Tommy. Eventually, we decided it would be best to pretend I didn't have a brother. I moved from his house into a hotel, using the last of my savings. But after a few days, I called him.

"Who is this?" he said. I hung up and took a handful of pills. When you're poor and on academic probation, there's no safety net. Every disruption to your routine becomes a crisis. One Friday evening, Tommy showed up outside at my hotel, which was in the broken-glass section of deep South Oakland. The receptionist called my room. I looked out my window and there he was, staring at the porch-sitters across the street. I lived on the third floor and appeared so quickly it startled him.

I didn't know how he'd spent the past few weeks, but he hadn't spent them on a couch drinking vodka and procrastinating. He looked different. His hair was longer than I'd remembered, pulled back in a ponytail. It reminded me of how some Native American men wear theirs. He was wearing all black: leather jacket, black jeans, and some wiseass sunglasses.

"You're mocking me," I didn't say, looking at his clothes.

"You're a mess," he didn't say, and I was thankful for that. He seemed eager to go inside, become less of a target.

"I've, uh, been..." was the first thing out of my mouth. *I've been looking for something...*

"You look like shit," he said. I shut the door to the apartment building, walked over to his battered car, and opened the door to the passenger side. He got in the driver's seat and the Latino gang members across the street stood and moved toward us.

"Drive," I said, leaning back against the leather headrest. Just drive. I told him I had a plan. We needed money (we both always needed money), and I knew someone who could get it.

"So, now what are we doing?" Tommy said. My plan had been to visit the doctor and Leslie. I figured they'd be too surprised by our visit to ask many questions. They'd give us money and we'd leave. But when we'd arrived at their house in Princeton, they weren't there. I found out later that they were away visiting relatives in New York. So, Tommy, Kate, and I were now driving home after our failed mission. I'd driven the last few daylight hours and we ended up spending the night at a bed and breakfast in New Jersey. I wore khakis and a polo shirt and Tommy had thrown on a pair of jeans he'd found in his car, an undershirt, and a green vest. We were downstairs sitting around a table and the elderly white couples were trying not to stare.

"Delighted to have you. Don't get many of you around here," they didn't say, sipping their coffee.

"Seriously," Kate said. She was talking to Tommy. I had no idea why he'd insisted on bringing her along.

"We're watching the leaves turn," I said, mostly to the five or six people sitting at the table. I was busy thinking of ways to salvage the weekend. The manager brought our food: Tommy had scrambled eggs on toast and I had the eggs Benedict.

"It's November," he said. I finished my eggs and told the manager she was an exquisite cook. Breakfast was over but nobody left the table. "You haven't answered my question," he said.

I mentioned how it was nice that Kate was here. Tommy

explained my identity crisis in a haughty and snide manner. He seemed surprised it hadn't resolved itself, as if it were supposed to magically self-heal. I told Kate about the term "banana," yellow on the outside, white on the inside. Did she know about that term? Whiteness, it's a strange concept. Race in general. "But now we have a mode of comparison," I said, motioning to Kate.

"What?" she said. Tommy leaned into her and said something quietly. She settled down a little. "I had things to do in Pittsburgh," she said. Her gray eyes stared forward blankly as she slumped in the chair. "I have projects—"

"Stop," Tommy said.

"You're here because Tommy couldn't stand to spend the entire weekend with me," I said, realizing it was true as I said it. I was still busy thinking of ways to salvage the weekend. Kate and Tommy were upset that I didn't call Leslie beforehand. They weren't satisfied with my answer that: a) she rarely left Princeton; and b) it would have killed the surprise factor.

"He thinks he's white," he said, pointing at me with his fork. "Does he look white to you?" he asked the people around the table. No one answered.

"I bet these people were having a lovely time before we showed up," Kate said.

"Why are we here?" Tommy said. I pulled the Identity Chart from my wallet, written on a small sheet of construction paper. I held it up. "You haven't answered my question," he said.

"Think about this: People with bullets in their heads usually have something in common," I said, drawing out the first few words.

"Death," Tommy said. Everyone else at the table stopped talking.

"Living ones, though. Think about it. Some act of violence, some unspeakable tragedy. They're survivors. Capital S. They have people they can go to. Support groups. People like them."

"You've had a tough life," Tommy said.

"Probably on vacation, maybe celebrating like their 75th wedding anniversary," Kate said, poking at her hash browns with a fork.

"Living ones, though. Think about it," I said.

"Throwing bullets in a fire isn't—?" Tommy said.

"That was chance, not directed specifically at me. Not cocked and aimed, not *get on your knees, fool, or I'll*—"

"Why are we here?" Tommy said. I held up the Identity Chart again. "What did you notice about my neighborhood?"

"That you were the only white person? Is that what I'm supposed to say?" The owner refilled our drinks without looking at us. Someone coughed and we finished our coffee in silence.

We slowly made our way west toward the Pennsylvania border. Tommy had been driving for a few hours and it was about two o'clock.

"I choose where we eat lunch. You picked that gay hotel," he said.

"Gay? Was the bed and breakfast *gay*? I didn't know that—"

"Here," he said, slowing as we passed a Korean restaurant at the edge of a strip mall. He turned around and pulled next to it. It looked expensive.

"How much money you got?" he asked me.

"Check the door. Do they take cards?"

"Yeah," he said, squinting at the door.

"I kind of wanted spaghetti."

"That's interesting," Tommy said, getting out and walking toward the restaurant.

The restaurant's lobby had a large fish tank and a bulletin board filled with pamphlets written in *Hangul*: all straight lines and circles, blunt and Spartan compared to China's pictograms or Japan's six alphabets. Inside, everything was shaded and earth-toned. It was a strange hour when everyone was just leaving and the hostess smiled to see us. It seemed like everyone else knew each other. For the first time during the trip, Tommy seemed at ease, joking with the hostess as she led us to our table. She pointed at the paintings and sculptures as if we were touring a condo we'd just bought. Finally, she seated us in what seemed like a reserved section at the back of the restaurant, the floor slightly elevated and the area around our table surrounded by a carved wooden railing. The table itself was thick, dark cherry with white placemats. It glowed pleasantly in the track lights.

I could only read half the menu. Our father told us stories and taught us the language, but I shed Korea like a coat. Korea. "Too much sadness," he'd said when I asked my father why we moved. My mother was dead and he'd lived to see his country divided. It was the oblivion of a new culture: He'd wanted to lose himself in it. And here, Tommy thought he'd taken the most after our father.

"Are there places you could learn Korean? Or, like, campus organizations?" Kate said. There were. But even if I learned Korean, then what? Picture me in Korea, stepping off the plane into a crowded market, full of bubbling earthen pots, cell phone vendors, primary colors. What did I have in common with those people? No, the rift was too wide, the distance irreconcilable. I couldn't explain that to Kate, so I didn't bother. She stirred her drink and looked at the round, earthenware sculptures.

The waitress came back and said things to me in their language but Tommy intercepted, folding the words back into their conversation. She left and returned with a spoon, knife, and fork, placing them across the table for Kate and me. It was a nice restaurant, so I sat politely and tried to smile. Kate slid further down her seat, very aware that Tommy was pretending she didn't exist. The whole scene must have looked hideous. I pointed to something on the menu and she nodded. From the look she gave me (mostly pity), my brother had excused me either as retarded or as a deaf-mute.

"You think you're doing me a favor," I said after she left.

"I think I'm doing me a favor," he said. I'd kept a few insulting phrases from our mother tongue and we traded those for a while. I was about to switch to English when the restaurant's owner approached us. If you're Asian, generic-looking (it's easy to distinguish whether a woman is from China, Korea, or Japan—harder with men), and you frequent Asian restaurants, this sort of thing happens all the time. The owner comes up and asks if you're Chinese or Korean. I don't know why. The owner was older, silver hair at the temples. He was venerable-looking; prosperity suited him well.

"Are you Korean?" he said, although it sounded like "Ah. You Korean."

"No," I said. He gave me a strange look.

"Oh," he said. He looked around at the restaurant, at the paintings as if he'd never seen them before. Then he walked away. The whole exchange lasted maybe ten seconds.

"Because I'm not," I said to Tommy. I looked over at him and reached into my pocket for the aegis of the Identity Chart but hesitated. While we were arguing about something on the menu, he'd picked up Kate's butter knife and waved it around as he called me an effeminate, mouth-breathing dogfucker in *Hangukmal*. But now, the dull blade and the look on his face—I've never seen anger like it.

Several incidents came to mind, but I'll only share one. When I was ten, Tommy tried to decapitate me—tied a length of rope around my neck while I was asleep, tied the other end around a doorknob, got a running start, and kicked the door shut. He'd previously removed one of his teeth in much the same way, and the sheer force ripped me from the bed and onto the floor. Snot and tears, I looked up and saw him, arms folded as he disapprovingly observed my survival. For some reason, he was wearing only underwear, bright white, and from a strange cinematic angle I pulled at my neck and watched him stare at me. A few days later, I returned the favor by knocking a bookshelf onto his head while he was doing push-ups in the living room. Three more inches and I would have had it. But · these were everyday experiments, playful in their violence. We put thought into them, yes, but never thought much about them.

In the restaurant, though, there was something I'd never seen in Tommy before: genuine malice, tight and seething. My hands were always shaking, but usually I could control it somewhat. I put them on my lap. When Dylan went electric, the guy shouting "Judas" didn't really mean it. Tommy meant it—the entire restaurant steeped in the ugliness. Not speaking the language was one thing, but to deny my heritage in this place, *here*, with the kingdom's glory spread around us. My dismissal was beyond ungrateful. It was betrayal, almost unspeakable in its callousness. I really thought he was going to kill me, drive in the knife in my throat, blood spurting slow motion in a chrysanthemum bloom. He stood up slowly and walked past. Everything in me contracted.

"You're paying for this," he didn't say. He walked through the restaurant, still carrying the knife, and out the door.

Drive. "We're almost there," I said. We'd passed Saturday with small talk and now it was Sunday morning. We were somewhere in Connecticut and had school in less than 24 hours. Now was the time, mostly because I figured he couldn't attack me and drive at the same time. At the very least, his power to ridicule me would be lessened.

I pulled out the Identity Chart, unfolding it on the dashboard. "This will require theory," I said.

"Oh my god," Tommy said.

"Otto Weininger was a social scientist, philosopher. Jewish fellow, sort of."

"What does that mean, sort of?" Kate said from the backseat.

"He renounced being Jewish." Tommy didn't say anything. He didn't have to.

"He also committed suicide at 23. But anyway, Weininger believed in spectrums. Instead of being purely one thing or another, we fall somewhere on a scale."

"Please stop," Tommy said.

"In order to heal from the trauma of adolescence and to face uncertain adulthood, I must first come to terms with my identity," I read, quoting the mission statement at the top of the paper. "All the answers are on this scale," I said, pointing to the ladder-like drawing of the Identity Chart. "On one end, there's pure Korean-American-ness."

"Drawn in red crayon."

"Burgundy represents Korean-Americans. And see the nice color spectrum in between..."

"Pink. Cute," he said, looking over. He didn't look at the chart—or at me—for the rest of the drive.

"And then Caucasians, represented by this white color here at the opposite end. The paper itself was already white, so I just drew the outline. So, I'm here," I traced a circle with my finger in the middle of the chart, "adrift in this vague ocean."

Eyes on the road, he shook his head. *How are we related?* the look on his face said.

I said, "Look, just because you don't understand something doesn't...Weininger influenced Freud. He might have been flawed and his ideas controversial, but that doesn—"

"Shut up. You've spent your entire life obsessing over—"

"People like binaries. White and black, Korean, Japanese, Chinese. But seriously, who's one hundred percent anything? Are you? Weininger challenged a lot—" Tommy drove the car across the grass median, the Dart's frame rattling, and into the opposing lane.

"Okay, okay!" I said, raising my hands in surrender. His foot pressed down a little on the accelerator. I yelled at him and stuffed the Identity Chart back in my pocket. The highway wasn't busy, but several cars honked as they swerved out of our way. He pulled back into the correct lane.

"Have you ever tried talking to people instead of studying them? You really should!" he shouted. He was angry.

"Thanks, Oprah," I wanted to say, but didn't.

"Wherever we're going..." There was a pause which lasted about a minute. "How is this going to solve your whatever issues?"

"Identity," Kate said.

"Hence the Identity Chart," I didn't say. His anger calmed to irritation. I took a picture of him with my cell phone.

"On the way home, I'm going to tell you what I really think about all this," he said.

A few minutes later he turned down a dirt road. The shocks on his car weren't very good and he had to slow down dramatically. There were trees on both sides of the road and we couldn't see anything beyond. The road ended in a gravel parking lot. While we were arguing about whether this was the right place, someone got out of the van next to us. He was a portly fellow wearing a thick blue coat lined with polished brass buttons and a tri-cornered hat. He was also wearing a leather sash, from which hung a decorative sword. He pulled a small snare drum from the back of his van, shut the door, and carried it out of sight, whistling.

"What the fuck?" Tommy said, each word a sentence. We got out and I walked to the end of the parking lot. It was a historic landmark, according to the sign. We were on a hill looking out over fifty acres of tall meadow. At the far end, a rustic wooden fence separated the field from the forest. There was a stone path which led down to a campground, which had several canvas tents. We watched our blue drummer make his way down toward them. It was too far away to make out any people, but we could see smoke from several campfires.

"Well?" Tommy said, making a sweeping gesture with his hand. Kate was smoking a cigarette. Her eyes followed his hand. He looked over at me.

"Mildred told me about this. The owner. At the bed and breakfast. Her son's into this. So was the doctor."

"Really?" Tommy said. "His adoptive father," he said to Kate.

"He was a medic in the Sixteenth New Jersey Regiment," I said. I remember helping the doctor carry his equipment. When I was twelve, he let me carry his musket to the car. It felt like my arms were pulling from their sockets, but I got it there unscratched, without even looking like I was struggling. I breathed in the damp New Jersey air. "Sometimes things just work out. The trees, the colonials we passed on the way here. Revolutionary War reenactors—these are the whitest people doing the whitest thing possible. It's either this or line dancing night at an Elks club in Vermont."

"Stereotypes," Tommy said.

"Not stereotypes. Purity. And look at his neat tri-cornered hat," I said.

"So your white friends do this?" he asked.

"Where would one buy such a hat?" I said.

"Do you have any white friends?" I gestured to Kate, but he said, "Aside from my girlfriend? Any...friends at all?"

That one stung, but I let it go. I took out the chart and

smoothed it on my leg. I calmly told him that one has to go to extremes when calibrating an Identity Chart. "I got the Korean part from the restaurant—that was by accident, but it worked out beautifully. After this, we can go celebrate in a Presbyterian church, practice *Hwaorang-do* in a vat of *kimchi.*"

"I think if I punched you hard enough, it would fix everything," Tommy said.

"The X on a map—*you are here.* People need that. It's important," I said, refolding the Identity Chart and putting it back in my pocket.

"But where?" he mused.

"Take enough cynical steps backwards and everything looks silly," I said.

"I'm going to take some cynical steps away from you." I followed him down the trail. The stone path ended in a broad field, upon which stood a line of tents. There was a flagpole with a colonial flag and a bespectacled, panting man taught a group how to lower, fold, and raise the flag. I hadn't wanted to get this close, but Tommy pushed further into the camp.

"Here we go," he said. He walked over to a young woman in a white bonnet. She was hollow-cheeked, thin, with short blonde hair. She wore a long dress and apron and tended to a cast-iron pot hanging over a small fire.

"What odd manner of dress," she said, staying in character. She looked at our shoes for a long time. Hers looked like moccasins. "Which colony are ye from?" I don't think she actually said "ye," but her voice had a strange tone, a flutter of certain vowels. Accurate for the time period, I suppose.

"Pennsylvania," Tommy said.

"Oh my. Are ye loyalists?" She looked at us with what appeared to be genuine suspicion.

"Tell her you're a loyalist, Jay," Tommy said. I ignored him. A man carrying a long musket walked over to us. He was wearing the same thick white pants as the rest of the soldiers, but instead of a coat he just wore a white collared shirt and a brown vest. Sort of looked like the guy on the Samuel Adams bottle. He greeted us warmly and shook our hands. He introduced himself as Bucky (he was missing both front teeth) and the cook, his wife Virginia. The thick-cut beef, onions, and carrots in the stew smelled wonderful. The camp was a maze of smells: food bubbling in cast iron, the lightness of smoke. I told Bucky we were doing a report for a class project. On period weaponry.

"Oh!" he said. "Well, you'll want to see this." He picked up his gun and held it in front of him. I took a picture with my cell phone. "Like hefting a fencepost," he said, resting it on his shoulder like a sentry. "This is a Brown Bess, carried over from Great Britain. Seventy-five caliber muzzle-loader."

"Seventy-five," I said.

"Add courage and ye have a revolution," Virginia said.

"Muzzle-loader, meaning one loads from the end of the barrel." He sat down on a wooden camp chair and held the gun on his lap. Virginia brought him a canvas bag and he pulled out a tube of paper the size of a shotgun shell. "Little known fact: A great number of patriots were missing their front teeth. Because—" he handed the tube to his wife, who stuck it in the side of her mouth and bit off the end.

"Fastest way to open a gunpowder tube is with the incisors," Virginia said.

"Can't whistle anymore," Bucky said. He pointed the musket at the ground. "This here is the flintlock." He poured a little black powder from the tube into a hammerlike contraption above the trigger. On a bolt-action rifle, this is the area where the bolt would be. He gave a long description about how the firing mechanism worked, using the words "frizzen," "pan," and "ignite."

"You're not writing this down?" Virginia said.

"My cell phone's recording everything," I lied.

"They're good boys." Bucky tilted the barrel up—the gun itself was about five feet long, made of dark, stained walnut. He poured the rest of the powder into the barrel and slid a brass ramrod from beneath the barrel. He pushed the paper cartridge down into the barrel. "Normally, one would include a lead ball with the cartridge, but we're not that dedicated in our reenacting."

"Not like the Civil War reenactors," Virginia chirped. Yes, chirped. This was some kind of inside joke. A bell rang out.

Bucky and his wife looked over toward a churchlike building near the edge of the woods. Virginia gathered not one, but *three* camp chairs and Bucky set the gun across them.

"It's five. Time for the safety meeting. Then we'll have some demonstrations," Bucky said.

"So...we'll go back to the car," Tommy said.

"I'll gladly trade you some stew to keep the fire going," Bucky said. Otherwise he had to put it out. Starting a fire with flint and tinder was not easy, he told us. Kate opened her purse and offered a lighter, but he politely shook his head.

I promised to keep the fire going. Bucky looked at his gun, but we made sure not to look over at it, or him. "They're good boys," he said as he walked his wife to the safety meeting. They met up with others and went into the church.

"What the fuck," Tommy said after they were gone.

"Bucky and Virginia obviously don't have kids," I said, picking up the gun. It was surprisingly heavy, almost as tall as I was. It was an elegant weapon, and it was a relief to hold a gun without worrying whether my brother was going to use it for a killing spree. It felt different in my hands, like a gift. It felt proper, the way my fingers curled around the wood. But I didn't want to shoot it. I knew what had to be done the moment I saw it but couldn't speak it until now.

"I want you to shoot me," I said. I handed the gun to Tommy, suddenly feeling helpless without it. It didn't take much for him to point it at me. The barrel was really wide: The lead shot must have been bigger than a marble.

"Wait," he said. He looked at the campground to see if anyone remained. Kate stayed by the fire, making it clear she wanted nothing to do with us. The bronze-colored metal below the flintlock and the metal of the barrel glowed dully as we walked down the field and into the shade.

"Man, this thing is heavy," he said.

"So, wait..." I moved about ten feet away, then fifteen.

"And you're sure this doesn't have a bullet in it."

"They shoot lead balls, not bullets. And no, he only loaded a blank."

"Because they were talking about loading these with real

bullets," he said. I'd been watching carefully, I told him. Obviously, it was loaded with a blank. This debate went on for a while.

"Wait, why am I doing this?" he said.

I told him, "This is going to solve everything. I didn't even plan this, but it's so perfect. People with bullets in their heads...remember that conversation? I have effect—" I pointed to my forehead, "but not cause. This is cause. Oh my God, this is perfect."

"What?" Tommy said.

"It's like Chekhov's rifle. *I'm* like that story. It must be fired," I declared. Chekhov once said that if a rifle is introduced in the first act of the play, it must be fired by the third. All this time, my life had felt out of balance. And now, I was ready to finally set things right. I started to explain Chekhov, but he sighed and took out the rubber band which kept his hair in a ponytail. He lifted the gun and pointed it at my face. "If this is what you want," he said.

"Wait," I said, taking a few steps backward.

"I thought so," he said.

"What?"

"Ready?" he said. I closed my eyes and held my arms outstretched. I could feel the air stir, a breeze from the forest. I took a deep breath. I was ready.

My brother was not. "We're going to prison for this," he said. Or, at least I am. You'll probably be dead."

I told him, "If this doesn't happen, I will never have this chance. Ever. Again. *Courage.*"

"Goddamn it."

"Courage."

He said something I didn't understand. "Go," I said. He seemed about to protest when he looked at something over my shoulder. I thought it was a joke, so I didn't look.

"I love you," he said.

I opened my eyes and he pulled the trigger.

A man wrapped in smoke, that's what I remember. I'd fallen, knocked backwards by the rush of everything. The shot's deep thunder was still echoing off the hills, inside my skull. The smell of gunpowder—it felt like I'd been inside the explosion. On the ground beside me were flaming ribbons of paper. *I love you.* Everything echoed.

"Do you feel reborn?" Tommy yelled as if I were really far away. I stared at the trees as if I'd never seen them before.

"I don't know," I said, but no sound came out. Everything looked new.

Tommy was shouting something. Had been for who knows how long. "Run! You fucker!" and I looked over my shoulder. Apparently, the safety meeting was over and everyone had been calmly filing out of the church—until they heard the shot. Now, torches and pitchforks, they were running down the hill. Toward us. "Get up!"

I had a perfectly reasonable explanation and we had friends in this group. Surely they would understand. Surely I would be able to explain. With this knowledge, I somehow managed to stand and then did the most responsible thing possible: I ran the fuck away, up the hill toward the car.

Tommy and I aren't speaking now (for the record, this is entirely his fault), but I can picture myself someday calling him and hanging up. You make progress with identity one day at a time. And I am making progress: I destroyed the Identity Chart in a ceremony with my therapist, sent it burning down the Allegheny River on a raft made of popsicle sticks. Very cathartic.

As for my identity crisis, I did my best to leave it behind. It makes people sad when I phrase it like this, but my heritage became something I figured out how to manage, just like my headaches. But so many things I'd inherited had held me back, it seemed. No one goes into mournful gyrations or gets mad at Italian-Americans who can't speak Italian, who don't pine for Rome. Forgetting is inevitable with oceans and time between us. What I looked like wasn't going to determine my path—I was going to choose my own.

But when I remember that weekend, I think it's funny, the immovable objects we carry and what can knock them loose in the most epic of moments. And, as I picture my brother moments before our getaway, running up the hillside and holding that awkward musket aloft, I think—it's funny, the things you hold onto.

20

LIGHTNING

Shortly after we returned from Connecticut, I ran out of money and moved back in with Tommy. We'd ignored Kate while we were playing with muskets, but one night in Pittsburgh we completely misplaced her. The three of us went to a party at the Playboy Mansion and after some important brotherly discussion about Descartian geometry or perhaps boobs, we found a bottle of grain alcohol hidden in someone's bedroom and half an hour later we were stumbling blindly down the South Oakland streets. We'd actually arrived at this party on time, maybe 9 PM. On the walk home, we sang Grateful Dead songs. Tommy found a dead lobster in the trash behind some restaurant and stuffed it through the mail slot of his landlord's house.

We found her the next morning when we stopped by her apartment to apologize. Her place was tiny, barely even a studio and decorated in a minimalist style. I suppose this was her sanctuary from her multiplying aesthetics, the garage-sale sensibility with which she decorated Tommy's house. There wasn't much except three dressers, a shiny air mattress, and the Chinese-style lantern I'd given her hanging in the far corner of her room. A few months ago, she'd painted the interior museum-white and changed the room's color by changing the bulb. I'd bought the lightbulb as a joke, but now the room was bathed with red light, watery in the morning sun. The entire apartment smelled like vomit. Like acid, and Kate was sitting on the mattress, which sagged under her weight. Her jeans were mostly off and laid crumpled on the floor, still clinging to an ankle. I looked everywhere else as Tommy moved tentatively in her direction. The bathroom was a mess—the curtain pulled down, blood on the handles of the sink.

Tommy took off his jacket and wrapped it around her, positioning himself to block my view, as if I was trying to see her like that. The red light seemed a mockery of the entire scene, so I turned the lantern off. It was bright enough outside—the light that came in the room was filtered through the Venetian blinds and the plastic sheeting on the windows.

"Who?" Tommy said.

"Lightning." A puzzled silence. It hadn't rained that night. I peeled away the sheeting, opened the window, and it was suddenly freezing in that room, the reflection of cars shimmering over us as they passed. No one said anything else for a while as Tommy and I tried to figure out what to do. The entire thing passed in nightmare time. "I can't remember. It's so much prettier late at night," she said. Tommy managed to pull her jeans up, which, judging by the sound, must have been an ordeal. She moved her hands up her thighs, the friction on the denim making a chilling sound, which raised goose bumps on my arms. Tommy's voice somehow matched that sound, that whisper as he spoke to the 911 operator or whoever.

I turned away and ran as fast as I could, pounding down the stairs and onto the street and I didn't stop running until I was somewhere in a forest, maybe in Schenley Park and there was snow and leaves underneath. White exploded as I fell and then I felt a beautiful nothing in my head. I fell down a hill, I guess, saw the ground and sky tumble over and over as if the world had tackled me, and I didn't know or care how I'd gotten there or where I was, or who.

It wasn't guilt that pulled me from that room, although I hope Tommy and Kate thought so. I'd even accept cowardice, or nerves. And for a long time, I found some comfort by telling myself it was either. But, no, it was the feeling I couldn't escape through my college years. At Tower, Tommy and I had worked hard and earned a fair living. Here, we were just taking—there was a sense that every free meal, every IOU and extended assignment, every carton and case would crash down upon us. We certainly couldn't keep our respective worlds from falling apart. When it happened, I knew it would be as grotesque as a face imploding.

There was so much to run from, but I felt it. We'd broken too many rules, gotten away with too much for too long. The overcorrection was coming fast and hard and it had already caught one of us.

———

A week later, it was her birthday. It was the first I'd seen her since. Some long bruises had developed on her neck. She didn't bother to hide them but didn't mention them, either. From the look on Tommy's face—and maybe even mine—it was clear how guilty we felt about the whole thing. Tommy actually baked a cake, then bought her one after deciding his wasn't edible. For the first time since we met, there were long stretches of silence as we ate, despite how we tried to cover them with talk about anything. After dinner, Kate found some poster board and lacquer and brought it to the table. I didn't know whether this was some kind of penance—a confession of sins, or an attempt at nostalgia. Either way, Tommy and I would have gone along with anything she said.

"There's a definite shimmer to the air," I said, waving my hand in front of my face. I handed Kate another photocopy. She brushed lacquer on the picture and lifted it, leaving a ghostly afterimage behind. Running her hand over the poster board, Kate found an untouched picture of Tommy. With a gold marker, she drew a gold circle behind his head, coloring around the picture. Looking over at him, she slowly brushed solvent on it until Tommy's entire body dissolved, his face clouding into an abstraction of ink and gold. The chemicals soaked through the poster board, sticking to the table.

"Fuck," I said, blotting the collage with a paper towel.

"He looks better this way. Through the ether. Everything's so pretty when you're drunk. Right, Jason?"

"You're cut off. You need to stop breathing this air." She reached out and I warily handed another picture, a photograph of her with Tommy. "We only have so many of these," I said.

She grabbed it out of my hand. "Who took this, anyway?" Kate said, staring blankly at the picture. "I don't remember you being there, Jason." I told her I was and had taken the picture.

"God, it's foggy in here," I said.

"Everything's prettier when it's flammable," she replied.

"Whatever that means," Tommy said.

"Speaking of which..." I looked down at my lit cigarette.

"Shit. Go outside. Good God," Kate said.

"Yes ma'am." When I came back, Tommy was pressing down on his newly colored picture, gently brushing over it with his palm. He lifted the copy, leaving a ghostly blue-green blotch.

"We've never looked better," Kate said. Tommy looked up at me, and I ran off to make a round of martinis. An hour later, we were more or less finished with the collage, a spattering of vague impressions and facsimiles. In the background were some of Kate's family photos, untouched and uncolored. Tommy painted a wintry landscape in the foreground, a row of spindly trees bending under a heavy snowfall.

"Paint dad," I said for some reason. It seemed wrong to have Kate's entire family, Tommy and myself, but not our father.

"God no," Tommy said.

"What did he look like?" Kate said. It surprised me that he'd never talked to her about him. I went into the kitchen and mixed myself another drink, listening to the voices float in from the dining room. It sounded something like this.

Kate: "Then just paint him. Jesus, what's the big deal?"

Tommy: "Because he becomes real again, sort of. It's hard to explain. I don't want to talk about it."

Kate: "Isn't that why we talk about people? To remember?"

Tommy: "I don't want to."

Kate: "Don't want to talk or don't want to..."

Tommy: "Jason was lucky to get away and even my father

knew that. When I'm ready, we'll talk about it." As I returned to the living room, my legs felt weak. I went forward with slow and measured steps. Our pasts seemed like they were made entirely of guilt and we kept returning to them. That and the thickness of lacquer and alcohol set that night on an irreversible course. Tommy furiously swirling reds and grays, small drops flying onto his shirt and onto the collage. Tommy, asking me what color best represented fear and hatred. "And don't you dare say black, either." Tommy with that look in his eyes that said he was trying to outrun something. "Let's go," he said. He had the same look in his eyes when he held a gun, when he had a knife in his mouth. We were looking for lightning, had been all week. We'd know it when we saw it.

21

TRASH DAY

When the University of Pittsburgh was established in 1787, upperclassmen moved from dorms to local residential neighborhoods. Because they liked the comfort and convenience, they parked their horses and buggies outside their apartments, not moving them for weeks at a time. Eventually, the horses died and rotted, the air thick with flies. The buggies collected literally millions of parking/street sweeping tickets (*thou hast committed a parking violation—paye five pence to the Pittsburg court system*) and were quickly replaced by other buggies after the student graduated and left town. Over a century later, this tradition continues. Although it is an established fact that there is no parking in Oakland, people still try, driving to parties or local restaurants. As they try to park, they drive faster and more erratically, speeding and stopping as drunk college kids stumble across the street without looking. Especially at night, this turns into a game of vehicular musical chairs. A line of cars and beeping horns accompanied Tommy, Kate, and me as we walked, still dizzy from the lacquer fumes. The chaos outdoors was slightly preferable to the chaos indoors.

It was trash day and we walked through a corridor of garbage bags, tense and shiny. This was Atwood Street, where someone had torn open several bags and lit the contents on fire. Further down the road, some were still aflame, grisly luminaria lighting our path. Most of it was smoldering when we passed, a smell of charred paper and a thicker, sweeter smell. Tommy kicked a can, scattering a mass of smoldering trash out into the street.

"Can we not get arrested tonight?" Kate said.

"I was just putting it out," he said. We ducked into a corner dive bar, filled early evenings by the panhandlers who prowled the streets around the university. It was still early, maybe around eight. The college students were cozy in their dorm rooms, studying or playing videogames. Or sneaking out to light garbage on fire. We walked toward the billiards room at the rear of the bar and played pool for a while. Kate said she'd get us a pitcher and went to the bar.

Almost everyone in the bar wore those powder blue or neon tees, drinking Yuengling or Pabst almost in unison. But they all seemed so goddamn happy. I looked at Tommy, who had ordered a round of shots from the waitress. Tempted though I was, I passed. No money.

"She said she was getting us a pitcher a while ago," he said after our game ended. He put his cue down and looked for Kate. Looking over, I saw her talking to a younger guy with spiky dyed-blonde hair. He was laughing, minutes away from putting his arm around her. Tommy racked up the ball and took a shot, hitting the cue with a loud crack. They watched her as she walked into the pool room.

"This is Jeff," she said, pointing to her spiky-haired friend. Jeff was an overgrown version of the food court gangsta, the white kid in ridiculous baggy jeans looking very tough in his B-boy stance outside the Chick-fil-A. His crew consisted of three JNCO-jeans-wearing jackasses—a very intimidating trust-fund posse. They stood around, eyeing Kate. I lit a cigarette. One of them, a Mexican wearing a backwards visor, grabbed a pool cue and walked to the other abandoned table. "Jeff's a music producer," Kate said, hanging onto his arm. He made a strange hand gesture toward Tommy and his posse laughed.

"I'm going home soon," Kate said. It looked like Jeff and his friends were about to go home soon, too.

Tommy leaned in and said something to Jeff. None of us could hear it. Jeff nodded and backed off a little. His cell phone went off and he pulled it out of his pocket, flipping it open. He had lightning bolts tattooed on both sides of his forearms.

"Hey," Tommy said, looking at his arms. He had to yell over the Skynyrd on the jukebox but his tone had something new in it, a nervous strain. "I've seen you before. 'Playboy Mansion.' I ran into you on the way out," he said deliberately, almost carefully.

"Hells yeah," Jeff said. He snapped shut his phone and gave his crew a nod and a knowing look. He had nerve, I'll give him that. Or a sort of disturbing casualness.

"Last Friday?" Tommy said.

"Yeah," Jeff said, eyes narrowing a little. *Why?*

"Let's talk outside," Tommy said. Kate steadied herself, holding onto the table with both hands, staring at it like it had answers. She watched, her eyes moving from Tommy to Jeff. I could tell from the way she looked at him that she knew she'd met him before somewhere. I assumed she didn't remember, anyway. But I wasn't sure—as Tommy was—that he was responsible for what had happened to her at the last party. How much she remembered was still a mystery, since it was something none of us were willing to bring up. I'd like to believe she didn't remember anything, but the look in her eyes that moment as she looked at Jeff said she did. Tommy and Jeff started having a heated exchange and we went outside.

"Hey, where are you going with that?" the bouncer yelled, but I just kept walking. He followed me outside and grabbed the pool cue from my hand. I still had the bottle, though. He either didn't see it or pretended not to and went back inside, talking to himself. Besides rap music, car sounds, and drunken yelling, there was another sound that occasionally cut through the rest: the staccato of medevac helicopters carrying the screaming wounded to the hospitals on the hill. Coroners call ambulances *meat wagons*—I wonder what they call helicopters. I followed the chopper's red beacon as it soared across Oakland, and then the sound of nervous conversation, pre-game psych-up whooping brought me back to the moment.

We gathered in an alley behind the bar. Jeff and all his friends had left first, and Tommy stood in the alley next to the dishwasher's entrance, a small light above it. He stared at the group in front of him and a few seconds passed in which everybody could have left. Of course, we had all thought about just going home. But the moment passed, and Tommy began walking toward the group. He had a strange expression on his face as he walked to the fight and I knew he wasn't mentally preparing himself for whatever was about to happen. He was thinking about his own role in what happened, how things would have been different if he'd chosen to stay with his girlfriend a little longer.

"Let's just go home," Kate said. She was standing next to me. "It's really not worth it." But she was worth it to Tommy. He had abandoned her to the wild young men of Oakland once but never again. This was a blood oath he was going to make in front of her. Now he was throwing himself before the mercy of the nation's sharp young men, bulging with bovine growth hormone, testosterone, and date rape. "What are you guys fighting about, anyway?" Kate said, doing her best to pretend she didn't know.

Tommy moved into the narrow funnel of light and asked Jeff's friends politely to please stay the fuck out of this and then nodded to me, as if I could do anything about it. I nodded back, trying to look confident and tough. Looking back, it's obvious that no one—not Jeff and certainly not his friends—had done this sort of thing before. A few of us had seen this in movies. That was it. My hands tightened around the neck of the green bottle I held at my side. Jeff's friends took a few steps back.

There was something unnerving about how confident Jeff was. As if to confirm my suspicions, he took off his puffy coat, revealing a muscular chest. It was solid and utilitarian, like boxers in black and white photographs. Tommy took off his jacket and the result was not as impressive. He was wearing a red and blue striped shirt, a larger version of something a child might wear. "All right," Jeff said, taking a step forward. There was nothing else to say. He warmed up, sort of swung his arms, crossing them in front of his chest.

Tommy looked up from his jacket. "Wait, what did you say?" he said.

"What?" Jeff said and Tommy punched him in the mouth. It was spectacular, a sort of wet thump, and he staggered off to the side. I knew we had a problem when he stood back up, zombie like. He dipped his head and charged, tackling Tommy around the waist. They both fell to the ground with Jeff raining down punches as Tommy tried to protect his head. There was the sound of bone upon bone and something breaking. It must have looked hideous, me standing there, watching. I saw myself doing nothing but couldn't move. Tommy's movements, the desperation of his struggle, the way Jeff and the red hole where his mouth had been, and the red mist in the air as he breathed—the black of the pavement absorbed everything into its scaly depths. Still staring at them, my body seemed to function on its own as I handed Kate my beer bottle without looking at her. Jeff might have had the lightning bolts on his arms, but something else inside me jarred loose and there was a sudden electricity inside that pushed me forward. I didn't know where it came from—some animal instinct, but there was so much power in my legs as I shot like an arrow toward the man attacking my brother.

We wrestled for what felt like hours but was probably a less than a minute and he managed to push me off. Kate must have watched in confusion, maybe taking a couple steps toward us with the bottle in her hand, then backing off as Jeff and I crashed to the pavement again. Jeff got up and walked back to his friends. They started to walk away. There were sirens in the distance, but this was Oakland—sirens were always in the distance.

I looked back at Tommy, who had somehow gotten up and was crouching on the ground. He stood up slowly, looking at me with a bruised eye and bloody face. It was a blank stare to be sure, as dazed as me, but I felt a shudder of guilt upon guilt. How to explain that I'd been entranced by the gemlike sight of the broken glass behind him, the sparkles like the glint of the sun off water. The sheer poetry of it—this in an alley, and blood literally in the air. I'd spent so long watching Tommy throw himself against things that I'd become as helpful as a movie camera. His breath had a wheeze and rattle to it. "What's Kate doing?" he managed to say, staring at the ground. He crouched down again. Kate was throwing up—I could recognize that sound anywhere. Jeff's friends were all staring at her. Bent over and gasping—now maybe they recognized her.

"Nothing," I said.

Tommy sort of lurched forward. One of Jeff's homies saw this over his shoulder and slowed his pace. "Yo," he said to no one in particular. He stood at the edge of the alley, looking at someone we couldn't see. Then he turned around. They were coming back. I picked up Tommy's coat and held onto it. I knew he wouldn't think to pick up his coat. Jeff and his friends were coming back for us. The power in my legs was still there, tense and waiting to be released, but I was not going to run.

The bouncer must not have wanted to trip over bodies on his way home. The Pitt Police stormed the alley like a SWAT team, cars at either end. I did my best to get us out of there, both of us flinching at the lights. Jeff covered his mouth with the back of his hand as he walked past us, looking for another exit. Apparently the paramedics were busy pumping freshmen's stomachs because it took forever for them to arrive. We weren't under arrest, the cop said as he handcuffed me. We were being detained until they figured everything out. Tommy was slumped against a wall with two cops guarding him. A lady cop shined a penlight in his eyes, then walked away.

Kate knelt next to Tommy, the cops distracted as one of Jeff's crew tried to run. She stared into his eyes and I turned away as she started kissing him. I lifted my head toward the fuming, puffy-coated losers struggling with their handcuffs and then looked back at my brother. Someone pulled Kate off of him and I thought how strange love is, what it can suddenly pull from you. I watched the whirling red-and-blue atop of the police cars and winced.

A large black cop walked over to me. He had a police dog with him but handed it off to someone else before approaching me. But it was the way it appraised me, held its head as it sniffed the air. The markings—it recognized me. It was the same dog we'd once liberated. Too bad it couldn't talk, vouch for my character. I told the cop that Jeff and his friends had guns. "You need to do full body-cavity searches on them." I told him about the fight. The cop wrote something in his notebook, then ripped off the page.

"How is my brother?" I asked.

"Looks like a concussion and a broken wrist. Could have been a lot worse." He wanted to know what really happened and I told him the truth. I said I was never drinking again. "For your sake, I hope that's true," said the officer. "Yinz are in a heap of trouble. What you did tonight was what, stupid." I strained my neck to look at Tommy, who glanced over for a second as if he were trying to recognize me, then back to Kate.

22

COMMUNITY SERVICE

I dropped the letter in the river and watched the ink cloud and dissolve in the foggy green. Car exhaust fumes and cigarette smoke hung in the wet Pittsburgh air. On the floating paper was a lacquered copy of my report card and stats from the Korean Olympic judo team. I wrote about our trip to New Jersey, how I'd later gotten rid of that heavy musket in a drug-induced moment of paranoia. I'd drawn some of the city's bridges and my pretty neighbor whose cat sat in the window facing my kitchen, orange tail curling and twitching in the bright noontime sun. The rest of the letter read something like this:

My first day in Pittsburgh, Tommy and I went to see the Commons Room in the Cathedral of Learning. It's a normal stop on any tour, but Tommy insisted we go there first. The Gothic skyscraper suggested majesty, but it didn't prepare me for what was inside. The monastery-feel of the walls, carefully mortared limestone. And then we stepped inside a massive chamber three stories high, ribs of stone running the length of the vaults, which ended in elegant arches. Heavy chains lowered stained-glass lanterns that may have well hung there since 1787. The room was empty except for a few students studying at the broad wooden tables. It was late fall—outside, the maple trees had already shed their leaves, giving a different wintry splendor, and workers were decorating a tall

Christmas tree. Neither of us spoke. I could go on to describe the hidden stone hallways, the smell of the fireplace, the way the thick amber glass of the lanterns shone down on the wooden tables, the way my fingertips felt against their wooden finish. But the main thing I remember is the tall metal gate leading into the room, its doors forever open. Above the elaborate black metalwork was a verse shaped in iron Gothic letters:

Here is eternal spring; for you, even the very stars of heaven are new.

And there is eternal spring in Oakland. Landlords have been raising the rent for local businesses, which are shutting down and moving. Next year's freshman class won't get to sit beside tattooed bicycle punks and listen to bad Afrocentric poetry at the Beehive Cafe. No more art-rock at Club Laga—even the corporate punk bands have been banished. Now, students have the smooth jazz and corporate furniture of Starbucks. Next year's freshmen will never drink quarter PBR drafts at Cumpie's bar, they will never know the pleasure of getting alcohol poisoning for less than three dollars, then regurgitating Pabst Blue Ribbon in a zigzag trail through Oakland to the cheers of smokers standing on porches. There was charm in the student ghetto-fabulous lifestyle, in the glorious squalor that was South Oakland. And now that I've gotten to know this area, it seems like most of it is about to vanish. I know these aren't the things sons tell fathers, and they might not be things a father wants to hear. But I don't know what else to say.
  – Jason

The paper drifted featherlike until it disappeared. I looked up at the freshly painted yellow bridge. The concrete surface was worn down to the rebar—I could actually see the shoes and jeans of pedestrians above. This was less than five years into the new millennium, a time in Pittsburgh when the term "city in crisis" became a catchphrase on the nightly news. City inspectors gave interviews to local news teams saying they refused to drive their families over various bridges, including the one I was standing beneath. The American Society of Civil Engineers gave the city's bridges a "D" on their annual report card. Hell, even I usually did better than that. Maybe since my personal life was in decline, I was more attuned to the city's problems. I thought about that old bumper sticker: "Where are we going and why are we in this handbasket?"

I blew a stream of smoke up through the hole in the cement and walked away. Someday, Tommy and I would scatter his ashes and this letter, delayed in its journey, would reach him, everything coming together in an eternal handshake. It was a cold day in Pittsburgh and looking out from the city's edge, it was impossible not to think of loss, of oblivion. Tommy and I—what had been lost between us? My father and I? My father and Tommy.

I was still poor, though Leslie had graciously covered our court costs. The lawyer Leslie sent from Princeton got my brother and me off with fines and community service. It was something of a coup for Tommy—apparently, this wasn't the first time he'd shoved another man's teeth down his windpipe. His community service was downtown somewhere, teaching black kids how to play baseball. As for me, I was becoming a better person. Hour by hour, as a matter of fact. At the behest of the Allegheny County Judicial System, I was working at a soup kitchen. In exchange for the lawyer, Leslie made me promise to move out of Tommy's house, so I moved to an apartment building in North Oakland, the façade clean brick with cube glass windows. She paid the rent and I was in no position to argue.

I "volunteered" at the Jubilee House in the Hill District. The house was run by state funds, the food supply dwindling due to the city's newfound fiscal austerity. But you wouldn't think it the way everyone continued with their work. This had happened before, the director told me, and they'd pulled through. His name was Mason and he was a stout bald man. He wore thick curved glasses that had been out of fashion for at least thirty years. Black—everyone there was except for me and one Hispanic cook. "It's just like Port Authority," he said. The city's bus service. "They say they're broke every year and somehow they find the money." This time, though, the city council adjourned for the year without addressing the transportation budget. This sent the entire city in a panic and Port Authority was already announcing plans to cut weekend service. This was a problem, since I needed the bus to get to the Jubilee House. But Mason just laughed, as if to say *You just haven't lived here long enough.* "We'll be fine," he said. "And even if we're not, worrying won't help."

Easy for him to say. The Jubilee House was a strange place to work. I'd expected some kind of cheerfulness running amok, or at least some kind of pervading optimism in such a place, but there really wasn't. It was a calm atmosphere. Mason planned and scheduled everything so well that there wasn't a lot of chaos or stress. There were only six people on full-time staff and they knew each other so well that their conversations were usually brief. No need to speak for great lengths, or in complete sentences, when you've been working with the same group for 30 years.

I was the only one doing community service. At first everyone must have thought I was affiliated with a church. But after someone saw me handing Mason a time card, everyone knew. "Jaywalking," I said to Tamara, the older woman who always made me tea. She laughed and no one brought it up after that.

A youth group came to the Jubilee House every weekend. *Agapé: Mission Possible,* their T-shirts said. They were college students or around that age. They were from a Korean Presbyterian Church in Oakland and this was part of their mission, Mason told me. This was the group everyone thought I was with when I first arrived. I didn't have much contact with them at first because I worked as a cook in the kitchen and the youth group served food to our fifty or sixty "clients." When we were done working, I came out of the kitchen a little late that day. The full-time staff ate in the kitchen, but the janitor and I ate in the dining room because it was more convenient. The youth group was sitting together at the far side of the room and since I always ate by myself at the table closest to the door, I went there as usual. It's not that I was avoiding them. After I'd finished my mashed potatoes and beef, I noticed a couple of them staring at me. They were curious and uncomfortable watching me eat alone. They were going to ask me to join them, I just knew it. I didn't feel like being sociable or answering questions, so I picked up my tray and finished eating in the kitchen.

The next weekend, Mason assigned me to work with them. They were mostly from Carnegie Mellon but some were Pitt students, some still in high school. "Agapé" was the Greek word for "unconditional love," someone from the group told me as we walked in late together.

And there she was again. I didn't say anything, but I recognized her immediately from the Happy Happy Bistro. It was the way her hair shone in the overhead lights, her sensible canvas purse. Those friends she was with in the restaurant were also in this youth group. Her name was Laura.

"But we're not like fanatics or anything," the late kid told me as he changed into his work clothes. His name was Randy. I told him that was wonderful and we washed dishes together for a while. They didn't preach to me at all or mention Jesus, which I was thankful for. "Who was that guy with you?" he said finally.

"What?" I said.

"At the Bistro," he said. Of course Randy was there. Now I recognized him. Of course he remembered.

"My brother," I said. I was happy to talk about him, to be his biographer and recorder of deeds. I was tempted to tell Randy how somewhere Jeff was wearing dentures because of Tommy. Although I'm pretty sure Mr. Lightning was guilty of rape, we never got an answer when we explained it to the cops. These things are complicated, he told us. Had we followed the rules, things might have worked out differently.

No one asked why I was working there, although I sometimes caught someone staring at me. Sometimes I felt the urge to blurt out something like, "I stabbed a cop in the face with a pencil!" It was a weird pressure, the non-communication we shared. And it's a weird limbo, not being white or black—a uniquely American middle-child syndrome. This youth group was nothing like the Koreans I saw in restaurants or on the bus, foreigners full of hope with dirty hands, judging their progress through us. It's a strange weight, an entire generation pressing down on you, and they bore it well. In fact, this youth group seemed strangely fine. No one seemed unhappy or neurotic or overmedicated.

I don't remember what I thought of them at the time. It should have been refreshing to see healthy normal people. I did enjoy working with them. It felt natural somehow, and not just because we had the same color hair (although a couple had dyed their hair brown or reddish brown), lack of eye folds, smooth warm skin. There was something comforting, an unspoken camaraderie as we wiped down tables together or sat waiting for Mason to assign us something. A solidarity. I must have felt envy, though, to be honest. That they had each other for support, that they had so much in common they must have felt something like a family.

But for me, there was a house rotting somewhere across the state and I was happy to let it rot without me. Just because I'd inherited something didn't mean I had to keep it. I would keep walking my own path.

23

AGAPÉ

When I watched Laura, I was a fan—of the graceful way she walked, her feminine efficiency while cooking, the extra attention she gave when giving directions, a small touch on the elbow to reassure the poor lost soul before he went on his way. When we weren't in the same room, I went back to being a cynic, noting how the youth group's members were wealthy or upper-middle class at least. (As was I, I know.) I could see it in the way they looked at our patrons, even though they tried not to stare or judge. I could tell by their bored expressions, their inability to suppress their youthful longings to run outside and play Frisbee, or video games, or—anything else but cleaning tables and slopping pork barbeque to Pittsburgh's homeless. It pleased the cynic in me that they were there more or less because their families made them. It was something else we had in common, not wanting to be there. There was an unspoken complicity that held us together and tied us to that place, if only for a few hours each Sunday.

But she was different, Laura. It annoyed me at first. I wanted to label her an overachiever driven by a puppylike need to please some male authority figure. Even then, I couldn't dismiss her. Despite how she downplayed it, she was so damn attractive. She had sensible shoulder-length hair usually kept in a ponytail but sometimes when faced with a serious problem—such as a malfunctioning dishwashing machine or a little girl who wanted pancakes—she'd let her hair down, falling around her shoulders, and tuck a few stray strands behind her ears with a look of concentration as she gathered every one of her eighteen years of life experience to solve the problem. There was something innocent about it, and something in my chest contracted and ached when I saw her. I admit to telling a young homeless boy that we served pancakes and sending her to the pretty girl wearing the Mission Possible T-shirt.

Mason wouldn't assign me to work with her, so I had to be creative. Her friend Randy told me her name. "Why?" he asked. I shrugged and he didn't press me. I only had fifteen more hours of community service left, two more weeks. I would miss it of course: the people, the service. The free food. They found flour and eggs and Laura cleared enough space and time. Mission possible, indeed. The pancakes were a hit. If saving the world by making a difference doesn't work out, she can always open a diner.

Our relationship started awkwardly. I'm guessing there wasn't any adult input into Agapé's plan to save my soul, which involved using Laura as bait. She approached me while I waited for the bus and introduced herself even though we both knew I already knew her name. The entire youth group strolled by innocently on their way to the parking lot. Then, Mason and the kitchen workers. Suddenly, we were back in high school, pushed together by mutual friends. Or I was, because it turned out Laura was still in high school. She was a senior at Schenley, a high school in Oakland. She played basketball, so we talked about Pitt basketball for a while—I'd overheard enough to complain properly. Lack of three-point shooters. Even Shaq was better at free throws. Howland's salary, which was bigger than the president's. She changed the subject, which I was glad for. I was being deceitful anyway, and something in me didn't want to be dishonest with her.

"Well my father's advice finally panned out," I said. It started to rain and we moved underneath the glass bus shack.

"What's that?" she said.

"Ignore women—it drive them crazy." The best advice he ever gave me.

"And how's that working out for you?" she said. I motioned to us with my hand and she laughed and said, "Oh."

"Met nice Korean gorl," I said, mimicking my father.

"Well half of one anyway," she said. She asked me my major and I told her. "That's interesting," she said, which usually means, "I have no idea what a communications major is but I suspect you're going to spend the rest of your life cleaning toilets for six dollars an hour," but she seemed genuinely interested, waiting for me to elaborate.

The irony of being a communications major is not lost on me, but I didn't know what to say during the long silence which followed. At the time, I didn't realize she was waiting for me to discuss my major. "It's the necklace, isn't it? Drawing you close to me," I said, pulling at the Guido chain I was wearing. In happier times, Kate had bought it for me at a garage sale.

"Your thug chain. Definitely," she said, laughing.

"Gets the ladies. The next time you see me, I'll be decked out like Mr. T."

"Who's that?" she said. I stared at her. High schoolers. I pity the fools. I explained the A-Team to her, how Mr. T hated flying, so they always had to trick or drug him. She didn't seem impressed. I told her about the fight, about Tommy, and how I'd been arrested for resisting arrest and lying to an officer. I had to. The entire time we were talking, that unanswered question was between us.

"They charge everyone with resisting arrest," I said.

"I guess the concept of resistance is a bit vague," she mused.

"I'll show you the paperwork if you want." She promised not to tell anyone, even though I said I didn't care. We'd taken an important step, sharing something besides circumstance. My therapist would have been proud. I looked at my watch and leaned out to look for the bus. She said that her father was waiting and could drop me off in Oakland but I told her it was okay. I didn't want to jinx myself, ruin the nice chat we'd had so far. The bus would come, eventually. She looked over her shoulder, then at her watch.

"Well here's my dad," she said as the youth group leader walked over to us. Something told me he'd been watching us the entire time, his entire body tense with cell phone in hand, 9 and 1 already dialed.

Laura introduced me. His name was James Moon. "It's a pleasure," he said.

Mr. Moon offered to drive me home. He said the bus wouldn't be coming. He wasn't sure if the buses would ever run again.

"Come on, I promise we won't mention *Jesus*," Laura said.

"You just did," I said.

"From now on."

Her dad's blue SUV was warm and spotless and Laura and I sat in the back while he asked me questions about my major. I told him it involved speeches and composition, lots of writing. I hadn't thought it through when I gave him directions to Tommy's house. (Mine was in North Oakland, another ten-minute drive.) I'd been worried the trip was going to be awkward and Tommy lived closer. But as he pulled up, Mr. Moon seemed concerned with the state of "my" house. The metal awning overhanging the sidewalk had fallen—anyone walking down the sidewalk had to step around the sharp edges. Also, there may have been piles of beer cans and overflowing coffee cans full of cigarette butts all over the porch, cigarette butts on the sidewalk out front. After I got out, Laura rolled down the window and invited me to join Agapé that Sunday. I asked if she was going to be there and she just laughed. Before she could reply, I said, "Yes." I distinctly remember her smiling before they sped off. I walked home without talking to my brother. I hadn't seen much of him since the fight—I guess we were both keeping our distance, erring on the side of caution.

On Sunday, I got a ride with Randy to the youth group meeting. I didn't know what to expect and I wasn't particularly excited. The last church I'd visited was for my father's funeral. Laura's church was in a small town north of Pittsburgh, past the expressway, where Randy weaved under a series of underpasses and concrete ramps—an engineer's playground so massive that it blocked out everything else, leaving only concrete geometry and streetlights. The church was a stout white wooden structure, three stories high with a sort of Roman façade and a tall steeple. It looked like it had been medium-sized at first, but they had built annexes as the congregation grew. The entire thing had similar architecture and the building looked tasteful enough, comfortably worn, as things in small towns often are.

Hands in my lap, I sat in an upper room at a scarred plastic folding table. The room smelled vaguely of mildew and chalk. It occurred to me that Laura never actually said she was coming to this meeting. Randy sat across the table from me, pretending to read a magazine.

"It was a bar fight," I said after a good five minutes of silence.

"Awesome," he said, looking up. "Lee owes me ten bucks." He looked around, as if he'd disturbed the room's holy silence, and saved his follow-up questions for later. The youth room looked ghetto festive, like much of South Oakland, although cleaner and alcohol-free. There was a shag carpet in the middle, around which couches were arranged in a square, each from a different time period. The couch closest to me was purple and from Ikea. Another was red in the 70s but had since faded to pink. The couch to my left was very rectangular and the armrests were made out of brushed steel, although someone (Laura?) had carefully wrapped padding around them. Randy was sitting on a beanbag chair next to me.

The room itself was painted light yellow with a lot of music posters on the wall. Christian bands, from the looks of them. Christian boy bands, Christian hip-hop groups, Christian gospel singers. Maybe this was one of the churches buying all those Christian romance novels we made down at Tower. There was a cluster of bulletin boards next to the main entrance, all of them overflowing with pamphlets about mission trips and fundraisers. I stood and stretched my legs. There was a pool table in the room, a foosball table, and even a television with an old PSone attached to it, but I didn't touch any of them. I didn't know if they were for our enjoyment or to tempt us. Randy hadn't touched them, had he? I could see the parking lot through the windows to my right, so I watched for Laura, hoping she'd arrive soon. Of course she did.

The meeting itself was less painful than I'd imagined. It was laid back and Mr. Moon actually had a decent sense of humor. They talked about a mission trip they'd taken to Alaska and passed around a photo book of the group restoring houses and serving food. Laura stood up and gave a report, sounding so confident and mature it was hard to believe she was still in high school. Later, we sang Jesus songs and Laura sat real close to me holding a songbook, which was nice. Mr. Moon ordered pizza and we sat around and talked. I didn't have a lot to say and I was starving, so I just ate and listened to Laura's voice as she talked about someday planning a mission trip to Seoul.

Later in the meeting, we broke into pairs to look up Bible verses. We were supposed to relate them to our own lives somehow. Someone else picked Laura right away so I partnered with Randy. We looked up Mark 5:1-20, which is about Jesus stopping to heal a bleeding woman on his way to bring back a child from the dead. Randy and I puzzled over this, but I pointed out the next few verses, which were about Jesus sending demons into a herd of pigs. We were so fascinated by this story that we didn't have much to share when it was our turn. After that we all held hands and prayed and even though I'm sure they wanted to, no one prayed for me, which I was thankful for. Still, it was strange being an outsider here—outside of my own race and age, God. No one looking in could have seen this. I began to feel like a spy, a phony. That unfamiliar feeling again where every look and gesture magnified. Laura said something about welcoming me into this group and I opened my eyes. The awkward feeling dissipated as someone squeezed my hand. We dispersed. I wanted to thank her afterwards but didn't know how.

The church had a bowling alley in it. No one knew why. This was Pittsburgh, after all, an entire city awkwardly converted from steel mills into a crime-ridden cesspool and then into a postindustrial service/educational center. In Pittsburgh, they'd converted an old church into a brewery/bar (The Church Brew Works on Liberty) and another into a nightclub (Sanctuary on

Penn Ave.). Maybe Laura's church was slowly turning into a bowling alley. At any rate, it was an old-timey lane with smaller pins. "Duckpin bowling," Laura said, as if I knew what that meant. We had enough time for one game.

"You still have to set up your own pins, though," Randy grumbled as he walked down the other old wooden lane.

"So when do I get to see you without an armed escort?" I asked Laura.

"Hardly," she said, looking at Randy, who had set up the pins backwards. "When are you finished serving time?"

I told her I'd finished a week ago. She rolled the small ball slowly and it took out all but the front pin and one in the back to the left. She frowned and stared at the pins, looking to me for advice. I said I didn't know much about bowling.

"What would Jesus do?" she said, laughing as she curved the ball down the lane.

I was suddenly terrified, although at the time I didn't know why. It was a strange experience, being so close to something so attainable, the idea of a new romance. I also felt an exhilaration, which I hadn't expected. A possibility for joy, for something that might never decay or vanish.

24

THE GLASS PALACE

After two youth group meetings, Laura agreed to see me outside of a church. It occurred to me that I hadn't seen much of Pittsburgh lately except for the courthouse, whimsically designed to look like a giant stone castle. It seemed like a good time to take another look as the city began to thaw, cracking its joints as it yawned and stretched. Gone were the piercing winds that dip to the rivers before cutting into your face, gone was the phrase "winter storm advisory," gone was the salty road slush that soaks the cuffs of your jeans. Students stumbled out of their houses, looking around as though they'd woken up in the wrong city. We'd all forgotten the sun and everyone hurried outside, the winter trauma almost forgotten.

Laura and I were going to the Phipps Conservatory in Oakland. Neither of us had been there and she seemed pleased I'd thought to take her there. The idea of us discovering something together excited me. She wanted to walk, so we met by the bronze Diplodocus statue near the Cathedral of Learning. Nature was generous that day and the sun quietly warmed everything. I took her on a detour through Parkview Avenue, one of South Oakland's family neighborhoods. It was newly paved with well-kept lawns, new siding, American flags snapping in the wind. "Andrew Carnegie and Dan Marino grew up on this street—at the same time," I said. She laughed. "It's true."

"I bet they had a lot to talk about." This route took longer but she didn't seem to mind. A road led through the park and wound past green hills covered with trees. A few cars passed us and I watched a red sedan as it vanished over a hill and reappeared in the distance, slowly making its way though the park.

She laughed and I turned to her. The wind had pulled at her hair, which she was wearing down, brushed to the side. I don't know what she was laughing at, but the weather—its joy was contagious. I wanted to lie down, close my eyes, and spread out my arms on the park's lawn. Quite a few people were doing just that. "We only get about eighty days of sunlight a year," she said, adding that we should make the most out of each one. The road converged with a few others behind the conservatory. As we approached, she looked toward a distant hillside where several rectangular buildings were under construction. They sort of resembled the old steel mills, except made entirely of glass. We were too far away to see inside. She said, "I heard somewhere they were adding a basement tunnel with a transparent ceiling so you can see the roots of the trees above. And a couple new rooms. But I don't know if that's true or when they'll be done."

"Probably waiting for the Oompa Loompas," I said. The conservatory itself was a large Victorian greenhouse, metal forming an elegant framework around thick glass panels. From a distance, Phipps looked like a strange birdcage with its intricate domes and white metal. Two wings extended the main building, which was accented by a long pond which extended its length, sprays of crimson water lilies rising from the surface.

Inside was a maze of rooms, or a room of mazes, all organized by some great flowery intellect. There was a desert room full of cacti, green and yellow with silk-colored spines, leaves the size of playground slides. Entire forests towered above as we walked to the next room, full of tropical orchids. All this somehow contained by glass and steel. Heat, I remember a slight heat inside, but giant fans hidden in the framework drew a cool breath through the glass corridors as we walked.

"Have you ever seen *Bio-Dome?*" I said as we walked through a Japanese courtyard lined with bonsai trees. She shook her head. I told her it was a film starring the great thespian Pauly Shore and said, "Did it hurt?"

"What?"

"When you fell from heaven?"

"All right," she said, meaning "that's enough," but she was smiling as she walked away. And then we were in the butterfly room.

Malachite. Palamedes Swallowtail, Red Admiral, Pearl-bordered Fritillary, "fritillary" Latin for "dice," so named for the silvery dots flickering and bouncing in the air—tumbling dice. *Blue-footed Booby* and *Titmouse* notwithstanding, the most beautiful names were reserved for winged creatures. And why not, as winged flowers, winged jewels, orange-winged colors lighted and alighted on slender leaves, merging with the yellow and purple flowers before flying away. As they rose, they drew attention to the arched glass above, which didn't detract from the garden below—they seemed to point out, land on everything elegant. The path through the garden ran in a loop, if I remember correctly, and halfway through the room we paused at an exit leading to another room.

"Oh," she said, staring up at the door. I'd wondered how they kept the butterflies in one area, especially with no doors between the rooms. Jets of air blew in front of the entrance and butterflies would approach and hover for a few seconds before being lifted and sent back into the room. It was only a moment, but I remember seeing something in her face as she watched a butterfly return to the garden. It tried again to leave, was returned. It made sense a few would do this. I'm not sure how to describe the expression on her face. It probably loses all its power once named, anyway. A shade between pity and sadness, something mournful. I've spent hours thinking about that moment, the way she clasped her hands so she wouldn't reach out to help, as if there was anything she could do. The moment passed and she walked down the path, smiling at a little boy running by her side.

This look, it had nothing to do with being trapped between worlds, the silent-film angst of the half-breed. This was something else entirely, a different kind of untouchable sorrow. Maybe even then she knew, could see that I wouldn't change, that our paths had to diverge. Maybe she saw a parallel, a metaphor for the two of us.

The magic hadn't worn off, but she had a chemistry club meeting, and we eventually found the exit. "I wonder how many rooms we missed," she said.

"They probably have maps somewhere," I said.

"At the entrance. There was a table full of them. Next time." I didn't know a lot about dating but I knew it was a good thing we left wanting more. I said it was a whirlwind that ended in butterflies.

She nodded. "All whirlwinds should end so." After crossing the conservatory's lawn, we were faced with an intersection of several roads, each full of speeding cars. Must have been rush hour.

"Do all the parks in this city double as highways?" I said.

"Stop it." She saw an opening in the traffic, grabbed my hand and we crossed, breathless and charging back into the city.

After walking Laura home, I went to see Tommy. Someone had cleaned up the metal awning and moved a stack of phone books still in their plastic wrappers (it seemed like Oakland residents got two a week) into a makeshift coffee table in the far corner. The door opened and Kate walked out.

"Oh. It's you." Holding a cigarette with her purse hanging from her elbow, she leaned a little toward me as she reached back to the doorknob.

"Yeah," I said.

She stood up straight and put the cigarette in her mouth. "I gotta go. I don't know where he is," she said, walking past me. I watched until she turned the corner but she didn't look back. I tried the door—it was locked.

Things had changed between the three of us. When my number showed up on his cell phone's caller ID, she'd usually answer and say she didn't know where he was. Or that he was in the bathroom. Or passed out somewhere. Whenever I'd stop by, they'd usually be on their way somewhere. Eventually I stopped calling. I didn't expect it to get this bad. It wasn't that Kate didn't like me, I don't think. But how could my presence not remind them of the past, those long wasted days when we'd find some new destruction and cheer each other toward it?

When I wasn't around, she could pretend their relationship was clean and new. But Kate knew she'd never have the seemingly indestructible relationship Tommy and I had, even though I'd done little to earn it. It was a weird link I never really understood, either. But if my brother had to choose between needy, oft-estranged me or some chick he met at a wild ghetto party—well, in a way, he'd already made the decision that awful night he left the party with me.

But she forgot to lock the side door. I went upstairs to Tommy's room and knocked on the door. After listening for a few moments, I smelled something burning. Cigarettes, pot, brain cells—something at that house was always burning. But this was different. It was paper, but with a harsh edge. Fuzzy, dizzying. It was coming from downstairs, so I followed it.

From behind the couch, I could only see the back of Tommy's head, but he was holding something thin and cone-shaped. It was on fire. "Dude," I said. The flames seemed to almost reach the ceiling. He turned around, not terribly surprised. In that house, people came and went, vanishing as quickly as they appeared.

"I swear, I was just thinking about you," he said. The coffee table was stacked high with Ms. —— books. Now I recognized the smell. It was industrial glue; the books we'd taken from Tower were steeped in it. The cone, still burning as he set it down, was made from long paper sheets, aborted books from the press. I didn't think to ask why he'd saved them.

"You haven't heard," he said, anticipating my question.

"What?"

"Would've thought you'd have been the first to hear...or

maybe were you keeping it to yourself." The burning cone folded into itself and fell on the carpet. He wasn't going to put it out, so I moved toward it. Cutting me off, he kicked it into the air. "Feels good to send these up to paper heaven. Got a call from a friend back home. Tower's holding a ceremony for Cal during midnight shift on Thursday."

"It's about time," I said, pleased. "What, did he—"

"He died," Tommy said, graciously cutting me off. "Heart attack." It felt like he'd punched me in the stomach. I stared at the blackened papers for a while. What did this mean to Tommy? The expression on his face didn't offer any clues. He stood and gathered the papers. I lost track of time and must have wandered blankly around the room. When I looked up, I was standing in front of the living room window, watching scraps of garbage shiver in the wind. "Cal was good to us. I'm sorry. I really am," he said. And he meant it. For those of you keeping track at home, the score is: Tower 2, Jason 0.

I made some phone calls. "How's school?" the foreman asked. I was still on academic probation and had a macroeconomics test the day of his funeral. It broke my heart, it really did. I'd thought of any possible scenarios to postpone the test, but none of them worked. But I could still travel home, pay my respects.

25

WAIT LONG BY THE RIVER

Wilkes-Barre doesn't startle you like Pittsburgh. The Steel City directs you into a tunnel and appears fully formed after a tiled fluorescent purgatory, but Wilkes-Barre gives a mountain vista, a distance from which to admire the warm suburban lights below, the backlit squares and rectangles of its warehouse stores. Tommy gripped the wheel tightly as he drove. (He usually moved it lazily with one palm.) It had only been a couple days since I'd learned of Cal's death, but the smell of burnt paper was still heavy on his jacket. He stared forward. The car swerved a little and he stiffly steered us back into the correct lane. It was Thursday evening, and he said Friday at 7:30 AM would be the week's last shift. There wasn't overtime that weekend, meaning after we snuck in, we could spend all day in the factory if we wanted.

Tommy never made peace with Tower. He was still waiting for it to collapse under the weight of its own cruelty and incompetence. For him, the factory's continuing efforts were a badly acted death scene that was taking too long. I'm not sure why he'd agreed to return. Maybe walking the empty factory would be cathartic, if only as a visit to a simpler time, where our only concern was filling bins with books. At any rate, we both felt a change coming.

To be honest, I wanted to return by myself, mourn Cal in my own way. And although I knew it would be awkward to see some of my friends from midnight shift again as they filed out into the sun, I was looking forward to it a little. I missed the place. It wasn't Stockholm Syndrome or anything like that. There was something about the urgency of physical labor. There was the feeling that I belonged, that I was valuable, or at least difficult to replace. In college, you write your number on the scantron midterm to distinguish yourself from the 399 other student-drones around you and weeks later crowd around the results printout looking for your numerical percentile. There was some ghostly part of me that never left the bindery, only a sketch of a failure, and I wanted to seek him out in those iron corridors to ask where I'd gone so wrong.

"We're having the party to end all parties when we get back," Tommy said flatly. He was unusually thick-tongued. Had he been drinking before we left? Smoking? That would explain the silence. I thought about asking but didn't. I wondered exactly what "partying" meant to Tommy now. "This one ain't pretty, but it beats sleeping in the car," he said, pulling into a cheap motel. We had just enough money.

We both woke early, so I volunteered to drive. I passed the old house on the way to the factory. I expected to feel something as I slowed down in front of it, but nothing came. It was still there, empty. The front yard looked like a meadow, but otherwise it was the same. I looked at Tommy, who didn't say anything. I pulled into a parking lot across the street. "I'm still paying property taxes on the house. The market's still hot. I really think it's time to let go and sell it," I said, gesturing to it.

"I know what the house looks like. You didn't need to drive me here."

"I guess I want your blessing on this. Like I said, you'll get half."

"You seem content to let it sit abandoned. Why sell it now?" he said.

He knew why. Did I really have to say it? "Because I'm really in debt."

"It's not yours to sell," Tommy said. I was tempted to point out that, according to our father's will, it was. But I didn't. I knew Tommy wanted to honor him in the house during an ancestral ceremony, *Chuseok*. But he'd put it off for four years, and I'd hoped he had given up.

"You never seemed to care before," I said, irritated at his new sanctimonious attitude.

"Why are you in debt? No, seriously."

"Because sometimes things build up and you're overwhelmed, over your head. Drowning, and—" I said, struggling for words.

"You're in debt because you've spent your college years drinking, eating in restaurants, hanging out with my girlfriend."

"Wait a minute," I said.

"I'm not saying I'm innocent here. I *am* saying is that it's not right to sell our father's house, which he actually worked for, to cover your debt."

"Fuck you," I didn't say, even though I knew he was right. Still, the house was sitting there, no use to anyone. I decided to let it go, starting the car and throwing it into drive. "You don't have to come inside the factory with me," I said. Honestly, I wanted to leap out of the car, let it carry Tommy's searing new honesty off into the smoky horizon.

"I know," he said. The commute had stayed with me, worked its way into my muscles and I finished it without noticing anything new. The slag piles still looked as if nothing could ever diminish them. The junkyard didn't look any bigger or smaller. It felt strangely comforting to see nothing had changed, as if the area couldn't move forward without me.

Tower's parking lot. Tommy still wasn't in the mood to talk, so we waited out the final shift in silence. Half an hour left: There must have been a strange feeling inside. This was the time of exhaustion mixed with a strange energy with everyone waiting for the bell.

As the last few workers straggled out, we walked in. I had my old union key card, but someone held the door for us. I didn't know what we were looking for inside. It was the same factory. I walked my usual path: cafeteria, double doors, ugly gray cinder blocks and machines with fine layers of dust, Line

14. Our workspace, those three empty bins, the place our father probably decided to commit suicide. The place where I might have followed him had it not been for Tommy. We walked to the MSV line and I sat down at Cal's work desk. "It's strange," I said, spinning around in his office chair. The place was austere, the pneumatic lines in the machines silent and slack. The rows of production lines looked so orderly, so perfect without humans beating on them.

"The fluorescent lights must stay on all the time," Tommy said.

How strange that our memories, recollections, records are reborn in this dusty graveyard, full of scratched metal and blades. Spun in the press, books come to the bindery as doubles, then they're spit into the blade assembly, separated, and sent on their own wandering paths. But in the final act, they return in that final stretch down the line, right before the oblivion of shipping and receiving. It felt right that my brother was standing next to me, looking back at this place one last time before moving on.

"Why did you follow me to Pittsburgh?" It was a simple question, and I was tempted to answer because I wanted to leave Tower, because I wanted to leave the house I'd inherited. But neither of those was really it. If I wanted to leave the area, I could have gone anywhere. If I wanted to leave my past, I wouldn't have moved in with my brother. The answer was somewhere in the echoing deep of the factory. It was over the steaming mountains of slag, in the tangled fire-escape geometry of Oakland's alleys. Even then, I could feel the rush as it swirled around me, but to breathe it in and form it into words—back then, it would have been impossible. But Tommy knew why I'd kept myself close to him for so long. In the end, this was about our father.

"That house. Gravity worked differently there. Something about him would just come out, even when he wasn't drinking. Who knows what could set him off," he said of our father. And things would fly, glasses and ice in brilliant slow motion. The couch, causing those deep gouges I found in the hardwood. "We went through four or five couches. The arms, they break when you use it like a battering ram."

I suppose I would have attributed the changing furniture as a sign of prosperity if I'd noticed. Battering ram. I pictured my father pounding the walls, trying to break them down because something better had to be on the other side. It was a gambler's hope, a kind of slow drowning. In the end, all my father wanted, I think, is a quiet place to rest. And why did Tower have to be cruel and violent? After a lifetime as a blunt object throwing himself against the immovable industry, he'd worn smooth from the exhaustion, nothing to show for it but a punching bag son, an exile son, and broken furniture. And for Tommy to follow me through those bindery doors, into the source of the swirling ugliness in his life.

He told me about being caught in our father's storms, which were as unpredictable as his schedule. "Remember how he used to toss us around when we were kids?" Those were happy memories, that feeling of weightlessness and grass and sky. And that had been the whole story for me, a fortunate truncation. But they'd continued for Tommy. He didn't describe much else to me. The terror, I can imagine it. It was at the heart of Tower, that nameless fear. A hand caught in a hopper, blindsided by a forklift, the loud ring of gunshots from an automatic rifle, from a coworker to whom everyone but you had shown unspeakable cruelty. The fear you'd be in that place for the rest of your life, the fear the place would close tomorrow and the new reality of no jobs anywhere, ever. Tommy didn't think he could outrun everything, the past falling around him like a haunted house collapsing in the movie's final reel. You kind of fall in love with it, he said, our father with the anger and my brother with the running.

We talked for a while, but I'll only share a couple stories. When I was 12 and settling nicely in Princeton, our father got drunk at a company picnic held at a state park about twenty minutes from their house. The drinking itself was embarrassingly normal but when our father got in the car, he couldn't find the ignition. So it was either stay the night in a parking lot with imaginary wolves and bears prowling, or...Tommy got in, found the keys on the ground, and started the engine. "It was really hard to reach the pedals and see. So I'd step on the accelerator, then kinda stand up to see the road. So I would go about five miles per hour for a bit, then ten. It would have been fine except that, even though it was late, a car got behind me. Eventually, yes, there was a line of cars behind me. When they were finally able to pass me, you should have seen their faces when they saw me in the driver's seat."

And the other he told almost fondly: "Dad was a big guy, and eventually I bought some deodorant spray for the bathroom for obvious reasons. Lysol or something. Of course, had I known how much alcohol was in that stuff, we wouldn't have kept the toilet paper right next to it—you know, on the radiator." Weeks passed and the spray soaked into the toilet paper roll. "And one day, dad, also full of alcohol, goes into the bathroom. At some point during his business, he lights a cigarette. And when he reached for the roll, I heard yelling and hesitatingly opened the door. Naked with his khakis around his ankles—I swear it was like he was playing soccer with that flaming roll of shit-paper. Like Pelé. Somehow we didn't burn down the house. Your house. Whatever."

"Remember the college girls down at Tower?" he said.

"Ha. Becky and Tiff." I pictured their teenage breasts, barely contained by their cotton tank tops, bathed in a sheet of sweat.

"Tiff. Her boobs were terrific." We reminisced a while and the conversation turned serious again. "You made fun of them for dressing up for the union guys."

"I'm not sure I'd call it 'dressing up,' but yeah. Because flirting on midnights didn't count."

"And what about you? You've spent your time here with women you could never have," he said, stifling a cough. He rubbed his face. "A vague major, friends who don't remember you in the morning. I just want to know—what *you* are running from?" he said.

Running. And maybe was right. Part of the problem was the desire itself. I'd wanted to know why so few of my coworkers at Tower would talk about my father, why the son who grew up with him had a desperation behind his drinking and drug use that was, frankly, a little scary. I was looking for my own lost history in a way. I wanted to know who I could have been if I'd had the courage to stay. But I was terrified of the answer. So all this time I'd been running toward it, circling around when I got too close, looking at the flames from every angle.

Tower. Before, it was a cloudy black spot in my mind around which my thoughts and memories parted. Now, there wasn't the same danger, the union obligations of before. With Tommy by my side, I could reminisce almost fondly about the horrors. In my mind, management were loveable buffoons, cutely out of touch. The machine operators on 14 were beady-eyed, pig-faced simpletons. I felt I could finally wrap my head around it, shrink the place to fold, and unfold it at my leisure. Somewhere, my father and Cal were inside, waiting for a proper farewell. But the place held no terror for me anymore. Even standing in its iron corridors, the silence, the memories of distant grinding knives, a fist striking a forklift driver—Tower didn't have the same menace that caused splitting headaches, that knocked my heartbeat irregular.

Someday, Tommy would get that feeling of closure as he walked through the empty house, recalling whatever horrors and finally viewing them as artifacts, harmless. Even then, when we worked together at Tower, though I dared not give it too much thought, I sensed what Tommy's childhood was like. But soon, I knew, emptied of its ghosts, we would settle the estate.

We stood in separate bins, looking out at the factory. Fuck the money, I decided. I could wait to sell the house and we could honor our father correctly during *Chuseok*, the "Korean Thanksgiving."

"You know, they're probably meeting at the bar. For Cal," he said. Had I been away from the union that long—we'd had at least three post-shift memorials while I'd worked down at Tower. I drove quickly to Red Rock, a local bar. The truth is, I was a little angry with Tommy for not mentioning it before. It's not that we didn't need to have the conversation, but we could have had it at the bar while surrounded by my old union friends.

Maybe he'd purposely waited to tell me. I ran into a couple of my friends, but it was obvious that they were on their way home, tired, and I didn't keep them long. Some of them had become religious and were happy to tell me about it; some of them were getting divorced. Nothing really new. The foreman was there, but he was busy talking to someone. He was on cleanup duty, it seemed, and was holding the framed photo of Cal they'd displayed on the bar.

It only felt a little strange ordering beer at eight in the morning. "Well?" I said to Tommy as I handed him a Miller Lite. Bars. When you're young, you expect a lot. Movies and TV promise light-up counters, swordfish trophies on the walls which later become weapons in the inevitable bar fight, tits, and knives. Red Rock was just a dim neon-lit room with a broken pool table. Ol' Babyface was at a table with a couple other Tower workers. I'd never seen them before, but I could tell from the red eyes, the way they rubbed at the paper-dust grit on their necks. Aside from that, there were three people at the bar. They were older; maybe they owned the place. They were watching us, not bothering to look away when our eyes met.

That's the other thing about being back in the towns outside Wilkes-Barre—everyone's white but you. Even though I wore the smell of Tower's glue, I was still a foreigner. We didn't have the grit and we'd lost the edge that makes the general public back away, that anger the builds up through the shift and follows you home. How obvious to everyone that we didn't belong there. And there's that weird paranoia again: Someone plays Neil Diamond's "Coming to America" on the jukebox and you wonder if it's a joke at your expense. You watch each gesture, listen to every intonation because they might be clues to determine who really fucking hates you. If you keep thinking about it, you remember that some white people can't differentiate one Asian person from another. Maybe that glare is actually directed at the last Asian dude who drank here. Someone stands up and moves toward you and you tense up. Can't flinch, can't show that you're nervous.

"Are we done here?" Tommy said. He wanted the feeling of

motion again, to see the lines on the highway knowing in a blink they'd be long behind us.

"Bald fellow bought you these," the bartender said, setting down two Yuenglings in front of us.

"Thanks," I said, but Tommy sent his back. The bartender gave him a weird look and walked away. I drank mine quickly. My peace came from breathing the cold, metal-scented air and knowing none of us—my father, Cal, or Tommy—would ever have to walk through these doors again. I figured Tommy could tell Baby how he really felt about him or maybe just seeing two ghosts from the past would be enough. Our presence would haunt him for the rest of his life or something. One accepts his peace offering, one rejects it. What does it mean? Think about it, motherfucker, until it's all you can think about and you get ulcers and headaches from it.

"Can we go now?" Tommy said.

"You know, if someone buys you a drink, you have to talk to them for five minutes," I said.

"Whose rule is that?"

"It's an unspoken rule."

"Wouldn't that just apply to dudes buying women drinks?" We argued about how the rule might apply in gay bars and about the consequences for breaking it.

"Is that why you sent it back? So you wouldn't have to talk to Baby?" I said.

"Fuck off."

"'Cause I'll go talk to him. I don't care."

"What will you talk about?"

"NASCAR."

"Seriously, enough."

"Pickup trucks. The new Ford F-150."

"Well, he's gone anyway," Tommy said. I looked over and saw his table was empty. Some bills on the table and the smoking ashtray were the only signs anyone had been there.

"See that? Now he's gone. That means we can go," he said. But Baby was now sitting at the bar. He was on the other side of the older people, hunched over. *He's moving closer to us,* I thought. Pretty soon he'd be sitting at the next table. But he was doing so slowly, as if he were loath to come near us. I wondered if Cal ever got tired and even for a second hated the youthful tide that appeared at Tower summer after summer.

"You could explain why you sent back the beer," I said.

"I sent back the beer so I *wouldn't* have to go talk to him."

"So now you're punishing him by not talking? Why don't you spread rumors about him at the hairdresser's and ask for your clothes back?"

"I'm thinking."

"Come on," I said. He stood up and put on his coat. Our former line boss walked over and Tommy sat down, still in his coat, and stared at Baby with a look of pure hatred. Time had done nothing to dull his anger.

"How's it going?" I said to Baby. He nodded, not looking at me, and picked up his cigarette.

"I was gonna apologize for being hard on you boys," he said. He let out a long stream of smoke toward the ceiling. "So I'm sorry."

I didn't know what to say. I hadn't expected this—something cruel would have been easier to answer. In that empty bar, it would have been great to make a scene, throw some chairs around.

"It's all right," was all I could think to say.

"Do you even remember my name?" Tommy said, looking directly at him.

"We get hundreds of you...college kids and temps a year. Nothing personal. But I remember you, sure. Hard to forget," Baby said. He was trying hard, but I could tell he was glad there were witnesses, that there was daylight outside.

"Some of us...it's easier..." *Easier to make peace with the past, with guys like you.* That's what I was trying to say, but I let it trail off like a jet of smoke, dissipate in the air.

"The future, it belongs to folks like you," Baby said.

"Maybe," I said. I had no idea what he meant.

"It's a free country. That used to mean something else. Now it means we're giving everything away," he said. Tommy stared into my empty glass.

"Amen," I said, ready to store the next few lines of redneck-spew that came out of his mouth. On the drive home, we could draw a target on everything he said, mock it over those long five hours.

It was one of those "you kids have so much more to deal with than we did" conversations. Caught up in being the Bigger Man, I couldn't just walk away. He went on about the polar bears, anthrax spores, teenage pregnancy, black-on-black crime, the gangs with the body armor. "This city's infested with Mexicans. You know that, right? They used to only come out at night, like the roaches. But now they're—"

I just sat and nodded, fuming into my beer. He must have thought I was commiserating.

"You've got it together," he said, looking at the two of us. Whether "you" referred to Asians or my generation or something else, I wasn't sure. But he seemed confident I knew what he was talking about. "This whole area they've given over to people from the outside. Come down from New York to escape the crime, except now they're running drugs up and down our I-80. They get Section 8, they get every chance in the world. I don't mind if people leave a bad situation, but for Christ's sake. We're outnumbered, can't hold onto nothing. Guys like us, even good men like Cal—we know we're running out of time. They're gonna pull it all down. Just come in and take it. So, you know what you have to do."

"You're describing all this shit, these problems like they just magically appeared," I said. Baby, with his shallow breathing, drunk at 8 AM with coffee on his breath, the pot belly, desperate hope in the eyes. Who was this bloated racist corpse to ask anything of me? And what exactly was I supposed to do? I stood to leave.

"Does it matter?" he said. I threw a tip on the table for the sake of the next Asian guy who walked into this sorry place. "I mean, does it matter who's to blame?" he said. The peace I had earlier vanished and it must have showed. The foreman, perhaps sensing the cloud of ugly, walked over. Baby pulled him a new chair from a different table, then walked away.

"How you been, Jason?" the foreman said as he sat down. He was about to leave and was holding Cal's picture on his lap, under the table. I nodded, a little stunned by his sudden appearance. I always felt a little uncomfortable in his presence. I composed myself and told him I was doing great, really great. The foreman nodded toward Tommy but they didn't say anything to each other. "How's school going?" he said.

"It's really going well. I'm making a lot of friends, learning a lot in my classes. Pittsburgh is great. There's so much to do."

"All right," the foreman said, smiling. He paused. "Cal...would have been proud of you." Those words stopped me in my tracks. My mouth opened a little but I didn't know what to say. "Your father would have been proud of you," he said after a pause. He kind of looked down, as if embarrassed, as if this was a line he wasn't comfortable delivering. But then he almost nodded, feeling the truth of the words. And it was the truth, to him. "I'm not saying I'm not in love with the grit, but sometimes you wonder how things might have went," he said. "Especially at my age." He put his hands on the table and paused before he stood up. "Take care, Jason."

"You too," I said. We were basically the only customers left at the bar and finished our beers quickly. Tommy held the door for me and we left without speaking. I suppose it's an appropriate image for an old mining town—the cities of the dead below, where they huddle and whisper, their hopes and desires and mistakes forming its own energy that rises up to the surface with a gentle yet insistent pull. What did everyone want from me? That pull suddenly didn't feel so gentle—it became clear the world wanted something, quite possibly more than I could give.

26

THE PARTY TO END ALL PARTIES

Back to Pittsburgh, making a right turn toward Oakland just as the gray downtown skyscrapers emerge from the horizon. There was never any parking outside Tommy's house, so we made plans in the parking lot. He made some calls and Kate walked over to retrieve him.

"Hey," she said as she saw me. I had the passenger side door open and since Tommy was still on the phone, she sort of grabbed the roof and leaned over, looking through me. We ignored each other. Rows and rows of cars—the sun glinted nicely off their roofs. There was something appropriate about a parking lot being the center of Oakland. It gave a sense of interchangeability, the dynamics of motion sliding on a still black plane, leaked oil and gas seeping into the ground. And the immortal garbage that will blow through the streets long after we're gone. Two smells always present in Oakland: sewage seeping upwards from antique pipes and pizza from countless neighborhood shops. We breathed through our mouths. Kate must have finally gotten bored because she asked me, "How was Wilkes-Barre?"

"Still there," I said.

"You seem more laid back," she said.

"Really?" I was tired from the five-hour drive, sure, but I'd

220

spent most of it thinking about Tower, that funny little caricature in my mind. I wanted to explain to her what happened, what the trip had meant to the two of us. Looking at Kate, I wanted to repair the distance between us.

"I'm sure you'll find something new to worry about," she said. I felt my mouth twist and something nasty rise. I was about to respond when Tommy interrupted.

"Cancel your plans this weekend," he said, tossing his phone on the dashboard. "Lots of people coming over."

I'd done an impressive job leveling the chemicals in my body. It wasn't an exact science. Cigarettes counteract the alcohol, energy drinks slow the effects of vodka, and I could time the crash for when I absolutely need to sleep. But I gave all that up when I met Laura. I stopped drinking every night and almost quit smoking, quit smoking marijuana completely. It was strange, being healthy. I didn't welcome it at first. All that energy, sunshine in the veins. You feel the suddenness of a fast-moving world through which you'd previously trudged through, sleepwalking. But I had Laura as my Virgil—and what a world to step into. Rediscover, maybe, but finding something again still counts as exploration, if you ask me. I didn't get winded walking up a flight of stairs. Scrapes and cuts healed the next day—it felt like I'd developed superpowers. I walked to the party glowing with health.

Kate's recent words became a self-fulfilling prophecy—I became obsessed over spending my life worried. I stood on the fire escape of my North Oakland apartment and looked at the homeless people gathered around the dumpster below, the protests in the distance moving through the streets like an unruly dragon dance. I watched the shadow of the Cathedral of Learning lengthen. That weird sensitivity—I felt like an antenna constantly overloaded but I couldn't turn off the signal. Everywhere there was fear and panic. How could I just ignore it? It was a long walk and I arrived late to the party as usual. Kate walked out the door as I was coming in. I'd seen that look on her face before. She was storming out, angry at Tommy. We didn't speak.

Laura wore a dress made of a silk-like fabric, something one might wear to a homecoming dance. Someone had spent a lot of time with her hair—now, her bangs swept across her forehead, her hair curled at the bottom. She must have thought "TMI party" was some kind of debutante ball, something the older kids wore tuxes to. I was wearing a pair of jeans which were about an inch too long and caught under my shoes when I walked and a rugby shirt I'd bought at the Goodwill. I wasn't the sharpest dressed man there, but I certainly wasn't the worst. It was around eleven and Tommy was wall-hugging drunk. Laura seemed newly comfortable with the fact that she was overdressed and held a red cup full of water on her lap. I only caught the end of their conversation, but here's how I imagine the beginning.

Laura: "Where's Jason?"

Tommy: "Wow, you're heavenly."

Laura: "Ha."

Tommy: "I remember you. The restaurant, right?"

Laura: "That waiter. Jason and I've talked about you."

Tommy: "He's never said anything about you, really." He pretends to think, then dismisses it. "Thinking hurts. I'm more a man of action."

Laura: "So I've heard."

Tommy: "Yeah."

Laura: "So..."

Tommy: "Oh, right. You're looking for my wayward brother. He's probably doing a keg stand with a joint up his nose."

Laura: "I don't think so. He's changed."

Tommy: "Mmm. We were normal once, you know. Lived in a house together with a father. But then, something happened when he left us. And we've been on opposite sides of the line ever since, pushing and shoving. A couple inches here and there, but I'm not sure we've gone anywhere." There's a pause. "So, you two met at a soup kitchen? I know he likes free food, but I didn't think he'd stoop that far—"

Laura: "I thought he never talked about me."

Tommy: "Did I say that? Oh, he might have mentioned

something. My memory...my God, your hair is lovely. How do you women do that?"

Laura: "You know, he never said much about you."

Tommy: "Well, that's the thing about smooth talkers. In the end, that's all you're left with." He spills his beer on the couch, then gets up to sit next to her. "But you can't throw away everything, right? Like, sometimes you need to look at things real hard..."

———

"Get up, get up." Kate shook me, my head rolling from side to side. "Jason, wake up." I sat up, falling back to the pillow. Her face was inches from mine. She'd recently eaten an apple.

"Your door was open," she said. "Is all of your stuff still here?"

"Laura," I said, rolling over and closing my eyes.

"I don't know...where she is," Kate said. She pulled away the covers. "Come on, you have to get up." I did, feeling the room spin. Sometime in the night, I must have slammed into the wall, knocking down my bulletin board. I'd spent the night drunkenly kicking and rolling, swimming in concert flyers and photographs. Kate helped me stand.

"Tommy's on something bad," she said, brushing thumbtacks off the mattress. We both knew what this meant: drugs. Babysitting. I couldn't remember anything from the party.

"Not again," I said. My hands stung and I looked down at them. There were angry abrasions on my palms.

"And he has to give a speech today." I stifled a laugh and she glared at me. I stared at her big gray eyes and composed myself, imitating her seriousness in hope of absorbing it.

"For what class?"

"Speech midterm. I think he's on acid. And he won't listen to me. Come on, communications major." This is an agony every communications major can relate to. No one (and I mean absolutely no one) knows anything about the field of communications except that it instantly enables complete understanding of—and the ability to converse with—every single person on the planet. People think "communications major" and picture C-3PO. I've spent a considerable amount of time convincing people I am not a protocol droid, and still. "In my experience, classes are usually easier the second time around," I told her.

"He's already failed it twice."

"Third then." She waited.

"Well let's go." On the way out, I checked my messages. There was one from Laura, saying she still loved me and not to worry too much but I needed help and to call her back today (please it's important, her tone implied). I walked out the door, rubbing my face, which felt rubbery, not my own.

While Kate tossed a couple bagels in the toaster oven for me, I stared at Tommy, who sat more or less comatose. He was somewhere else entirely—the few times I'd seen him like that in college, I worried that he'd never return. We should have taken him to a hospital. When she returned from the kitchen, Kate laid out her plan.

"Obviously Mr. Shit-for-brains over there won't be helping us save his grade," Kate said. I looked up from the textbook she'd handed me. I'd never heard her curse before. "So we're gonna have to boogie here. Class in one hour. CMU is a ten-minute run from here. Do the math."

"Just because I'm Asian..."

"No time for that. Come on. She handed me a paper he'd already written. "Let's go, let's go." At the time, I found her manic energy cute. I like strong women and I'd never seen this side of her before, untempered feminine determination. Looking back, I think it was more desperation. She'd sought my help, after all. She must have felt it, too—Tommy was slipping away. He began to make a humming noise and she threw a book at him. "You need to graduate, jackass. Before you end up..." *Like your brother.* "Fucked."

For the next half hour, I tried to talk him back to reality, occasionally punching him in the chest. He sat glassy-eyed and uncommunicative. I imagined he heard my voice at first in the distance, floating above the clouds of his dream world. Then, slowly growing louder and distorted until something in his ears popped and then clarity. I read him the speech he'd written. (It wasn't clear exactly what it was about.) Time might have brought him out of this, but we didn't have any. I noticed a few signs of life, some attempt to return from whatever cold in which he'd spent who knows how many lifetimes. Kate dressed him, clipped on a tie. I spent the last ten minutes drawing arrows to emphasize points he should make, traced over his opening statement in red pen to make it more visible. As we hustled him out the door, I wondered if he had enough bullshit in his brain to fertilize this project. Lord knows we'd exhausted most of it throughout our college careers—I've always feared that, despite its ubiquity, bullshit is a non-renewable resource. But maybe he could pull it off. "Let's go," she said, grabbing Tommy's arm. He made a pained noise as we pulled him out of the room and down the steps.

The wind cut through the houses and corner shops, carrying the smell of garlic and dough. Kate looked at Tommy and noted that he looked a little saner, hopefully shaken from his stupor by the walk. As we reached the classroom, she grabbed Tommy's lapels and slammed him against a wall, holding him up with a strength that surprised me. "Listen to me. Just read what's on the paper. Look up every now and then, okay? You can't fail this, not again. *Do not fuck up.*" He nodded and she kissed him. We followed him into a classroom that looked more like a corporate boardroom. We sat in the back. There were about fifteen students, and a beefy kid wearing a black hoodie was giving a speech on massage therapy. As I sat down for a moment, flashes of the previous night returned to me with sickening clarity.

"Did you see him upstairs? With Laura?" I asked Kate.

"No. And stop talking," she whispered. When his name was called, Tommy shambled to the podium, the speech flapping in his hand like a bleeding wing. The students leaned forward, wondering who this newcomer was. Even the professor seemed surprised.

"Mister...Han, nice of you to join us." Tommy stared at the podium, no doubt watching the grain swim, the tiny black lines curling beneath his paper. "Any time, please." After smoothing out the paper, he closed his eyes. The students leaned in closer.

The party the night before. I remembered walking in on Tommy and Laura. They were in the living room, some of his sketches hanging above the orange couch. There were torchiere lights and a Naugahyde throw, college-student interior design. Aside from that, the room was empty, party-proofed to stave off theft and property damage. Rap music came from the basement. The way the floor was shaking from the bass during the choruses, the dust from the carpet rose with each heavy beat. Looking back, I picture roaches and beer cans leaping from the carpet in rhythm, the melted ice in the keg bucket rippling.

"We were just talking about you," Laura said, reaching for me.

"I was giving a Girl Scout troop directions to North Oakland," I said. I didn't want to admit that I'd spent the last two hours trying to exorcise the demon of worry from my system by burning a paper on which I'd written down my obsessions. You can imagine how effective that was. She didn't believe me, so I tried to kiss her on the cheek. She pulled away. "They had a cat with a broken paw. They were trying to heal it with cookies, but I told them they needed to go to a veterinarian. In the end, the vet put a neon orange cast on its little kitty paw."

Tommy couldn't follow my nonsense, so he continued their conversation. "It's really hard, you know. Growing up the way I did. You have all this…freaking…viscera, like broken glass mixed in with the happy experiences. And you can't help but resent everything. Even if you suspect it might not all be bad."

"Like what?" Laura said.

"Well, you know when you're trying to feed a wild animal—say, a bird. Right? And you're holding bread or whatever in your hand. And the bird wants to get it, but it doesn't trust you, so it flutters and jumps around, thinking about which direction to take?"

"Who wants a drink?" I said. I knew what he was doing. Right in front of my face. I saw it with absolute sober clarity. I had no idea what they were talking about but knew I had to break it up, and soon.

"Like, you know the right thing but don't entirely trust it," Tommy said. He'd mastered an earnest look and was focusing hard on maintaining it. Something in the eyes. He knew how to hold it just long enough to draw them in.

"You know exactly what you're doing," I said, and made sure he knew exactly what I meant.

"Sometimes I feel so lost. There's so much stuff out there...and all I need is just one thing—one light—to guide me through."

"But that's the thing—there are so many lights. How do you know which one is real?" Laura said. Now she was sitting up, and I could see that she wanted to take his hands in hers. She settled for putting a hand on his forehead and holding the other in the air, ready to receive His divine word.

"I've been so numb...what is that?" Tommy said.

"This is bullshit," I said. Laura looked at me with an expression I'd never seen before. Contempt for my unforgivable blasphemy. But I was cursing something else entirely—how to explain that to her?

"We're going upstairs," she said. Tommy didn't look at me. Things might have been much different if he'd seen the look on my face. But he knew enough to look toward his goal, his bed upstairs. And so they went, to their own private rapture. Below, I stood looking up the staircase, my hand on the railing as I put my foot on the bottom step. The dirt and roaches rose and fell in rhythm around me. Going upstairs to interrupt would tell Laura I had no faith in her. Did I?

Meanwhile at Carnegie Mellon University, Tommy's speech wasn't going well. "We are here to discuss the weight of things," he said, quietly tapping on the podium. This was not the speech he'd written, but I didn't care. I thought of a million other ways I could have spent that morning. Kate made a groaning sound, just loud enough for me to hear. This was it: He had fucked up irreversibly, for the last time. Again. He discussed love (capital L the way he said it) and hate, how they sort of mix, although he didn't put it as delicately or articulately as what I just summarized. I could have helped him as he repeated "people equals shit, think about it."

The professor was enjoying this too much to interrupt. To him, there must have been some justice to this spectacle: Here, watch the fuck-ups fuck up. A cautionary example for those who actually had futures. I could have stood up and said, "I think what he's trying to say is _____," I could have stood next to him at the podium, absorbed some of the laughter. "My brother is very sick..." But I did nothing, sat and watched him stone-faced. He looked at me and realized how much I knew. He stopped talking. Neither of us moved. He opened his mouth to add something, but the instructor finally cut him off.

People equals shit, indeed. I did go into Tommy's bedroom later that night. My stomach was in knots and the alcohol had finally done its work as I sat downstairs drinking. I'd thrown up twice as I ascended the stairs, practically dragging myself along the hallway and clawing at the wall as I pushed open his door and leaned in, holding onto the frame, prepared as I ever would be for the awful scene inside. My Laura was there, sleeping in his bed. She was in her clothes and Tommy was gone. Who knows how much time had passed since they went upstairs—certainly enough. Enough time. To. Everyone had gone home and the house was dark. What time did our parties usually end? Questions, and it was all I could do not to shake her and start screaming.

There were paintings I'd never seen before lying on the floor. Somewhere in the seduction, he'd trotted these beauties out. In the streetlight, there was something silver and weightless about them. They were mostly watercolors, skeletal like his sketches. His pencil outlines bloomed into reds and oranges. One showed sparse trees growing from the slag piles. Near the foot of his bed were two more: one of the inside of Tower, watercolors perfect for the rows of fluorescent lights that once floated above us. The last was of the two of us, Tommy and me. It looked nothing like the other two. Colors bled outward in strange outlines: We looked like silhouettes. We looked so young. Underneath the bed was a brass urn about the size of a football, the streetlight glinting dully off its smooth sides.

Carnegie Mellon University. Me, exiting the classroom. "Tell him I'm selling the house. He'll know what it means," I said to Kate, who obviously didn't know what it meant. She nodded absently and walked toward the instructor like she was going to her death. When I got back to my apartment, the blinking red light on my answering machine was the only light in my apartment. I ignored it and went to bed. If I closed my eyes for a few days and let the world move on without me, things would be better when I resurfaced. The chaos could wait. It made me sick just to think about Laura. To hear guilt in her voice when we talked would be so much worse than the constant questions: No she didn't, of course she didn't. They just prayed. It's the opposite of what you think.

Sometimes my phone would ring late at night and I'd answer, expecting to hear Laura's voice. But we'd both seen this coming. On our last date a week before the party to end all parties, we rode the inclines. We rode up the Mon Incline into Mount Washington, land of immaculate restaurants and flat surfaces. Land of beautiful views, where you can see the city spread beneath you in a bright electric triangle. We wandered and passed through what felt like the entire city and floated back down on the Duquesne Incline. It was a perfect night, like a dance, the last of the evening. Even now, when I picture downtown, I can still see the entire distance laid out between the glowing incline tracks. Those clean lines of demarcation—both of us knew we could only go so far.

27

I STILL LOVE YOU, MS. ------

It was April in Pittsburgh, two weeks after the TMI party. The city's lack of money led to a lack of police, which led to a drug war. Although my apartment was in a nice part of town, the other side of the street was mostly crack houses. I didn't want to be the fifth person gunned down on my street, so I moved back to South Oakland, finding a small studio apartment next to Club Laga. I busied myself with the logistics of moving, which kept my mind off other issues for a while. While I unpacked, loud music filtered through the pipes and insulation.

The gutter punks converged outside with their cardboard signs and body odor. One of them yelled, "Slap a skinhead. Onnne dollah." Next to him, a short, bald white kid *Sieg Heiled* passing doctors and professors. A woman pushing a baby carriage walked by and he put his hand down. The blind black panhandler up the street sang "There is a Balm in Gilead" while his homeless friends kept watch over his change cup. More gutter punks arrived. The new group had a pit bull. Someone lit incense and I slammed my window shut. I hadn't eaten in two days and my left hand was numb. Maybe there was a connection. I ate some ketchup packets in the fridge.

One of the messages on my answering machine was from my realtor. Someone was interested in buying the house. I signed lots of papers. She said there were more coming. I wanted to sell everything I owned or just throw it away. Pittsburgh felt so much like a monument to everything that had gone wrong in my life. I started to think about Laura and decided to take Leslie's offer to return "home" to Princeton, even though she'd made it five years ago. There wasn't an expiration date, I hoped. Despite how much I was relishing the freedom of being single, I needed to get out of the city. God forbid I should walk into Tommy and Laura on the street, a happy couple eating ice cream together. So, just as the sun came out from the clouds and a wicked headache started to bloom, I got in my car and drove. I hadn't slept in what felt like weeks and it was night by the time I reached Philadelphia. The highway lights hovered and exploded as I flew past.

As I reached Trenton, my car started to overheat. The engine was nearly aflame as I crossed into Princeton. As I drove up the doctor's driveway and stumbled out of the car, the world around me somehow felt lighter. Everything evaporated, the tension pouring off my body like steam after a long shower. Smoke poured from the hood and the hissing noise grew louder. Feeling returned to my legs and I stood. I knew the doctor and Leslie had taken on a new boarder—force of habit, I guess. We had a couple brief conversations when I called looking for Leslie and he went to find her. He was a thin shuffling man with wavy brown hair, bad teeth, and a hippie beard. He worked as an EMT in a city outside Princeton but had been laid off. The doctor volunteered at local hospitals, so that's how they'd probably met. Didn't ask. Didn't care. Dan was wearing a green T-shirt partially covered by a gray fedora resting on his chest.

"Nice hat," I said.

"Nice car," he said. He picked up the hat and fanned himself with it. "Quality American craftsmanship." My car was a Honda CRX.

"Are they home?" I said. He didn't respond, but I saw his eyes following something on the road behind me. I turned around. There was an older woman power-walking past the house. She was pale, dark-haired, maybe in her early fifties.

"Hi!" Dan shouted. She quickened her pace, turning her head to stare at the house on the opposite side of the street as she passed. "Hey!" he yelled as she almost ran into our mailbox. She turned just in time, sidestepping to avoid a collision. She stumbled and almost fell, trying to regain her balance, and careened out of view. Dan made a grunting noise and replaced the hat on his chest. I opened the screen door and knocked. A moment later, Leslie opened the door.

Borscht was probably the last thing I wanted, but once, over a decade ago, I mentioned that I enjoyed the cold beet soup she'd served. It was an offhand remark, meant to be polite, but she served that meal every special occasion, especially the rare times my father and Tommy visited. Dan came in and we had a bland conversation about what we were up to. Leslie returned from the grocery store with beets and said she was sewing her own clothes now, making them from patterns recalled from childhood. "Because I remember my mother doing it," she said. The doctor was doing volunteer work at the hospital. When I asked what Dan was up to, he made a sweeping motion with his hand, gesturing to the house in general, I suppose, and went back to his soup. Leslie was clearing the table when the doctor came home.

He looked the same—thinning silver hair combed straight back. His beard had thinned and there were deep lines around his mouth. He stuck his hands in his pockets as he looked me over. "How's school?" he said.

"Good," I told him.

"I see." He had a deep voice which, like a smoker's (though he was not) had grown raspier as he'd aged. His speech pattern had also changed. It was slower with more pauses. "And. What brings. *You*...to Princeton?"

"I don't know," I said.

"What?" he said, leaning closer.

"It's complicated," I said.

"Isn't school still in session?" Leslie said.

"About that. I'm not sure." I said. The doctor stared at me, waiting for an answer. He almost raised an eyebrow and walked off to join Leslie in the kitchen. I hadn't sent them my grades in quite some time.

"How *is* Pittsburgh?" Dan asked me. Leslie had already asked, but I gave him a more straightforward answer.

"The word 'nosedive' comes to mind."

"Got that right. Takes more than a fat man and a gay quarterback to reach the big dance. *Kordell Who?*" His knees popped as he stood and put his soup in the microwave.

I woke around 2 PM the next day. There were a bunch of pamphlets on the table about time management and positive study habits. Leslie's work, no doubt. This was how we kept in touch while I was away at college. I think she mistook my interest in communications for an interest in writing. She sent Langston Hughes poems and *New York Times* articles about the craft of writing. After I told her I was declaring communications as my major, she started sending me Ms. —— novels. I kept hoping for a signed copy but never received one.

I think I sent her one article in all those years, something about gardening I'd found in a campus newspaper. She occupied a strange place in my families. Because she was a cancer survivor, she had short hair, which puzzled my father. When I was fourteen, she got the idea to drive me to Wilkes-Barre to spend a special magic surprise weekend with my father and Tommy. The only comfort I took in that awkward visit was the fact that she seemed even more confused and out of place than me. After that, she never offered to drive me "home" and I never asked.

She had worked as a freelance writer once—features for newspapers, profiles of local fame and talent. I remember overhearing that at a party, one of those "do you still" conversations that drift into uncomfortable ellipses. I think she understood the point where things become irretrievable.

It was nice out. Humid, but not oppressively so. We were shucking corn and there was something pleasant about the smell as we threw the husks in the basket, something vague and pastoral that stirred childhood memories. They had a large front yard, perfectly rectangular and dandelion-free. The house was surrounded on both sides by tall elms, evenly spaced through the neighborhood. They gave a sense of order and timelessness. Across the street there was a large white colonial with black shuttered windows. Like the rest of the neighborhood, the front lawn was immaculate, as were the dark purple-black bushes that lined the stone walkway to the front door. "New neighbors—the Lindens," Leslie said. I nodded. "And those are Linden trees," she said, pointing to the pair of trees that stood on either side of their front door.

"Clever," I said.

"They're generally resistant to disease—the trees, not so much the family. But every year those trees attract wasps and Dr. Linden is allergic."

"Maybe not so clever," I said. She flicked a few strands of corn silk. The wind carried them onto the lawn.

"Here comes the Author," Leslie said, motioning to the dark-skinned woman again jogging past the house. Her hair was dark, almost blue, even at her age. There was an athletic wrapping on her left leg and she sort of shuffled, breathing heavy. She was carrying a magazine rolled in her hand. Eyeing our mailbox, she slowed her pace and swung wide of it. She looked over at us. Leslie waved. The Author let the magazine spring open and raised it to cover her like a suspect on the TV news. She kept it there as she passed. Leslie's eyes followed her until she was out of sight. She flicked another handful of corn silk into the basket.

"Is that..." I asked. I was sure I'd recognized her the previous day, but this strange jogger seemed different from the Ms. —— I remembered.

"The doctor once called her 'That Damned Author,' and it stuck." The photos on the back cover must have been decades old. Two generations of men in my family loved her. Even though I'd met her as a child, it was surreal to see her after reading so many of her books—it was like someone walking off a movie screen into the audience. But why was she covering her face?

"It's been like this ever since she moved here," Leslie said. "The whole thing started when you were about ten. Mrs. Parks and I had started our daily walk through the neighborhood. This was when the Author had just moved in. Well, Mrs. Parks and I were out walking and the Author saw us as she came around the corner. We waved and paused, hoping to welcome her to the neighborhood but as soon as she saw us, she literally turned her nose up and started staring toward the sky. And, still craning her neck skywards, she crossed the street—a completely graceless maneuver, I should add, and walked into a tree. We moved to help her but she got up and ran away limping."

"Weird," I said.

For a while, Leslie thought *she* might have been the problem. Or maybe there was a meteor shower or falling satellite. But after a few similar encounters and talking to fellow neighbors, she realized this is how the Author generally treated strangers. "We," meaning the doctor and she, "were dining at the Ferry House when we saw some friends—another surgeon he knew and his wife. Ms. —— was sitting at their booth and when we approached to say hello to our friends, she stared at the wall and began fidgeting. I half expected her to stand up and bolt, but our surgeon friend was sitting to the outside, blocking her. Ha." She made a victorious punching motion with her hand.

"So she has friends in Princeton," I said.

"I hear she's generous to her friends, although I'm not sure what the word means to her. I suppose she doesn't flee in terror when she sees them." I wondered aloud whether Ms. —— would talk to me. Leslie said she doubted it. "I think as a writer she uses her walks to compose and she's terrified of being interrupted. Or maybe she had bad experiences with people before. But you should have seen her, Jason. I really think that if she was sitting to the outside, she would have ran. And we weren't even there to see a famous author. As if anyone in this town would chase her down to have a book signed." I remembered something when she mentioned a book being signed, but I pushed the thought away. "It's a sad case, though. Dan told me he's dyslexic, among other things, and never enjoyed reading. But during high school, he picked up one of her books and spent an entire weekend locked in his room with it, which was completely new. It was through this that he came to realize what people enjoy about reading, what he'd been missing. Since then, he's moved on, but you should have seen him when he heard she lived nearby. He's always wanted to thank her, let her know what it meant to him. But, of course..." She finished shucking the last ear of corn and placed it in the basket.

"It's gotten better. Sometimes, depending on which way I walk, if she can't avoid me, I can get her to wave. I have to use a certain tone, though. It took a long time. It took years for her even to look at me." She glanced around at the street, as if she was expecting the Author to pass by. She stood up and opened the screen door.

"What time do you usually go walking?" I asked, following her into the kitchen.

Shortly before eleven that night, I was brushing my teeth when I noticed the bathroom window was open. I heard someone coughing and saw Dan sitting on the roof, his back to me. I climbed out and joined him, making enough noise so he didn't startle and fall when I sat down next to him. He had something in his hand. "That looks like a marijuana pipe," I said.

"Really?" He stared at it incredulously, rotating it in his hand.

"I've seen them in movies. Also, read about them in literature."

"This one doesn't have a carb. Like a crack pipe," he said apologetically. He passed it to me, but I just handed it back. In our present location, we were shielded from most of the night breeze by the roof of the house's east wing. To our other side was a row of tall elms which formed a black canopy above us. The streetlight fell through the branches in irregular shapes like camouflage. The roof outside the bathroom was recessed a few feet, which heightened the feeling of being hidden from the world. The smell of marijuana still lingered faintly, but underneath was the pleasant smell of old wood and dry grass. He dumped out the pipe's contents, nearly upsetting his beer.

"Your mother wants to know how your writing's going. I told her you've won several local awards." Dan was amused at Leslie's misunderstanding of my career choice. For her, books meant communication. For me, communication meant communication.

"Pitt's renaming their library after me," I said.

"Have they erected a statue in your honor?"

"It's like Penn State's obnoxious Paterno statue, only I'm holding a book as I burst through the wall. Here, allow me to show you this year's writing journal. I should point out that it's a Moleskine journal, the preferred brand for Hemingway and Picasso. And Chatwin."

"Holy shit. Must have cost a fortune," he said, flipping through it. He held it up, trying to catch the light. There were five pages of notes taken from a research project on women, followed by three pages of conjugated Italian swear words, followed by a few drawings of penises. After that, it was blank.

"Someone else drew those," I said. He handed it back to me. There was a long silence, during which he flicked his lighter several times.

"Who's Chatwin?"

"I don't know," I said.

"I'm writing a play," he said, flicking his lighter again. "Did I tell you that?" I told him no, I hadn't heard. "It's about a man who hates borscht. But no, seriously." I offered to take a look at his work when he was done.

"Same to you," he said.

"You just saw this year's *oeuvre*," I told him.

Around noon the next day, the doctor took me for a drive around Princeton. Before we left, he tried to invite Dan but there was no response when we knocked on his door.

"How is Pittsburgh?" the doctor said as we drove into town.

"Pretty wretched," I said.

"Really? Wretched," he said, drawing the word out. He frowned and tapped the steering wheel. "I knew it was in decline in the 80s after the mills closed. You should have seen the rivers back then. The whole area was, as you say, *wretched*. My understanding is that they'd cleaned it up, though. Dr. Linden's daughter Nancy went to school there in the early nineties and liked it. But you say it's in decline."

"She went to Pitt?" I said.

"Duquesne." He turned left at a brown three-story mansion. "There's Grover Cleveland's estate. The president. But yes, Nancy went to law school at Duquesne. Is that near your school?"

"Not really. It's closer to downtown Pittsburgh. Maybe wretched is too strong a word."

"You lived there, paid taxes, maybe voted. You're entitled to your opinion," he said. He asked if I worked while I was in school and I told him "not really." Stealing ketchup packets never felt like an actual job. He nodded, leaned back and said, "In Carnegie's steel mills, they worked twelve-hour shifts. Every other week you worked a double shift, which meant twenty-four hours before the blast furnace. The floors...so hot the workers nailed boards to the soles of their boots."

"Ouch," I said, nodding. I'd seen enough movies to imagine hissing molten rivers that occasionally crested to spray liquid metal into exhausted faces, churning machinery raining sparks onto one's exposed neck. I'd seen the abandoned mills in Homestead. From the looks of the imposing, barnlike shells that seemed to stretch forever and from the looks of the abandoned train yards and rusting hooks outside, it wasn't hard to imagine the horror inside. "...but it's the foundation from which one builds. That's how men *create*," he said. I nodded even though I missed most of what he'd said. I rolled down my window and stuck my hand out to catch the wind.

We passed through an old neighborhood, stately trees towering over the houses. I thought about my neighborhood in Pittsburgh, the smell of blooming gingko trees. I pictured the graffiti and noise from the legions of college students packed into low-rent rundown housing.

"No, wretched fits." He offered to drive past Einstein's old house and I nodded, genuinely excited. When I was younger, we visited Einstein's house every trip.

"Mercer Street," the doctor said. "There it is." The house looked nothing like my boyhood memory; for a few moments, I thought he was mistaken. Through the years, the house had grown in my mind and taken on embellishments. But I recognized the house number and the general shape. It was a yellow, two-story house. Simple. Dark bushes hid some of the front porch's neo-Greco columns and there was a stone walkway leading to the front door. As I got out to take a picture with my cell phone, it struck me that the front yard was roughly the same size as the row houses in Pittsburgh.

The doctor stayed in the car. I asked if I could take a tour of the house and he shook his head. "Einstein was a modest man," he said by way of explanation. Crisp leaves blew around my feet and when the breeze blew, I could smell someone cooking in a nearby house. A homey kind of smell. Fish, maybe.

As we drove back to the house, it struck me that there was some kind of majesty here, strength in the symmetrical rows of trees that guarded each neighborhood. In my childhood, there was something magical about the parks and tall fountains, but they still evoked something. But there'd been a shift somewhere inside me. Princeton, the city I'd grown up in, felt like a prize I hadn't earned yet. Just an idea of *home*, of rest and peace. Until then—well, I didn't know what to do.

Back at the house, I walked into Dan's room. My room was pretty much the same, but they'd turned his into a sort of terrarium—hanging plants in all the windows and a layer of potted plants sitting on the radiator near the far wall. Clothes and papers and comic books were piled around his bed and desk. He was sitting at his desk in front of an old computer. "This game's called *Castles*," he said. He pointed to a large brown square surrounded by swarming green pixels. See, I'm building that."

"Are those green things your peasants?" I said.

"I think so. The graphics are awful," he said.

"It's a Commodore 64. You're writing your play on this?" I said, flipping through a stack of five-inch floppies.

"No, on my laptop," he said, pulling a PowerBook from beneath a pile of dirty clothes. "The disc's here somewhere," he said.

The doctor walked in, holding a glass of water. "Did I ever show you the lemon tree?" he said. "Christ," he said, almost tripping over a mound of clothes. He picked up a small pot from a windowsill and held it up. It was a small bonsai tree about a foot high which had a few yellow orbs the size of marbles growing on it. "Lemons," he said, holding up the pot as if toasting me with it. "Here," he said, meaning for us to follow him. We walked into the kitchen. He made tea and plucked three lemons from the tree, cutting them in half and putting them in our teacups.

"Did you study Buddhism in school?" the doctor said. He looked at Dan for a long time, then back at me.

"Not really," I said. The tree was in the middle of the table. He picked the last remaining lemon and rolled it between his forefinger and thumb. "Maybe you'll get this anyway. They use riddles to teach. For example: *The lazy boy isn't lazy enough. If he was truly lazy enough, he would be* energized," he said, stretching out the last word. He looked from Dan's face to mine as if expecting an answer. He squeezed the lemon. Two drops fell into his tea.

"Is this like the one about one hand clapping?" Dan finally said. The doctor gripped the table and stood up, carrying his tea down the hall.

"Is it?" he asked me.

We went walking the next morning around 10 AM. It was me, Dan, and Leslie. She had threatened to burn the clothes I'd arrived in and maybe she had after she took them to wash. I was wearing some of Dan's old clothes, a pair of khakis and a thin jacket. It was dark blue and had a thick, creased collar and straps that buttoned on the shoulders, sort of like a Boy Scout uniform. It was worn and comfortable, something a respectable person might wear. Dan wore a pair of cutoff denim shorts and a blue Broncos T-shirt. Leslie wore a sort of mauve tracksuit made of material that swished when it rubbed against itself.

After we'd walked a few blocks, I looked back at Dan, who looked as if he'd just run a marathon. "How do you feel?" Do you. Feel...*energized*?" I said.

"Less talking. More walking," he said, motioning to the street.

"Why are you talking like that?" Leslie said to me. I stopped—she knew why. The neighborhood is essentially a circle with a few roads jutting out like spokes. We'd made it about halfway before encountering Ms. ——. We were rounding a corner with Leslie in front and Dan wheezing behind me. The Author almost ran into Leslie, who made a startled noise and moved aside, leaning into the bushes next to us. And there, I caught a good look at her face. She had a squarish face with high cheekbones—Indian blood? Her hair was tucked underneath a knit cap. The windbreaker she was wearing was too small, which made her look even thinner. She regarded us with horror and immediately crossed the street. She had a grim expression on her face and stared down at the sidewalk as she did this, repeating something to herself. When she reached the other side, she turned her back to us and disappeared down a side street. "Are you okay?" Dan said to Leslie, who was brushing her sleeves. We turned around and quietly walked home.

And there was an old memory, almost buried under the rest of my embarrassing childhood moments: I'd met our famous neighbor before, twice. The first time, I had been in Princeton for a year, so I must have been about 11. I was bored, the only possible result of living in such a tranquil neighborhood. I was outside on a walk when I spotted a gray cat and started following it. This wasn't due to my youthful adventurous spirit—I had stolen a pinecone from Leslie's craft room and wanted to get closer before I beaned that furry gray fucker. I found myself behind a large tan house. I distinctly remember a birdbath, a sliding glass patio door, a newly finished patio made of square stones. Ms. —— was outside and the cat ran to her. We exchanged names and she asked if I liked cats. I told her yes, I liked cats very much. I was holding the pinecone behind my back and knew she was going to get suspicious, so I decided to be clever. I held it out in front of me and asked, "Do cats eat pinecones?" as sweetly as I could.

She laughed and said something like "My heavens, no." I probably mentioned, as I told everyone back then, that I was the doctor's son. This confused people for several reasons. But she seemed impressed and fixed some hot chocolate, which she brought to me outside. We talked about cats for a while and my memory fades after that.

The second time I met her was about six months later and just as accidental. We were in a bookstore outside of town, the only major retailer at the time. It was large, two stories with an escalator, but still crowded. Leslie hated crowds but went upstairs for some reason. The Author was there. I recognized her voice and saw her standing at the podium. At first, I was only vaguely interested that the stupid woman I'd tricked and I happened to be sharing the same space again. Even as someone listed the awards she'd received, I still wasn't impressed. Almost won the Nobel Prize? Almost doesn't count. But then she started to read.

There was something about her voice—not quite as commanding as a teacher's, but somehow more powerful. How was that possible? In my memory, everyone around me was completely silent. She was reading about caves and oceans. I didn't understand half the words but there was something captivating about the story, the way she managed light and shadow on each character, the prismatic way she could describe one moment so precisely, pull so much reflection from it. I knew I was hearing something important. There was something magic about the words, as if I'd never heard those sounds before. Everyone was listening. Not just people in the store, but people all around the world were leaning toward her, straining to hear. In my mind, even the cash registers and cars outside had gone silent. Who was this woman who could freeze commerce and traffic with just her voice? I'd started the reading looking smugly at the rest of the audience but soon realized that I, too, was in her grasp. It was wonderful, a sort of surrender. She hadn't even finished when I decided that I needed to speak with her, receive the blessing of her words. Of course she would remember me. The reading concluded and the announcer indicated there would be a book signing following the reading. I didn't know what a book signing was, but I quickly found the most important book I knew and decided to present it to her. It was *Moby-Dick*, the doctor's favorite book, and Dan's.

When it was time, I made my way to the front of the line and ceremoniously presented it to her. She didn't seem to remember me. To be fair, there were many people in line. She opened the book, looked at the cover, and quickly wrote something. The person behind me went and I opened my book, expecting some kind of magic, like fireworks, to erupt from the drying ink. I squinted. Inside the front cover, she'd scribbled:

I didn't write this. Asshole.

My eleven-year-old mind reeled and I left the store immediately. Wide-eyed, I waited outside next to Leslie's locked car, my hand automatically pulling at the handle.

The next day, Leslie and I passed by the —— household on our daily walk. It was a log-cabin-style house, set back in the woods so it had an expansive front yard. In the lawn were two floodlights which were turned on the house. I could make out a Honda Accord with a mangled bumper in the driveway. In my memory, the house was made of wood: a rustic combination of long, interlocked planks and tall panes of glass. There was a fireplace inside, somewhere. I'd seen it. I told Leslie this and she squinted at the house. "Maybe they remodeled it," she said. "Let's go. I know the people across the street."

That night, the floodlights were still on. Moths swarmed around them, their frenzied shadows magnified and cast on the white arch above. It was almost dark out. The road and lawns and unlighted houses vanished as I walked home.

"What do you think a whale's belly looks like?" I asked Dan when I got home. He said he didn't know. I didn't tell him that the streetlights flickered on as I passed her house. I didn't tell him that for a second, I thought I'd seen someone peeking out through the curtain.

Two days passed and we still hadn't seen Ms. ——. When we got home from our walks, Dan would check the neighborhood through the telescope in his window, but we never caught sight of her. By the end of the week, we weren't optimistic about seeing her again. There were a lot of parks around town through which she could take a peaceful stroll and Dan was almost sure he'd seen her driving back from one.

A couple days later, Dan had a job interview. We went walking later that day. "How was your interview?" I said. He waited until our house was out of sight to answer.

"Didn't go," he said simply. We walked down a side street that didn't have a sidewalk. A blue minivan passed us. The driver waved and I waved back. Dan sat heavily on the sidewalk, back resting on a tree trunk. He was breathing heavily and slumped back. He was having a heart attack, it dawned on me. I froze, staring at him. He said no, he wasn't and stood up. Then he sat back down. "I'm okay. Seriously," he said. I'd never seen a human being so exhausted in every sense of the word. Idly, I wondered about him, the same way you look at homeless people at night when you're safe in your car and passing by. He asked how old I was and I told him. "God, I'd kill to be 22 again."

"And know what you do now?" I said.

He stood up with a little difficulty and paused before he continued walking. "Doesn't even matter."

He talked the entire walk back, but I only caught a few sentences. "Got a job lined up back in Kansas. Just have to talk to a buddy of mine. No more of this humidity and boredom. No more of the doctor's cock-blocking." I wished him luck and we circled back to the house. When it was in view, I said something like, "I'm glad you weren't having a heart attack. I wasn't about to give you mouth to mouth." We both laughed, even though neither of us thought it was funny.

The next day, Leslie served borscht again for dinner. We were halfway done eating when the doctor came in. He seemed short of breath. "That damned Author crashed her car again. Right into a pole this time," he said.

"Is she okay?" Leslie said.

"Where?" Dan said.

"I don't know. On Baker. You know how the telephone poles on Baker have patches of foliage around them. I was passing by the Silvermans' to deliver some coffee. She was already outside the car, which wasn't too badly damaged. She was sitting on the ground. I got out and asked if she was okay."

"What did she say?" I asked.

"She didn't respond. She wasn't looking at me. I think she was dazed. I told her, 'Ma'am, I'm a medical doctor,' to which she said nothing. I told her I was her neighbor, *et cetera*." He waved his hand dismissively, imitating the Author. "Finally, I told her, 'Ma'am, you're sitting in poison ivy.' She looked up and told me to go away."

"Did you call 911?" I asked. He glared at me, refusing to dignify this incredibly stupid question, then glanced over my shoulder at my bowl.

"Would you like some borscht?" Leslie asked him.

"I'm feeling rather sick," he said, walking down the hallway. "I'm going upstairs to rest a bit."

I looked at Leslie. She was folding up her towel. Dan was quiet, staring down the hall, even though the doctor wasn't there anymore. He picked at the shoulder of the orange throwback Elway jersey he was wearing. I put my silverware on the plate next to my bowl. Leslie took out a pen and started to write something on the newspaper she always kept at the table. The doctor's door slammed shut and we ran to the garage.

"You'd better drive," Dan said, motioning to his car. "Come on, Baker's only three minutes away," he said, pushing me toward the driver's seat.

"Wait," Leslie said. She walked into the garage and returned with a quilt, which she folded and placed on the passenger seat. "There," she said. "Let's go," she almost yelled at me. The unnatural volume and her clear, almost-panicked tone startled me into action. While she was in the garage, I was nervously considering the situation. I got in and started the engine, backing down the driveway.

"Turn here," Dan said. "This is Baker." We passed three or four small houses and then there was just forest on each side of the road. And there she was, still sitting in the middle of a viny patch about three yards from the telephone pole and her wrecked car. I stopped the car and backed up. Dan got out before I did.

He called Ms. — — by her first name and walked slowly over to her. She didn't stand up, but once she saw him she looked away, into the forest. "I'm an EMT," he said, which was true. She looked over at him. From the look on her face, she would have been less surprised if he'd introduced himself as John Elway. Leslie got out of the car and introduced us. She offered to drive her to a hospital. It would be quicker and would save money on the ambulance trip. It would also be more discreet, she said. Ms. —— nodded and Leslie told Dan to stop pestering her. After he backed off, she let Leslie walk her to Dan's Chevy Nova. "This is for you," Leslie said, smoothing her hand over the quilt she'd placed on the backseat. Ms. —— stared at it and, after a brief hesitation, got in.

"Well, Jason. What are you waiting for?" Leslie said. I started the car and drove. Ms. —— sort of slumped in the seat next to me, staring out the window. "Turn right at the stop sign. That'll take you to the highway," Dan said.

"You don't know how to get there?" Ms. —— said, looking at me with a tired, disapproving glance.

"Of course he does," Leslie said. "My son is not an idiot. Or an..." *asshole*, she didn't say. I silently thanked her for that, although, at the moment, I felt like a complete asshole. I didn't have a lot of time to reflect upon the situation because I was busy driving. Having never been there, I had no clue how to find the hospital. When there was a turn coming up, Dan would make a noise or nudge the seat and I would glance in the rearview mirror to see him indicating a direction, usually by jerking his head.

You know how when you're sitting in the backseat you can see the face of the person in the passenger seat reflected in the side mirrors? Well, Leslie was in perfect position to stare at her face and did so, intently. This wasn't lost on Ms.——, who looked over her shoulder a couple of times. Leslie kept on staring.

"Hello," she said sweetly, calling the Author by her first name. Leaning away from me, Ms. —— went to rest her head against the window but pulled away. She sat straight up, facing the road with me, and closed her eyes.

"You're good," Dan said out loud after another left turn. Ms. —— opened her eyes and looked back at him. We were on a sort of minor highway now, passing a few deserted restaurants. Everyone was silent for the next few miles. It was a growing, unhealthy kind of silence that reminded me of the situation in which I'd been placed. Or in which I'd placed myself. It was the kind of silence that makes one want to scream. No one seemed interested in breaking it.

"Have you ever written a play?" I blurted out, louder than I intended. Ms. —— looked over at me. "My—"

"Shut up," Dan called from the backseat.

"Never mind," I said. We were on a straight path and I spotted the sign for the hospital exit. Now that I didn't have to expend so much energy on driving, I relaxed a little and began to think. I knew I'd already blown the situation. If I had the chance, I'd have explained the situation to Ms.——, how we first met. I'm sure she'd remember me. I'd relate the second meeting in an ironic, wasn't-this-hilarious/I'm-not-pissed tone to put her at ease, and then offer to drop by her house and show her the autographed copy of *Moby-Dick* she'd signed. But as I sat next to her, I knew I couldn't enact this plan. I'd missed my chance and, and even then I knew deep down that this wasn't going to end well. Still, I could salvage it. She would remember me. When all of this was finished, she'd remember that she owed me a favor. Her mind plus my looks and charm? I couldn't even begin to imagine.

"No," I heard Dan say. But I was going the right way. I knew it. I looked back at him and the next second I felt the car swerving to the right as if of its own will. I knew I'd scraped against something and quickly pulled to the side of the road. Dan had actually said, "Whoa!" From the look on her face, the Author was screaming, but no sound came out. It was surreal, really. Maybe she'd lost most of her voice in the first accident.

"Okay, okay," I kept repeating. I took a step out of the car to see what I'd hit. There was a police car directly behind me. I'd hit a police car. I quickly got back in and shut the door.

"Fuck. Fuck me. Fuck me," Dan said to nobody in particular. Today had started with such promise. And then the cop appeared. He was young with a shaved head and, of course, sunglasses. I handed him my license and registration.

Any hope that he'd have sympathy for my situation evaporated when he looked back at Dan and said, simply, "I fucking hate the Broncos." I didn't dare look over, but I saw the cop's expression soften a little as he looked past me. "Please calm down ma'am," he said to Ms. ——. I could feel the car sort of vibrate from the gyrations she was making. "Stay in the car," he said, walking back to his squad car. His partner walked over, looked at Ms. ——, and let out a long whistle.

The car stopped shaking. Leslie said relax, everything would be fine. I looked over at my favorite Author, who was now sitting calmly, staring out the window. Her one leg was shaking, but other than that she seemed calm. I apologized. They were taking a long time back there, Dan noticed. How long had it been? I started to tell Ms. —— the story about the book signing but it all came out wrong. My hands were shaking, so I sat on them, then put them on the steering wheel in case the cops were watching and thought I was hiding drugs, although I was not. Leslie said, "Maybe it would be better if we were all quiet for now." What were they doing back there? I looked in the rearview mirror but couldn't see either cop.

I couldn't take the silence, any silence. "Do you still have that gray cat?" I asked Ms. ——. "What are you talking about?" she said, looking over at me. I shook my head and stared at the digital clock on the dash. Six minutes passed. "How do you know about Buttons?" she said finally, looking me directly in the eyes, as if this was the first thing she'd actually heard me say.

"What?" I said. There was more silence, and her leg really started bouncing. She looked in the rearview mirror, then leaned against the door. Seriously, what were those cops doing?

"Who are you?" she said, looking at me. I think she genuinely believed we were going to kidnap and murder her.

"Nobody," I said. Maybe I sounded a little bitter or threatening, because as soon as she heard me, she opened the door and rushed out, back toward the cop car. I suppose the human mind can only take so much. In hindsight, I probably should have just stated my name: "Nobody" *is* kind of a creepy response. The tan cop spotted her and started yelling for her to *Stop running, Police! Stop!* She looked back but didn't stop. I watched in the rearview mirror as they disappeared from my line of vision. I could have turned my head to watch, but I just closed my eyes and let my head fall against the headrest.

Things slowly settled the next week. The doctor and Leslie went about restoring their reputations and I quietly prepared for my trip back to Pittsburgh. Dan fixed my car and after it still wouldn't run, the doctor paid to have it towed into the city and repaired.

I spent my last few days in my room successfully avoiding trouble. On the day I left, I joined Dan on the roof for an "important meeting." His words. "Watch this," he said, leaning over the edge to empty his last dime bag. "I'm finished. There." And that was it. I congratulated him heartily, even though I knew he had a spare dime bag taped under his desk. When the doctor saw us both leaving the bathroom at the same time, his expression didn't change. He just kept walking to his room and slammed the door behind him. Leslie hugged me and said the doctor would eventually get over it, that the family honor hadn't been too badly wounded. I thought I saw him waving from inside the house as I drove off.

I couldn't help one last look at the —— house. I'd bought a fruit basket when I was picking up my car, although I didn't have the courage to sign the card and doubted I could present it in person. But when I drove past her house, I saw she'd installed a chain-link fence, the kind with plastic barriers so you can't see inside. I slowed long enough to carefully place the basket in the middle of her driveway, then sped off.

It would be too easy to compare myself to Jonah, careening toward Nineveh with a newfound faith in some divine plan. Pittsburgh was waiting with its headaches and consequences, alleys and long smokestacks. I flew toward it now, welcoming the return. I would finish college. I would call Tommy. Laura flooded into my mind and I had to shut her back out. The pain was absolutely blinding and I had to focus on driving. I told myself that with a clear head and some courage, anything was possible.

28

DEAD FLOWERS

When I returned to Pittsburgh, the first message on my answering machine was from Kate. She was crying, saying I had to come to Tommy's house. It was an emergency. The rest of the message didn't make sense. Bates Street. Tommy's house. Kate crying, kneeling beside the horror show in Tommy's bed. Tommy, hair wet like a decomposing animal. A sheen of sweat, skeletal face. His room had changed, accumulated a number of dark objects. A couch and two dressers were stacked against the far wall, blocking out the sun. The barricade took up half of his room, the other half empty except for his bed, which was now just a box spring and mattress on the floor. Beside it was Kate's field hockey stick. For protection, I suppose, but from who? He'd stuffed clothing around the windows where the light shone through, concealing the filthy carpet and takeout boxes. The only other light source was an old movie projector casting a white rectangle on the wall opposite the bed. The empty reel was still spinning, the film's tail slapping with every revolution. It was hotter in that area, with a smell of burning metal. I unplugged it. The lights weren't working, so I unplugged a few holes, tossing a dirty pair of jeans from the barricade. Purple light spilled into the room, created by the shower curtain tacked to the window frame. The room smelled like dollar-store incense, body odor, and a strange mushroomy stench. Kate forced open the windows, which helped a little. "What happened?" She looked under the bed, picking out a baggie filled with a brownish powder. Mick Jagger's voice floated in my head: *I'll be in my basement room/with a needle and a spoon.* *And another girl to take my pain away.* "He's still alive," Kate said. She held his hand, staring at him. The scene reminded me of those old British mysteries, the family agonizing over their deathbed patriarch. I could recognize only parts of him: his hands, the same hands which had traced sketches and pulled color seeping across canvas, electric. The scarred knuckles. I did not recognize the constellation of punctures up his arm.

"My God," I said, looking around the room.

"Fuck, Tommy," Kate said, throwing the bag at his head. He strained to sit up. There weren't any covers and although he was wearing jeans and a tank top, he looked naked, somehow exposed.

"What," Tommy said in a hoarse breath.

"Don't," Kate said. "Just don't."

He tried again. "*Wait,*" that's what he'd been trying to say. But whatever he'd been trying to put off had caught up to him and we moved in a new frenzy. Motion, anything as long as we were moving forward. Kate left the room and I dumbly followed her downstairs. She lit a cigarette. Did ambulances call the police with cases like these, the same way they report gunshot wounds? We didn't know. Exactly what was his criminal record, and how long might he spend in jail? We didn't know. Did any of us have money for the hospital or an ambulance? No. There wasn't a debate he had to get to a hospital. My car was still unreliable, so I retrieved his from the parking lot, dripping sweat as I pulled in front of the house. Kate busied herself with emptying the car, throwing fast food cups and papers onto the street.

"You're driving," Kate said as I got out and ran upstairs to help my brother to the car. I told her it would just take a second. She lit a cigarette and waited by the door. "We broke up, but that's happened before," she said. "I don't understand this." The upstairs was about ten years ahead of the downstairs in terms of architecture and decoration. Even the molding was different. There was the framed modernist photograph of a metal cube and a painting of blue and white dots probably hung in the hall since 1986. I'd never really noticed them before, but they struck me as appropriate, a compartmentalization like the dramas above and below. I walked to his room feeling a sense of dread, a new shaking of the hands and voice.

"Christ, Tommy, how did we get here?" I said. I didn't know how I was going to get him downstairs. "We'll talk later. I'm driving you to the hospital," I said.

I waited for him to respond, but he said nothing. "Shut the door," he said finally. I sat down and looked at him. Years ago, he'd saved me from Tower, reliving the worst parts of our father's life to offer his hand to me, a way out. And now the world balanced itself so I could return the favor.

"Is it locked?" he said.

"What are you doing?"

While we'd been cleaning his car, he'd slid up his sleeve (he was wearing a T-shirt soaked with sweat and a mix of fluids) and pulled a shoestring around his bicep. He'd already prepared the needle. I hadn't seen him grab it. I had been staring at the window, thinking about how the few rays of light were almost solidified by the room's filth.

"One last hit before rehab," he said. "Plus, I'm not facing Kate again sober." I took the bag from him, candy from a baby. He didn't resist much but I could see the hate in his eyes.

"So now you have the power," he said.

"Sucks, doesn't it? Someone taking something that belongs to you," I said, as if Laura were a shirt or a book. He didn't say anything.

Kate knocked on the door and looked in on us. She turned away, recognizing this as an important family moment. "We're almost done," I told her. *Why*, the expression on her face asked Tommy, but he didn't answer. She closed the door.

I rolled down his sleeve and prepared for the task of moving him downstairs. "What's that on your arm?" I said, pointing to a splotch on the outside of his bicep. He held it up to the light. I'd worried it was an infection, but it was too smooth, too old. "Crucifix," he said, rubbing it with his hand. In high school, my friends...we'd do them with cigarettes." He shrugged weakly, admiring the scar. "I did this one myself. Patrick, my best friend, did a four-leaf clover on my other arm. He's dead now."

"Didn't it hurt?" I said, rubbing my own arm.

"We were pretty drunk. Afterwards. Plus, stuff got in it. Dirt and ashes."

"Damn." I examined the cross-shaped blotch. In the thick rays of sunlight it looked like a birthmark.

"You want one," Tommy said. I lit a cigarette, taking a deep drag, considering my own unadorned arm.

"I do," I said, but that sounded too serious, even though I felt like this was a very important moment. "Yeah." Burn Jesus into my arm. I say this in all seriousness: It seemed like a wonderful idea. Like this was the best way we could be spending our time.

It's a sharp, stinging pain, the kind you violently pull away from. A dull beating, like when someone punches you in the shoulder—that, you can take for a while. This was unbearable the whole time.

"Jesus won't forgive you," Tommy kept saying when I tried to pull away. He thought it was hysterical. He wasn't very strong, so I had to hold perfectly still.

"You don't have any alcohol around here?

"Drank it all."

"I don't need it to dull the pain. I'm just thinking about sanitizing it. Kill the germs."

"His divine presence is enough." He went through the rest of my pack. By the end we were breathing through our mouths. The pain of the last cigarette felt the same as the first. At the end—this must have been how Sir Edmund Hillary felt, staring down at whatever countries lie below Mount Everest. It was fire on my skin, yes, but the whole process felt mysterious, significant. This was something we had in common, this time by choice.

Kate yelled something up the stairs. I told her it was a family meeting and we'd be down in a second. "Laura'd love this," I said. I walked over to the window, moving closer into the light. In the sunlight, the blisters were an angry red, flecked with spots of gray ash. I blew on it, watching a line of clearish blood run down my arm. "Where's his head?" I said, inspecting the crucifix in the daylight. He picked up my pack, which was empty.

"Hey, what the fuck are you doing up there?" It was Kate again.

"We'll be out in a minute," I said.

"They're towing your car," she said, threatening to come upstairs.

I opened the door a crack and looked down the hall. I couldn't see anyone. At times like this, you really have to prioritize. I told her our family meeting was about to adjourn and called down: "Do you have any more cigarettes?"

PART III

MOONLIGHT MILE

29

THE QUEEN OF PITTSBURGH

Late in April, I got a phone call telling me Tommy had disappeared from rehab two weeks into his treatment. I sat on the roof of my apartment building, looking down as I barbequed some cheap burgers and potato slices doused with butter and garlic. The summery smell drifted down and generated good-natured envy from students in sandals and tank tops passing below. The sun was finally out after weeks of rain. I hung up the phone. The burgers were overcooked, with a consistency like tofu. I ate a couple and left the rest for the pigeons and rats.

In South Oakland, most rooftops are close enough to step across. At that point in the evening, the shingles were offering up their heat to the oncoming night and were warm enough that I could walk barefoot on them. I hopped a small brick divider and strolled across my neighbor's roof. I pictured them looking up at the tap of my footfalls, pausing before going back to their business: TV, screwing, or maybe even starting homework for the upcoming summer semester. I reached an alleyway and stopped at the end of the street, looking at the abrupt drop ahead.

Turning around, I caught a glimpse of someone in a window across the street. His head was cocked and he was talking on the phone. His back was to me and from behind he almost looked like Tommy. He was about the same height, same haircut—he even stood the same way talking on the phone, leaning with the back of his head against the glass. He moved away, leaving behind a frame of blank wall with peeling green paint. I lit a cigarette and breathed in the calming smoke. The way it sunk from my mouth in the damp evening air when I exhaled somehow settled my stomach a little.

The day she learned of his disappearance, Kate walked to Tommy's house and started airing out the rooms. She went into his bedroom and hauled out one piece of furniture at a time, reviewing her memory to set them to their right places. Re-hanging curtains and folding his laundry, hauling trash bags, cleaning the windows—she let in the early spring to light the swirling dust around her. I saw her through the windows at night, the entire house glowing as she moved from room to room. Every day for a week she wiped the counters, leaving behind the scent of pine and bleach.

At my apartment, the calls came in, friends of his with sighting reports. I made a list and followed up if the voice on the other end wasn't shaky or monotone. It was obvious some people just wanted to talk. Sometimes, I swear I'd see him just ahead of me in a crowd. Sitting and watching TV, sometimes I heard his stomping footsteps coming up my stairs and my stomach would drop. I would stand, anticipating his return. The feeling would pass but I always opened the door. My head felt like the inside of the drum, staccato guilt with long echoes. Even when it wasn't raining, there was a noise in my ear like the hiss of a phone line. Sometimes I followed Tommy into buildings, only to find a different face and turn away, my own flushing with embarrassment.

The second-to-last week of April, the neighborhoods around me buzzed. The students living in the surrounding neighborhoods hastily overpacked their cars, leaving bookshelves, vacuum cleaners, and microwaves piled high on the curbs. Parents toured the neighborhood, gawking at the mountains of waste and pretending not to see the panhandlers.

At end-of-the-semester frat and house parties, the nation's future traded cell numbers and screen names, making promises they wouldn't keep about staying in touch. All over, appliances, utilities, cables were being unplugged. An arc hung in the air for a split second before vanishing.

By Thursday, everyone was gone, leaving ample parking on the streets and four months of quiet for their neighborhood's old folks. That day, I picked up my burden and carried it to Tommy's house. Leaning my body and face against the old, cracked wood of the doorframe, I slid my student ID against the lock and crawled up the stairs. Kate must have just finished cleaning. The living room was empty except for the table and a neon orange lamp shaped like an owl. Kate had found pieces of a stained-glass window in the closet and had placed the shards against the windows, casting a bordello haze on the walls of the lamp-lit rooms. I collapsed on the couch, setting down the heavy bundle beside me. Looking around, I thought, *maybe he'll actually get the security deposit back.* I walked up the stairs to see his room.

"I guess I don't have to ask how you've been," Kate said, standing up when she saw me. She was cleaning the Venetian blinds with a rag. How sterile the house was now, cleaned as if for a museum exhibition. They could project us on the walls, working on collages or smoking hash while Miles Davis blared orange through his trumpet.

"I've been meaning to ask you—" she said flatly as she walked into the bathroom, the last couple words muting as she closed the door. There was a fight coming when she finished that sentence—I pictured her running the water as hot as possible, purifying herself. She'd been backing away from the white heat of it, earning the right to walk away. The question hung and glowed like a crescent moon.

She opened the door. Her hair was in a towel, but she unwound it, letting heat into the apartment that I felt in my throat, stealing my breath. She stood in her underwear, pulling on a pair of cargo pants. I turned my head. She was over me: Was I on the floor, the way I'm looking up at her? No, I wasn't that drunk, not yet. I was kneeling, resting my head on the coffee table, the old absorber of smoke and candle wax. There was enough light for the stained glass window to project a marbled white on the walls—maybe a tinge of yellow—and the steam rose off her arms and neck as she stood framed in the doorway, refusing to look away.

The T-shirt clung to her—it was as if she were baring herself to me, goddess-like, daring me to do the same. The energy of so many possibilities flashed through the room. Maybe she thought I'd do it, break down and answer her unfinished question. Explain any number of things. That rifle, for example. Sometimes, I still laugh about what she must have thought of that. How we pick up and abandon things so quickly.

Flashback to a few hours before that moment. I didn't know Kate would be at Tommy's house. I didn't know this would be my last day in Pittsburgh. I didn't leave my house hoping to be transformed, bathed in the white flame of epiphany. I grabbed my backpack and some other things and left with a tangible sense of purpose, my feet slapping the concrete with a newfound conviction.

I have the utmost respect for people who can face themselves sober, but I'm not one of them. There were several bars on the way. This is Oakland, after all: Plan it out right and there are always several bars in your path. There's Cumpie's, whose name is technically pronounced Cum-PEEs but everyone preferred the more appetizing CUM-*pies*. That night they had the twenty-five-cent Pabst Blue Ribbon drafts. Someday when it's twenty-five dollars a pint, I'll tell my grandchildren about that. But anyway, the ambience and company left something to be desired as I made little trophy pyramids of plastic cups on my table. After three or four dollars, I was ready to go, the heavy-metal taste of cheap beer in my stomach. I washed it all down with a Black and Blue. That's the South Oakland equivalent of a Black and Tan, except instead of half Guinness and Harp, it's half Guinness, half Pabst. And yes, it's every bit as delicious as it sounds.

There were a couple other bars I stopped at, telling myself I was just going in to mentally catalogue them, because it would be a long time—maybe never—before I returned. I wanted to see the burned CD I'd put in the jukebox down at Denny's pub, my own Senior Year mix. The pool tables at Bootlegger's, where I'd easily spent two hundred dollars, one quarter at a time. The tables at Jimmy's, which celebrated and educated patrons with laminated newspapers from the 1960 World Series. "Twin Killing," Bill Mazeroski's homer. Soon, the glorious squalor of these places would be replaced by respectability, flavorless bland plastic. Oakland one year from now would be almost unrecognizable. It felt like the world was constantly shifting around me. Even Princeton looked so different now. Would life always be like this, one step behind the world and feeling like everything would vanish the moment I touched it?

Kate and I stood downstairs looking at the bundle I'd left on the couch. "What am I supposed to do with this?" she didn't say. She didn't have to. "I don't want it," she didn't say, barely looking at the heavy urn I'd lugged from one bar to the next. The bronze band in the middle glowed—I'd recently polished it. "You know, he would never believe it was you," she said, my father a silent witness to this exchange. "After a while, I stopped trying." In an act of quiet hate and seething, I stole the urn and put the house on the market, taking what my brother needed most: his escape routes. Afterwards, he turned to what must have felt like the last option. I put the urn in my backpack and sling it over my shoulder, heavy. The door to Tommy's house closes, not even a glimpse at the back of her head. "Goodbye, Jason," she doesn't say.

30

THE WALKING LANTERN

"Sometimes. People asked when I started, but not anymore. Where are you from, anyway?" My backpack and confusion—he thought I was a tourist. I'd never ventured down to the Southside before—in my drunken state, I should have fit right in, but I wasn't drinking to celebrate. I was the grinning death's head behind the party's magenta curtains. I should have been calm, symbol that I was. But this was Mardi Gras smeared after the rain, and not in a good way. Talking, it was important to keep talking.

"The sign. Do people try to steal it?" I asked because I'd been thinking about stealing it and wondered if the bouncers watched for this.

"Lost and find? What does that mean?" He didn't give out his real name and, yes, a lot of people try to steal the sign. Even though it's heavy, neon, and plugged in. Occasionally, he'd lean down from his perch on the bar when necessary to repeat himself over the bad vocoder R&B blasting through the place. "Man-Child" was his stage name.

There's a blank space between Kate's house and this place, Tommy's favorite bar. He'd been going there since before I'd come to Pittsburgh and there was an unspoken agreement that this was his sanctuary. There was a P. T. Barnum-esque neon sign next to the door that read "Midget Inside." It had an oversized Confederate flag hanging on the mirrors above the bar. There was a broken jukebox and several neon-orange poster boards on the walls advertising handwritten drink specials. Every now and then a waitress came around with a tray of fluorescent tubes. A few months ago, even, this would have been great fun.

"I have a fashion line," he said. What had we been talking about? Maybe he misunderstood a question I'd asked. Now, they were blasting AC/DC from a little boombox at the bar, pointed directly at the two of us.

"What kind of clothing do you sell?" I said.

"Bar sells it. I have a whole line planned. Mockups and a distributor. They're going to sell it at Kmart." I couldn't tell if he was kidding. "It's an easy job, though. What I do." Man-Child was Pittsburgh's three-foot-tall bartending prodigy. Every Wednesday and Saturday, if someone paid ten dollars, an air-raid siren went off along with a spinning yellow police light. It was then Man-Child's job to walk along the bar and pour a shot in everyone's mouth. It must have been Saturday because a woman approached and leaned on the bar long enough to toss two fives in front of him. He pulled a cord (I couldn't help but notice his short arms—every movement fascinated me) and everyone ran over to the bar, mouths open like baby birds. It was weird and there was something intentionally lurid about the way he poured the shot into the women's mouths, lingering a bit longer as he poured, wiping the edge of the bottle on some lucky young woman's lower lip.

"Ever do that to a guy?" I said after he finished and everyone returned to their stools or tables.

"No. If you want, I mean—"

"No, no. I was just wondering...seriously, never mind." He had a little "house" set up for him, a curtained wooden box about the size of a refrigerator at the far end of the bar, a few feet behind the spot where he was sitting Indian-style on the bar. I was on a stool close to the door. It seemed like he usually didn't talk to people. After all, the place had two or three other (regular-sized) bartenders he could talk to. Man-Child. When he started working at this bar, he was a novelty, or worse—a freak. But once they got used to him, he became something like a mascot. Cheer when the midget serves drinks. After that, something else. Not even a servant, really, or a subservient curiosity. He became a sort of decoration, something people are glad to have around, but not much else. For this shifting public, he would become part of the ambience, a color to enliven the mood. It might have been comfortable, but there was something about it that enraged me. To spend his life silent and wandering, dragging chains of shame and lost potential—I can't think of a worse fate for anyone. I wanted to warn him, save him. Because if he could be saved, maybe there was hope for me. But there in that bar, with the hideous truth finally out, I was the object of Kate's disgust and Laura's pity and my brother was missing. For myself, I didn't see much of a way out.

"This place is packed," I said. He moved closer so we didn't have to shout. The song on the boombox skipped and someone unplugged it. There was a momentary silence as people paused in their conversations. My ears rang, a hollow vacuum quickly filled by shouts and whistles, then conversation. I looked at the grotesque crowd pressing against us.

"Why do you do this?" I asked. He gave me the same look you see on TV shows when a cop asks the hooker why she does it. I apologized. It was none of my business. "You might as well ask me why I drink," I said.

"Tommy?" a woman shouted into my ear. I don't look anything like Tommy, but I supposed (with the Rebel flag and all) I might have been the first Asian in that place since Tommy. You know how we all look alike. I shook my head and she put her hand absently on my shoulder, perhaps in apology, and disappeared back into the crowd.

The crowd parted quickly as two large bald men moved through it. The pub was shaped like one large hallway, the bar in the front to the right and directly behind it were some arcade games and pool tables. Behind that were the bathrooms. There was a stairwell to the side leading up to who knows where. The men ran upstairs. I didn't have the energy to follow whatever crisis they were rushing to.

"Things get violent here," Man-Child said, nodding his large head. The bell rang and he stood, walking his stiff little legs across the bar, dutifully pouring shots. I watched one man get a shot at the far end of the bar, then run to the other side to get another. *It's hard to refuse a drink when a midget's pouring it into your mouth,* he yelled afterwards to his girlfriend. After the commotion and chants died down, Man-Child sat back down in front of me.

"You wanted to know why I do this?" he said, holding up a green bottle of cheap liquor.

"I mean, if you want..."

"I converted." He said this as if it explained everything. I had no idea what he meant. "To Judaism."

"Ah," I said. That's the kind of person Man-Child was. One day you're not and the next day you're Jewish. That's Pittsburgh. One day you wake up and you're talking to a bartending midget about Judaism.

"Hey, Tommy?" someone said. Apparently I wasn't the only person in Pittsburgh looking for him. I shook my head again and he walked off. Man-Child explained Judaism to me but I was too tired and drunk to pay close attention. His sister turned him on to it after marriage. He used that exact phrase, "turned me on to it." But he went to the synagogue with his sister and her husband a couple times out of curiosity and something appealed to him. Some higher truth, and then it happened.

"How long have you been Jewish?"

"That's the thing, friend, just a few months."

"You're not wearing the hat," I said, ordering a drink from a different bartender.

"Don't have to. And do you think I should, here in this holy place?" he said.

"How does one become Jewish, anyway?" I said. I wouldn't have put up much of a fight if he'd wanted to convert me then and there.

"Promise not to laugh?"

"Wading pool." I stared up at him, not comprehending.

"How does that work?"

"Oh, you don't know. When people convert to Judaism, they

strip naked and everyone turns their backs and there's a big ceremony. Like a big baptism, kind of. Washing your old religion off, that sort of thing."

"Turning your back on—"

"It's not like that. And can you completely turn your back on the past?" I shook my head. He drank some water from a pint glass. "They usually do it at a congregation member's pool, at his house. But as you can see," he gestured to indicate his height, "I'd drown. Hence, wading pool."

"Wasn't that degrading?" He looked at me. "Oh."

"But, you see..." The alarm sounded and Man-Boy angrily got up, grabbing a bottle of Old Crow. He walked along the bar holding the bottle high, not bothering to aim for their mouths. A few people got whiskey in their eyes, stepping back and flailing around. It was awesome.

"I still haven't answered your question," he said to me when he returned.

"I'm not in a hurry," I said. He stretched, reaching his arms behind his head.

"How much do you think I make here?"

"An obscene amount," I replied.

"Well, sort of. More than I'd make at the circus," he said with a short laugh. "Or Hollywood. I'm going to travel. Bethlehem, Jerusalem, Rome. I'm saving up."

"Plan ahead when you pack," I said, holding up my heavy backpack. I finished my Yuengling and waved away the other bartender when she returned to refill it. I was done for the night.

"I'm not traveling just to travel. There's a purpose. Truth and beauty aren't just on a vase. They're out there, waiting. But in shards, little pieces. And as a seeker, as a member of the faith, it's your—well, my—job to seek it out. And it's there in those holy cities. Someday I'm grab all that light, gather it together. Like a Lite-Brite. That'll be me." He motioned to the dark bar, lit by the glowing ends of cigarettes, candles on tables, the glint of light reflecting off belt buckles and watches. "You can't imagine."

"I love traveling," I said. And what had I been doing throughout my college career but testing boundaries, exploring? The world grew closer to its full size in my mind and, standing on it, I shrunk when I realized how little I'd seen. I pictured myself trudging down the sepia-hued streets of Jerusalem. I pictured them made of smooth broken stone. Me moving into the crowded marketplaces, hemp ropes, tents and camels, drawn like a magnet toward the sacred and undiscovered.

"Hey are you Tommy?" someone said to me. This time I said yes. Here I was, sitting in his bar. I'd coveted his girlfriend—why not pretend to be him for a few minutes? The man was the jolly old-school, middle-management boorish-type. Graying hair around the temples, thin frameless glasses.

Man-Child craned his neck to watch something to the back of the bar. He'd been doing this the entire conversation, keeping watch. "Listen to me. You need to leave." I should have listened. But I was too drunk to turn and follow what he was seeing. It felt like I was never going to leave. That was a time where everything was swirling. I was chewing gum—had he given it to me? I didn't see it coming, but I saw it on his face—someone grabbed my shoulders and pulled me to the ground. And then I learned what it felt like to be Tommy. I did my best to protect my head, curl into a ball.

Gasping for air, I hoped above hope that Man-Child would pick up his green bottle and leap down to vanquish my enemies, but he had retreated into his shelter, closed the curtain. *I understand,* I wanted to say, even though I understood very little at the time. And then I was trying to grab a boot near my ribs, jerking my body with sharp electric pain. The candied lights in the bar popped and ran as something slammed into my jaw, jarring my teeth. I clung to someone's leg and eventually someone got me out of there. One of the bouncers, maybe.

Man-Child must have come back out because he was above me yelling, maybe even directing the rescue. I wanted very desperately to ask him his real name, something to hold onto. Willowy shapes floated at the edges of my vision. The smell of blood and asphalt. Soaking into it. I closed my eyes. And then I remembered my backpack was inside. The doorframe was just within my vision—Midget Inside. My watery eyes melted the sign. Somehow, I managed to stand. Story of my life. And then I remembered my backpack was inside.

"Support the head," someone said in another language. I listened, trying to make out the words. Someone, no a few people, were carrying me, abstract shapes.

"How are you?" someone asked me in Korean—now I could make out the sounds. Each word was a sacred vowel, rounded and deep. I tried to respond but couldn't move my tongue. Whoever was carrying me had the deepest, rumbling voice. It sounded like a mountain talking. My head swam. My entire body was limp, my ear resting on someone's chest. Someone stumbled and they were all pulled off balance, dumping me onto a dirt path next to a road. I made out a girl's blurry face as she ran her fingers through my hair.

"Sorry," whoever stumbled said.

"I think he's dead," another voice said, floating alongside.

"Where's my backpack?" I managed to say.

"See, he's not. He's coming 'round. I have your backpack here. No, you're not in any condition to carry it."

"Ask him where he wants to go."

"Where do you want to go, man?" the mountain asked me.

"Bus stop," I said in Korean. It must have been an older phrase—I hadn't spoken the language in so long.

"Train station?"

"Bus stop," someone said in English. I looked up at the clouds. They sat me down on a wooden bench and offered words of encouragement and warnings about not to do whatever I'd been doing. I didn't belong there. They spoke Korean, mostly, and I listened without moving. Their voices echoed slightly off the glass-covered shelter as the words seeped into the oblivion of night. I sat there, late into the night, my head against the back of the cold metal headrest, watching the stars. Overhead, the moon continued its descent.

I don't know how much time passed before Laura arrived. "You called?" she said. She picked up my backpack and held it on her lap. I didn't remember, but I must have made it to a payphone and called her. If you lean forward right, you can stumble forward in a straight line for a surprisingly long distance. She must have sent the youth group ahead of her—maybe some of them lived closer. Mission possible. If the youth group members were still around, I couldn't see them. "What time is it?" I asked. "Two in the morning." "Last call." She didn't know what that meant. High schoolers. "It means the bars are closed," I said. She nodded. "So what are you doing here?" she didn't say. I said I was looking for my brother. "When did you call him last?" I didn't know. In reality, I hadn't. Even though I'd been looking, I kind of hoped I didn't find him. What would I have said if I ran into him at the Confederate Midget Bar? *Sorry for ruining your life. Buy you a drink?* But I knew I had to find him. "Well, where do you think he is?" she asked. "Back home. Wilkes-Barre." She offered a hand, but I rolled off the bench and stood up slowly. She looked at me for a long time. "My dad's van is a block away. I can't drive you the whole way, though." I told her thank you, and of course I understood. We knew we could only travel so far together.

31

MY THIRD LETTER

The man walking on the side of the highway, he must be freezing. I woke with my head at an angle, caught between the seatbelt and window—for the second he's in view, it looks like he's falling past at an incredible speed. It's raining tonight, dense, the only thing I can hear. We're driving past a long concrete bridge spanning the horizon, blocking out the arc of streetlights behind it. A curved overpass rises above the bridge and follows the highway for some length with its long rectangular supports. From this distance, they vaguely resemble a harp. Pennsylvania's highways are ribbed with stone and so is tonight—slate, the rain falls just to kiss it.

"Are you okay?" Laura asks. I nod, my face still against the window. There's no way she sees him. Once, a state over, I fell from the doctor's roof. It was a tall mansion and I must have bounced and here I am, pressing my face against the cold. Outside, there's gravel and some flowering weeds, but not much else. The asphalt would have been hot this morning, the first drops of rain dissolving inches above the ground. Now, the water slides and creeps atop the highway, absorbed and now it's barely even a gloss. "Hey, roll down the window if you're going to throw up."

Pittsburgh's a hovering mass behind me. Before the van and the youth group rescue, I was walking along the freeway, just like that falling man, cold. I felt just a little worse than I do now: There were feathery shapes at the corners of my vision and my body felt like it was vanishing. My left arm and shoulder, the fingers on my right hand. My face. For all I knew, I was leaving them behind as I walked. I remember a backpack slung across my shoulder, a heavy, a stinging ache. I'd cough and points of light would explode, driving away the dark shapes for a few seconds. Flattened iced-tea cartons and plastic bags floated by me, little flags of paper lit ghostly by passing cars. All these lights on the freeway tonight, streaks of white and red. Sitting in the van, I composed my last letter to my father. If I could have written it down, it would have looked like this:

Father,
How long I've spent in your midnight world of dust and ash. For me, Pittsburgh was a chance to leave everything behind, the baggage of coarse black hair and *kimchi*. The sweeping, clawing spawn of our nation's history—real and imagined wrongs, murder and handwritten signs. Fear with static around the edges, hi-res pixelated fear pumped through fiber-optic cables, blood spilling into the Tigris and Euphrates, the plume of ground zero, a lone plane's fiery arc into Somerset County. Debt. Freed of all this, I thought I would soar above the city, my jeans flapping in the night air. Pittsburgh from above: the orange glow atop the Koppers building, the white disc of the Bayer sign, the angles of the lighted incline tracks. A blue-skinned rocket forever accelerating beneath the constellations.

But I hadn't thought it through, Laura would say. You'd like her, I think. The air's cold among the clouds. And where would I go, all by myself? Who would I share all it with? Who would I talk to? I don't know. I guess no matter how fast I flew, through the stratosphere, I'd feel pretty much like I had beneath that massive Rebel flag, searching through the crowd for my brother. In Pittsburgh, all I knew was the life I hadn't chosen, a life I'd wandered into and accepted. I could coast on the spiral and see where it leads, but there has to be another way. I need to gather courage beyond what I had known, bind together in me all that is good and worthwhile.

The last thing I have to face was the anger I'd inherited from you, a slow twisting of the Korean temper, something I brought with me over the long ocean. Borne of compressed fear and anxiety, it crept like oil into my heart. It was borne of jealousy, because Tommy was so sure of himself, because he belonged and was comfortable belonging. It was something so ugly I still barely recognize it as my own. But even now, I see it when I hid my brother's water on boiling days down at Tower, when I plotted to steal his girlfriend, when I stole the urn, when I stole your ashes. I'll see all of it reflected in my brother's face and I will ask forgiveness.

We'll travel west together. Tommy wants to meet at our house, and so we shall return home to bless the dead. I own your ashes now, if such a thing can be owned. Eventually, the only thing you can do is let go. The lunar calendar places *Chuseok*, the harvest festival, in September this year. A traditional day of remembrance and thanks, one of the high holidays. A gathering of families, the highways in Korea crowded and slow as the entire nation makes its way home. We have a little time to prepare the house. We have forgotten much, which will complicate the ritual, but that only seems appropriate for such a family as ours. I doubt Tommy the firstborn has ever built a Confucian shrine, and I kind of dread cooking with him, peeling fruit to stack in little bowls. The whole thing may turn into a fiasco, but we will get through it, and get through it together.

Below, the consecrated dead received everything the rain brings, paper and sand through the porous fabric of everything. At my feet, the unburied dead are wrapped in light, the occasional spark of gathering truth. It shimmers and swarms, that kind of light, here in the drab interior of this metal box. We are moving fast, *energized*, as the doctor would say, tons of steel atop the slick highway.

32

SECOND ACTS

Pittsburgh. I've said it's a monument to my failures, the whole city a museum of ghosts and could-haves. But there was beauty there. It was a destination once and even though I view it as a detour, I will return someday free of debt and guilt.

The old joke about Pennsylvania—there's Philadelphia on one side, Pittsburgh on the other and in between: Arkansas. We're driving through that kind of Arkansas, nothing but blue fields on either side, a guard rail, occasionally a barn. The landscape a flat plane devoid of color and light. I love it, but it creates a kind of longing for the city, to be pulled closer to the edge of the spectrum.

Tommy, my brother, who has borne my vindictiveness again and again. How did it become so easy to hurt each other? And we were always doing the easiest thing. You've found someplace quiet, I know, but there are things I need to say. And someday you'll return to Oakland to pick up your art portfolio and car, which has been collecting parking tickets for quite some time.

Laura and I are surrounded by fields, the sky a dark blue. It's almost morning, about six. She drives past a house along a lonely stretch of farmland. It has a white picket fence with

PENN STATE written in the official quasi-futuristic font along with the pensive Nittany Lion, which suspiciously resembles the ThunderCats logo. I think of those T-shirts they sell in Oakland. Front: *What does a Penn State student say after graduation?* Back: *Want fries with that?*

"All I know about Penn State is that when Paterno dies, they're gonna hire a psychic and Ouija board so he can coach from beyond the grave," I tell Laura. Nothing.

"You think we had sex, didn't you?" she says finally. Speaking of ghosts.

"The two of us? I'm 100% positive we didn't—" *Stop*, the look on her face says. She's serious. She wants to have a Serious Talk. I suppose I owe that to her.

"Did you?" I say. As long as we're going for closure here.

"You think we..." she says. "You think we were upstairs that night...*fucking*?" She says the last word quieter than the rest, then repeats it as if realizing it for the first time.

The look on her face. "I know you weren't," I said. That whole night was full of betrayals. All this time, my jealously blinded me, but I know Laura was never capable of that kind of betrayal. I tell her that. I watch her legs shift a little, and the van swerves a little. She wants to slam on the brakes and yell at me, but she exhales slowly and continues driving.

"You think I gave up on you," she said finally. We're in the city now—Penn State city or whatever it's called. The downtown businesses are all getting ready to open. We drive along a long street adjacent to an academic building with several columns and a long flagpole. "Things aren't always what they seem," she says, slowing down. She looks at me and suddenly I get it.

"You're dropping me off here?" I say. She gives me an admonishing look.

"They have a bus station. It's nice."

"Seriously? In Penn State? Enemy territory?" I say a little quieter. Maybe she doesn't know about the Pitt-Penn State rivalry. "You look tired," I tell her. She's already driven two or three hours. And she has church tomorrow—or rather, today. But she doesn't look tired—she looks as focused as when I first saw her, pulling her hair back in a ponytail. She's not changing her mind. "You got a mean streak," I say as a tease.

"New city, new beginning," she says.

"I'm beginning to think the city was never the problem," I say, laughing.

She pauses, wavers. "You still don't look okay. Why don't I drop you off at a hotel?" she says. "I can cover it." She's beautiful, in case I haven't already made this clear, and there's something about her that makes my heart ache. Her earnestness, the innocent longing to help. I've seen it before in another lifetime. It would be so easy for both of us, but I only hesitate for show. It's been a long drive indeed. I shake my head. "Thank you. It's been..." And she nods. We leave much unsaid. She pulls a little closer to the curb and I open the door.

"Wait," she says. "You have no money—"

"Fourteen cents," I say.

"You've been holding out on me. But seriously, you're not even dressed for...and you look like you died a few hours ago," she says.

"In some ways, I did," I tell her, doing my best Oprah-guest voice.

"Oh ho. That's cute." I'm done hitchhiking. She realizes there's no way to change my mind and kind of flops, pushing herself back against the seat. She stares forward. I offer my hand and she shakes it.

"Your hand is freezing," she says as she takes it in hers. She knows my cell phone is lying smashed somewhere in Pittsburgh and writes her home number in pen across the back of my hand, followed by a little smiley face. The cars behind us grow impatient. She nods, satisfied with the finality of the act. I wave and she's lost in the morning rush. Outside, a thick fog celebrates the meeting of day and night and I use the moisture in the air to smear the number on my hand into a darkening of veins, and then nothing. It feels like a callous dismissal, but I think she would understand. The cold against my skin, seeping through my shirt—this is what it feels like to be alive. Here I am, walking east, toward my brother. There's fog all around me, rising up from the pavement like the end of a magic show.

ABOUT THE AUTHOR

Photo credit © Dyanna Warner

Robert Yune was born in Seoul, South Korea. As a Navy brat, he traveled around the world, moving 11 times by the time he turned 18. Yune's fiction has appeared in *The Kenyon Review, Avery,* and *The Los Angeles Review,* among others. In 2008, he received a fellowship from the Pennsylvania Council on the Arts. In 2012, he was a finalist for the Flannery O'Connor Award in Short Fiction and was one of five finalists for the Prairie Schooner Book Prize, selected by Sherman Alexie and Colin Channer. From 2010-2013, Yune served as fiction editor of *The Fourth River.* He has worked as a behavioral health researcher, a census enumerator, and a stand-in for George Takei. He currently lives and teaches in Pittsburgh.